Colder Than Ice

Helen Macpherson

Quest Books

Nederland, Texas

ISBN 1-932300-29-5

First Printing 2004

9 8 7 6 5 4 3 2 1

Cover design by Donna Pawlowski

Published by:

QuestBooks
PMB 210, 8691 9th Avenue
Port Arthur, Texas 77642-8025

Find us on the World Wide Web at
http://www.regalcrest.biz

Printed in the United States of America

Acknowledgements

Okay, let me just lay some historical or technical issues to rest. The Sixth Geographic Congress did meet, but it was in 1895, not 1894. Why the change? This was to allow a time line that would see Finlayson's base in Antarctica, before the actual first base in 1899. Next, the possibility of Antarctica having solid pack ice in late November that an icebreaker couldn't get through is unlikely. However, to make that part of the story work, this change was necessary. I hope you'll be gentle with me over that one! Finally, Australia hasn't worked in imperial measurements since the early seventies, when a very nice female teacher replaced my imperial ruler with a metric one. In deference to my predominantly American and United Kingdom audience, I have kept to the imperial system, rather than mix between the two.

As is often the case, so much has gone into writing this story. I spent about three months reviewing numerous written and audio sources about Antarctica to ensure the story's integrity. They're too many to mention; suffice to say, if you're interested there's a lot out there on the subject of Antarctica. Understandably, the research would have amounted to nothing had I not written the story; and this wouldn't have happened without an excellent support crew. Casey, thank you for your editing support. Lori, thanks for your sage guidance on the nuances of copyright and registered trademarks. Barb, thanks for your continued support and sanity checks during the writing the story. Joan, I honestly don't believe I would have finished this in the time I did, without your unflagging support and confidence in me. My very sincere thanks for your ongoing positive reinforcement. Last, but certainly not least I'd like to thank my partner Kate, for her support and patience, and once again being a writer's 'widow' during the writing of this story.

~Helen Macpherson

Publisher's Note:

This novel is written by an Australian and is about Australian characters. Therefore, we have allowed many of the Australian spellings, phrases, methods of address, grammatical differences with American English, etc. to remain in the text rather than remove that voice during the editing process.

Expeditioners wanted for long, dangerous journey to Antarctica. Conditions at sea will be extreme. Conditions on the land will be perilously cold, with endless winds and the ever-present threat of blizzard. Risk to life will be a constant factor and only the most hardy need apply. Wages will be small, however, deserving acknowledgment and reward will necessarily follow upon the success of the expedition. Interested parties may write to E.R. Finlayson, Expedition leader.

~Notice in the *New York Tribune*,
1st March 1895

Prologue

Antarctica July 1896

My Darling Charlotte,

This will be my last entry for I am becoming too weak to write. After so many months of hardship and heartache, I grieve at the thought that I have led my men to their deaths, and I will soon join them. Lying here alone, I understand now where I failed and have endeavored to record these lessons for those who may find me, so that any future Antarctic expeditions will not suffer the same fate. It pains me to think that after so long I have achieved so little.

However, of all the pain I suffer now in silence, of all the loss we have experienced and the regret at not achieving what we set out to achieve, I have one regret above all else. That regret is that, Charlotte, I will never see your face again, your warm smile and your sparkling eyes. It pains me to think we shall never again share a cup of tea by the fire, discussing the everyday events that course through our lives. I will never again lie in the warmth of your arms, feel your soft caress, like butterfly touches to my face and limbs. I know you cannot read this and I can only hope you can hear my thoughts. Please do not mourn for me my love—you are too young to sentence yourself to premature widowhood. Find someone new to share your life with. However, know this: I will always love you, until death and beyond.

E.R.F

Antarctica, 2009—nine days out of Wills Station

THE VEHICLE, A barely discernible orange speck on the Antarctic landscape, made its slow, deliberate way across the white expanse. Inside, the rumble of the tractor made it difficult for Sarah Knight to catch the driver's words.

"I missed that, Rob. What did you say?" she shouted in his ear.

Without taking his eyes from the unchanging vista, Rob turned his head slightly and yelled, "I said, after days of travelling at this bloody slow pace, are we there yet?"

Sarah smiled. She'd previously worked with Rob and was used to his teasing questions. "Okay, enough. We're nearly there. Of course, lugging around an ice core drill that weighs as much as this one has slowed us down."

"Really? You don't say," he replied with light-hearted sarcasm. "I've dragged this baby around before and I'm intimately aware of how heavy the bloody thing is. I suppose what I should be asking is why not just take core samples from the Law dome, instead of coming all the way out here?"

"We're trying to do a comparative study of the information we've found in core samples from the Law dome with samples that are further along the inner coastal fringe. We're investigating the extent of damage done to the environment through the spate of worldwide nuclear tests conducted in the 1950s. Think of it as an integrity check of information collected from a site which has been relatively untouched by humans over the past hundred years." She slapped him on the shoulder, hardly registering against the multiple layers of clothing. "And besides, who else would I have out here except the best driller in all of Antarctica?"

Rob laughed. "Flattery will get you everywhere. It's just a shame you've never taken me up on the offer. We'd make a great team you and I. Me, the brawn, and you, the brains of the outfit."

Sarah shook her head in mock exasperation. "Mate, as I've told you before, there's one slight problem with that. You're not kitted with the gear for my kind of interests. And besides, how could you put up with my constant nagging? I'd drive you to drink in no time."

Rob spared Sarah a glance. "You can't say I didn't try. But you're right; you nag a bit too much for my liking. How do the ladies put up with you?" He dodged another blow from Sarah.

"You should know that women are always right. It's only men who can't do things correctly the first time."

"You keep on like that and you're likely to find yourself walking home. And trust me, it's a bloody long walk." He checked the instrument panel and scanned the area through the vehicle's icy windscreen. "By my calculations, I think we're where we need to be. Now, would Little Miss Perfect like to check that this mere male hasn't got it wrong?"

"Very funny." Sarah checked the readout against the data in her logbook. "If you just head over that way about another five hundred yards, we should be where we want to drill."

"Five hundred yards? Five hundred yards? We're in the middle of bloody nowhere and you want to move another five hundred yards? Thank God I've never moved house with you. I can just see it: 'No, just a little more to the left. No, too much. Just a little more to the right.' No man in his right mind would put up with you." Rob gave her a cheeky grin.

She grabbed a thatch of hair below his cap and pulled it hard. "Yeah. Just do as you're told mister brawn or I'll start doing this by inches."

"Ow! Just for that, I'm only going to go another four hundred and ninety yards. If you want this bad boy any closer you'll just have to get out and push." Despite his threat, Rob parked as close to the target position as possible.

As they climbed down from the vehicle, they took a moment to brace themselves against the biting cold of the wind that was a constant factor on the continent. They worked silently together, ensuring the stabilising legs of the drill piece were in position before they took samples. Satisfied the drill was ready for operation, Rob checked the mechanics of the machine while Sarah looked over the drilling requirements for the sample to be taken.

"If it's okay by you, I'd like to do a couple of samples

about twenty yards apart." Sarah held up her hand at Rob's incredulous look. "I know. Call me anal retentive, but I want to make sure the data we collect will be worth the trip."

"It better be worth it. Stuck for days having to listen to your voice is enough to drive anyone to drink." Rob ducked behind the safety of the drill as Sarah propelled a small chunk of ice at him. "Okay, okay. I give up. But before we start, we've been travelling over some pretty untidy terrain. Do you mind if I do a quick test drill to make sure everything's working? I'd hate to get down to any sort of depth and have the damn thing seize on me."

"No. That's fine. It'll give me a chance to assess what the composition of the ice is like at this early depth. Let me get some photos and data on what we've found at the other sites and I'll be right with you." Sarah covered the ten yards from the drill to the door of the vehicle's front cabin. Struggling against the force of the wind, she opened the door and retrieved her backpack.

Not waiting for Sarah to return, Rob flicked the switch and brought the drill to life. He checked the blades encased in their titanium cylinder to ensure they were rotating before he positioned the drill to take its first bite of the ice.

Rob bore a small hole and was satisfied that the drill had not been affected by the long journey to the drill site. He raised the drill out of the hole in the ice, turned the machine off, and removed the test sample from its confines. He exchanged a surprised look with Sarah.

Sarah removed bits of a darkened material from the relatively blue-white hue of the rest of the specimen. "What the hell is that?" She sniffed it and shook her head before taking a closer look. Bewildered, she turned to Rob. "What's wood doing in an ice sample?"

Rob took the specimen and sorted through it with a gloved finger. "I was just thinking the same thing. We're not on a historical site are we?"

Sarah walked the small distance from the hole, to where her pack lay on the ice. She removed from her pack the data relating to their drill site. "Have you got the GPS?" Rob nodded. "Can you do another check of where we are? I'll just recheck the maps to make sure I haven't misread them. There really shouldn't be anything in this location." She scratched her head in confusion.

They carefully checked and crosschecked their position, and validated it was correct. Both of them returned to the small hole and looked down into it. Rob scanned the immediate landscape for any clues and found none. "If we're in the right position, what's wood doing here? There're no records of early expeditioner's huts in this location. Plus, the depth where the wood appears in the core sample dates it from at least a century ago. So, come on, woman of multiple doctorates and child prodigy, what's your hypothesis?"

Sarah paced the ice. Possible answers entered her mind but were rationalised and just as quickly dismissed. She stopped pacing and her eyes widened before she shook her head. "No, it couldn't be. That was never substantiated."

Rob grasped Sarah's arm. "What was never substantiated? What are you talking about?"

Sarah broke out of the mental check and crosscheck she'd been running through and turned to Rob. "For as long as I've been involved in Antarctica and well before that, there's been talk of an expedition that was never proven to have taken place. It was thought to be the first expedition that ever settled on Antarctica. Many had circumnavigated the continent before it, but no one had ever established a base on the ice. It was supposedly headed by an explorer called Finlayson but nobody's ever found proof of his expedition."

Rob wrapped a well-padded arm around a perplexed Sarah. "I'd say they have now. I suppose that means no more drilling, hey?"

Chapter One

My Dearest Charlotte,

The meeting of the Sixth International Geographic Congress seems like a lifetime away and yet it has only been ten months. Do you remember how excited we were, gaining their blessing in support of my expedition—to be the first person to establish an expedition base on Antarctica? And here I am, a day's sailing from our last port of civilisation, heading for the adventure that lies ahead for my faithful crew and myself. The people of Christchurch in New Zealand were very helpful, sometimes a little overly so. I have more lamb than I know what to do with; thankfully it has made cook happy. The New Zealand people's gracious provisioning of our coal and oil supplies were of extreme benefit and I shall not forget them when naming areas of the great white continent, or indeed in my memoirs when I arrive home.

Oh, my love, you should have seen the crowds; they lined the wharves ten deep in places! And the pleasure boats on the harbour, faring us well on our journey, were a sight to behold.

The swell rises, my dear, and so I must cut this entry short. I did send you and Robert junior a short letter before we sailed yesterday and by the time you receive it we should be well and truly established on Antarctica. My loving thoughts go out to you.

ERF

Sydney, Australia—2009

AS ALLISON SHAUNESSY ran up the well-worn steps of the Museum Station, she mentally berated herself for her late departure from home. She was well aware of the Museum's faculty meeting that morning, not to mention the items on the agenda. Today the faculty, under the iron guidance of the Museum's patron, would decide the key projects to be funded for the upcoming year.

Securing a position on the staff of the Flinders Museum of Australasian Exploration had been no mean feat. The doctorate in Archaeology Allison had gained from Sydney University certainly held her in good stead. This, coupled with the entrée provided by Rick Winston, her partner of three years, had made the transition from academia to practical application of her knowledge that little bit easier. She'd worked hard to establish her own credible niche and, as time progressed, people ceased to refer to her as Rick's girlfriend and instead called her Dr. Shaunessy.

Allison took the hundred year old sandstone steps of the station two at a time, stubbornly ignoring the signs that her stamina was flagging. Without warning, she tripped and instinctively threw out her hands to break her fall. Almost simultaneously she watched her bag erupt as it hit the stairs, sending a stream of pens, papers, books, and fruit flowing back down the steps.

Allison gingerly rubbed the pain throbbing through her shin and hands and muffled an embarrassed curse. She carefully made her way back down the stairs, picking up everything and graciously thanking those people who returned to her the contents of her bag. At the bottom of the steps she found her grapefruit and orange, their progress halted by a newspaper stand. She shoved her bruised breakfast into her bag, shaking her head at how late for work she was now going to be. Deciding she may as well take the time to pick up the morning paper, Allison glanced at the tabloid flyer on of the newspaper stand and nearly dropped her bag again. Bold letters declared what she'd sought to prove for so long:

FINLAYSON EXPEDITION NO LONGER A MYTH!

She paid the owner for the paper and walked up the steps, this time one after another, her eyes eagerly scanning the article's contents. Nearly slipping again on the worn sandstone, she decided to stop reading until she'd emerged from the underground railway exit.

As Allison walked through Hyde Park, she barely noticed the beautiful autumn day that greeted her. The changing colours and the encompassing morning's warmth scarcely touched her awareness as she brusquely walked to work, nose firmly ensconced in the paper.

> 27 March 2009—Dateline Antarctica. A random discovery made last week may well have laid to rest over a century of speculation surrounding the true existence of the first explorer to establish a base in Antarctica. The remains of an expedition's hut were found during ice core research, in an area previously recorded as not containing archaeological relics.
>
> Dr. Sarah Knight, the glaciologist who made the discovery, said she'd never expected to find anything in such a remote location, some nine days from Wills Station. When she discovered wooden elements within a test ice core sample, she conducted a GPS check of the drilling location and confirmed that the position was not a historical site.
>
> When asked to speculate on what the actual remains might be, Dr. Knight was confident in her reply. "We've mapped and recorded every explorer to have traversed the continent of Antarctica, with the exception of one who, until now, was thought to have perished in the Southern Ocean long before reaching Antarctica. I believe these remains can be no other than from the hut of Eric Robert Finlayson."

"Good morning, Dr. Shaunessy," Arthur Packham greeted.

Allison looked up from the newspaper and realised that she was in the Museum.

She grinned. "Hi, Arthur, how are you?" She always enjoyed chatting with Arthur, who was one of the museum's oldest and most well-informed guards, and, as always, smartly dressed in the charcoal grey uniform of the Museum's employees. Allison waved the newspaper at him. "Did you see the news this morning?"

Arthur smiled. "I'm fine, Dr. Shaunessy, and yes, I did. I'm sure you're very excited by this possible find."

"After so many years of speculation, it looks as if my research has been vindicated. My theory regarding his supply ship must have been correct. They did manage to unload both men and cargo onto land and then the ship must have perished on the return journey," Allison said wryly, and shook her head. "The odds of finding the hut's location are astronomical. I'd love to speak with this Sarah Knight and see if there're any other telltale signs around the site."

Arthur tapped his watch in gentle remonstration of Allison's enthusiasm. "Now that you mention talking to people, Dr. Shaunessy, isn't there a faculty meeting today?"

Allison scowled and lightly cursed as she trotted to the elevator, leaving a chuckling Arthur behind her. She turned to give him a quick wave goodbye and smiled. His attention was already focussed on a small girl, who tugged on the hem of his jacket. From inside the elevator, Allison watched the scene and softly laughed at Arthur's patience with children as the doors quietly closed.

ALLISON DUMPED HER gear on the desk in her office in the rear area of the Museum and wheeled for the door. She'd barely taken two steps when she ran into a six-foot-two immovable object, the scent of its aftershave unmistakable.

Rick Winston took a step back and absorbed the impact by encasing Allison in his arms. "Ooof! Alli, where are you going in such a hurry? And where's my good morning kiss?"

Allison disentangled herself enough to brush Rick's lips. "I'm as late as all hell. The alarm wasn't set this morning, I woke up late, missed my train, and then dropped everything on the way to work and now I find out that part of my thesis may have been proven. And, of course, to make matters worse, I'm late for the only appointment I need to keep on a regular basis."

Rick gently shook Allison's shoulders. "Slow down or you'll burst something. Old Pedant Peterson was held up leaving Melbourne. His plane was fogged in and he's not due for another twenty minutes or so. Come into my office and we'll have a cup of coffee and compare notes." He stepped out of the embrace and headed down the hallway.

Allison resignedly sighed at the way he naturally expected her to follow him.

"You do remember the purpose of the meeting today don't you," Rick called over his shoulder before entering the wood-panelled room of what could only be the office of a man.

Allison rolled her eyes—as if such an important meeting could be forgotten. The faculty members of Flinders had only been preparing papers for it for the past two months. And now, the one paper she should have had ready to present wasn't ready at all. "Of course I do. Today is the day old Peterson spreads his largess over the unwashed masses, namely us. What have you heard about the projects the old geezer's likely to sponsor this year?"

Rick's eyes quickly flitted toward his open door and then back at Allison. "For Christ's sake, Alli, keep your voice down. I suspect the old man already knows that you think he's an ignorant prat, without you calling him names. The last thing you want is for someone to hear you."

Allison flung her head back and then forward, her short brown locks falling into her eyes. She impatiently brushed them away. "What, like blimbo you mean?"

Rick stifled a laugh. "You're going to get yourself in so much trouble one of these days. Di will hear you and then that'll be the end of it."

Allison insolently shrugged. "Well, what would you call her? All that flouncy, curly long blonde hair and a body shape like an advance party for a famine. As for her wardrobe, what self-respecting academic would be caught dead looking like they'd stepped off the pages of a fashion magazine?" She shuddered. "Ugh. The woman makes my skin crawl."

Rick laughed and gently closed his door. Walking past Allison, he playfully ruffled her hair with his fingers. "You, my dear, have a terminal case of non-diplomatic foot and mouth disease." He poured steaming filtered coffee into two mugs and handed one to Allison. "About the possible projects to be considered at the meeting today, I've heard of the combined proposal from the meteorology and geology department; I think it's called the Simpson project. Have you heard of any others?"

Allison sat down and nodded as she took a long sip of her first coffee of the day, its strong aroma teasing her senses. "Hmm, the Simpson Project. If I was a betting woman and given the amount of discussion at last year's meeting, I'd say it's a shoe-in. There're also others. One is the Mungo Project. It's a dual one between the Palaeontological and the Anthropological departments. They've taken a holistic approach and pooled their resources in order to study the ancient environment, its fossils, and the culture of prehistoric man existing during that era. I've no doubt that tightwad Peterson will be more than willing to support two outcomes for the price of one."

Rick nodded. "You're right. It seems to be the way things are these days. Man, I liked it so much better when the Departments were at each other's throats. Divide and conquer, that's what it should be about."

Despite the logic in Rick's words, Allison was unsettled by the vehemence of his tone. She cared little about how many academic departments there were to a project. To her it made sense to pool projects where possible. She filed away his reaction for a later discussion. "There's one other and it's almost guaranteed to receive funding. About two hundred and fifty miles southwest of Riversleigh they've found another dinosaur field that rivals Dinosaur National Park in the States. By all accounts it's an ancient water basin, full of pristine fossils."

Rick drew his eyebrows together. "I don't get it. We dug at Riversleigh years ago and got a mountain of samples out of there. Why bother doing the same thing again?"

Allison smiled at Rick's sometimes single-minded approach to life. "Yes, we did, and got some excellent samples in the process. Stop and think. Where's Riversleigh?"

Rick gave her a perplexed look. "Riversleigh is in the middle of Peterson's brother's electorate. Remember, he's the sitting member? What better way in an election year to secure re-election than to ensure a guaranteed injection of funds into the community?" Allison sipped her coffee. "Aside from those, I don't know of any other projects."

Rick shook his head. "Then why are we wasting our bloody time this morning? We all know the old man only funds three projects a year. This meeting's a done deal."

Allison nervously shifted. "Not exactly. There's another project I'd like to table, but given my paper's incomplete, I may require the support of others."

Rick frowned and then his eyes widened. "You've got to be kidding. Have you anything you can put in front of the old man about the Finlayson expedition? You know he's a stickler for detail and he's not likely to be too happy with a verbal briefing."

"If I'd have known what this morning's headlines would be then I'd have been prepared months ago. This vindicates key elements of my thesis." She stood up and paced the small office. "Even though the University Faculty accepted my exposition, I could see doubt on the faces of some of the Panel. There can be no better closure than to go down there and conclusively prove Finlayson's presence as the first person to expedition on the Continent."

Rick caught Allison's hand and gently pulled her to him. "Calm down. You've got my support and I've no doubt in the excitement of the moment you'll have the support of others in the meeting. But you've got to present this as diplomatically as possible and you know you're not good at that. Choose your words carefully or you'll never have a chance with this. In the extreme case he says yes, are you sure you can pull this off? I mean, Antarctica isn't like the middle of Australia. The expedition cost alone is going to be astronomical."

"Don't you think I know that? If I can just get some sort of commitment from him I know I'll find a way. Can you imagine the excitement of such a project?" Allison managed to stop herself before she yet again launched into her pet topic. She caught Rick's barely stifled yawn. "What happened to you last night? I thought you were coming over to my place?"

Rick stifled another yawn. "Sorry about that, I got caught up here at work and, given my apartment's only two blocks away, I went home instead."

Allison opened her mouth to ask about the project that had kept him so late when the telephone rang.

"Flinders Museum of Australasian Exploration, Dr. Rick Winston speaking. He is? We're on our way. Thank you, bye." Rick hung up and grabbed the half-full cup of coffee from his desk. "The old man's arrived, so we best get a move on."

With a determined glint in her eye Allison took a step toward the door. Rick put himself in the doorway, halting her progress.

"What's wrong?" Allison asked.

Rick pushed a stray lock from Allison's eyes. "Remember what I said. I'll support you, but you've got to present your case clinically and don't rise to his goading. Don't interrupt me, you know he does. Let's get going." Rick patted her backside and pushed her out the door in the direction of the conference room.

Being the last to arrive in the deeply stained wood-panelled room, Allison and Rick took their seats at the antique cedar table.

Allison listened with detached enthusiasm to the projects briefed to the Museum's Patron, Alastair Peterson. It wasn't that she thought they weren't deserving. But every nod made by Peterson took her further away from her intent to present the idea of support for an excavation of the Finlayson hut.

As the meeting droned on she mentally worked on plans on how the dig might proceed. Certainly it would be different from any others she'd participated in before. There'd be a greater degree of isolation, not to mention the extreme environment. Rick kicked her shin. She blinked out of her mental preparations and scowled at him.

"So, if there are no objections or additions to the three proposed projects I believe we have our planning mapped out for the year ahead." Alastair Peterson tipped the ash of his expensive cigar into an ashtray.

Trying not to cringe at what she believed to be a filthy habit, Allison cleared her throat.

Peterson condescendingly smiled at her. "Yes, Miss

Shaunessy, is there something you wish to add, seeing as how you've daydreamed through the majority of the meeting?"

Allison reined in her temper as the others around the table suddenly preoccupied themselves in their own papers. Peterson persisted in calling her Miss instead of Doctor. This usually didn't bother her, but he seemed to take a perverse pleasure in not recognising her academic achievements. *Why, he wouldn't know the difference between a duck's thighbone and a Hesperomis' thighbone from the late Cretaceous period. In fact, I bet if I asked him that now...*She mentally slapped herself. There were times to start an argument and clearly this wasn't one of them.

"Thank you, Dr. Peterson," Allison said as she inwardly cringed at her use of his honorary title. "I know your day ahead is no doubt busy, but I was wondering if you'd seen the papers this morning?" Peterson nodded. "Then I'm sure you read with interest the story about the discovery of evidence of the Finlayson expedition."

"Yes, I did. However the information provided was typical of the meat and vegetable journalism of the newspapers of this country. Sensationalism, damned sensationalism, that's all they're ever interested in."

Rick loudly blew his nose and Allison made a mental note to thank him later for halting the old man's rant.

"Unfortunately, they very rarely give the full story and this one's no different," Allison said. "As I'm sure you're aware, in the late nineteenth century there was a race between the civilised nations to see who'd be the first to explore the Antarctic region. Captain Cook is widely thought to be the first recorded man to sight Antarctica, or at least the edge of the ice pack in 1773, and Jules Sebastian was credited as being the first person to set foot on Antarctica in 1840. However, no one had comprehensively explored or established an exploration base on the continent. There's anecdotal evidence that before the turn of the nineteenth century whaling ships found themselves locked by the pack ice, forcing the ships and their men to face a frigid winter in the region. But, it's generally agreed no one had spent any great deal of time on the ice.

"In late 1894 the delegates of the Sixth International Geographical Congress met in London where it was universally declared that exploration of Antarctica and its environs was the greatest geographic exploration still to be undertaken. The congress urged that this should commence before the end of the century. At that meeting was an eccentric called Eric Finlayson, who'd explored most of the world's continents. He was an unconventional type, shunned by American society for his forward-thinking views on women and social democracy. It seemed a quirk of fate that Finlayson should attend the meeting as he was planning an expedition to Antarctica, one that supposedly left early the following year.

"Until now his presence on Antarctica has been hotly debated. After his ship departed from Christchurch in mid-August, he and his crew were never heard from again. It's widely believed the small ship perished in the southern ocean's treacherous waters, and that Finlayson never actually set foot on the continent. The 1899 expedition led by Carsten Borchgrevink was thought to be the first expedition to spend winter on Antarctica. That was until this recent discovery."

Alastair Peterson narrowed his eyes. "If my memory serves me correctly, all the drilling team found was wood. How could a piece of wood possibly be conclusive evidence of Finlayson's presence, if indeed he made it there in the first place?"

Allison forced herself to remain calm. Sometimes explaining anything to this man was like talking to a petulant child. As she surreptitiously glanced across the table, she saw the warning signals in Rick's eyes and collected herself. "Dr. Peterson, Antarctica has detailed maps which record all historical sites on the continent. This has been made possible by the fact that expeditions were widely publicised affairs. This, and the diaries the explorers kept, made it easier to plot their presence. Given that remains of every other expedition have been uncovered and duly recorded, it would be reasonable to expect that the site discovered in the past few days is Finlayson's."

"Well, *Miss* Shaunessy, that's all good and fine, and thank you for your history lesson. However, what has that got to do with this morning's proceedings?"

Allison bit the inside of her cheek to check her verbal retort and arranged her papers. *Sometimes men can be so*

*obtuse, or is it he knows full well what I want and is just wait-
ing for me to beg for it? Hold it together or you'll lose the battle
before it's really begun.* "If this is the Finlayson expedition
then its importance is tantamount to finding Hatshepsut's
gold, the Ark of the Covenant, the discovery of Earhardt's
final resting place. I couldn't think of any other organisa-
tion more imminently qualified to conduct such an excavation than the Flinders Museum of Australasian
Exploration."

Allison nervously took a sip of water as an uneasy
silence enveloped the room. She tentatively glanced across
the table at Rick and caught his quick reassuring smile.
Looking back at the head of the table, she was accosted by
Peterson's squinting features, encased in a semi-opaque
halo of expensive cigar smoke.

"So let me clarify what it is you're asking. You'd like
the Museum to fund such an excavation?" Allison nodded.
"Have you any idea how much such an expedition would
cost? Or are you suggesting we cut one of the already
agreed upon projects in favour of yours, only verbally
briefed, with no supporting documentation, unlike the
others presented today? And what about the logistics of
the matter? Going to Antarctica will require specialist
training and equipment, long before you even get close to
what may amount to no more than a wild goose chase. Fur-
thermore, if my memory serves me correctly, under a pro-
tocol ratified by the Antarctic Treaty, people undertaking
research in Antarctica must first prove they're mentally
and physically capable of actually operating on the continent. Your project costs alone would be tantamount to can-
celling at least two of the projects on the table this
morning." He coughed through the miasma surrounding
him.

"I think this would be a wonderful idea."

Allison turned her head and looked in shock at the
woman beside her. Not once since taking up tenure at the
Museum had Dianne Peterson, the daughter of the
Museum's Patron, supported her in any conceivable way.
If anything, Dianne often went out of her way to make
things difficult for her. *So why is blimbo so interested in this
all of a sudden?*

"What is it with young people these days?" Peterson

demanded in a booming voice. "Dianne, do you think I'm made of money? This archaeological chasing of rainbows would cost a fortune."

Dianne benignly smiled. "I understand that. But think how academic institutions and society would regard the Museum. Surely such an undertaking has the potential to attract more patrons to the Museum, which in turn would increase its credibility in both national and international circles?"

God, she's good, Allison thought. *She's clearly identified the critical vulnerability of this man and has him wrapped around her finger.* Allison recognised the references to the Museum and its credibility as a thinly disguised allusion to how Peterson's credibility would increase in society's eyes. She knew that while Peterson had grudgingly been the Museum's patron for so many years, the main reason he held such a position was the doors that it opened for him in political, business, and social circles. *But why? Why is she so interested in this? I'd think that somewhere a hell of a lot warmer would be more to her liking.* She glanced at Rick and found him entranced by Dianne's words. *Why doesn't that surprise me?*

The room collectively held its breath as Peterson considered Dianne's words. "I've no doubt there'd be a lot of positive publicity, not to mention first rights to any viewing of retrieved artefacts. However, Dianne, the matter is one of economics. I simply cannot afford to solely fund such a venture.

"The costs of this would be astronomical. But, I'm willing to provide in-principle funding for two-fifths of the costs of the excavation." He imperiously held up his hand. "I want to see numbers; a more concrete proposition of the finances involved. Then and only then if I agree, you may seek the additional funding and make the appropriate press releases. If it proves too expensive then the damned hut or whatever it is can remain down there for another hundred years."

Before Allison could reply, Peterson stood, signalling an end to the meeting. Allison watched as Dianne's svelte figure followed behind her more rotund father.

Allison smiled at the effect created by Peterson's departure. A positively joyous atmosphere quickly replaced the tense and business-like mood of the room. She watched as those around the table congratulated each other on their project's funding successes. She congratulated each team, in turn receiving offers of support for her expedition. She acknowledged their support and then looked across the room and sent a non-verbal cue to Rick that she wanted to leave.

As they entered Allison's office, Rick went straight to the top drawer of the filing cabinet. He retrieved her secret cache of whiskey, poured a small measure into the two tumblers, and handed one to her. He raised his glass in a toast. "You know, you could talk the legs off a chair."

Allison winced as the liquor traced a mercurial path down her throat. She leant against her table, silently yet begrudgingly acknowledging it hadn't been her efforts that had given her a foot in the door. "If I can talk the legs off a chair, that woman could charm candy from children. The way she pressed her father's buttons, not to mention some of the other men in the room was amazing."

Rick took another generous sip of the eighteen-year-old malt. "What do you mean the other men?"

Allison laughed. "When I looked at you, you couldn't keep your eyes off her, nor could anyone else, including some of the women. It was as if she'd bewitched you all." Allison contemplated the effect Dianne had on the gathering. "In fact, maybe she's not a blimbo at all. Maybe she's that witch from that old sixties television program. You know, the blonde headed one."

Rick chuckled. "Sometimes you make me laugh. I look at a number of women and yet Di always seems to get under your skin. You're seeing things. I think that whiskey's already gone to your head."

"No, I'm not, but it's a little early for this stuff, no matter how good it is." Allison returned the bottle to its hiding place and sat down behind her desk. She scratched a small spot above her eyebrow, an unconscious habit when she couldn't figure something out. "So why did she decide to support my proposal? She's never done that before."

Rick shrugged. "I don't know, but obviously she's interested in the project. Who knows, maybe it's her goal to go to Antarctica and look at the geology there. Apparently the formations are quite amazing, not to mention among the oldest in the world."

"If she hadn't been there, I've no doubt Peterson would've refused the project outright."

Rick nodded. "If we're to have any chance of success with your proposal then she's going to have to be part of the project team."

"You've got to be kidding. You know what we're like when we're put together. I don't know if I could put up with her moods on a regular basis. It's bad enough when I only see her for a few hours every day."

Rick held up his hand. "That may be the case, but face facts. Do you want to get this project off the ground?" Allison nodded. "If you want to succeed then you have to ensure you minimise any potential hurdles, and this includes a possible about face by the old man. Di may be the key to ensuring this doesn't happen."

Allison objected to the idea but she could see the inherent sense in Rick's words. She'd worked with difficult people before so, at least, she was in practice. She picked up the phone. "B...er Di, it's Alli. Do you have a minute? Rick and I are in my office brainstorming the proposal for the Finlayson Project and we were wondering if you were free to join us? Great. We'll see you in a tic. Bye." She hung up and smiled at Rick. "There, I did it."

Rick smugly grinned. "Yeah, but how long can you remain level-headed about the whole thing?" Allison's answer was belayed by a knock on the door. Dianne entered without waiting for a response.

Allison joined the two at her small coffee table. She silently laughed as Rick gallantly offered Dianne a chair. "Di, thanks very much for supporting me this morning. It was really touch and go there for a while."

Dianne graciously tilted her head. "No problem. I was very excited by the discovery and think it would be a great project for the Museum. So how do we tackle what needs to be done? Father said he was keen to see something in writing by Monday week and that leaves us six working days."

Allison bit her tongue over Dianne's use of "we." *I haven't even asked her to join the group and yet she's already trying to run the damn thing!* "I think the rule here will be

divide and conquer. I'll work on the written proposal if
you, Di, can canvass your social contacts regarding possible funding. Rick, you can work on the academic contacts
and see if we can get any from those groups. In fact, both
of you should work together to avoid any possibility of
doubling up. I want this to look as professional as possible. I'll work on a short presentation brief that could be
used to explain the aim, objectives, and outcomes of the
expedition."

Rick nodded. "How soon could you have the briefing
pack complete?"

Allison stood up and went to her bookcase. "My Doctoral papers are here somewhere. They contain the Finlayson information." She knelt and attempted to pull a well-
lodged wad of notes from her over-flowing bookcase. "On
one of these shelves is also the funding proposal I did during my first year here for the refurbishment of the south
wing. Now if I can only lay my hands on it."

"Hopefully it won't take you all day to find it." Allison's withering glare halted any further sarcastic comments from Rick. "What about trusts? Should we be
targeting these guys as well?"

Allison straightened. "That could be a difficult task.
There's a heap of them and trying to ensure the right ones
are targeted may be more trouble than it's worth."

"No, it's not really," Dianne interjected. "It's a matter
of knowing where to look. There's a group called the Australian Philanthropic Society for Educational Research and
they list all the trusts, along with their aims and objectives.
Father's a member of the society."

How convenient that must be. Allison nodded and
smiled. "Great. If you two can look at the list and divide it
between you, I'll get in touch with the Southern Hemisphere Antarctic Division regarding logistic and legislative requirements for the excavation."

Rick's eyes reflected his amusement at Allison's
restraint. "You might also want to try the Archaeology
Department at the Uni of New England. Weren't they the
initial group involved in the McKinley expedition?"

Dianne looked at Rick and then Allison. "What was
that one about?"

Hah! And you call yourself an archaeologist? Any first

year student knows about that. Allison's conscience again kicked her in the butt. *Hmm, gotta stop going there.*

"It was an expedition first conducted in the 1980's that involved excavating Sir Daniel McKinley's hut," Allison said. "He was the first man to lead a small team to the South Magnetic Pole. The information's a little dated but it's a start point." Dianne nodded. "I'll need some time to get this pack together. How about we meet tomorrow morning to nut out what we've got so far? How does a working breakfast in the conference room sound?"

Rick nodded. "Oh, great. I'll bring the coffee."

Dianne's perfect picket fence smile was almost too much for Allison. "Oh great! I'll bring the croissants and French pastries."

Allison nodded, like the head of a plastic dog in a car's rear window, as she ushered Rick and Dianne to the door. *Oh great! God give me strength.*

OVER THE NEXT six days Allison worked her small team hard and they met regularly, providing each other with updates. Allison spent the time preparing a brief that would satisfy Peterson, but as the days passed one thing became clear. The information she'd gained from both the University of New England and the Southern Hemisphere Antarctic Division highlighted the need to start detailed preparation now, if they were to work in Antarctica during the upcoming summer months.

Allison started her planning by securing, in principle, limited logistic support from Wills Station, one of three permanent Australian stations on the Antarctic continent, and the closest to the dig site. She also received an e-mail from Sarah Knight, advising her that the station's tracked vehicle assets could be relied upon for the transportation of the dig's larger items. Despite such support, a surface distance of nine days between the site and the station meant her team would have to be self-sufficient. This would mean dividing among the group the more routine tasks, while still maintaining a focus on the dig itself.

She also identified the need for any Antarctic team to undertake suitability testing, to ensure they could actually operate in extreme conditions without tragic or adverse outcomes. Allison checked the companies conducting such testing and tentatively booked a fourteen-day camp in Mount Cook, New Zealand.

Allison couldn't help but wonder at the seemingly endless list of tasks. There was the transportation of the team, their stores, and equipment to the white continent to deal with. She had to establish the site, conduct the dig, and finally extract the team and any artefacts in only eight weeks. Then when she had the team and the artefacts home, she had to oversee the creation of an artificial Antarctic environment to ensure the artefacts didn't deteriorate in the museum's different climatic conditions.

After the frantic pace of the past week, Allison's presentation to Mr. Peterson felt anti-climatic. She was grateful for Dianne's smooth handling of Peterson's belligerent interjections. It was obvious to Allison that Dianne had worked on her father before the project brief.

Allison collected her papers as Peterson slammed the door on his way out. "Two-fifths of the funding. At least that's a start. Still, it seemed to go a little bit too well, especially given the old, er, Mr. Peterson's objections last week. Rick, how did we go with securing private funding?" Her stomach sunk at the look on Rick's face.

"No go on donations from the business sector. All the institutions I approached have locked in their donations for the next financial year and have published those bequests. To go back on their word would be very untidy. That, and the recent economic downturn, meant they weren't all that keen to part with any more funds."

Allison shook her head. "Great. Is there any good news?"

"A little. Financial donations might have been hard to come by but we've gained some attractive material donations and sponsorship, including clothing and accommodation contributions for the duration of our stay on Antarctica. Another company has agreed to provide some specialist equipment and air fares to our departure point if we get past the selection stage in New Zealand," Rick replied.

Allison smiled. "Well, at least that's something, but it's not going to cover all the expenses. What about you, Di? Did you manage to drum up any support from Sydney's social community?"

Dianne shook her head. "It's the same story as Rick's. But I did get an offer from the Double Bay Ladies Croquet Club to knit some lovely woollen socks for the expeditioners."

Allison shrugged. *Great, just what I need.* "At least that's something. Please thank them and let them know we'll be in touch. What about the Trusts, any luck?"

"Same, same. Wrong time of year. Those who were most interested are more focussed on seeing if they could fund an expedition themselves."

Allison searched her mind for any other funding options the team hadn't already exhausted and then it dawned on her. *That's why the old bastard looked so smug during the presentation. He knew that even if he committed funds to the excavation, we'd never be able to fund the rest.* She forced herself to refocus on the problem at hand. "What about a Government Grant? Surely the State and Federal Governments would be interested?"

Dianne looked down at her briefing points. "State Government, no. They suggested that the discovery was one of national significance and should be funded by a Federal Government Grant. I wasn't having much luck with the Federal Government either so I spoke to Uncle Conrad. You remember, he's a Federal sitting member?" Allison and Rick nodded. "He spoke with his party members and they've agreed to fund our team accommodations on one of the Antarctic ice breakers. We'll have to pay for cargo space though. He didn't think the Party's generosity would spread that far."

Bloody tightwad politicians. Of course they'd support the least financially draining aspect of the journey. Then they could say they'd done something. "That's better than nothing. But where do we get the remaining three-fifths of the funding before someone else gazumps us and gets there first?"

Chapter
Two

My Darling Charlotte,

It seems days since I have been able to share my thoughts with you. The sea swells I mentioned in my last entry developed into one of the most ferocious storms I have ever encountered. The sea itself boiled in an ugly green anger, as if affronted at our small craft's incursion into its territory. The waves, like towering mountains, were bigger than anything I have ever seen before. It was not unusual for our little vessel to enter the trough of a wave, and for us to look up and see nothing but water above the highest point of the ship. It was as if the ship was no more than one of little Robert's toys, being tossed about in the frothy water of his bath at home.

Seasickness then struck the crew. Although they were reticent to take even the smallest morsel of food, I ordered cook to prepare a light meal for consumption at least once a day. To lose one's stomach and strength in such foul weather may well have been our undoing. As for cook, he was magnificent. Regardless of his seasickness, he soldiered on—I bless the day I signed him to the expedition's company.

Perhaps the most tragic outcome of this horrible storm was the loss of six of our dogs. The lashings on the deck could not withstand the force of the waves and sadly the dogs were swept to their death. It was a terrible loss for the crew, but thankfully the rest of us remain intact.

We are in relatively calmer waters now and hoping for a safer passage for the rest of our journey. God bless.

ERF

Houston, Texas—2009

MICHELA DeGRASSE'S FOCUS on her digital tablet was broken by the arms that traced a path down her shoulders before coming to rest on her chest. "Hey there."

A soft kiss grazed Michela's cheek.

"Hey yourself. What's keeping you up so late?" Natalie asked.

Michela glanced at the clock in the corner of her screen. "Is that the time? I didn't realise. I was looking at the *Antarctica Today* website. There's a report suggesting they've found the remains of an historical expedition, previously thought to be a myth." Her voice command took Michela to the pertinent area in the article. "He's an American called Finlayson and they're saying if the remains are genuine, then his would have been the first party to actually have spent time on Antarctica."

Natalie ruffled Michela's hair. "Still ruing not seeing a winter out on the Continent? I thought your current job would occupy enough of your time."

Michela shrugged and shifted in her chair. "It wasn't my fault my leg broke when it did. Instead of my own studies into humans in extreme environments, I ended up having to rely on the findings of others."

Natalie leaned forward and squinted at the screen. "I don't understand. What's this got to do with you?"

Michela wiped an invisible speck of dust from the side of her digital tablet. "The name of the glaciologist who made the discovery was mentioned and so I e-mailed her. Apparently there's a group in Australia attempting to mount an expedition to excavate the actual hut and surrounds. But they're struggling to raise funds."

"This isn't getting any clearer," Natalie said.

"If they manage to get the funding, Sarah, the glaciologist who made the discovery, said the archaeological team would be going down to Antarctica for about eight weeks to conduct the dig. It would be a great opportunity for me to conduct the practical aspects of my Mars mission research. The Institute might even agree to provide some funding." Natalie abruptly disentangled herself from Michela. Michela turned in her chair and looked at her. "What's the matter?"

Natalie bitterly laughed. "How many years have we been together?"

"Four-and-a-half. Why?"

"During that time, how long have we actually been in the same location?"

Michela sensed where the conversation, no argument, was heading. She stood and reached for Natalie's hand but Natalie backed away. Michela tilted her head and crossed her arms. "Honey, you're a model and I'm a psychologist. We've both got established careers. We've always known that travel would be a part of our jobs and that sometimes we'd be away from each other."

Natalie snorted. "That's an understatement. We've spent less than a year-and-a-half in the same location and I'm getting a bit tired of it."

"We've been able to spend a lot of time together lately," Michela said calmly. "Besides, you've had your fair share of trips away. Why don't we sit down and talk about it over a cup of coffee—"

Natalie glared. "God damn it! I'm not one of your subjects. I'm your lover. Every damn time I try and discuss something you make me feel as if I should be looking for a couch!"

"I do not. I've never spoken to you in that manner. And while we're on the subject, what's this obsession with me being so far away from you?" Michela unfolded her arms and took a step toward Natalie. "Regardless of where I am in the world, it's you I love. Do we need to be in the same place for you to know that?"

Natalie paced. "Hell, yes, I do! On top of never knowing when you're going to return, everything you do is damn dangerous. In Alaska you were nearly killed by a Polar bear. And then there was Nepal and your altitude sickness, just so you could assess the effect on the thought processes of humans. That trip almost killed you."

Michela inwardly cringed. *But this is what I do.* "You've always known my job came with the occasional occupational hazard. But, at no time has my life been actually threatened."

"Oh, really? So you being captured and held hostage by guerillas in Borneo and being one of only nine to survive doesn't constitute a threat to your life? It was six months before you could cope with a full day of work."

Michela's memories of barely surviving the thirty days of terror and privation were as clear as if it had happened only yesterday and she gently took Natalie in her arms. "Darling, this trip may never get off the ground. The complete funding is yet to be guaranteed and if that doesn't happen, then obviously they, and possibly I, won't be going anywhere."

"Yes. But if they, and I guess now *you*, do raise the funds, you'll leave me again, won't you?"

Michela stroked Natalie's long black hair. "Yes. But this will be the last time, I promise."

Natalie propelled Michela out of her arms. "Right. And that's what you said last time." She stormed out of the office, nearly dislodging the door from its hinges as she slammed it behind her.

MICHELA REVIEWED HER notes one last time before her meeting with the Institute's Director. She'd thrown herself into preparation for this meeting and yet the troubles she was experiencing at home still invaded her thoughts. She was so preoccupied with last night's attempt at reconciliation with Natalie that she almost missed the polite tones of Dr. Reilly's secretary.

"Excuse me, Dr. DeGrasse, Dr. Reilly will see you now."

Michela stood and gathered her notes. "Thank you." She gently knocked before entering the office.

"Good morning, Dr. DeGrasse." Dr. Reilly stood up from his desk and picked up his coffee cup. "Please have a seat."

"Thank you," she said as she sat in a plush leather seat at the coffee table.

Dr. Reilly took a seat across from her. "What brings you to the more mundane administrative offices of the Institute?"

"I was wondering whether you're aware of the recent discovery in the Antarctic," Michela said.

"Which one are you referring to? They regularly make so many discoveries down there."

Michela sat forward, barely masking her enthusiasm.

"Around two weeks ago a discovery was made that suggested the remains of the Finlayson expedition had been found. The glaciologist who made the discovery confirmed there were no other historical sites in that area."

Dr. Reilly sat back. He stroked his upper lip in thought and then nodded. "He was an American explorer of the late nineteenth century. A bit of an eccentric, I believe. If I remember correctly, it's thought he didn't make it to Antarctica."

"That's correct. The Flinders Museum of Australasian Exploration is currently trying to raise the money needed to fund a dig. To date they've managed to raise two-fifths of the entire amount."

Dr. Reilly smiled and picked up his cup. "Given we're talking about the proposed expedition, I'm assuming this has some remote link to your research."

"Yes, it does. Apparently, the initial group that will go won't be very large. They'll be very isolated for the greater part of the dig. To achieve their mission they'll have to be self-sufficient in an environment and conditions unfamiliar to them. This expedition would make a perfect practical medium to confirm some of my research theories."

"That might be so, but surely these people aren't going to be on the continent for over a year-and-a-half, which is the suggested duration of a mission to Mars. And besides, these people aren't astronauts."

"I know that. But like the crew being proposed for the Mars mission, they're a small team of professionals, thrown together in less than desirable circumstances. As individuals they'll no doubt have differing priorities regarding the excavation and its goals. Regardless of these priorities, they're going to have to work together. I believe this is an opportunity we shouldn't miss.

"From discussions I've had with Dr. Knight, the Australian team is going to be at the actual site for around eight weeks. This should be more than ample time to conduct my research." Michela placed a brief in front of Dr. Reilly. "This is an executive summary of what my study would cover. I've also attached a more detailed overview of the project and its outcomes."

Dr. Reilly quickly scanned the executive summary. "Supposing I agree to your submission. What are the costs involved?"

Michela nervously swallowed. "The Flinders Museum website has established a page that specifically relates to the expedition. The site is run by the head of the Flinders Museum team, Dr. Allison Shaunessy, and she's set the funding for the expedition at half a million dollars."

Dr. Reilly's eyes widened. "Half a million dollars. There's no conceivable way the Institute could afford such a large amount."

"I understand, but the Institute wouldn't be asked to provide all the funds. According to the Flinders Museum website, two-fifths of the money has already been donated. I was wondering whether the Institute could afford to fund the remainder."

Dr. Reilly stroked his chin in thought. "Even three hundred thousand dollars is a large sum, especially after we lost the first Mars spaceship to that damned terrorist plot. If this second attempt hadn't been a global undertaking, it's unlikely any one country could have covered the costs."

Michela nodded. "Financial circumstances aren't the best at the moment. But is there any possibility of funding?"

"I don't know. But you've picked your time well. Our weekly global status report is this afternoon. I'll put your proposal on the agenda but I can't make any promises." Dr. Reilly went to the door and opened it. "I'll advise you of the outcome in the next couple of days."

"Thank you very much."

Michela went back to her office. She dropped her notes on her desk and pressed the button on her intercom. "Frederick, can you come in here for a moment?"

Michela had barely settled herself at her desk before Frederick strolled into her office. "How did it go?"

"It's as I suspected. It's a great opportunity that might never see the light of day because of lack of funding," she said. "I'm beat. There's nothing here that I can't do from home, so if you need me that's where I'll be for the next few days."

"Sure, boss. You do look as if you've been burning the candle at both ends. Give me a call if you need anything."

Michela smiled as Frederick left the room. If anything,

he understood the work she did, unlike Natalie.

As she packed her briefcase and grabbed her digital tablet, Michela hoped the break from work would provide an opportunity for her and Natalie to reconcile their differences. The silence between them had gone on longer than ever before and this made her unsteady.

Her hopes of reconciliation were dashed when she arrived home to find a coldly succinct note from Natalie, stating she'd be at a fashion shoot for the next few days. She picked up Natalie's cell phone from the counter and shook her head. It was obvious that Natalie was still in no mood to talk. Michela put the note and phone back on the counter, took a hot shower, and got some well-deserved sleep.

THE FOLLOWING MORNING Michela's slumber was interrupted by the warbling tune from her cell phone. Barely awake, she answered, "Natalie, is that you? What time is it?"

"Dr. DeGrasse. I'm sorry to bother you. It's Dr. Reilly's secretary. He wishes to speak with you. Could you hold please?"

Michela vigorously rubbed her face.

"Michela, glad to hear you're taking a bit of a break," Dr. Reilly said. "I thought I'd contact you regarding your proposal. I've spoken with the other Committee members and they agree with it."

Michela's hopes sank at Dr. Reilly's pause. "Let me guess. They agree to the proposal in principle but funding is impossible."

Dr. Reilly chuckled softly. "Such pessimism at your age. The news isn't all good, but the Committee has agreed to fund a fifth of the expedition costs. You can speak with my PA regarding the e-funds transfer. You'll also need to submit the findings of your research to the Committee when you return—that is if the remaining monies are found."

One-fifth still left the expedition two hundred thousand short. Still, it's better than nothing. "Thank you, Dr. Reilly. I'll keep you informed."

Michela dragged herself out of bed and walked to her

office. She sat down, picked up her digital tablet, and dictated an e-mail to Sarah Knight, who she'd been in touch with over the last few days.

Hello Sarah,

I've some good news and some bad news. I've spoken with my Director, and the committee's agreed to provide $100,000.

Last time I checked the Flinders Museum website, they'd raised $200,000. Do you know whether they've had any further success? I'm at my wits' end here. If the remainder can't be funded out of Australia, I don't know whether the dig will ever get off the ground.

Keep me posted and I'll do the same.

Regards,

Michela

Michela sent the e-mail and then took a hot shower. As the water cascaded down her broad shoulders and over her body and sculpted legs, her thoughts turned to Natalie. Whenever Natalie was on a shoot she'd phone at least once a day, whether she had her own cell or not. The lack of communication with Natalie was unsettling.

After her shower she checked the phone and was disappointed by the absence of messages. Sighing, she retreated back into her office. Ignoring a number of work e-mails that needed her attention, she eagerly opened a new message in her inbox.

Hi Michela,

I bet you're surprised at the quick reply. I'm currently on my way home to Australia from Antarctica and I was busy sending some e-mails when your message came through.

That's great news. I know your Institute's donation isn't going to get the project off the ground, but at least the group's more than half way to its goal. Have you spoken with the team leader in Australia yet? Her name is Dr. Allison Shaunessy and apparently what she doesn't know about Finlayson isn't worth knowing. In case you haven't, I'll attach her work e-mail at the end of this message.

Re the remaining funds, have you approached the Finlayson family? I was speaking with my ex-girlfriend a few days ago and she's a computer geek. She mentioned something about the family being a giant in Information Technology in the States. Maybe they'd be interested in providing a financial donation.

Anyway, I've got to go. There's a big party tonight for the homeward-bound expeditioners and I don't want to miss out on free beer. Keep me posted.

Regards,
Sarah

Michela smiled at Sarah's casual reference to her ex-girlfriend. "Hmm, obviously family." Getting back to Sarah's suggestion, Michela opened a browser.

"Let's see what the business links bring up." Michela entered the business listings area and uttered *Finlayson*.

"I'll be. Go to Finlayson Enterprises, annual report." Michela scanned the screen. "Sarah, you were right. A top five hundred company no less, and look at those profits. So who is it that I should be talking to about a donation?" Her voice command took her to the Board of Directors and Michela laughed at what she found. "A company this size headed by a woman. I'll bet there aren't too many of those." She touched the photograph that defaulted to Charlotte Elizabeth Finlayson's abridged biography.

Michela shook her head. "The best schools, married and divorced, chair of a number of charities and still running a world-wide company. I wonder how she manages. A home in the country as well. Now that would be nice."

Charlotte Finlayson's contact details were at the bottom of the page. Taking a gamble, Michela picked up her cell and punched in the long distance number.

"Good morning. Finlayson Enterprises. May I help you?"

Michela was so surprised at actually reaching a person that she was momentarily speechless. "I'm sorry. Good morning, ma'am. My name is Dr. Michela DeGrasse."

"Good morning, Dr. DeGrasse. I'm Virginia Blainey, Ms. Finlayson's personal aide."

"Please excuse my surprise, but I'm amazed at actually getting through to her offices," Michela said.

Ms. Blainey softly laughed. "Ms. Finlayson believes

she should be contactable to anyone who has a sound reason to speak with her. I filter any undesirable calls she might receive. You're not one of those, are you, Doctor?"

"I assure you I'm not. I understand how busy she must be but I was wondering if it would be possible to actually speak with Ms. Finlayson about a small matter."

"May I ask what you wish to speak to her about?"

"Yes. I was hoping to talk with her about her ancestor, Eric Robert Finlayson, and the recent discovery down in Antarctica."

"You're not a reporter are you?" Ms. Blainey asked.

"No, I'm not. I work for the International Space Research Institute, in Houston, Texas."

"Would you please hold the line?"

Michela's ears were at once filled with a beautiful piece of classical music. As she tried to place the melody she was interrupted.

"Good morning, Dr. DeGrasse." Charlotte Finlayson's tones were warm and yet businesslike. "I'm between meetings and have very little time. What is it you wish to know about Eric Finlayson?"

"Good morning, ma'am. I'm a psychologist currently working with the International Space Research Institute."

"Yes, you mentioned that to my PA."

Michela couldn't be sure, but she was almost certain that Charlotte Finlayson was sassing her. "I've no doubt you're aware of the recent possible discovery of proof of Finlayson's expedition to Antarctica. What you may not be aware of is that there's a team in Australia attempting to organise an archaeological dig at the site. I'd like to be part of that expedition and was hoping to speak with you regarding any interest you may have."

"You're not suggesting a woman of my age would be interested in going down to Antarctica are you? No, of course you're not." Charlotte chuckled. "I'd like to discuss this further, however, I'm expecting a group of overseas delegates in my office at any minute. Hold the line will you?"

Before Michela could respond her head was again filled with classical music.

"Dr. DeGrasse, are you there?"

"Yes, ma'am."

"Virginia tells me I have a free couple of hours on Saturday afternoon. Do you think it would be possible for you to come up and discuss this matter with me? I'll have you picked up from the airport if you like."

Michela barely managed to contain a loud whoop of excitement. "Certainly, ma'am. What time would suit you? So I can book my flights."

"I'll put you back on with Virginia. She's so much better at that than me. I'll see you Saturday then."

After agreeing on the arrangements with Virginia, Michela checked the net for a low-cost flight to New York. She would fly out on Saturday morning and return early the following day. Michela quickly e-mailed Sarah with her news and then composed an e-mail to Dr. Shaunessy.

Hello Dr. Shaunessy,
We've not met. My name is Dr. Michela DeGrasse and I'm a psychologist working with the International Space Research Institute in Houston.

I read with interest the recent discovery by Sarah Knight of possible evidence of the Finlayson expedition. I contacted Sarah and she advised me you were attempting to raise funds to support an expedition, but from the progressive totals on your website, it would seem that you're having difficulty in securing the funding.

I'm writing to advise you I've managed to secure $100,000 worth of funding out of my Institute. Understandably this still leaves you $200,000 short, however I have a meeting this Saturday with the CEO of Finlayson Enterprises and I'm hoping she'll be interested in financially supporting the expedition. I'd like to discuss this with you and I'd be very grateful if you could contact me.
Regards,
Dr. Michela DeGrasse

Michela stretched as she read the e-mail. Satisfied, she touched the send icon on the screen. *Now I think it's time for some breakfast.*

Breakfast was a quick affair and it wasn't long before Michela grabbed a progress report from the Institute off her coffee table and flopped onto one of her living room chairs. She barely finished the first page when a high

pitched sound from her office heralded incoming mail. She
went into her office.

Good morning Dr. DeGrasse,
I've just finished reading your e-mail and am excited
and grateful beyond words. We'd really hit a dead end
here with funds. Notwithstanding, we've managed to pro-
cure some fairly high tech equipment from interested parties, so at least that's something.
One of the things I really hate about e-mail is the
inability to include a tone of any sorts in what I'm trying
to write. Having said that, I really don't know how else to
pose this question, so I'll be blunt. I'm very grateful for
your assistance in securing the additional funds. But why
is someone from a space research institute interested in an
archaeological dig?
Anyway, I must get back to business. Things to do and
not enough time—I look forward to receiving your reply.
Regards,
Dr. Shaunessy

Michela wryly smiled at the straightforwardness of
Dr. Shaunessy's message. Realising she'd been less than
direct in explaining her interest in the project, she set
about dictating a response.

Good afternoon Dr. Shaunessy,
Thanks for your reply. I hope you don't think me too
forward but Dr. DeGrasse is my mother's name, although
she's a medical doctor, not a psychologist. I'd prefer it if
you'd call me by my first name—Michela.
This takes me to the question from your last message.
As I've mentioned, I'm a psychologist with the International Space Research Institute. My work involves the psy-
chological group dynamics of how humans respond to
extreme and isolated environments. This study is prima-
rily focused on identifying possible problems likely to be
encountered by astronauts during space travel, and reme-
dying them before any spacecraft leaves the ground. Currently I'm undertaking research on problem-solving and
decision-making, at the small group level in stressful environments. This includes reviewing decisions made in iso-

lation of normally established support mechanisms a team might fall back on. I'm also looking for the presence of possible triggers or warning signs that might indicate a possible team breakdown.

In terms of extreme environments and isolation, Antarctica has previously been used as a test bed to undertake similar research. I'm sure you're aware that the International Space Research Institute is currently working on a manned mission to Mars. The information I'm collecting will be used to aid the astronauts who will crew that mission.

From the perspective of your archaeological dig, you'll be working in isolation, in an extreme and unfamiliar environment, with a multi-disciplined team who haven't all worked together before. This would provide me with an invaluable opportunity to validate the theoretical side of my research.

Again, my apologies for not clarifying this in my initial e-mail and hopefully this brief explanation makes matters a little more clear. I'll be flying to New York this Saturday and hopefully I'll have some good news for you after my meeting with the Finlayson Enterprises CEO.

Regards,
Michela DeGrasse

After sending her reply into the Internet ether, Michela headed back to her living room and the progress report that awaited her.

MICHELA PUT THE finishing touches to the presentation for the following morning when the phone rang. "Frederick, is that you?" She had left a message on his voice mail, advising him she was going to New York.

"No, it's Natalie. Were you expecting to hear from him?"

Michela cringed at Natalie's clipped tones. "Yes. I wanted to let him know I'd be out of town for a couple of days."

"Isn't that convenient. And here I was hoping I could talk with you when I return tomorrow morning. So, when will you be home?"

"I should be home by mid-morning Sunday."

"Fine, I'll see you then."

Michela winced at the abrupt end to the conversation. Before she could give it any further thought, the phone rang again. "Hello, Frederick? Listen, I've got to go to New York for a couple of days. Could you keep abreast of things? Yes. There may be the opportunity for some funding. I'll fill you in when I return. Thanks."

She gathered her notes and headed to her room to pack for the day ahead.

VIRGINIA BLAINEY MOTIONED to the waiting area of the CEO's offices. "Take a seat, Dr. DeGrasse. I'll let Ms. Finlayson know you're here."

Michela picked up a copy of the Company's quarterly report from a side table and made herself comfortable. She scanned the preliminary information and turned to a page containing a photograph of the CEO. Charlotte Finlayson was an imposing, yet elegant woman, her soft green eyes radiating comfort and trust. Before Michela could study the picture any further, the door across the room opened.

Charlotte Finlayson, elegantly dressed in a grey flannel suit, strode toward Michela. "Dr. DeGrasse, welcome. How was your flight? I hope it wasn't too bumpy. My last flight from Houston was so turbulent I nearly lost my dinner. But I'm sure you didn't come all the way here to discuss my fear of flying. Please, let's go into my office."

Michela followed, smiling at Charlotte Finlayson's Yankee pragmatism. *I can see how she manages in a man's world.* She admired the understated executive elegance of the office and found herself drawn to the painting hanging behind Ms. Finlayson's chair.

Charlotte followed Michela's gaze. "That's a portrait of my grandparents and their son, Robert. In fact I'm named after my grandmother. Please, have a seat."

"Thank you. I didn't realise you were a *direct* descendant of Eric Finlayson. You must be very excited about the discovery then."

"Yes, I am. It would be good to put to rest the stories that have abounded over the years of his success or otherwise, not to mention allow Grandmother Charlotte to finally rest in peace." Charlotte handed an ornate silver photograph to Michela.

Michela smiled at the picture of a small child, no more than twelve months, sitting on the knee of a woman of advancing years.

"That's my grandmother Charlotte and I. She died when I was young, but I know she went to her grave believing Eric made it to Antarctica. Enough of my talk. Please sit down and explain to me just exactly what it is you're seeking."

Michela gave her presentation in the same format she'd used with her director and finished with a request for much-needed funds.

Charlotte sat back and considered the request. "Despite the current profitable state of my company, what you're asking for is quite a sum of money. What might I gain from this venture?"

Michela ran through a number of slick responses and found herself drawn to a simple comment made by Charlotte. "There's no direct profit to be gained by you from this. But I believe there's more to this expedition than my studies and the recovery of artefacts." She gazed at the imposing painting of Finlayson and his family. "You said your grandmother always wondered whether Eric made it to Antarctica. If his body is there, this would confirm her belief in his success. At last you and your family would have closure."

Charlotte Finlayson scrutinised Michela. "I like you. I've had some business pitches thrown at me over the years and every once in a while it's nice to see that put aside for simple honesty.

"I'll agree to the funding on two conditions. I want you to head the expedition. It's not that I don't trust the team in Australia. But it's a large sum of my money and I want it managed by someone who won't run off and purchase every fancy piece of excavation equipment available." Michela reluctantly nodded. "The second condition is personal." Charlotte turned and looked at the portrait holding pride of place in her office. "Bring my ancestor home."

Michela couldn't help but be affected by the gravity of

Charlotte's request. "Ma'am, if he's there, I promise you I will."

Charlotte Finlayson cleared her throat. "Now, I'll have my lawyers draw up the papers and Virginia will give you the contact details you'll need to access these funds. Please keep me updated on the project's progress." She stood, motioning for Michela to do the same. "I look forward to speaking with you when you return. Now, if you'll excuse me, I've another business appointment. The car's still at your disposal for the remainder of the day; just don't do anything illegal in it." Her eyes twinkled as she escorted Michela to Ms. Blainey's desk.

Michela felt if she was walking on air as she left the imposing art deco style building. She barely noticed the driver in front of her.

"Where to, ma'am?"

Michela looked at her watch. "I didn't realise the meeting would be so quick. Could you take me to the airport? I might try to get a flight home tonight."

"Ma'am, there's a phone in the centre console if you'd like to check."

Michela sank into the plush leather. "Thank you." A quick call confirmed a late flight. *It's better than nothing. At least it might give me some time to talk through things with Natalie.*

IN THE AIRPORT, Michela sat in one of the business cubicles of the Club lounge. She made herself comfortable, released an excited breath, and narrated an e-mail to Sarah.

Hi Sarah

I've got great news! I've met with the CEO of Finlayson Enterprises and it so happens she's the grandchild of THE Finlayson. She's agreed to fund the remaining two-fifths, so now it's only a matter of coordinating things with the Flinders Museum.

I've been in touch with Dr. Shaunessy about the initial $100,000 from my Institute and she was very grateful. But there are some conditions to the Finlayson Enterprises donation, which I'm sure she won't be terribly happy about. I think I'll give it some thought before I e-mail her. At last, I can feel it coming together!

Regards,
Michela

She touched the send button and then called home. No answer. Disappointed, she returned the PDA to her jacket pocket. *Natalie must still be at work.* Michela picked up her briefcase and went into the lounge area. After grabbing a bite to eat, she made herself comfortable for the long wait before her flight.

GIVEN THE LATENESS of her return, Michela wasn't surprised to find a darkened house. She quietly closed the door behind her, put her briefcase and overnight bag on the couch and went up the stairs. She smiled in relief at the muted glow emanating from the door to their bedroom. She tiptoed down the wooden-floored hallway, opened the door and absorbed the scene before her.

"Frederick. I'm certain when I told you to keep abreast of things over the next few days I wasn't referring to my partner. And Natalie, what a surprise. It seems you weren't so lonely during my absences after all." Before either body on the bed could respond Michela turned and trotted down the stairs. She grabbed her overnight bag on her way out the door and walked into the moonless night.

Chapter
Three

My Darling Charlotte,

After being tossed around like a cork in a bathtub, it was wonderful to again stand on solid ground. We are ten days into our journey and yesterday morning we awoke to the comforting view of Macquarie Island. It is a rather barren place. However, after sailing on churning seas, it was a pleasant interlude. Using our rowing boats we were able to step onto the shores of the island, with no one to greet us excepting the penguins. You would love them my dear; with their small wings and predominantly black and white colouring—they look like gentlemen dressed for dinner. There are some amazing varieties among them; one possessing a crested plumage on its head, making it look as if it wore a wonderful wig or, as was the case with one small bird, as if he had flared eyebrows.

They share the beach with sea lions and seals and it is no surprise this Island attracts the oilers that it does, collecting seal oil from these innocents. Of course, I cannot complain too readily, considering a complement of my fuel is just that.

Tomorrow we will put this small interval behind us and set sail for Antarctica. I am sincerely hoping the weather is kinder to us this time, for I don't know if the crew could take any more of the horrendous seasickness they have suffered through so far.

My thoughts again go out to you and Robert. Take care, my love,

ERF

Houston, Texas—2009

THE SHRILL RINGING of the cell interrupted Michela from her work. "Hello, Michela speaking."

"Hey, sis, how's everything going?"

Michela smiled at the sound of Christine's voice. "They're going as fine as could be expected. I've spoken with my lawyer and he's currently discussing the settlement with Natalie's lawyer."

Christine let out a mock cheer. "I'm glad to see you've learnt from your last break up. I can't believe you walked out and left that other woman everything."

"There's a lot more to this relationship, especially from a material perspective. My lawyer's preliminary meeting with Natalie's lawyer indicates she's still hoping for a reconciliation."

"You've got to be joking. Surely she can't think that you're willing to take her back. Or are you?"

Michela collapsed into a chair and dragged her fingers through her hair. "No, definitely not. I know that over the past few months things weren't good between us, but after this I don't think I could ever trust her again. I expect the possible Antarctica trip may well have been the excuse she was looking for."

"So how are the preparations going? Have you heard from Australia yet?"

Michela looked across the room at her digital tablet, aware she was woefully behind in answering the e-mails that sat in her inbox. "To tell you the truth, I haven't been in touch with them. I've been so busy with this thing."

"I'll let you get back to it then. Make sure you let me know if you're about to disappear on another of your trips. Okay?"

"No problem. I'll drop you an e-mail as soon as I know." Over the telephone came the sound of an intercom calling Christine's name.

"Sorry, sis, I'm being paged. You know what it's like. No rest for us surgeons."

"I thought the saying was no rest for the wicked. I'll talk to you later. Take care."

Michela walked to her digital tablet, sat down, and reviewed the messages in her inbox. There were a number of increasingly insistent notes from Sarah, the last one a short note, asking Michela if she'd dropped off the face of the earth.

For the first time in days Michela laughed. She composed a quick reply.

Hi Sarah,

I'm sorry I've been off-line for a while. There have been some personal issues I had to take care of. Re whether I've spoken to Dr. Shaunessy since my trip to New York, no I haven't. But it's on my short list of things to do today.

I'm happy to hear Dr. Shaunessy's offered you a position on the expedition. It would be great to finally meet you and discuss a few issues over coffee (or something stronger)—not the least of which is one of the conditions surrounding Ms. Finlayson providing the additional funds.

I'll make this e-mail short so I can check what the good doctor has to say. I'll keep you posted.

Regards,
Michela

She touched the send button and shook her head. *This project is difficult enough with today's technology. I'll never understand how they ever got an expedition off the ground over a hundred years ago. What a nightmare.* She opened the e-mail from the Flinders Museum. It was a quick message from Allison, asking Michela whether she'd had any success with Ms. Finlayson. Michela closed her eyes and groaned. *I just know she's not going to like what I'm going to tell her. Can this week get any worse?* She checked her world clock and found it was morning in Australia.

Good morning Dr. Shaunessy,

My apologies in not getting back to you sooner but I had some immediate personal business to see to. You'll be pleased to know that Ms. Finlayson has agreed to funding the remaining $200,000 and I'll be speaking with a representative from her company regarding the arrangements for the money.

Unfortunately her donation is conditional. She's asked

that should you find the body of her ancestor that he be returned to her. The second condition is that I lead the expedition. I would have preferred to discuss this with you in person, however distances make this a little difficult. Rest assured that I see this position as one of managerial oversight only and do not intend to interfere with the actual dig.

I look forward to your reply,
Michela

Hoping she'd explained herself without sounding too abrupt, Michela sent the message and then settled down to answer the remaining messages in her inbox. She was two-thirds of the way through the task when her phone beeped.

"Dr. DeGrasse, it's Eric Stephenson. I've just had another meeting with Natalie's lawyer and it seems they're ready to sign the settlement papers. Would you be available this afternoon?"

Michela looked at the digital tablet's screen. "I do have a bit of work to do, but I'd really like to get this over and done with. Did they suggest a time?"

"They'd like to meet at two. Does that suit?"

Michela looked at her watch. An hour to travel what was only a small distance, at least practically, if not emotionally. "Yes, that's fine. I'll see you then."

Michela hung up, went upstairs to change, and prepared herself for another painful closure in her life.

Sydney, Australia—2009

ALLISON PICKED UP her stress ball and launched it at her door. "For Christ's sake!"

Rick Winston ducked and just managed to avoid the forcefully thrown missile. "What's wrong?" He picked up the sponge ball and placed it on Allison's desk.

Allison furiously pointed at the digital tablet's screen. "We've got the money."

"That's great news." Rick looked at the firm line of Allison's mouth and the scowl on her face. "It's not?"

"We only get it if DeGrasse can head the expedition." Allison turned the screen. "Here, read for yourself."

Rick scanned the e-mail. "I think she's made it clear that she sees the role as only a coordinating one."

"That's not the point. She's a bloody psychologist and has no experience in leading an archaeological dig," Allison said with a pout.

Rick laughed. "I think you're forgetting something here. Correct me if I'm wrong, but it's the $300,000 she's managed to get that's allowing the dig to get off the ground."

Allison shook her head. "That's not the point. This is my dig."

Rick laid a soothing hand on Allison's arm. "Be reasonable. You might see yourself as the leader. But you'd be the leader of nothing if she hadn't gained the additional funds."

Frustrated, Allison slapped Rick's hand. "Damn it, Rick. Can't you humour me and be on my side for once? I hope this bloody Yank doesn't turn the whole thing into a social experiment."

Rick stepped away, rubbing his hand where Allison had hit him. "Oh, for heaven's sake, Alli, grow up. I doubt she's going to make it anything like that. In fact, I'd be surprised if half the time you know she's even there." He turned to leave.

"Where are you going?"

"Di and I have to go over to Greeton's and pick up the first of the equipment for New Zealand training. We shouldn't be more than a couple of hours."

Allison crossed her arms. "So it's Di now. What happened to blimbo?"

Rick tilted his head to the ceiling and closed his eyes. "I give up," he muttered and closed the door behind him.

Allison again picked up the stress ball and threw it at the closing door, gaining satisfaction as it hit the polished wood with a resounding thud.

Houston, Texas—2009

MICHELA POURED HERSELF a glass of red wine and went to her digital tablet. The meeting hadn't been as bad as she expected it to be.

She worked through the messages in her inbox and cringed when she saw the response from Dr. Shaunessy.

Dr. DeGrasse,
You can imagine my surprise at your last e-mail. I accept Ms. Finlayson's conditions but I believe we need to be clear where your delineation of responsibility lies. As you've already mentioned, your role as leader will be purely managerial. The oversight of the dig is my responsibility.

We will only be a team of eight. As well as your research and oversight, you'll be expected to help with everyday tasks. Hopefully you won't mind getting your hands dirty.

There's also a legislative requirement for any group going to Antarctica to undertake training prior to arrival on the continent. I've approached the Christchurch office of the Southern Hemisphere Antarctic Division and they're willing to provide their training location near Mount Cook in about two week's time. Regardless of Ms. Finlayson's donation, if you're to be part of the team you'll have to attend this training. The rest of the team will look at meeting at 2.00 pm, New Zealand time, Friday 8 May at Christchurch Airport. You should meet us there.

Regarding e-funds transfer, I've placed at the bottom of this e-mail an electronic encoder that will allow you to access the expedition account. If you've any problems operating this, let me know.
Dr. Allison Shaunessy

Michela snorted at Allison's officious response. It was obvious from her words that Allison had assumed she'd be the team leader. *So you'll accept Ms. Finlayson's conditions. When should I point out that if you didn't, you officious twit, then this expedition wouldn't be going anywhere.* She shook her head at the direction regarding the training requirements in New Zealand. *So, Drill Sergeant Shaunessy, I'm to report at 1400 hours and no later, to Christchurch Airport in order to undertake my induction training? If your last e-mail is anything to go by then two weeks at Mount Cook is just going to be a ball.*

She chuckled as she formed a mental image of a short

woman in horn-rimmed glasses and sensible skirt calling the roll at Christchurch. *The things I get myself into,* she thought, before returning to her work.

New Zealand—2009

MICHELA SMILED AT the furiously waving figure standing off to one side of the helipad at Mount Cook. The blades had barely stopped rotating when the person made their way to the craft's side. The door opened and Michela was exposed to the crisp mountain air.

"Michela, I'm Sarah Knight. Finally we meet."

Michela smiled at Sarah's broad Australian accent. Sarah's well-tanned features belied a twelve-month stint on the Antarctic continent. She managed to break her stare from Sarah's sparkling green eyes. "The feeling's mutual. Sorry about the delay. There was a storm over Los Angeles that temporarily grounded all flights. I was lucky to get out when I did."

"Luckier than you think. The weather's closing in here too."

"Then I'm glad I managed to get here while it's still fine. The scenery here's breathtaking. The turquoise colour of the lakes here is amazing."

Sarah pointed to the snow-capped mountains around them. "That's caused by the glacial run off from those beauties. The flat glacial valleys are created in much the same way. Let's get your bags and get inside before it gets too cold."

Sarah walked to where Michela's bags had been stored and Michela followed her.

Michela hefted her bag strap over her shoulder and pulled on a pair of gloves. "When did you all get here?"

"We flew in late yesterday afternoon in two helos. It's an interesting group. You'll see what I mean shortly. From what Allison said last night, she intends to focus their work on the main building, once its structure's been iden-tified." Sarah opened the door to the building's enclosed porch. "You'll hear more about the dig this afternoon at our first team meeting with the training staff. The sleeping arrangements are fairly Spartan and not very private but I think that's all part of preparing people for what to expect down south."

Michela followed Sarah down the hallway and into a room that wasn't terribly bigger than the one she'd had during her first year at university. She silently chuckled as Sarah grabbed a pile of clothes off one of the beds and moved it to the one that was obviously her own.

"You'll be bunking with me. I hope you don't mind."

Michela placed her bag on the bed. "No, not at all. So where and when is this meeting being held?"

"Four doors down the hallway on the right, in the common room." Sarah looked at her watch. "We've probably got enough time to grab a quick brew before it starts."

Sarah led the way to the kitchen, where they prepared their hot beverage of choice, and then made their way to the common room.

Sarah opened the door and stepped aside, allowing Michela to enter first. "Look who I found out at the helipad. It's the long lost Dr. DeGrasse."

With all eyes on her, Michela drew on her years of training and managed a calm welcoming smile in return. Before she could say a word she caught movement in her peripheral vision. She turned and looked into the most amazing deep blue eyes she'd seen in years. Sparkling with energy, they suited the somewhat unruly brown locks of the woman before her. As if to validate her thoughts, the woman unconsciously ran her fingers through her hair before extending her hand to Michela.

"I'm Dr. Allison Shaunessy. It's good to see you could make it."

Michela returned the firm handshake. *Was that a comment about my lateness or is this a continuation of your last e-mail? Just what I need, a woman who thinks the world revolves around her. I thought I just left one of those behind me. And what's this insistence on Doctor? Surely she knows I'm aware of who she is. Maybe it's about time you came back down to earth, Dr. Shaunessy.*

"Allison, it's nice to meet you at last." Michela gave herself a personal high five. The slight twitch around Allison eyes confirmed the power game Allison was attempting to engage in. Michela elected not to apologise for a delay she'd no control over. "At least, I'm here now."

Before Allison could reply, the door opened, allowing what was obviously the training group leader and his team to enter.

"Ladies and gentlemen. Welcome to what will be your training camp for the next couple of weeks. I'm John Bryson and my team and I will be preparing you for your expedition to Antarctica. Now I won't bore you with my credentials. Just be aware that my team and I have been doing this for eight years now.

"During your stay here, you're going to be very busy. We'll cover a number of areas, including survival techniques, search and rescue, communication, plus living and travelling on the ice. My team and I will observe you in terms of suitability to actually spend time on the continent."

Dianne held up her hand. "You make it sound like if we don't pass the test, then we don't get to go."

John nodded. "You've about got it in one. The camp serves the two purposes of training and observing how you interact as a team. If I feel that one of you is a potentially destabilising influence on the rest of the group then I won't endorse your travel down south."

"So what's to stop us from going anyway or going somewhere else to get an endorsement?" Rick asked.

"There's a list of people's names and their signatures held by the customs people in Hobart, which is where you sail from. If one of those signatures isn't on your documentation then you won't get on the ship, let alone get to Antarctica. Think of it as an in-country visa if you will."

Michela watched the group uncomfortably shift in their seats.

John held up his hand. "I think you're getting ahead of yourselves. From your paperwork, two of you have had previous experience on the continent as well as one who spent a little time there. You're a group of professionals and I've no doubt you'll conduct yourself in that manner."

The group breathed a little easier.

"So let's get on with it shall we? I think we'll start with introductions before I give you a broad overview of the continent. Tonight we'll have a welcoming dinner and tomorrow we'll start our training with a short walk to the snow line, so I can gauge the fitness of each of you." John's gaze tracked around expectant faces in the room. "So who'd like to start?"

Michela slipped easily into her role of observer rather than active participant. She wasn't surprised when Allison was the first to stand up.

"As you know, I'm Dr. Allison Shaunessy, Allison or Alli will do. I'm an archaeologist who currently works with the Flinders Museum of Australasian Exploration. Apart from the obvious archaeological interest I have, I'm also interested in the man himself. My doctoral thesis was based on Finlayson."

Hmm, Michela thought. *Nothing like establishing credibility through academic snobbery.*

Michela watched as the man beside Allison stood and casually patted her on the backside and then self-assuredly folded his arms. "I'm Rick Winston and like Alli, I'm also an archaeologist with the Flinders Museum. There's a lot more to me than that. I've no doubt you'll get to know more about me throughout the week." He resumed his seat.

Michela inwardly sighed. *Very sure of ourselves, aren't we? There has to be at least one Alpha male in every group. As for the way he patted Allison's butt, you'd think she was his property or something.* Michela schooled her features and smiled as the woman on the other side of Rick stood.

"I'm Dianne Peterson and like Rick and Alli, I also work at the Flinders Museum. As well as having a degree in archaeology, I also have one in geology." Dianne gracefully flicked her blonde locks and smiled. "I guess I couldn't make up my mind which discipline I liked the best."

Michela silently laughed as Dianne wove her spell. *And at least one Alpha female as well.*

Sarah literally bounced out of her chair. "G'day. I'm Sarah Knight and I'm a glaciologist and a physician, with a side-interest in forensics. So I suppose if any of you get ill down there, I'll be the person you'll be seeing." She started to sit down and then stood again. "Oh yeah. It was me and that big buffoon in the corner who made the discovery of the site."

Michela sipped her coffee. *What you see is what you get. She may well be the glue that binds this group. Despite her*

*qualifications, she still seems to have a good rapport with those
she works with. I wonder if she can give lessons to the first
three?*

The man Sarah had alluded to now stood and poked
his tongue out at Sarah. "Big buffoon is it? We'll see who's
the big buffoon next time you want to get something off
the top shelf, shortie." The man looked well over six feet
and Michela doubted he'd ever get lost in a crowd. The
group laughed. "I'm Rob Shearing and like Sarah, I've finished my second stint down south. I'm an engineer by
trade, but I'm also a driller, specialising in ice drilling. Oh,
I'm also a carpenter—a jack of all trades you might say."
Rob folded his lanky form back into his seat and the man
beside him stood.

"I'm Michael Gribbin and the cook, so when we get
there if you've any complaints about the cooking then
come and see me. I won't change the way I cook, but if it
makes you feel better to complain, then fill your boots. I'm
also a jack of all trades, having worked as a jackaroo for a
few years."

"What's a jackaroo?" Michela asked.

"I think you know them as farm hands or cowboys.
It's about the same thing." Michael sat down.

"G'day. I'm Ewan McMillan and I'm a mechanic and
electrician. Like Rob and Mike, I'm also a bit of a jack of all
trades, so when we get there, I'm willing to help in any
way I can."

"Thanks, Ewan, that's great," Allison said as Ewan sat
down.

Michela stood. "I'm Michela DeGrasse and I'm a psychologist, working with the International Space Research
Institute in Houston, Texas. I'm involved with the current
Mars program and am studying how teams operate in
extreme and isolated environments."

"Great, a shrink!" Rob called out. He suggestively
wiggled his eyebrows. "Just show me your couch and I'll
be there as soon as I can."

Sarah snorted. "You're a pig, Shearing. You know
that, don't you?"

Rob grabbed at his chest in mock embarrassment.
"Stop it, you're making me blush."

Michela chuckled. "Rob, I'll remember your offer, but

I don't think they make couches that big."

John Bryson stood and briskly rubbed his hands together. "Right then, let's get underway. I'll start by telling you a bit about Antarctica. Some of you may believe you've been cold before, but you haven't been cold until you've been down south. Antarctica is the coldest continent on the earth. While it's gotten down to as low as minus one hundred and twenty eight point six degrees Fahrenheit, where you'll be working, the daily temperatures, wind chill included, will be between nineteen degrees and minus two degrees Fahrenheit. So, you'll need to ensure you're wearing the appropriate clothing at all times. Hypothermia and frostbite are a real threat in Antarctica, especially if you're not prepared. We'll cover layering and what you need to wear over the next few days.

"It's not only the temperature that'll cause you to freeze. There are Katabatic winds and they whip down from the inland, bombarding the coastal regions. The speeds have been registered as high as one hundred and ten miles per hour, but they normally blow at a constant nine miles an hour, with wind gusts greater than that.

"You'll be exposed to infrequent blizzards or white outs but hopefully not many during the time you'll be there. All the same, you need to be prepared for them as they can hit with very little notice and then rage for hours, even days. Once you've set up your base camp you'll need to ensure you establish blizzard ropes or guidelines around the camp. In a blizzard if you haven't done this, you can be within six paces of a building and not be able to see it.

"You'll sleep in small fibreglass huts, known as googies and apples, depending upon their size. They're comfortable enough to house two to three people and their belongings. Having said that, the living arrangements will be tighter than what you're used to. During the trip from Wills Station to your base camp, you'll be living in tents, so we'll also spend time teaching you how to erect those.

"Spread over the continent are long term field huts and remote refuges. They're plotted on all maps and should you find yourself stranded, they're fully equipped to cater for emergency accommodations. In an emergency the huts can be located using GPS.

"Some people think Antarctica is no more than a big block of sea ice. Wrong. The ice is actually fresh water and under the ice are mountains, valleys and lakes. It's an amazing place and, once you've been there, you'll never forget it. It's the largest repository of fresh water in the world and yet it's the driest continent on earth." John took a drink from a steaming mug. "Are there any questions at this stage?"

Dianne raised her hand. "If it's so cold there and all, how do you, well, you know, go to the toilet?"

John allowed the inexperienced group members to finish chuckling. "A reasonable question. There are portable toilets in Antarctica, however during expeditions away from an established base, all human waste is bagged in plastic and brought back to the station for destruction. For times when you don't feel like getting dressed in multiple layers to walk out to the portable toilet for a quick pee, women are given a funnel."

"A funnel? My God, you mean I have to pee down a funnel?"

Sarah joined in the polite laughter of the others. "It's not as bad as it sounds, Di. It doesn't mean you can't get up and use the toilet. But it takes about fifteen minutes to get dressed, ten minutes to get your clothes into a position where you can pee, ten minutes to re-robe, and then fifteen minutes to get undressed again. Give me a funnel any day. Trust me, after the first few days you'll think you've been doing it all your life."

"I doubt it," Dianne muttered.

"Are there any more questions? If not, I'll hand you over to my crew who'll teach you about the clothing you'll be wearing while in Antarctica."

The group spent the afternoon learning how to dress and undress, Antarctica style. The many layers of clothes made them look like a group of overweight tourists rather than doctors, scientists, and tradesmen.

Michela watched the group's interaction through the afternoon activities, and did her best to avoid getting into a situation where she and Allison worked together. The few times when she couldn't avoid the inevitable resulted in derisive and condescending comments from Allison. *It's obvious she's still got a problem with the team leadership issue.*

I think I'm going to have to speak with her before this comes to a head.

Sarah lightly tugged on Michela's sleeve. "Is everything alright?"

Michela turned and blinked at Sarah. "At the moment, yes. But I need to speak privately with Alli and I'm not looking forward to it."

"Knowing the signs and symptoms of hypothermia is essential." The look the instructor gave Michela alerted her that he wasn't happy with the interruption.

Michela shrugged at Sarah and they returned their attention to the lesson.

MICHELA FLOPPED DOWN onto her bed. "My God, I don't believe we've been going all afternoon. We haven't even done anything physical and I'm already tired."

Sarah reached across the span of the two beds and softly patted Michela's leg. "It's probably the jet lag. We've only got two hours time difference to cope with. You've got a day or more. You'll be right by tomorrow."

Michela gently removed the hand from its resting-place on her thigh and sat up. "I never did thank you for that lead regarding Charlotte Finlayson. Without Charlotte's funding, this expedition would never have gotten anywhere."

Sarah dismissively waved her hand. "Don't thank me, thank my ex-girlfriend. If I hadn't mentioned it to her then I wouldn't have been able to suggest it to you in the first place."

Michela's attention strayed to the recent events between her and Natalie and she nearly missed Sarah's words.

"Michela, are you alright? You look as if you're off on another planet."

Michela ruefully chuckled. "No, I'm fine. I was just thinking about you and your ex. It must be nice to stay in contact with each other. I don't think my ex-girlfriend and I will be contacting each other in the near future."

"Sounds bad. Is it recent?" Sarah asked.

Michela nodded. "Too recent to be talking about just yet. Besides that, my lifestyle's something I don't want the rest of the group to know about." She stopped at the slightly offended look on Sarah's face. "I'm sorry, it must be the jet lag. That didn't come out the right way. I mean, your e-mails indicated that you're open with your life-style, whereas I prefer my privacy."

Sarah held up her hand. "You don't have to worry about me. I understand your preference to keep it quiet."

"Don't get me wrong, plenty of my friends and work colleagues know I'm a lesbian, I just don't think everyone needs to know about it." Michela rubbed the back of her neck. "This conversation's getting far too deep for me. I think I'll try and wash off some of this jet lag."

Sarah laughed. "I better try and find something to wear to dinner among this bloody great pile of clothes." She plucked a pair of crumpled jeans off the floor and placed them on the bed as Michela headed for the door. "Michela."

"Yes?"

"I know we've only just met, but if you want to have a bit of a rant then I'm happy to be a sounding board," Sarah replied.

Michela smiled. "Thanks. I might just take you up on that."

ROB SPRAWLED HIS large frame into a chair. "That was the best meal I've had in ages. That venison was fantastic. And the Shiraz really topped it off. I wonder if there's another bottle around here somewhere."

Ewan sipped his port, a contented look on his face. "I wouldn't get too comfortable if I were you. There's still the washing up to be done."

"You're kidding aren't you?" Dianne said.

"He's only teasing," Rick replied. "I'm sure there's someone else here who's paid to do that stuff. And besides, I'm definitely not cut out to be a bottle-washer."

John Bryson laughed. "That may be the case, but in Antarctica you're all going to have to pull your weight. Obviously, you'll be busy with the dig, but with a group this size, you're all going to have to help with the more mundane tasks, such as washing up and emptying the toilet."

The group groaned in protest.

Rob nodded. "John's right. That's how things are down in Antarctica. We'll all have to learn to pitch in and accept the jobs that Allison gives us, hey Allison."

Allison disdainfully glared at Michela. "Why ask me, Rob. I'm just an archaeologist on this dig."

Rob's response and Allison's defensive body language signalled to Michela that Allison had yet to explain the leadership of the team to the rest of the group.

Like spectators in a tennis match, the group's focus alternated between Michela and Allison. Michela nervously rubbed the tip of her nose. *Why couldn't we resolve this like two adults?* "Allison."

Allison shook her head. "How can a shrink lead an archaeological expedition?"

"I don't think it has anything to do with who should rightfully lead the expedition. This is the basis behind Charlotte Finlayson providing the money." Michela watched Allison's features cloud over. "Look at it this way. As team leader you'd be responsible for a number of daily tasks. Tasks that potentially would take you away from the principle job you're there to do. It would be to your advantage not be team leader."

Allison stood up. "Well isn't that just peachy," she declared.

Before Michela could reply Allison was out the door.

Rick placed his glass on the small table and stood. "Maybe she shouldn't have had that last glass of red." He closed the door behind him as he went in search of Allison.

"Shit," Rob said. "If I'd have known such a simple question was going to result in after dinner entertainment then I never would've asked."

John stood. "There you go. Never a dull moment. Michela, have you got a moment please?"

Michela rose and followed John to his office.

"Is that true? I must admit, given the nature of the expedition, I naturally thought that Alli would lead the team," John said.

Michela nodded. "Frankly, I'd be just as happy not to have the position. As much as it would interfere with Dr. Shaunessy's work, it will do the same with mine. And besides, she obviously isn't happy with the arrangements."

"That's an understatement. But it does answer the question that's been plaguing me all afternoon when I saw how she reacted to you during the training. You're going to need to resolve the conflict between you and get the team to work together. If you don't, no amount of donations will have me sign off any paperwork to get either of you to Antarctica."

Michela nodded and yawned. "I understand, but at the moment if I don't find a bed, I'm likely to collapse. I think my jet lag's catching up with me."

John rose. "If you want to discuss this further, my door's always open. But, with your particular background, I'm sure you're more than qualified to find a solution to the problem."

SARAH TURNED AS Michela entered the room. "That was a show and a half."

Michela sat down and pulled her boots off. "I don't know if I'd call it that, but I do know I'm in no mood to go another round with her tonight." She felt her upper back twinge, and she reached for her shoulder in an attempt to massage the pain.

Sarah sat beside Michela and moved her hand away. "Here, let me do that."

Michela turned and tiredly smiled. "You're not trying to have your wicked way with me are you?"

Sarah snapped her fingers. "Darn, foiled again." She held up her hands and wiggled her fingers. "No, I'm a trained masseuse and I love my sleep."

"I don't follow," Michela said.

"Well, I figure if I can ease the pain then you won't be tossing and turning all night and then I can get some sleep."

Michela turned around and allowed Sarah to ease the stress from her shoulders. "Women and their ulterior motives, I should have known."

THE FOLLOWING DAYS were a flurry of activity as John and his team trained the group. They covered a num-

ber of topics, including snow and ice travel, both in vehicles and on foot, how to survive in extreme conditions, and
how to erect a tent in a snowstorm. The day for the tent
construction was made to order, and a gale blew for the
duration of activity. Although the final tents were reasonable, they would definitely not suit any long-term habita-
tion.

Despite Michael's presence as the cook, each member
was taken through the ration packs that would be the primary source of food during their eight-week stay. The
cooking lessons resulted in some interesting culinary cre-
ations, and the group learnt to eat what was prepared
regardless of its palatability.

A full day was set aside for rappelling down as well as
climbing up ice walls. In time of emergency this would
allow the group to extract a team member from a crevasse.

Navigation took up another day, as the group learnt
how to navigate both with map and GPS. Despite its size,
the GPS was capable of guiding a person to within one
yard of their destination. The team was equipped with
GPS that "talked" directly with a vehicle, through a simple
docking port. The result was the ability to pre-program a
journey and allow the GPS and vehicle to make subtle
shifts in the journey to cater to changes in terrain, while
ultimate control still rested with the driver.

"ALLISON, HAVE YOU got a moment?" John asked.

"Sure," she replied and followed John to his office.
She took a seat and waited while he closed the door.

"I thought it might be a good idea for me to clarify a
few issues before we begin the final two-day activity
tomorrow. Let me start by saying you display an amazing
ability to adapt to the training we've provided."

Allison smiled and made herself comfortable. "Thank
you. I've always been a bit of a fast learner."

John nodded. "But there are some issues I need to discuss with you. There's no way to do this diplomatically, so
I'll be blunt. You're great as an individual but your interaction with the team is appalling." He held up his hand.
"You're obviously disappointed about not being team
leader. But I believe you've allowed this to compromise

your working relationship with Dr. DeGrasse. She's tried every possible means to draw you into the group and you've resisted every olive branch she's extended. You continue to challenge her over the smallest of things. Just now, during the washing up, you were finding food specks on plates that even a magnifying glass wouldn't have been able to pick up. As a professional you need to overcome not being the team leader. If you can't get past this then you won't be part of any team going to Antarctica."

"But I know everything there is to know about this man," Allison protested. "I'm more than qualified for this job."

"That might be so, but you're not working as part of the team. That's more important down there than any amount of skill or knowledge you may have. I'll be assigned to your group for this next activity and I'd like to see a marked improvement in your attitude. If not, then I'm sorry but you'll leave me no other choice."

Allison tamped down on her frustration. "I'm sorry if I've been acting poorly and you're right. It was wrong of me to allow personal opinions to compromise my perspective. I'll do everything in my favour to ensure Dr. DeGrasse and I get along."

"I'm not saying you have to like her, but you do have to work as part of a team. That's what I want to see: professional courtesy and teamwork."

Allison nodded and left the room. His revelations were like a shock of cold water to her ego, forcing her to prove to him that she could rise above personal dislike to secure her place on the expedition.

MICHELA PULLED HER pack onto her shoulder. "Well, team, another task bites the dust. At this rate we'll be home in no time."

"I think that leaves the final navigation leg from here to the small peak over there." Allison indicated the way. "I'll plot the next leg if you like."

"Thanks, Allison." Michela looked at the tired faces of the people around her. "If the rest of you can take a quick break, I'll check in with John." She walked away from the group to the team supervisor.

"Why the confused expression?" John asked.

"I hope you don't mind me saying but I feel as if someone's stolen Alli and replaced her with someone a hell of a lot nicer and much more accommodating."

John chuckled. "Let's just say we had a talk the night before we started this final activity and there was a tiny bit of attitude adjustment involved."

She looked at Allison and shrugged. "Hell, I don't care what you did, she's a different person. A heck of a lot more polite and very easy to work with. Thanks for your help."

"No problem. I just think she needed to be set straight on a few matters."

Michela checked the position of the sun. "By my estimation this is the final leg. Allison's plotting the bound and we should be okay to go. Are you happy for us to leave, or would you rather we camped here tonight?"

"No, carry on. There's enough daylight left, especially if Allison's navigation is as good as it has been. If not, then I suppose it will be tents again."

Michela groaned. "Camping is highly overrated. I think I'll go and ensure the navigation's on the mark."

Michela walked to where Allison was briefing the group and waited until there was a pause in the conversation. "What's the plan?"

"Rather than go up and down these mountains, I've decided that contouring around these peaks might be the way to go. We'll start here and then move to that point." Allison motioned toward a re-entrant three hundred yards in the distance. "We'll cross that and then make a steady climb toward Berester peak. What do you reckon?"

Michela checked her map and nodded. "Sounds fine. Lead on."

John interrupted before the team went any further. "Remember what I said about things you can't see. I've allowed you to walk without you being belayed together mainly because I was familiar with the ground we were traversing. But this area's had a lot of new snow and I haven't been out here for at least a few weeks. I suggest we tie a belay rope between each member of the group."

Michela supervised the activity, ensuring there was the required thirty yards between each person. Allison stepped off, with Michela directly behind her. She watched as Allison infrequently disappeared up to her waist in the snowdrifts, and then continued ankle-deep in the snow.

Michela turned to answer a question from Ewan. Almost simultaneously her feet were swept from beneath her, and she slid uncontrollably along the snowy slope to where Allison had just been standing. Michela vigorously hacked into the snow with her snow axe to find purchase and halt her progress.

With desperate effort, she finally managed to stop. She quickly rigged a makeshift anchor point and ensured the rope was secure and under the control of two other team members. Hearing Allison's screams, she cut herself out of her belay rope above the anchor point, and carefully edged forward.

Seeing a break in the white, Michela lay on her stomach and slowly crawled to the lip of the hole. She watched as Allison swung precariously by the rope attached to her waist. "Whatever you do, try not to move around too much."

Despite Michela's calming words, Allison continued to struggle as she attempted to gain a foothold on the icy walls. "Don't let me go. Get me out of here!"

"Alli, stop moving around, honey. Alli, look at me." Michela waited until she had Allison's attention. "Honey, I'm not going to let you fall, but you must remain still. John's anchoring off and he'll be down there in a second, but you must remain still."

Allison nodded, the look of panic barely masked on her face.

Michela looked up in time to see John step off the edge of the crevasse. He slowly manoeuvred himself into a position that would allow him to attach a safety harness to Allison, and it was a measured crawl back up the icy face before John finally delivered Allison to the safety of the snow above.

Allison's shaky hands fought to release the clips of her makeshift safety harness. Michela placed a reassuring hand over Allison's. "Here, let me help," she said softly.

Michela removed the harness and placed it to the side before turning back to Allison. "It's okay, you're all right now."

Allison wrapped her arms around a surprised Michela. "Thank you for saving me. I don't know what would have happened if you didn't stop my fall."

Michela gently stroked Allison's back, strangely comfortable in her embrace. "It's okay. We all worked together and that's what being a team's about. You'd have done the same for me had the tables been turned."

Allison looked up at Michela, the realisation reflected in her face. "Yes I would."

John lightly touched Allison's shoulder. "Are you okay?"

Allison stepped out of Michela's arms. "Yes I am. I'm sorry about that. I guess I didn't look where I was going."

John shrugged, as if the near disaster was an everyday incident. "No harm done as long as you learn the lesson. Never be distracted so easily and always check the ground in front of you."

Shoulders slumped, Allison looked down at the snow, avoiding John's gaze. "I suppose that seals my fate then, doesn't it? No going to Antarctica for me."

John gently tugged on Allison's jacket and waited as she raised her head. "On the contrary, as far as I'm concerned you're going. You proved over the last two days that you can rise above personal issues and get the job done. And this incident, despite you being on the receiving end, you worked as part of a team, listening to your team leader and doing as you were told. I'd say you've more than passed the test." He picked up the coil of rope used in the rescue. "In fact I think you all have. I don't know about you lot but I could do with a good bath. Let's head back."

With a small cheer, the team collected their belongings, tied off, and headed for the lodge.

Chapter
Four

My Darling Charlotte,

Despite our most fervent prayers, we again encountered rough seas past Macquarie Island. I had often heard it said the waters of the southern ocean were among the most foreboding in the world and it is true. Fortunately this time half the group managed to master their horrible bouts of seasickness. You can imagine the relief of the men when the seas finally abated. That is, everyone except cook, who is back to having to provide three meals a day for the lads.

After so many days of rough seas, we finally found ourselves on what could only be the Antarctic fringe. Chunks of ice abound, and every so often a small iceberg sedately floats by the ship. While I understand some of these to be of mammoth size, we are yet to see such a monster. However, the ones we have observed are still of decent quantity, one such being approximately half the size of our ship.

The days grow longer here as we approach the continent, with little darkness to speak of. This hasn't been without its difficulties, as men struggle to sleep, while their body perceives it to be the middle of the day. It will only be a matter of time before we reach the pack ice and commence our steady traverse, for a break that will lead us to the continent.
All my love,

ERF

Hobart—2009

RICK PEERED TOWARD the harbour through the
hotel window that offered the smallest glimpse of the
orange-coloured ship that would transport them to Antarctica. "Are you sure that ship's going to be okay to sail in?
It hardly looks big enough for the trip."

Allison looked up from her work and smiled. "Of
course it will be. It's one of the newest icebreakers the
Norwegians have. We're fortunate the Southern Hemisphere Antarctic Division is chartering it. If we'd ended up
on a smaller ship we most likely wouldn't have had secure
storage space for our equipment and provisions."

Rick scratched his head. "If she's one of the most modern there is, why couldn't we have gone sooner?"

Seeing she was unlikely to get any work done, Allison
put her pen and notepad on the bed and sighed. "During
the late autumn and winter, Antarctica almost doubles in
size. This makes it almost impossible for the icebreakers to
get near the bases they support. The first couple of weeks
in October are when the first ships start their journey.
Hopefully by then the ice has begun to break up. And the
third week of November was the earliest we could get on
the ship. This is all in your information pack. Didn't you
read any of it?"

Rick shrugged and snatched one of the complimentary
biscuits from the top of the bar fridge. "I would have if I'd
more time. We've been flat out since May." He opened the
fridge door and was disappointed to find it empty. "I'm
going to head up to the bar for a quick drink. You coming?"

Allison shook her head. "No. There's still a lot more
stuff to go through here. You go on and I'll meet you there
later. I think we're all supposed to be there by five anyway."

Rick was out the door before she finished her sentence. She rolled her eyes before returning to the mess on
the bed. The non-stop roller coaster of preparation for the
dig hadn't been made any easier through the planning that
had been conducted from opposite ends of the world. Coupled with the basic logistic requirements of the expedition,
Allison had needed to ensure that the equipment to be

used at the site was environmentally friendly. This had been a challenge she'd struggled with.

She mentioned one such problem to Michela, who had included it in her regular brief to Charlotte Finlayson. Charlotte's resourcefulness and business contacts solved the issue almost immediately. One of the U.S. bases was in the process of testing a portable means of providing solar powered energy to remote expeditions. They'd developed a unit robust enough to face the rigours of extreme climate but were yet to test the equipment. A word from Charlotte had secured the unit, as well as its delivery to the site. Allison couldn't help but think how fortunate it was that Michela had been providing regular updates to her patron, or they may have never solved the problem.

Allison reflected over the months since Mount Cook. While there'd been disagreements, she begrudgingly admitted the two of them made a good team when they worked together. *Still, she can be bloody stubborn at times— it's a wonder anyone puts up with her at all. She's not bad for a Yank I suppose.* Allison smiled and returned to her work.

MICHELA WALKED TO the hotel reception desk and waited for service.

"Hey, stranger, long time no see."

Michela turned around. "Hey, Sarah. It seems you're always my welcoming committee."

"I often lurk in hotel foyers, waiting to pounce on unsuspecting women."

"Pounce away but after the last six months I'm about dead on my feet. I tried your suggestion and spent a couple of days in Melbourne before coming here, but I still feel as if I could do with a week's sleep."

Sarah sympathetically patted Michela's back. "Alli didn't give you too much trouble did she?"

Michela chuckled. "I'll be honest, there were some days when I felt I was dealing with more than one woman. There was one disagreement where I nearly had to utter those awful words 'I'm the leader and that's the way we're going to do it.' But most of the time we seemed to work well together." Sarah picked up one of Michela's suitcases. "Do you want a job as my valet or something?"

"Very funny. Hey, how're things on the personal side?"

Michela shrugged. "Not too bad. At least having to work long hours has meant little time for a personal life. I never did thank you for your sympathetic ear in the flight lounge in Christchurch."

Sarah waved away the thanks. "No worries. It was obvious you needed to talk about Natalie. I didn't think you could drink so much."

"I usually don't," Michela said. "Seriously though, it was good to get it off my chest. And thanks for the motivational e-mails since then. Some days they were just what I needed." Michela smiled as she recalled Sarah's regular correspondence, and the many hints that Sarah was more than willing to take their friendship to the next level. Michela knew that Sarah would only ever be a close friend—a friendship Michela wouldn't jeopardise with a night of what would most likely be passionate sex.

Sarah checked her watch. "Hey, it's about time to meet for drinks. How about I stop bugging you and let you get into your room and I'll head on up to the bar."

"Sound's like a plan. I'll see you there shortly."

MICHELA ENTERED THE top floor bar and was captivated by the floor-to-ceiling glass panelling that offered an unrivalled view of Hobart, its harbour and surrounds. A collage of pleasure boats liberally dotted the Derwent River, while the colourful Battery Row markets were full with a teaming mass of people.

She turned around and scanned the room, finally locating Sarah and the rest of the team.

"Hi, guys. Sorry I'm late, but when I got to my room I found I'd been put in some sort of hostel part of the hotel." The others laughed and Michela joined them. "I had to explain to them that I'd be living in a shoe box for the next couple of months and I wanted my final days before departure to be as palatial as possible."

A drinks steward approached the table. Michela sat and waited until the others had placed their orders and then placed her own.

"It won't be long now before we're finally on our

way," Michela said, after the steward walked away. "Has everyone checked in their stowed luggage?" The group nodded.

Rob nudged Sarah. "So, did you manage to fit all that booze within your weight restriction?"

Sarah mocked punched him. "Yes, mate, I did, thank you. I suppose weight restrictions won't be your problem, given those blow-up dolls don't take up so much room do they?"

Allison joined in the laughter. "What about you, Di? I swear you had a fashion wardrobe in Mount Cook. Are you going to get under restrictions?"

Dianne smiled. "Very funny, Alli. I'm prepared to meet any contingency. After all, you never know when you may meet the man of your dreams, isn't that right, Michela?"

"I don't like your chances on Antarctica—the people who work there year round have a tendency to become a little feral," Michela replied. "Seriously though, if you can't meet the restrictions then you'll need to fix it in the next couple of days before we sail. And that includes any duty free you might purchase before we go."

Michela took a sip of wine. "We're also required to attend a pre-departure briefing on the ship the day we sail." The group groaned. "I'm sorry, but this is compulsory. Anyone who isn't at the meeting won't be allowed to sail. I'd also like you all to be on the ship and settled before the briefing. Is everyone okay with that?"

The others murmured agreement and Allison raised her hand. "I've about squared away the stores and equipment for the expedition and I can have the cargo manifests to you by tomorrow morning if you like."

"Thank you," Michela said.

"Was there anything else that needed doing?"

"No, not really. But I was wondering how you all felt about having a team dinner tonight. Nothing fancy. I thought we could take in one of the seafood restaurants on Battery Point—a sort of last decent meal before we sail."

Rick snagged a chip from the bag on the table. "Sounds like a great idea, Michela. Have you got anywhere in mind?"

"Last time I was here there was a place called The Net.

It's casual but the food is to die for. How about we meet in the foyer at, say, seven-thirty? It isn't that far from the hotel and afterwards, those who want to can hit the night clubs."

Ewan rubbed his hands together. "Sounds like a plan. Fine food, fine women, who could ask for more?"

He ducked as the group threw serviettes and chips at him.

DINNER THAT EVENING turned out to be just as Michela promised. The finest seafood Tasmania had to offer, complemented by wines from the Tamar Valley made the group's evening a pleasant one.

Michela spent the meal silently observing the interaction between her comrades. They all seemed in good spirits, keen to start their journey regardless of the relative uncertainty that awaited them. As the meal drew to a close, Ewan was good to his word, pulling the men away, less Rick, for a tour of Hobart's seedier hot spots.

Michela was relieved at Sarah's suggestion of something a little more sedate, and Sarah guided them to a coffee shop, well known for its wonderful desserts.

The coffeehouse's soft musical tones and muted lighting were a welcome change from the noise they'd left behind at the restaurant. Michela searched for a seat in the stained wood booths that lined the walls. Before she could find one, Dianne pulled back from the group. "I think I'm going to have to take a rain check. I feel a headache coming on. You lot stay though. I'll find a cab to take me back to the hotel."

Allison turned to her. "Don't be silly. You've never been to Hobart before and you're not feeling well. We'll take you back to the hotel. We can get a coffee in the bar upstairs."

Rick lightly grabbed Allison's sleeve. "There's no need for everyone to miss out. How about I take Di back to the hotel and you girls have a bit of a night of it. I'll be fine. Ewan mentioned where the men were going. I'll track them down and keep them honest."

Michela internally cringed at Rick's use of "girl." *Why is it they're men, but we're girls?* "Are you sure?"

He quickly kissed Allison and patted her backside. "It's fine. Alli, honey, you hang onto the key and I'll get a spare one from reception." He gently guided Dianne to the door. "You girls have a good night."

Allison pointed to a vacant booth along the opposite wall. "I'll grab us some menus and meet you over there."

Sarah made herself comfortable along the length of one side of the booth. "I swear to God if he calls me girl again I'm going to flatten him."

Michela chuckled. "I thought it was just me. I wonder if he consciously does it? As for that damn patting on the backside thing, what's that all about? Anybody would think Alli's his property."

"It's so bloody condescending. If he was my partner, he'd have lost his arm by now."

Allison tossed the menus on the table and slid into the booth beside Michela. "Who'd have lost their arm?"

"That waiter at the restaurant. If he'd stroked my arm one more time I'd have decked him," Sarah replied.

"I thought he was merely trying to be polite." Allison smiled at Sarah. "I think he fancied you."

Sarah shifted. "He's bloody-well not my type."

Michela laughed at Sarah and the three took time to peruse their menus. After the waitress finished taking their orders, Michela glanced up and found her eyes locked on the blonde headed woman heading toward their table.

The woman stood head and shoulders above the other patrons, her confident walk testimony enough to acknowledge the eyes, both male and female, that followed her. Michela's body instinctively responded to what she saw and she barely managed to school her features before the woman stopped in front of them.

"Sarah Knight, as I live and breathe, don't you ever get enough of this place?"

Sarah propelled herself from her seat and into the woman's outstretched arms. "Maddi Walker. The things you see when you don't have a gun. What are you doing here?"

Maddi cast an appreciative eye at the two women at the table. "Just having a drink with some of the old crew. What brings you to this part of town?"

"Shit, where are my manners. Maddison Walker, meet Dr. Allison Shaunessy and Dr. Michela DeGrasse. We're part of a team going down to the Finlayson site."

Maddi's hand lingered in Michela's. "Maddi will do fine. Pleased to meet you both. That means you'll be on my territory, so you better behave. I'm the Team Leader for Wills Station and I'll be your immediate backup during your stay. So, Sarah, all the crew are here from your last tour. Got time for a quick hello?"

Sarah was torn between catching up with old friends and deserting her new team.

"I'm sure Alli and I can look after ourselves. Go and see your friends and we'll catch up with you later," Michela said.

"Are you sure?" Sarah asked.

Allison stood and sat where Sarah had been. She stretched her legs out on the bench. "There. Now you've got nowhere to sit, so you're going to have to go."

Nodding her thanks, Sarah took Maddi's hand and they wove their way around the tables and across to the group of women.

Maddi looked back at Michela's booth, nearly causing her to run into one of the tables. "So, are they a couple?"

Sarah laughed. "No way. Allison's straight. Her partner's currently out with the boys. As for Michela, she's family but let's just say she's not out and proud."

"What, she's not closeted is she?" Maddi asked.

Sarah shook her head. "No. She just doesn't see the need to share her private life with those who don't need to know about it, that's all."

Maddi laughed. "Ooh, I'd like to share her private life with her. By the way, that young biologist who you were all over last year is here, so be prepared for a heartfelt welcome."

"Sarah." A young woman stood and pulled Sarah into a long kiss and hug.

Sarah chuckled to herself. *Well, I never said I was discrete.*

MICHELA WATCHED ALLISON'S curious eyes follow Maddi and Sarah as they approached a crowded table. Allison's expression turned to surprise as she witnessed the display between Sarah and the short woman who greeted her.

Allison returned her gaze to Michela and struggled to conceal her embarrassment.

"Are you all right? Do you want to go home?" Michela asked.

Allison picked at a paper napkin. "No, I'm okay. Surprised that's all."

"About what?"

Allison motioned toward the loud group on the other side of the room. "I didn't realise she was gay. I mean, it's not as if I haven't met gay people before, it's, well, it came as a bit of a surprise."

Michela accepted her coffee from the waitress and directed Sarah's coffee to where she was now sitting. She sweetened her drink and looked at Allison. "Each to their own, I suppose."

Allison silently sipped her coffee. She surreptitiously looked at the group and then turned back Michela. "Doesn't it bother you? You know, to know you'll be bunking with her when we get to the continent?"

Oh, if only you knew the full story. I wonder what your reaction would be. "Firstly, I haven't finalised the accommodations arrangements and secondly, no, it doesn't bother me at all." Allison tilted her head. "Just because Sarah's gay doesn't mean she's interested in every woman she sees. For example, do you like Rob? Would you like to take things a little further with him?" Michela laughed as Allison's lip curled up in disgust.

"You've got to be joking. I mean he's nice guy and all but, well, he's not my type." Allison smiled and nodded in understanding. She took a sip of her coffee and boldly regarded Michela. "So what's your type?"

Michela's features sobered. While she'd had occasional partners, Natalie had been her one and only long-term relationship. *If only I'd spent more time at home.*

Allison touched her on the arm. "Michela, is everything alright?"

Michela put her hands to her face and rubbed it vigorously as if to scrub away sad memories. "It's okay, I'm fine. It's just I had a bad break-up after four-and-a-half years of what I thought was love ever after. I think your question shook me, that's all."

"When did it happen?"

Michela smiled in resignation. "Oh, not long before I flew out to Christchurch. Not the best timing I'll admit."

"I'm terribly sorry. It can't have been easy coming all that way, when there was unfinished business at home."

Michela shook her head. "That's the good thing about high paid lawyers. They managed to come to an agreement that suited us and didn't involve too much financial acrimony. No, coming to New Zealand happened at the right time."

A comfortable silence descended between them as they retreated into their own thoughts.

"I've never really thanked you for saving me that day," Allison said.

Michela frowned before realising Allison was referring to her fall at Mount Cook. She shrugged. "There's no need to thank me."

Allison took Michela's hand. "No, I'm serious. I don't know what I'd have done had you not acted so quickly. I was a right royal pain in the backside over there and you never once lost your temper. I'd hate for you to think I was ungrateful as well."

Michela looked at the smaller hand softly clasped around her own. Despite the lightness of touch, the heat between them was palpable, forcing her to wonder if Allison could also feel it. She locked eyes with Allison, seeing something there she couldn't readily discern. *Was it recognition or fear?*

"I don't know about you two but I'm about ready for bed and if I stay here any longer, someone's going to try and get me into theirs." Sarah cocked her head toward the group she'd just visited.

Michela smiled as she removed her hand from Allison's light grasp. "Yes, well, you will get yourself into these situations, won't you? Alli, you right to go?"

Allison stood and pulled her purse from her bag. "I'll just fix up the bill."

Sarah watched Allison until she was a safe distance from the booth. "What was that all about? Did I interrupt something?"

Michela quietly laughed as she stood. "Not at all. She

was merely thanking me for saving her in New Zealand."

Sarah smiled. "That's a relief, because I'm here to tell you, you've got a not-so-secret admirer in Maddi."

Michela glanced at the group and straight into Maddi Walker's appreciative gaze. Gallantly tilting her head in Maddi's direction, she smiled and turned to Sarah. "Yes. Well something tells me she'd be a bit of a handful and not one after long term commitment."

"Maddi would be devastated to discover you'd worked her out in less than one meeting." She nudged Michela good-naturedly. "Given she's on the same ship as us, you'll have to tread warily."

Michela visibly cringed, while at the same time a twinge of excitement coursed through her. "Great. Just what I need. An over-sexed God's gift to women on the same boat as us. Give me strength."

MICHELA LET OUT a relieved sigh that her team was present for the ship's final brief before sailing. The final day on the Australian mainland had been a frenzy of activity, with cargo manifests confirmed and personal equipment checked one final time.

The authoritative tones of *Durville's* captain forced her mind back to the meeting.

"Dr. DeGrasse, are you with us?"

Michela looked up. "Yes, I'm sorry, captain, I was doing one final crosscheck. What was it you said?"

"I was recommending that your team get a final good meal inside of them before we get into open water. If you remember from your first trip to the continent, maintaining your energy is important, especially if you suffer from seasickness."

"Thanks, captain. By the looks of some of them, they've indulged in nothing more than a liquid diet over the past few days and could do with some solid fare." Michela looked at Ewan. He was already green and they hadn't yet left the harbour.

Feeling a tug on her arm, she turned to Dianne. "You didn't mention you'd been down to Antarctica before."

Michela realised she had the immediate attention of her group but was reticent to yet again upset the captain.

"Yes. I was down there a little while ago, but I broke my leg in the opening days of training and was evacuated home," she whispered.

Michael Gribbin groaned and held his head in his hands. "Not more bloody training! I thought we finished that in Christchurch."

Michela patted his shoulder. "Don't worry. There won't be too much. I'm sure you'll be over your hangover by then."

The group chuckled lightly, resulting in the captain clearing his throat. They again returned their attention to the front of the room.

"I KNOW DINNER isn't going to seem like such a good idea, but at least try to get some food inside of you. If you're unlucky enough to be seasick during the voyage then the last thing you're going to want to do is eat." Michela turned to Sarah, who was busy tucking into her meal with gusto. "Did you manage to chat with the ship's doctor?"

Sarah swallowed and nodded. "Yep. He's more than happy to have some of the workload taken off him. So after dessert it'll be needles all round."

Ewan dropped his fork. "Needles. What for?"

"It's only a precautionary measure, but there's a greater chance of fighting seasickness if you have a needle while you're still well." Sarah wickedly smiled. "I promise I'll be gentle."

SARAH WAS ONE of the first of the group to recover from seasickness and she quickly checked on the rest of the team before volunteering her services to the ship's over-taxed medical staff. After an hour of confined spaces filled with less than savoury aromas, she was in dire need of fresh air.

She walked to the bow of the ship, and was surprised to see Allison, clothed in her wet and cold weather gear, standing legs astride as she rode the rise and dip of the ship in the mountainous waves.

As if sensing someone beside her, Allison turned. "This is great. It's just like catching one of the old Sydney-

Manly ferries on a really rainy day. You could stand at the bow of the ship, open to the wind, and get soaked by the spray as you crossed in front of Sydney Heads. It was terrifying and yet exhilarating at the same time."

Sarah laughed. "I remember. I think all Sydneysiders did that at some point in their life." She motioned with one hand at the rough seas, leaving the other hand safely grasping the railing. "But I don't think they were anything like this—this is magnificent."

Allison nodded as she hung on and rode the waves, like a cowboy riding a bronco.

"How's Rick coping? Has he managed to keep anything down?"

"He managed to keep down a little broth this morning. But at the rate he's going, he's going to run out of clothes. I swear he deliberately misses the bloody barf bag and throws up on himself." Allison shuddered.

Sarah shook her head. "I don't know how you put up with him."

Allison shrugged. "I suppose it's something you don't have to worry about."

"You saw what happened at the coffee house then?"

Allison snorted. "It was hard to miss it."

"Does it bother you?" Sarah watched Allison give the matter some thought.

"It did at first, but I don't think I was looking at it from a total perspective. I was more focussed on the fear factor."

Sarah chuckled. "Ah, yes. Evil lesbian openly preying on unsuspecting straight women."

"It sounds awful when you say it like that, but I guess that's how I felt," Allison said. "Michela gave me a different perspective on it though, asking me to see it from a heterosexual viewpoint. It made sense when she put it that way."

Sarah nodded. *That must have been a new concept for you, Michela.* "Yes, she's a smart woman, our Michela, and fortunately she seems to be recovering from her seasickness as well." Sarah pointed to the doorway. "Maybe we should go in now. I don't think it's all that good to spend too much time out here."

SARAH WATCHED AS the *Durville's* pilot boat struggled against the waves surrounding Macquarie Island. She wasn't surprised to be joined by Allison. "How's Rick?"

Allison shrugged. "He's not too bad. He's upset that the rest of the team are up and moving and yet he's still suffering. Sometimes he can be such a baby. So where are we in terms of our trip?"

"We're about half-way. In fact, it mightn't be a bad idea to try and get Rick onto some solid ground. Macquarie Island's annual stores have to be unloaded and that should take a while. A walk on solid land may be just what he needs."

Bending over the railing, Allison watched the stores preparation on the deck below. "So how do we get there?"

"There're two options. The first is the pilot boat." Sarah pointed to the small craft valiantly battling its way toward shore.

Allison groaned. "Given his condition, I think that's out of the question."

Sarah laughed at Allison's frustration. "I know what you mean. There's the air option. There'll be a helo that will carry under-slung loads between here and the station location." She stopped, suddenly aware of Allison's silence. "What's wrong?"

Allison hunched her shoulders and shoved her hands into the pockets of her wet weather jacket. "I can't go up in one of those things."

"What do you mean? They're quite safe."

"They may be but I had a bad experience with one once. I was in one that crashed into water. If we hadn't been taught the crash drills before I went up in the damned thing, I don't think any of us would have made it." Allison shuddered. "Planes, yes, helicopters no way."

"That leaves a small problem. Rick's too ill to be walking around Macquarie Island alone and I wouldn't trust any of the guys not to get him into more trouble." Sarah went through her list of options. "What about Di? Do you think she'd mind?"

Allison shrugged. "I don't think so. In fact she said something about wanting to see some penguins up close, especially the ones that look as if they're wearing a bad toupee."

Sarah laughed. "You mean the Royal Penguin? I like the Rockhopper Penguins myself. They're the ones with really outrageous eyebrows."

"Are you going to go ashore?"

Sarah nodded. "I'm going hiking with Maddi." She paused at Allison's doubtful look. "I can see what you're thinking but it's purely platonic. There's a nesting breed of albatross called the Light Mantled Sooty albatross and they're beautiful. The sailors often referred to them as the Blue Albatross because of their remarkable colour. The weather was so bad last time I was down here I never got a chance to see them."

Allison stepped back from the railing. "I think I'll wait until you download the photos. I better go and see if Di's available to take Rick onto the island."

MICHELA SAT AT the small desk in her cabin as she reviewed the trip to date. *The break on the island proved to be just what the team needed.* Even though the team had only been together for a short while, they were already finding the surroundings a little close for comfort. *This is just the sort of research that will aid my thesis.* She sighed at a knock on her door. "Come in."

Years of inbred courtesy and more than a modicum of nervous tension forced Michela to stand when Maddi Walker entered the room.

"Dr. DeGrasse, what are you doing here, locked in your room on the evening of such an inauspicious event?"

Michela shook herself out of the awkwardness she felt at Maddi's presence. "Catching up on my research. What's the occasion?"

"The captain tells me tonight we're to cross the Antarctic Convergence. You remember what that is, don't you?"

"From what I recall, it's the down south version of crossing the equator, or something like that. I'm a psychologist, not an oceanographer."

"And a very good looking one at that." Maddi laughed as Michela realised she was blushing. "I'm sorry if I've embarrassed you. I believe in speaking my mind."

Michela stumbled for words that wouldn't make her sound as if she were the oldest love starved teenager on the planet. "I'm sorry, I mean thank you. It's been a while since I've received such a compliment."

Maddi shook her head in mock disgust. "If others are blind, I'm certainly not. Anyway, I was wondering if you wanted to go to the Convergence initiation ceremony. There're a few drinks afterwards and it might be my last chance to unwind."

Michela knew Maddi was hopeful of more than merely her presence at the party. While she'd never been so forward with a woman, she found Maddi's approach exciting and her body reacted to the thought of the evening ahead. "After an offer like that, how could I refuse?"

"YOU KNOW, I think Rick would've loved to see this," Allison shouted into Sarah's ear.

Sarah looked at the group dressed in varying degrees of gaudy clothes. "It's unfortunate that the short break on Macquarie Island didn't help. I swear we were no sooner under way than you were looking for me to give him a shot."

"So what's this about?" Allison asked.

Sarah leant toward Allison to be heard over the rowdy gathering. "Have you ever crossed the equator?"

"Yes. I was on a cruise years ago. We celebrated the crossing with a big party and a bloke dressed up as Neptune blessed us with his alfoil trident."

Sarah laughed. "This is much the same. Technically it's known as the crossing of the Antarctic Convergence. It's where the colder southern oceans of the Antarctic Circle meet the warmer northern waters, forcing the southern waters to plunge below the warmer waters. These proceedings are probably a little more feral than your crossing of the equator. No one gets hurt, but there are some very suggestive comments made at times. If you're easily offended, now might be a good time to leave."

Allison shook her head. "No, I'm not that easily offended. Besides, I've spent enough time looking after Rick. At least tonight I'd like to see a little more than the smelly insides of our small cabin."

Sarah nodded. "It'll probably do you good to have a break from each other. I suppose he's pretty tired of being treated like an invalid, as much as you're tired of playing nurse." She pointed at Neptune's first victim. "Here comes the first unfortunate soul now."

Allison was so absorbed in watching the first victim pledge allegiance that she was surprised when two men manhandled her into the line of worshippers. She crawled on all fours until two guards at the foot of Neptune stopped her. She took Neptune's lewd directions with good grace, giving as good as she got, and at one point she caused Neptune himself to blush. After gracefully accepting her liquid punishment, Allison went back to where Sarah desperately swatted at two guards who were trying to force her into the receiving line. Before she could come to Sarah's rescue she felt a tap on her shoulder. She turned to Dianne.

"What's wrong?"

Dianne wrung her hands. "It's Rick. He's been ill again and he's calling for you. I'm sorry to spoil your fun but he looks like he's in a bad way."

Allison turned to Sarah. "Sorry to spoil your evening but I better go and see what's going on. You stay here."

Sarah gently grabbed Allison's elbow and guided her to the closest hatchway. "Now what sort of doctor would I be if I stayed here? Let's go and see my patient. It's a shame he's a non-paying one. I could have retired on his referrals alone." Sarah smiled as they went to the ship's accommodations area.

MICHELA FELT LIKE a ball in a pinball machine as they bounced from wall to wall in the narrow corridor. Her next comment was muffled by Maddi's hand, which softly covered her mouth.

"Ssssh. At this rate you'll wake up the rest of the ship."

Michela tried to put all her concentration and effort into walking down the middle of the corridor while leaning heavily on Maddi. *Geez. I was sure I only had two scotches. Maybe I should have eaten today.*

After managing to walk in a relatively straight line, she was relieved when Maddi finally leaned her back against the wall. Michela closed her eyes in relief but quickly opened them again as Maddi's hand plunged into the back pocket of her jeans.

"Just looking for your access card," Maddi whispered close to her ear.

Michela shuddered at Maddi's closeness. As she leant forward to increase the contact, Maddi removed her hand from her pocket.

Disappointed, she watched Maddi slip the card into its slot on the door. As the door was pushed open, Maddi wrapped an arm around Michela's waist and helped her into the compact confines of the cabin and closed the door.

Michela's inebriated gaze scanned the small cabin, before finally coming to rest on Maddi. She smiled broadly as Maddi slowly walked toward her and insinuated her body between her legs. Maddi's thumb gently stroked the small dimple in Michela's cheek.

"God, you've the most amazingly calm eyes." Maddi lightly ran her fingers through Michela's auburn hair. "Have you any idea how beautiful you are?" She entwined her hands at the nape of Michela's neck.

Michela felt Maddi's lips on her own, and giving into the sensation, she parted her lips to Maddi's soft insistent tongue.

As the kiss deepened, Michela felt Maddi's hand on her jeans and the top button gave way under Maddi's strong fingers. The feather light touches of Maddi's fingers against the soft skin of her stomach seemed to sober Michela, and she broke off the kiss. "I don't think I can do this."

Maddi encircled her arms around Michela's waist and pulled her closer. "Why not? You were doing fine a moment ago."

Michela's physical side reacted to Maddi's touch, while her more practical side struggled to answer. "I know we were. It's just we barely know each other." Her breathing hitched at Maddi's soft fingers against her lips.

"I know we barely know each other, but I also know you're an exceptionally intelligent and beautiful woman. I'm not asking for commitment. There's a spark between us that we both feel and I'd really like to do something about that. But I'm not about to take this anywhere you don't want it to go." Maddi withdrew her arms from Michela's waist. "Would you like me to leave?"

The sudden withdrawal of intimate warmth was like a dash of cold water. *For God's sake you're single, in a room*

*alone with an incredibly attractive woman, who's offering you
sex and God only knows that's something you've been missing
over the past seven months. At least she's being honest with her
intentions. What are you doing?* Michela looked up as Maddi
reached for the door handle.

Realising her silence had been misinterpreted, Michela gently grasped Maddi's arm. Maddi turned, her questioning eyes scanning Michela's. "I'm sorry. I zoned out
there for a moment." She reached out her hand, palm
upturned in offering, toward Maddi. "No, I don't want
you to leave."

Maddi smiled and drew Michela to her. She tugged
Michela's shirt clear of her pants, and traced a path over
her muscled stomach.

Michela released a shuddering breath and consumed
Maddi's lips with her own. Maddi lightly cupped the soft
silk fabric that encased Michela's breasts before she
slipped her hands around Michela and unclasped her bra.
Michela groaned at the sensation, as Maddi took her soft
breasts in her hands.

She pulled Maddi's T-shirt from the confines of her
cargo pants and ran her hands under the shirt to her
breasts, moaning with pleasure at the absence of a bra. She
softly rubbed her palms across the already hard nipples,
causing Maddi to uncontrollably buck against her thigh.

Maddi wrapped her arms around Michela's waist and
lightly rested her forehead on Michela's. "I swear to God if
I don't lie down I'm going to fall over."

Michela chuckled as she snagged Maddi's T-shirt.
"How about we get rid of some of this first?" She slowly
pulled the shirt over Maddi's head.

Maddi quietly laughed as she in turn peeled off Michela's shirt and bra. "Now why didn't I think of that?"

MADDI SILENTLY UNTANGLED herself from a
softly snoring Michela before retrieving her clothes from
their various resting-places throughout the room. She
tucked her T-shirt into her cargo pants and turned to
where Michela was sleeping, only to realise she was being
observed.

"Good morning." Michela's voice was thick with sleep

and a slight hangover.

Maddi glanced around the room, as if looking for an escape. "Good morning to you, too. I'm sorry, but I've got to go. There's some work I have to get done before we arrive at Wills."

Michela breathed a silent sigh of relief. Despite Maddi's assurances, she'd been a little worried about whether Maddi would be true to her word. "It's okay. I understand. No strings attached."

Maddi released a held breath. "Thank God for that." She winced. "Sorry. That didn't quite come out the way I meant it to. As I said last night, you're an incredibly beautiful and intelligent woman and I could feel something, almost primal, between us. I'm very grateful we can be adult about this."

Michela laughed at Maddi's struggle for diplomacy. "I think you better go before I have to get Sarah to extract more than the one foot that's already in your mouth."

Maddi gave her a cheeky shrug and a quick kiss on the cheek, and then slipped out the door.

Michela took a quick shower and dressed. She closed the door behind her and headed to Sarah's room for her daily report on the state of the team and their seasickness. While Ewan had managed to see half of the previous day through before retiring to bed, Rick was still a concern.

She quietly knocked on the cabin next to hers before entering. "Hi. How goes things this morning?"

Sarah, a smug look on her face, folded her arms and leant back against her chair. "Don't you think that's a question I should be asking? My my, we can be a little noisy, can't we?"

Michela blushed. "Sorry about that. I forgot the walls were so thin. Don't worry. There won't be a next time, so I don't think we'll be bothering you again."

Sarah shook her head. "Don't get me wrong. I think it's a great thing you and Maddi finally scratched the itch you've both been carrying around for days. And don't look so surprised. It's pretty obvious there's something between the two of you. All I'm saying is, well, I thought you were more discrete than that."

Michela ran her fingers through her hair. "I said I was discrete but I never said I was a nun. You're right though.

It won't do any good if the others were to find out. Thankfully Allison didn't come and see me this morning as she usually does."

"She's a little preoccupied with Rick at the moment. She was here only a short while ago getting some more medicine for him."

Michela frowned as a chill filled her stomach. "How long ago was that?"

"Oh, about fifteen minutes. Why?"

Michela creased her brow as she recalled the discussion at the coffeehouse that she and Allison had shared about Sarah. "That's about the time Maddi left my quarters and she didn't look as if she'd been paying a morning visit either."

"Let's hope for the sake of peace she didn't see Maddi," Sarah said.

MICHELA JOINED THE crew and excited expeditioners on deck at the first sighting of icebergs. She made her way through the crowd to Dianne and Allison, who were snapping off photographs of the glistening blue-white crags of ice. "They're beautiful, aren't they."

Dianne turned. "Hi, Michela. Aren't they magnificent? I mean, I've read about them but to see them up close is amazing. And to think the majority of these biggies are actually under the water."

Michela laughed at Dianne's enthusiasm before pointing at the blue hue of an ancient berg off the ship's bow. "That's a small one. Years ago one calved off the Ross Ice Shelf and it was the size of Tasmania. Quite unbelievable to think of a block of ice that size, not to mention what lies beneath the water level, hey Alli?"

Allison turned to Michela, her cobalt blue eyes piercing Michela's hazel ones. "Yes, it's surprising, isn't it? When you think you've seen all there is to see, there's so much hidden below the surface. A bit like deceit don't you think? It's so amazing what lurks beneath, where it can't be seen. Excuse me. I've got work to do. Dianne, Dr. DeGrasse." Allison disappeared in the crowd.

Michela watched as Dianne, preoccupied with getting a better shot, moved closer to the ship's railing, nudging people out of the way as she went. Sensing someone beside her, she turned to see the rueful smile on Sarah's face.

"If that's anything to go by, the good Dr. Shaunessy didn't miss a trick this morning. I'd say you've been well and truly caught out."

Chapter
Five

My Darling Charlotte,

After what seems like days of searching, we have finally found the coast of Antarctica. I will only admit this to you my love, but there were moments when I thought we would never sight land. Navigating through the pack ice was treacherous. More than once we found ourselves backtracking on the path we had taken in order to move forward. At times I could not help but wonder whether we were stumbling along the coastline like a group of drunken sailors, rather than the expeditioners we are. We were not without our false sightings of land either. On one such occasion we found ourselves beside an ice cliff, which we paralleled in the hope of finding an inlet. Imagine our surprise to find that after half a day's sailing we had merely reached the end of what was a mammoth iceberg.

When all seemed to naught, through the mist we stumbled upon a rocky inlet, large enough to provide shelter and allow us to commence the difficult task of unloading our stores and provisions for the long months ahead. I have decided that we will push inland five miles or so, rather than remain close to the shoreline. I feel this will provide us a better staging base, as well as protect us from the fierce storms of the coastal fringe. There is so much to do that I must prematurely finish this entry. Again, my thoughts are with you and dear Robert,

ERF

Antarctica—2009

MICHELA WATCHED AS the last of the stragglers entered the ship's briefing room. She gazed around the gathering. The expeditioners buzzed with curiosity, but she'd been through this before and had some idea what this meeting was about.

"Good morning, ladies and gentlemen, and welcome to Wills Station," the captain said. "Well, as close as we're going to get to it. We're about six miles from the station, but an unusually late thaw has meant that the depth of the ice between here and there makes it too difficult for the ship to safely cover the distance. So we'll off-load stores and personnel going ashore from here."

Michael Gribbin raised his hand. "You mean you're going to put gear down onto the ice? We've just crashed through the stuff. What stops it from cracking the moment we set foot on it?"

The captain chuckled. "That's a question often asked by newcomers. We're going to off-load the stores onto ten feet of solid ice and this is as stable as concrete. The weight is evenly distributed and no one point carries any great deal of pressure. Last season I off-loaded a twenty ton arctic tractor onto the ice and the surface held its ground. I don't think you've got anything to worry about.

"The movement to Wills Station will be in two phases, with the stores moving by ground and personnel by helicopter. Despite the fact you'll be travelling over pack ice, there's always the chance the helo may find a break between here and the station. Because of that, you'll all be trained in wearing an immersion suit before you fly out. For those of you unfamiliar with the suit, think of it as a sort of skin-tight garment with big boots. It's not the most comfortable thing to wear, but it's better than the alternative. In the unlikely event of a crash..." He paused as Allison quietly got up and left the room. He met Michela's eyes, and she nodded at his unspoken request.

"As I was saying, in the unlikely event of a crash these will keep you alive in the water. Without them you'd last for ten minutes. With them you can expect to last for eight hours. Off-loading will commence tomorrow at six in the morning. Will the Team Leader for Wills Station and the

Team Leader for the Finlayson expedition ensure there's someone present to supervise the off-loading of stores at the other end? The first flights will carry these people." Michela made a note of the timings for tomorrow.

As the meeting broke up Michela walked to the front of the room. "Captain, I'm sorry that Dr. Shaunessy left. I'm not sure what the problem is, but if you leave it to me I'll try to resolve it."

The captain smiled. "Not a problem. Just ensure she's fully aware of the requirements for tomorrow."

"Leave it to me."

MICHELA HEADED TOWARD her quarters, knocking on the doors of her group as she went. She gave them ten minutes to meet her in the mess.

When everyone had gathered, Michela allocated tasks for the following day. "There'll be about a two-hour delay between when the first stores depart by land and the main body of people depart by air. This will give enough time for the equipment to be on its way, while also catering for the two-person advance party to meet the stores at the other end. Alli and Rick, I'd like the two of you to be on the first chalk made available to us."

Rick tilted his head. "What's a chalk?"

"It's just a name given to a list of people who are flying by helicopter from one point to another. You and Alli can check the stores as they arrive and ensure they're placed in a separate bay, away from the others. Di, you and Rob will be first to leave in the main body, followed by Michael and Ewan and finally Sarah and myself. I've already spoken to the Wills Station team leader and she's confirmed we can rendezvous in the station's conference room once we've arrived. From there we'll be allocated our quarters for our stay. By eight tonight I'll post the flight details. The brief on immersion suits will take place about a half hour before you fly tomorrow. Any questions?" Michela hadn't missed the look on Allison's face at the reference to Maddi.

"I'd rather go by road," Allison said.

Michela turned to Allison, who stood in the corner, her arms tightly folded across her chest. *Oh dear, here we go. I'm sure this won't be the last time we'll clash swords over the next couple of months.* She took a calming breath. "I'm sorry, Alli. I don't know that we were given any option. The vehicles used to move stores aren't people carriers. They've space for a driver and that's all. If you were to travel in one you'd freeze."

Allison shook her head. "I don't care. I'd rather go by road and freeze. In fact if it's only six miles, why can't I walk?"

The group curiously watched the argument, and Michela gave Sarah a questioning look. Sarah quickly shook her head.

Rick put his arm around Allison's shoulders and gave them a good-natured shake. "What's wrong, Alli? It's only ten kilometers. It's not like it's going to hurt you know."

Allison forcefully shook away his arm. "What would you know? Your first helicopter ride was only a few days ago."

"God, what's wrong with you? Are you pre-menstrual or something?"

Michela silently groaned at Rick's short-sighted nature. *I can't believe you said that, you damned Neanderthal. There's something else bugging her, can't you see that?* She caught herself, realising that she hadn't initially picked up on what was now obvious.

"That wraps it up," Michela said. "Tomorrow will be busy and I ask you to follow the directions from the crew. We'll meet again in the Wills Station conference room tomorrow night. Now are there any more questions? Fine. The time's now your own." Allison strode out the door. "I guess that means the meeting's over." The remainder of the team filed out, leaving Michela and Sarah.

Exasperated, Michela ran her fingers through her hair. "What the hell is going on? First she walks out on the captain's briefing and now she walks out on mine. Obviously you know something I don't."

"It took you a little while to pick up on her body language. And you call yourself a psychologist."

Michela rolled her eyes. "I know. I think I'd prepared myself for a confrontation and was blind to anything else. What's the problem?"

"I'm not sure I should be telling you this, but Alli was

in a helicopter that went down over water. From what she's mentioned, I think she's lucky to be alive. Remember when we went to Macquarie Island and she stayed on board?" Michela nodded. "That's when she told me what had happened."

Michela mentally kicked herself for being so blind to what, given her profession, should have been obvious. "You're right. I should have picked up on her mood. But it doesn't change things. She's still going to have to leave by helo. Any suggestions on how we achieve this?"

"Short of tying her up and throwing her on the chopper?" Sarah laughed at Michela's outraged expression. "Seriously though, I think if we could talk her into taking a light dose of a relaxant that should be enough to calm her for the short journey."

Michela nodded. "That sounds like a possible solution if she'll listen to it. I can rearrange the chalks so that Rick and Alli fly second last and Di and Rob go on the advance chalk. Di's more than capable of supervising the checking of the equipment. I better go and mend some bridges with Alli."

MICHELA QUIETLY KNOCKED on Allison and Rick's cabin door. As she mulled on how to broach the topic with Allison, Rick opened the door.

"Michela, did you forget something?"

"No, I need to speak with Alli regarding a change to the chalk arrangements tomorrow." Michela wondered how much she should tell Rick. "I intend to fly Alli out in the second last chalk tomorrow to give her a chance to get used to the idea. Don't worry. I'll make sure you can fly out with her."

Rick smiled. "I understand what you're saying, but I think this is one of Alli's moods. We're here now and I'm keen to be off this tin can. Can't you reorganise it so Di and I fly out first and, say, Rob fly with Alli?"

Michela was lost for words. *You obviously don't know about Alli's fear of flying, do you? And you couldn't give a damn over why she feels the way she does. You selfish prick!* She struggled to rein in her temper. "I'm sure it could be arranged," she curtly replied. "In the meantime, do you know where I can find Alli?"

"She's in the cargo hold, doing a final equipment check. I swear the girl can be so single-minded sometimes that she just lets the rest of the world pass her by."

Michela thanked Rick before heading to the hold. *Sometimes that's not such a bad idea. And she's a damn woman, not a girl you misogynistic creep.*

Michela quietly walked to the bay holding the stores for the Finlayson expedition. Realising her presence was still unnoticed, she took the opportunity to watch Allison work. Her face was a picture of concentration as she ticked off items from a checklist. Allison curled her hair behind her ear, offering Michela a view of her high cheekbones and strong features. Michela's eyes traced a path up Allison's compact body, lingering on the tight waist, concealed in jeans and complemented by a long sleeved woollen skintight top that nicely outlined her breasts. *Breasts? Back up there a minute, woman. She's straight, remember? And what's more, you're not exactly on her Christmas card list at this moment.*

Michela cleared her throat. Allison turned around.

"What do you want?" Allison demanded.

"Good afternoon to you, too." Michela bit off any further sarcasm. "I hope you don't mind, but Sarah spoke to me after you left the meeting. Why didn't you tell me about your dislike of helicopters? We could have worked something out."

Allison shrugged and returned her focus to the tablet in her hands. "I really didn't think it was any of your business."

Michela took a calming breath. "It is when it concerns one of my team."

"Don't worry. *You* needn't worry about me. I'm sure you've got other more pressing issues or *people* you need to speak with."

I swear she's baiting me. Michela resisted the temptation to be equally sarcastic. Losing her temper would get her nowhere. "Sometime over the next few days I'd like to sit down and discuss a few things with you but we don't have that luxury right now. I'm sorry about your experience with the helicopter, but it's the only way we can get you from here to the station. If you wish, Sarah can give

you a mild sedative, enough to calm you for the journey."
Allison shrugged. "If I could, I'd move you by land. If you
want the sedative please speak with Sarah about it. If you
need to talk with me, I'll be in my cabin. Feel free to drop
by."

"Should I knock first, just in case you're preoccupied?"

Refusing to take the bait, Michela left Allison to her
work.

MICHELA RAISED HER head as the door to the Will's
Station conference room opened and Sarah entered. "First
here. I hope you don't want a gold star. Hey, how did
things go with Alli?"

Sarah leant against the desk that dominated the room
and removed her jacket. "Things went fine. I was surprised
to hear that Rick wasn't flying with her. I can't believe all
he wanted to do was to get here. If she was my woman I
wouldn't let her out of my sight."

Michela laughed. "Why does that not surprise me?
You're a softy at heart, aren't you?"

"Rick's, oh I don't know, a bloke and a single-minded
one at that. I spoke with Rob and gave him the bare facts
about Alli and flying, and he couldn't have been more
helpful. Now there's a real softy, even though he doesn't
look or act like it most of the time. And anyway, Rick got
his comeuppance by being in the first chalk."

"What do you mean?"

Sarah chuckled. "Just before the first flight was due to
take off there was an almighty gust. The Katabatic winds
were playing up again. I swear he was green before he
even got on the helo. Thank Christ I wasn't flying with
him."

They both laughed. "So, how's Alli?"

"She's fine."

The rest of the team filed into the room.

Michela quickly glanced at Allison, reluctantly thankful that her sullen features indicated the effects of the sedative had worn off. Rubbing her hands together, Michela
smiled at the group's expectant faces.

"We're finally here," she said. "Now, Michael, I know

you're not all that keen on more training, but there's a little bit more we've got to do. This will involve a quick brief on the Station's safety procedures, followed by training on one of our four ski-demons and our sno-trak."

"What's a ski-demon and a sno-trak?" Michael asked.

"A ski-demon is like a SKIDOO, just a different brand name," Rob replied. "A sno-trak, to put it politely, is an all terrain, tracked and heated washing machine that can fit four to five people per cycle, as well as tow a payload of about two tons."

Sarah laughed at the look on Michael's face. "Rob's right. They're very capable machines, but riding in them is like being tossed about in all different directions. For those of you who have read about the equipment in Antarctica, they're a lot like the HAGGLUND, which for many years was the vehicle of choice down here."

Michela nodded. "Rob will be the driver for one of the two sno-trak's travelling with us to the dig site. The other will carry the rest of the group and will return to station once we've been dropped off."

Ewan held up his hand. "What about the rest of the stores?"

"Some of our equipment has been pre-positioned. The portable solar power plant organised by the Finlayson Corporation has been put in place and will be waiting us on our arrival." Michela held up her hand, waylaying the outraged response that looked about to erupt from Allison. "Using Sarah's coordinates and resonance testing of the ground, they've made sure they weren't putting it anywhere near the actual historical site. In fact, it's a good forty yards from where Sarah took her core sample, Allison. If historical records are any indication, you're not going to find a building that big in Antarctica.

"On top of that, the hut that will serve as our kitchen and office will move by air. Weather permitting, this will be flown out tomorrow to our base camp by a Chinook as an under-slung load. Using the trailer on the sno-traks and a sixteen ton BOB-trak 5000, we should be able to move the remainder of our equipment."

"I'll be the bunny. What's a BOB-trak 5000?" Ewan asked.

Sarah chuckled. "It's more commonly known as BOB,

which stands for beast of burden. Think of an enclosed rectangular tractor on tracked wheels, like a tank. Like the old NODWELL, if you're familiar with that." Ewan nodded. "They're a very handy piece of transportation for scientific expeditions because of the heavy loads they can tow."

Michela nodded. "Sarah's right. It will be our workhorse. Unfortunately, because of the speed of the BOB-trak and my intent to travel as a group, our movement will be relatively slow. Loaded, the vehicle's top speed is about twelve-and-a-half miles an hour in good conditions. Only experienced operators are allowed to drive these so we'll off-load our stores and then the driver of BOB will return to base, accompanied by the driver and the second sno-trak."

Dianne stifled a yawn. "That's fine but where are we sleeping tonight? I'm about ready for bed."

"Long term expeditioners are allocated a room in the building we're in," Michela said. "Because we're only going to be here for a short while, we've been put in two of the dongas outside. And Michael, before you ask, these are the living vans. You'd have seen them when you arrived."

"You're not talking about the refrigerated containers outside? God, we'll freeze," Rick declared.

"First off, you won't freeze. Each of the vans has a heating unit. And second, get used to the conditions. On the move to the dig site we'll be living in tents. I'm sorry people, but this place doesn't have a five star rating."

"I think we all know that," Allison interjected. "Why don't you just tell us who has what container and we'll be on our way."

Michela pretended to check the papers in front of her instead of reacting to Allison's belligerent tones. Deliberately avoiding Allison's eyes, she replied, "Because of the number of people here at the moment, we've been allocated two vans of four beds each—one for the men and one for the women. They're vans one and two, just down the stairs, off the main building."

Allison flung her head back. "Isn't that snug. I can't wait."

"What are the shower arrangements? I feel like a nice long soak," Dianne asked.

"Sorry, Di," Michela said. The shower arrangements here are pretty tight. They're set to a timer and automatically turn off after five minutes. We've been allowed a shower now and one before we leave, so think of the other people on the station and use the water sparingly." She quietly chuckled at the shocked look on Dianne's face. "Now, if there's nothing more, the women will be in van one and the men in two. Training starts at nine tomorrow morning, with breakfast at seven-thirty. I'll see you then."

She'd barely finished her final comments and Allison was out the door. She studied her digital tablet. As the door closed behind the departing group, she growled in frustration, only to hear Sarah's laughter.

"I take it all back. You have the patience of a saint," Sarah said.

"She's driving me crazy. If she's angry over what she saw then why doesn't she damned well come out and say it? I swear to God, she's the most frustrating woman I've ever met."

Sarah patted Michela on the back. "Look at the positives. It'll be good for your study."

ALLISON PULLED HER beanie from her head, removed her jacket, and sat down in one of the conference room chairs. She watched as other members of the group also disrobed as they laughed among themselves.

Derek Fowler, the second-in-command of Wills Station, cleared his throat to gain the group's attention. "It was good to see that so many of you were familiar with a ski-demon. It doesn't matter that not all of you managed to master the art of driving the sno-trak. I assume Rob'll be doing the bulk of the driving there and back.

"I know I gave you a quick brief on the station emergency procedures, but I'd like to remind you about the emergency huts that are located throughout Antarctica. If you pull out your maps we'll go on." Derek waited until there were at least two team members to a map.

"These are a lot like the dongas you slept in last night. They carry emergency rations and bedding, enough for a group to sit out a blizzard. As you can see, these are already pre-plotted on your maps. Now, if there are no

questions, I'll run through the emergency evacuation procedures to be used when recovering a team member from a
remote site back to the base."

Despite the importance of the information being presented, Allison's mind wandered. *Were all the stores ready
for travel yet? Had anything been broken in the move?* She was
dying to get back to checking the equipment.

At the next break she looked around the room,
attempting to locate Michela. *I really do need to get back to
checking those stores. The idea of asking that woman to be
excused riles me no end, but if I have to sit through another
briefing I may commit a murder.* She turned to Rob.

"Where's Dr. DeGrasse?"

Rob shrugged. "Buggered if I know. The last I saw of
her she was heading off with the Wills Station team leader.
They were deep in discussion about something or other."

Allison thanked him and turned to the window. Looking over the white landscape, randomly dotted with a cornucopia of modern and not-so-modern buildings, she
mentally vented her spleen. *That's all this group needs is a
bloody oversexed woman on it. For Christ sake, can't she keep
her mind on the job at hand? If she can't, then one of us will.*
She quietly took her leave and went to the warehouse and
the expedition's stores.

MICHELA TICKED OFF her task list on her digital
tablet.

"I've gone through your two primary means of communication, but unfortunately if we get solar flare activity
you won't be able to contact us. If this happens you should
re-establish comms at the next available opportunity.
You've got enough backup fuel should your solar power
unit not work. But in deference to the environment, I'd
prefer you keep fossil fuel use to a minimum." Maddi
rubbed her hands on the back of her jeans. "That about
covers it. Any questions?"

Michela shook her head. "I don't think so. I'm sure the
occasional issue will come up, but I'll deal with those as
they come along."

Maddi smiled. "Yep. Down here thinking on your feet
can be the difference between success and failure. By the

way, what's the matter with Alli? I said good morning to her this morning and she gave me a look so scary that it could convince small children to eat their veggies."

"I know what you mean. Apparently, she saw you leave my quarters the other morning and she's had a bee up her ass ever since."

"So, why should it bother her, what you do with your social time?"

"I think it's got more to do with the fact she's made a wrong assumption," Michela replied. "My dealings with her over the past six or so months indicate she's a little proud and doesn't like to be wrong. I mean, you should have seen the accommodations hut last night. Di and Alli occupied the two beds down one end, with Sarah and I down the other end. In between was an assortment of hanging towels, as if Alli was afraid that Sarah and I would spend our time gawking in her general direction."

Maddi patted Michela's shoulder. "It sounds like you've got your work cut out for you. A word of advice. Clear the air before you leave here. The last thing you want is dissent at a remote site. And, of course, if there's a problem with the sleeping arrangements, you could always bunk with me tonight."

Michela grimaced. "Oh, right. That would be a great solution." They both laughed. "You're right about solving things. I wish she could be a little more adult about it."

Michela left Maddi to her work and went to where the rest of the team was training. She wasn't surprised that Allison was absent and, guessing Allison's location, headed to the warehousing area of the station. Seeing Allison in the far bay, Michela calmed herself as she searched for a benign way to begin the conversation. Allison, wearing a less than savoury expression, acknowledged her presence.

Pasting on a smile, she walked to Allison. "You seem to have your work cut out for you here. How's the stores reconciliation going?"

Allison glanced at Michela. "I'd have thought that was the least of your worries, given your obvious preoccupation with Maddi."

All thoughts of rational discussion left Michela as she fought to retain a calm appearance around the other people in the bay. Aware of prying ears, she moved close enough so that only Allison could hear her. "That's it," she uttered through clenched teeth. "Come with me, now." She turned, not bothering to see if Allison followed her.

Michela walked out of the warehouse and into the main building, in search of the nearest vacant room. When she found one, she waited by the door for Allison to enter, and then closed it quietly behind her. "Just what is your problem? You've been like a damned bear with a sore head for days now and I've just about had enough."

"You've had enough? You're bloody well not the only one. You must think I'm so terribly gullible buying your story of lost love. I can't believe I was so stupid to even believe you. I've no doubt you and Maddi had a good laugh on my behalf. I think the thing that pisses me off the most is that you lied to me."

Michela shook her head. "I've never lied to you about anything."

"Bullshit you haven't," Allison replied, hands on hips, legs apart.

"Seeing as how you think I have, when did I supposedly lie to you?" Michela asked.

Allison laughed. "At the coffee house of course."

Michela squinted as she tried to recall the discussion they'd had that evening. "I never did. We discussed Sarah's sexuality and you asked me questions about what my type was. At no time did you mention gender, not that it's any of your damned business anyway."

Allison threw her hands up and wheeled around the room. "Isn't this a fine state of affairs? Two bloody lesbians in the group. I suppose the two of you will have a fine time together, keeping each other warm. I hate to think where that leaves poor Dianne in the sleeping arrangements."

Michela could feel the last of her control slide away. "Didn't you listen to *anything* I said that night regarding choice? I'm not interested in Sarah and I'm sure as hell not interested in Dianne."

Allison closed the distance between them. "Of course you're not, you're more interested in Maddi. It's a shame she's not part of the team."

Michela looked at the ceiling, her teeth and fists

clenched in exasperation. *Woman, you've walked a fine line long enough and you've just crossed it.* She returned Allison's steely gaze. "Just what is it that really bothers you, Dr. Shaunessy? That I had great sex or that it wasn't with you."

Allison slapped Michela and the sting caused Michela to take several steps back in surprise. Allison closed on her. "How dare you! Lady, you certainly have an unrealistically high opinion of yourself and you must be blind as well. I prefer men not women and even if I did prefer women, if I woke up with my arm around you I'd gnaw it off to get away."

"For Christ's sake, what is your problem then?" Michela roared.

The door opened and Sarah's head popped in. "I was passing by and thought I heard world war three starting. What's going on in here?"

Allison pushed past Sarah. "Why don't you ask her? She seems to have all the answers."

Sarah stepped into the room and closed the door behind her. She silently watched Michela run her hands through her hair and rub her neck in an attempt to calm her emotions. Michela turned to Sarah, the red mark still evident on her face. "What the hell happened to you?"

Michela gingerly touched the mark. "She slapped me."

"She what?" Sarah carefully checked Michela's face for any permanent damage. "I think you need to reassess her position on the team. If this is the way she responds to authority, then you don't know how she'll act out in the middle of nowhere."

"No, I deserved it. I lost my cool and said something entirely inappropriate. It's a wonder she didn't do any further damage."

Sarah leant against the door. "What did you say?"

"You know there's been tension ever since the incident with Maddi." Sarah nodded. "It came to a head this morning and I asked her what her problem was. Things got a bit out of hand and she started carrying on. I got angry and asked her what her real problem was. I asked her whether it had to do with the fact that I had great sex with another woman or the fact that it wasn't with her."

Sarah cringed. "Ooh, no wonder she tried to deck you.

Why did you say such a thing?"

Michela rubbed her forehead with the heel of her hand. "I don't know. She drives me crazy sometimes. I managed to control it in Mount Cook, but, lord, she can be so damned painful."

Sarah tilted her head and her eyes lit with understanding. "I don't mean to be rude here, but I'm wondering whether I was right about the sexual tension thing between you and Maddi. Or was Maddi merely a release for something you're feeling for someone else?"

Michela whipped her head around and stared at Sarah, prepared to deny her suggestion. Try as she might, she couldn't. "Aargh! The woman frustrates me to hell and back." She rubbed her forehead, closed her eyes and then once again opened them. "But damn it all to blazes if I don't like her. And what's worse, she's with that useless piece of crap that treats her like a doormat and she's happy to be with him. Look at him. She nurses him through a voyage and as soon as she's better and she needs him, he's too busy wanting to be the first of the team to land on Antarctica. I swear he drives me crazy and she drives me insane because as an intelligent woman she can't see through his façade."

"I'm not going to give you a lecture on the dangers of falling for a straight woman. I'm sure you've heard all those before," Sarah said.

"Thank you," Michela curtly replied. "But it does raise some accommodations problems once we get to the site. Allison made a passing comment regarding us sleeping in the same hut. You know I trust you but I don't want to add fuel to the fire."

Sarah snapped her fingers. "Damn it. There goes my chance to have my way with you." Michela gave her a withering look. "The answer's simple. Obviously Alli and Rick will be in one hut, Ewan and Michael in another. Rob and I are used to close quarters, so we can share. That leaves you with Dianne. Something tells me she's not your type, so Alli should have nothing to worry about. And, besides, Di's clueless to the developing situation here. In fact her mind's been elsewhere through the whole voyage."

Michela nodded. "You're right on all counts. That

should solve our long-term arrangements, but can you imagine the look on Alli's face when I explain the tent arrangements for the trip to the site? Females in one tent, males in the other."

Sarah chuckled. "If I were you, I'd have that discussion in a room full of people. Less possibility of damage that way. I better go find Allison before she beats up on anyone else. And you keep your nose clean and stop starting any more fights."

IN A STATION the size of Wills, it didn't take long for Sarah to locate Allison, who had retreated to their temporary accommodations. She closed the door on the prevailing outside wind and walked to the middle of the small room, giving Allison her space. "Say, slugger, that's a mean right hook you have there."

Allison looked at the offending hand. "I don't know what happened. I've never hit anyone before but she pushed me too far."

"Look, obviously there's some ill feeling between you two, but I don't intend to spend the whole expedition running back and forth dressing your wounds. You two need to learn to work together and sometimes that means biting your tongue."

Allison picked up her jacket and pulled it on. "I can't believe what she did with that other woman."

"She's an adult, she can do what she likes." Allison snorted. "Just hear me out. Regardless of what you may think, she's still a professional."

"Really? Is she?"

Sarah shook her head, silently acknowledging how frustrating Allison could be. "If that's the way you think about Michela, what do you think about me?"

Allison waved away the comment. "That's different."

"No, Alli, it's not different at all. Michela and I are both lesbians. But that doesn't mean for one moment we're less professional than you, Rick, Di, or anyone else on the team for that matter." She watched Allison struggle with the concept. "Look, I'm not telling you what you should and shouldn't think or do. All I'm asking is for you to think about your actions today and the effect they could have on a small group in the middle of nowhere. And before you get on your moral high horse, I've said the same thing to Michela. Besides, I've no doubt that the last thing you want is to return to Australia with nothing to show for your efforts other than a group of splintered people."

"IT'S BEEN HOURS," Rick shouted over the din of the jostling vehicle to Allison. "It was fun when we first left Wills Station and all those old buildings were great to look at. But, bloody hell, how long before we get there?"

Allison leant closer to Rick. "If the weather holds we should be there in about nine days or so." Rick nodded and Allison returned her gaze to the view outside, only to have her arm pulled by Dianne.

"I thought these things went a lot faster than this. They did the other day when we were training," Dianne said.

"We're travelling in convoy, so we only go as fast as the slowest vehicle. The slowest vehicle is BOB, the tractor thing out there."

Looking disgusted, Rick shook his head. "Who made that bloody decision? Hang on. Of course, it was Michela. Why can't we cut away and let the damned thing catch up with us? We're wasting time."

"It has to be that way. Things are different out here and people move in groups," Allison said. "It's a lot safer. What's more, the stores we'll need to start the dig are on that tractor. So even if we got there early, there's very little we could do."

Rick shifted in his seat and attempted to get more comfortable. "I don't care. It's a pain in the backside. And what am I supposed to do, stuck in this damned thing for that long? At this rate I won't have an intact bone left."

"I think Michela's decision makes sense," Dianne said. "After all, she's only looking after the good of the team, right Allison?"

Allison nodded. Despite her anger with Michela, she'd not discussed their disagreement with either Rick or Dianne. *After all, how do I explain to them that two of their team members are gay?* She was certain they knew about

Sarah, who'd refused to conceal her sexual preference. But she was sure neither Rick nor Dianne was aware of Michela. *She may be the biggest pain in the ass, but that's no reason to discuss her private life. If only she didn't rub me up the wrong way so often.*

Seeking some privacy, she returned her gaze to the view outside. It was white as far as the eye could see, with an occasional shift in the flat surface, signalling an ice field that resembled frozen waves, commonly known as sastrugi. Rising to sometimes a metre high, the sastrugi had been the bane of many of the early expeditioners who had been forced to go over them with dogs and sleds in tow. Twice that morning they'd been forced to diverge from their course. The first had been because of sastrugi and the second had been to dodge a crevasse field. While they could have gambled and taken the sno-trak across the ice bridges that sometimes formed over a crevasse, the risk outweighed the possible gain.

She returned her gaze to the vehicle's interior and closed her eyes as she thought about the sleeping arrangements for the move to the base.

Michela had broken the news before they'd left. As Allison watched Michela make the announcement, she wasn't surprised when Michela looked directly at her. *It was as if she was daring me to speak out.* For the majority of her adult life, Allison had either slept by herself or with Rick. The sleeping in the dongas still gave her a degree of space but the compact tent would be cramped with four people and this would certainly be different to what she was used to. This, as well as the animosity between her and Michela, made the arrangements all the more uncomfortable.

Despite the time approaching six at night, it was still broad daylight outside. *Summer in Antarctica.* Allison sighed. *It's certainly going to be strange going to bed and waking up in the light.*

MICHELA WATCHED AS Michael breathed a sigh of relief when the vehicle they'd been tossed around in all day finally shut down its engine.

"Thank Christ. That noise is worse than any nagging

I've ever had to put up with," Michael said.

Rob laughed as he checked the brake. "I don't know about that, mate. You should reserve your judgment until you've heard Sarah in full voice."

"Are you right there, gob on a stick," Sarah retaliated in mock tones. "I've heard your fair share of whinges when we've been stuck together. In fact there're times when you've almost driven me to drink."

Michela attempted to work the cricks out of her back. "Anybody would think you two are husband and wife the way you carry on. Now comes the fun of setting up camp for the night. How are the winds out there, Rob?"

Rob tapped one of the vehicle's panels. "Pretty calm at the moment. She's blowing at about ten mile an hour, with gusts up to fifteen."

"Good. I guess we better get set up," Michela said. "Rob, can you check with the other two drivers to ensure they're okay?" Rob nodded and left the cabin.

"Ewan, can you, Michael, and Rick start setting up the men's tent? Sarah, could you see to the setting up of the blizzard lines between the tents and the vehicles, in case we're hit by a storm? I'll organise Di and Alli to help me put up the women's tent. Cooking tonight will be under tent arrangements, using the small gas stoves we have. Other than that, we'll look at a seven-thirty departure tomorrow morning."

FLAT ON HER rapidly freezing backside, Dianne struggled to hold the canvas in the prevailing wind. "Did you say this was a pretty calm breeze?"

Michela nodded as she centred the main pole. "Yes. This is pretty tame."

Alli battled to control her edge of the tent. "It's a bit different to the one we put up at Mount Cook. At least there was shelter there. This place is flat as a pancake and other than the vehicles, there's not much to protect us from the bloody wind."

Michela masked her surprise at Allison's contribution and preoccupied herself with the tie down ropes of the tent. *Maybe things have settled down a bit. I really should apologise for what I said the other day, but I think I'll wait until things are a little more private. And who knows, her moods can change so quickly. This might be just a lull in the storm.*

"What are you doing?"

Michela looked up from her work. Rob, obviously finished with his discussion with the other drivers, looked ready to kill Rick, Michael, and Ewan. The three were getting ready to throw their belongings into a tent that looked like it could be blown over by the first decent wind to blow their way.

Michela, Allison, and Dianne watched in amusement as the four men argued until Rob proved his point by kicking one of the tent anchors. The tent collapsed on cue, and Rob made sure it was erected correctly.

Michela ensured the blizzard rope connected the three tents to the vehicles and a field toilet—for anyone who wanted to brave the cold—was secure. After a makeshift meal of re-hydrated pasta and vegetables, accompanied by a cup of hot chocolate, the respective groups settled for the evening.

ALLISON WOKE FROM a relatively sound, yet cool night's sleep and found a sleeping Michela uncomfortably close to her. At first startled, she realised she must have rolled into the centre of the tent sometime during the night. What now greeted her was Michela's face, snugly encased in the loft of her Antarctic-weight sleeping bag. Careful not to wake her, Allison took a moment to observe Michela.

Sleep softened Michela's face, making her seem even calmer than she usually was. *That's one thing that does bug me. Apart from the other day and despite my goading, she always remains calm. How does she do that? What do you hide behind that beautiful mask of yours, Dr. DeGrasse?*

Allison's eyes widened in surprise. Despite their disagreements, she couldn't help but admit that Michela was attractive, and even more so when she was angry. Michela's exasperated words echoed through her mind: "What is it that really bothers you, Dr. Shaunessy? That I had great sex or that it wasn't with you?" At the time she'd been outraged at the mere suggestion, but as she replayed the scene in her mind, she was unsure that her first reaction was an honest one.

Allison knew they reacted to each other like fire and ice, always fighting for the upper hand. But as she recalled the fleeting moments when they touched, she swore she felt a current pass between them. Remembering her rescue from the crevasse fall, she couldn't help but admit to the comfort she'd experienced in Michela's arms. While the moment had been fleeting, the warmth Michela had generated had stirred something in her, something that had been dormant for so long.

And then there was the incident in the coffeehouse. When I touched her hand I felt something and, by the look in her eyes, I think she felt it too. Allison returned her thoughts to the present. Michela was so close, her hot breath lightly tickled Allison's face. Warmth filled the pit of her stomach.

The shaking of the tent interrupted her thoughts and Rob's concerned tones filtered through the canvas. "Sarah, are you awake in there?"

Michela awoke from an exceptionally erotic dream and found herself mere inches away from Allison. Still half-asleep, Michela reached out to Allison but her hands were trapped in her sleeping bag.

"Sarah, get your sorry ass out here. We've got an emergency!"

Michela unzipped her bag, sat up, and quietly cursed as she pulled her ice-cold boots on. "What's the matter?"

"It's Michael. When I woke up this morning he was complaining of pains in the chest."

Sarah pulled the remainder of her body out of the bag and headed for the door.

Michela put a hand on her arm. "We can't afford two patients. Please put your boots on before you head out."

Cursing, Sarah grabbed her boots. "Did he say how long he'd been suffering the pains?" She drew the laces tight and stuffed them in the top of her snow socks instead of tying them.

"He said he thought he had indigestion for a while, but figured it had something to do with the meal last night. Rick cooked and I swear he takes cooking lessons from you," Rob replied.

Sarah pulled on her beanie and sunglasses and left the tent with Michela. "Rob, under the front passenger seat of

your vehicle is my medical kit. Can you get it? I'll meet
you at your tent."

Sarah crawled into the tent and found Rick and Ewan
sitting in their sleeping bags. Michael, in obvious pain,
was on the other side of the tent.

"It wasn't my fault," Rick declared. "How was I to
know that red stuff wasn't tomato but chilli sauce."

"I don't think this has anything to do with your cooking. Now if I could please have a little quiet." Sarah barely
acknowledged Michela as she passed the medical bag to
her. "Can you tell me how you feel?"

Michael grimaced. "My chest hurts like all buggery."

Sarah reassuringly rubbed his arm. "Can you describe
the pain?"

"I feel as if someone's put a huge concrete block on
my chest and I've got a hell of a pain down my left arm.
Damn it, if I could just get comfortable, this bloody feeling
might go away."

Sarah quickly took Michael's pulse and temperature
and checked his breathing. She retrieved a small bottle of
pills from her bag and spilled one into her palm. "There're
a couple of things this might be, so I'm going to try and
rule out these as I go. This," she motioned at the pill in her
hand, "is glyceryl trinitrate and is commonly given to
angina patients. If it's going to work, then it will do so in a
very short period of time. Now, I'm going to place it under
your tongue."

"What if it doesn't work?" he asked before Sarah put
the pill under his tongue.

"If it's not successful then you may be having a heart
attack. Either way, we're going to have to get you back to
Wills Station where they've much better medical facilities
to deal with this. Ewan, can you keep an eye on Michael? If
there's any change in his condition, can you let me know?
Michela, could I have a word with you outside?"

They crawled out of the tent and went to the shelter of
the cold, but windproof sno-trak. Sarah closed the door of
the vehicle and faced Michela. "Mate, I don't think the
angina tablet's going to do any good whatsoever, but it
can't do any harm at this stage. In fact it may calm him a
bit." Sarah removed her beanie and vigorously scratched
her head. "My guess is he's having a heart attack, how

serious I'm not sure. But we need to get him back to the station and fast. If he crashes here I've got no hope of saving him."

Michela nodded. "I'll contact Maddi. She mentioned the long range helos they have at the Wills. Let's hope our comms are working."

Sarah snapped the lock of her medicine bag shut. "There're two helos at every station and they always fly in pairs because of the conditions down here. They'll be able to cover the distance. It'll be more an issue of how soon they can get here. I better go and see how Michael's doing."

Michela pulled the satellite phone from where it had been secured for the journey. "While you do that, I'll contact Maddi and let her know what's going on. Can you get Rob to give me a GPS reference so I can relay our location?"

"Sure." Sarah closed the door.

As Michela fiddled with the phone, she felt a blast of air.

Allison climbed in and struggled to close the door. "Rob says Michael's had a heart attack. What are we going to do?"

"Yes, he has, but Sarah's got it under control. In the meantime I'm going to call back to station and get him evacuated to Wills."

Allison nodded as she rubbed her cold hands together. "Is there anything I can do?"

"No. Hang on, yes. You can keep everyone busy by getting the camp ready for travel. Pack everything except the tent Michael's in. In the off chance we can't establish communications we're going to have to return to Wills Station."

"But if he's suffering a heart attack, won't that be too long? Won't he die?" Allison's unease was evident.

Michela looked into Allison's eyes and covered her hand with her own. "He's going to be fine, but I need you to keep everyone else busy. Can you do that for me please?" Allison nodded. "Good. Now I've really got to see if I can get this phone to work."

Alone in the sno-trak, Michela pressed all the necessary buttons and flicked all the required switches and then attempted to place a call, only to get static. She silently cursed. *What had Maddi said about solar flares?* Michela searched her memory. The flares had the capacity to knock out communications for hours or possibly days. *Great. We're in the twenty-first century and our technology is still thwarted by something completely beyond our control.* She tried the phone again and got the same result. Forcing herself not to scream in frustration, she tried one final time. This time the connection dropped through and Maddi's disjointed tones echoed down the line. Michela wasted no time in explaining the situation.

"So Sarah thinks it's a heart attack?" Maddi asked.

"Yes," Michela said.

"If that's the case we'll send the long range helos out to you. They should be there in just over an hour. Do you have a GPS reference for me?"

"Yes, Rob's passing it to me now."

"Got it. Hang on a minute." Maddi shouted a series of instructions to someone. "Right. They've got the info and they'll be there as soon as possible. There's no sign of bad weather so it should be smooth sailing. I'll send the station's doctor so he and Sarah can do a quick medical assessment before Michael's transported back here."

"What's the plan once you get him back there?" Michela asked.

"The Yank Chinook we've been using to ferry some of the stores from the ship to the station's still here. There's a medical facility at Kennedy Station with a surgical capability and it is better equipped to handle such cases. I'll speak to the pilots about the possibility of flying him there for treatment. Depending on how he responds will determine what happens next. Suffice to say, I strongly doubt he'll return to the expedition."

"I sort of expected that. We'll have to reallocate tasks and share the cooking. My main interest is his health."

Heavy static echoed down the line. "I'm losing you so I'll sign off. The helos will be there shortly. Have the guys mark out a landing zone for them. Both Rob and Sarah know how to mark out a LZ. I'll keep...ou...osted on Mi...aels...dition."

Before Michela could reply, the line went dead. She returned the hand-piece to its cradle and went to make preparations for the helo's arrival.

In little over an hour the helicopters landed on the makeshift LZ created by Rob and Ewan. While Michael's condition hadn't deteriorated, it hadn't improved. After Sarah's quick briefing with the Wills Station doctor, Michael was put on a stretcher and loaded onto the first helicopter for the return journey to Wills Station.

When the helicopters were no more than specks on the horizon, Michela marshalled the team and refocussed them for the journey ahead.

Over the ensuing days Michela received regular updates from Maddi about Michael's condition. Some days she managed barely thirty seconds of discussion with Maddi before the communication link went dead. But it was enough for Michela to relay to the rest of the members that Michael had stabilised and was going to be okay.

Michela was relieved at further good news—that the U.S. Army had volunteered to fly him out in about a fortnight on one of their re-supply flights to Christchurch. From there he'd be repatriated to Australia.

WELL INTO THEIR ninth day Rick shook Allison awake.

"What?"

Rick pointed out the window. On the horizon, they could just make out the orange rectangle that would be their mess and work area over the ensuing weeks.

Allison smiled. "After so many damned months, we're finally here."

Chapter
Six

My Darling Charlotte,

It seems so much has happened since my last entry. After five days of continual unloading, we managed to have all our stores on solid ground. There was time for one final festive dinner on the craft that had so bravely ferried us here. The following morning we watched as it slowly made its way through the pack ice and onwards toward Tasmania. The captain has agreed to rendezvous with us in four months time, before the colder weather closes in and makes movement by water impossible. This should give us sufficient time to make our observations of this great white land.

Our movement to the camp was slow and not helped by the prevailing winds that seemed to blow from the continent's inner regions. The dogs that survived the sea journey proved a blessing, speeding up what would have been a long traverse if made by men alone. The establishment of our base has been my first priority, however this hasn't always been the focus of the rest of my crew. I can hardly blame them and their eagerness to explore, however we must finish our accommodations before we can even consider exploration.

All my love,

ERF

Antarctica—2009

DIANNE, RICK, AND Allison scrambled out of their sno-trak before it had barely come to a halt and scanned the landscape in an attempt to see the remains of the building. Ewan joined in the excitement, kicking the ground, as if trying to unearth hidden treasure.

Michela and Sarah waited until Rob shut down their vehicle before joining the rest of the team.

"Where is it? Is this the right spot?" Dianne asked.

Sarah nodded. "We're in the right location but the hut's completely buried by over one hundred years of snow and ice."

Rick headed back to the BOB-trak and the team's stores. "Let's break out the blades and start digging."

Michela lightly grabbed his arm. "Not so fast. There's a list of things that have to be done before you even start digging, not the least of which is setting up our camp. There's no point in starting to dig if you've got nowhere to sleep and eat." She looked at the disappointed faces of the group. "I know how you feel but trust me. Finlayson's hut's going nowhere."

Rob rubbed his hands together. "Okay, boss. What needs to be done? The sooner we finish, the sooner we can start on this digging stuff."

Michela nodded her thanks to Rob. "First, we have to off-load the stores from the two vehicles returning to Wills Station. Once that's done there's accommodations, electricity connection, toilet construction, establishment of the mess and work area..."

"God, we'll barely be finished and it'll be time to leave," Dianne said.

Michela held up her hand. "If we all pitch in it should only take a few days to get the base camp completely established. Then there'll be plenty of time for you to start your excavation."

Sarah stamped her feet; her gloved hands firmly wedged in her armpits. "So who's doing what? I'm getting cold standing around here doing nothing."

"We'll all unload the two vehicles returning to base and then the tasks will be as follows. Rob, I'd like you to be responsible for rigging electricity to the mess hut and the accommodations huts." Michela made a map in the light covering of snow. "This is how I'd like the camp laid out. You can all see the mess hut and the solar panels behind it." The group nodded. "I want you to think of the mess hut being at twelve o'clock. At nine and three o'clock, I'd like each of the apples to be set up. Alli and Rick will be in one and Di and I will be in the other. At six o'clock will go the googie and that's where Ewan, Rob and Sarah will bed down. Ideally I'd like to see the distance between the buildings to be no more than thirty yards. I know this sounds close, but once the weather sets in it will make safe movement around the site a lot easier."

Rob scanned the area where the camp was to be established. "So, boss, you want me to run power to each of these huts?"

"If you could. The other building to be set up is the toilet." Michela made a mark in the snow. "This is to go about thirty yards downwind of Rick and Alli's apple. A reinforced blizzard rope will be put out to the toilet and it's to be checked every day."

Ewan rubbed the stubble on his cheeks. "Bugger me, could you imagine it, dying because you got stranded on the toilet in a blizzard. What a way to go."

Rob laughed and slapped Ewan's back. "Don't worry about it, mate, it'll never happen."

"While Rob's seeing to the power, the rest of us will focus on setting up our accommodations. Because the googie's a bit bigger than the two apples, if you finish first then please go and give Sarah and Ewan a hand. Rick, once your hut's up, could you ensure the field toilet is erected?" Michela wasn't surprised by the sour look on Rick's face.

"You want me to set up the toilet? You've got to be joking," Rick said.

"It shouldn't take you very long and then you can help the rest of us establish the working and eating areas." Michela ignored the disgusted snort from Rick. "There'll be a task rotation for the duration of our stay. Probably the most unattractive of these is bottle washer and slops person. They're responsible for washing up after each meal and ensuring the kitchen waste is appropriately bagged for when we return to base. Law requires us to leave here as we found it. That means all our rubbish, both food and body waste will need to be bagged for the return journey. So, the final task of the slops person will be cleaning out the toilet every second day."

Dianne screwed up her nose. "That's gross. You can't mean we're all going to have to do that."

Michela shrugged. "I'm afraid so. Once the toilet's erected we'll do a dry run, so you can all get an idea of what's required. For the first seven days, I'll be the slops person. We also have to re-allocate the cooking. I'm going to need a volunteer for that as well."

Rick cast his hand at the females. "That's women's work. You should be able to easily spread that amongst yourselves."

Keep calm. He's an idiot but that's no reason to want to do him bodily harm. "That's not the case, Rick. Everyone will get a go at cooking, no matter how bad they are. Now, do I have any volunteers for the first week's shift?"

Rob nudged Michela. "I'll do it, boss. I'm a reasonable hand at cooking even if I do say so myself."

"You'd be the only bloody one saying it," Sarah said in jest.

"Thanks for the offer, Rob, but I want you to focus on the electricity, at least in the first few days. This is an experimental system and it will no doubt have its problems. Any other volunteers?"

Dianne sighed and held up her hand. "I'll do it. But don't expect five star cooking. And if you don't like what you get, then you can go without."

Michela smiled. "Thanks, Di. I'll make up a slops and cooking roster and post it in the next few days. Okay team, let's get to work."

ALLISON MADE YET another trip from the pile of stores to her hut and opened the door to find Rick asleep, spread-eagled on one of the two single beds. She put her bundle on the small desk in the middle of the room, went to Rick, and gently tugged on his foot.

"Come on, sleepyhead. There's a heap more to be brought over here before you can doze, you know."

Rick turned his head toward her and opened one eye. "I've done about as much as I'm going to do today. The rest can wait. And talking about tomorrow, why can't someone else bring our gear here? We're archaeologists for heaven's sake. Why can't the workers set up camp and let us get down to business."

Allison sat down on the bed. "It doesn't work like that here. As Michela said, we've all got to pitch in and get the camp established before we can do anything else."

Rick sat up, leant against the wall, and drew his knees to his chest. "I don't care. I didn't come here to be employed as a lackey. And what's with you anyway? Why are you agreeing with her all of a sudden? It wasn't so long ago that you couldn't string the words together to speak a civil sentence to her."

Allison rolled her eyes and sighed heavily. "It's not about personalities, it's about getting the job done. If we all pitch in together then there'll be ample time to get the dig under way."

"I don't care. I've done all the moving I'm going to do today. You can suit yourself." Rick lay back down and made himself comfortable.

Allison shook her head and stood. "Fine. I'll do that." She said in clipped tones as she walked to the door.

"Where are you going?"

"Where do you think I'm going? I've still got gear out there that I need, including my clothes."

Rick crossed his hands to make a pillow for his head. "Could you pick up my backpack while you're out there?"

Allison wheeled. "Listen, you bloody lazy mongrel. I turned a blind eye earlier today when you skulked off for an hour, leaving me to tighten the bolts of our hut. I didn't even say anything when you came back with one cup of hot chocolate and then drank it all, without even offering me a sip. But, if you think for one minute I'm going to get your gear because you're too lazy to get it yourself then you've got another thing coming. Get off your lazy ass and get it yourself!"

Rick stood and towered over Allison. "What's wrong with you? You've been like a bear with a sore head for most of this trip."

"There's nothing wrong with me that wouldn't be fixed by you pulling your bloody weight, rather than expecting everything to be done for you." Allison closed her eyes in an attempt to rein in her temper. "Listen, if you want to spend the whole time here in those same clothes because you're too lazy to get your backpack, that's up to you." Allison opened the door, stepped outside, and slammed it behind her. Looking across the compound, she caught Michela's questioning eyes and then she turned and skulked toward the stores area.

MICHELA SHIVERED AS a blast of wind signalled the opening of the mess hut's door. Sarah struggled to close the door against the wind and then flopped down opposite Michela.

"Hey, there. What are you up to at this time in the morning?"

Michela smiled. "Just completing a few entries in my diary. My duties as slops person have kept me otherwise occupied."

Sarah removed her gloves and squeezed some warmth back into her fingers. "So how do you think it's going?"

"I have to admit I was a little worried by that temperamental solar powered unit. After all the effort to get it here, I thought it was going to be a white elephant. Thank God for Rob's ingenuity and perseverance with the damned thing."

Sarah nodded. "Yeah. There's a lot more to him than meets the eye."

"And then there was the drama with the recharging of equipment. I swear to God, for a group of academics, they certainly lack common sense."

Sarah threw her head back and laughed. "I know what you're talking about. I thought Dianne was going to have a cow when Rob told her there'd be a forty-eight hour delay before they could start digging, to allow the equipment to fully recharge."

Michela joined in the laughter before looking around the hut. "They seem to have spent the time making a darn great mess of this place. I mean, the office is supposed to be at the far end, the kitchen area in the middle and the eating area here." Michela picked up a bag of electronic equipment she'd moved to the side of the table when she sat down. "I'm sure this thing should be down at the other end. It's interfering with my research."

Sarah leant forward, attempting to read Michela's tablet. "So, have you analysed us to death yet?"

"I've already signed your admittance papers to the funny farm." She laughed at the look on Sarah's face. "Seriously though, it's a great test bed for the Mars expedition. Take for example the group working together. There are some definite personalities in the team and some which are already interfering with group cohesion. But, like space, we don't have the luxury to change them and so we have to make the best with what we've got."

"What do you mean?"

"Look at the dynamic, in particular the men. Rob is mister flexible and nothing seems to phase him. Ewan craves acceptance among the three archaeologists and has just about bent over backwards in trying to please them."

Sarah leant forward and crossed her arms on the table. "So what do you make of Rick?"

Michela rubbed her eyes and then ran her fingers through her hair. "Now there's a problem if I ever saw one. I'm sure he's gifted in his profession, but he's changed since we've arrived."

Sarah let out a breath. "Thank God you said that. I thought it was just me. Since we've got here he's become demanding, almost dictatorial in his moods. The other day Rob had to physically coax him into checking the blizzard lines."

Michela wryly smiled. "If I didn't know you any better I'd say you've been reading my notes. He's really changed and become incredibly chauvinistic as well. I can't believe this didn't surface during the training. One of my report recommendations will be a much longer training camp to hopefully weed out the likes of him."

"It looks like you've got your work cut out for you finding any positives."

Michela tapped her tablet to a page. "It's not all bad. I was pretty impressed with the way everyone coped with Michael's early departure. I've got to say, I don't understand how he ever passed the physical in the first place."

"I agree. I don't know about you, but it's obvious some people are finding the confined spaces difficult to cope with. At this rate, it'll be interesting to see how they're coping by the end of the dig."

Michela recalled the minor issue Rob and Ewan had argued over at breakfast that morning. "I know Rob and Ewan have been at it, but like most men, they seem to have resolved it pretty quickly. I'm more concerned over the shouting that's coming from Rick and Alli's apple. Even with the wind, they can be heard clear across the compound."

"It can't be anything to do with the sleeping arrangements. With the increased size of the single beds, I'm sure they can fit on one bed. Last night I actually rolled over and didn't touch the edge." Sarah looked at her watch. "So tell me, why aren't you getting any sleep?"

Michela shrugged. "I'm not all that tired. I usually exist on about four hours a night and this constant daylight isn't helping."

"I know what you mean," Sarah said. "If there's anything I can give you for it let me know."

Michela yawned, stood up, and gathered her papers into a neat bundle. "Thanks for the offer. I might try and get some of that sleep you obviously think I need."

"That'd be about right. I start to chat up a pretty woman and she leaves me." Sarah raised her hands above her head in mock supplication. "What's this going to do to my reputation?"

Michela laughed, knowing Sarah was one team member she wouldn't have to worry about.

ALLISON SILENTLY CHUCKLED at the confused look on Ewan's face as he looked at the myriad of wires spread on the ice.

"What exactly is this electronic spaghetti?" Ewan asked, eyebrows furrowed.

"It has a technical name, but its common name is the Web. It's a series of electronic nodes that are counter-sunk into a surface, this one being ice. The nodes are connected by an infra-red beam, hence its name." She picked up the wiring. "This wire is then attached to the mother node, which feeds all the other nodes, and vice-versa. The other end of the wire is attached to a digital tablet. The program sends electro-magnetic pulses through the network, causing a sound wave to bounce below the surface of each node causing a ripple effect, like when you drop a pebble in a pond. The digital tablet's program's configured so that it can remove the surface from the picture. The end result is a shadow, which in this case I hope will be the outline, or part of Finlayson's hut."

"What a great piece of kit," Sarah said. "I wonder whether it could be adapted for research on the ice domes down here."

Allison shrugged. "I wouldn't know. As a geologist, Di would be the best person to give you an idea whether the Web could be adapted for other use. I just know it makes my job as an archaeologist so much easier."

Sarah turned and scanned the vicinity. "I might do that. You don't know where she is do you?"

"She's setting up the electronics for the equipment in the mess hut," Allison replied. "There's no real point in standing out here in the cold with a digital tablet if you can as easily do it in the warmth and comfort of a hut."

"Thanks." Sarah strode to the mess building.

"So, you set up the Web, but how do you work out where to start?" Rob asked.

Allison slapped Rob on the back. "That's where you and Sarah come in. The GPS reading you guys took when you were out here all those months ago will be the datum point where I position the mother node. I'll spread the rest out in a circular radius of about five yards, to see what we pick up. From there it's like a jigsaw puzzle, only you work your way outwards. If we can find the edge of the building, we mark it and trace that line until we come to a corner. We'll continue to trace the next line until we finally have the rough outline of a building. This is then pegged out and we take the dig from there."

Rob nodded. "Bloody amazing. Now I know you guys normally go at this sort of stuff with shovels and the like. I suppose that's where these blades fit into the picture." He pointed at the blades resting up against one another.

"Right again. I hadn't seen these used until we gave them a trial in Sydney, but I reckon they'll speed up things quite a bit." Allison turned a blade over and revealed a small switch. "They're battery operated and work much like a delicate flat-bladed jackhammer. The difference between this and a normal jackhammer is that the actual blade is super-heated, allowing it to cut through the ice like a knife through butter. You adjust the heat and power by flicking these two switches." She pointed to a green and purple switch.

Ewan carefully took the blade out of Allison's hands. "I can't wait to give this bad boy a try. But isn't metal brittle? What's to stop it from being affected by the extreme cold conditions?"

"You see how light they are?" Rob and Ewan took turns holding the tool and nodded. "The metal in the casing and the blade is aircraft grade titanium. This means it's non-corrosive and can withstand extreme variations in temperature as well as pressure. Super light and super strong and I might add super expensive. That's why Rick will run you through a couple of lessons before we unleash you on the dig site."

Rob handed the tool back to Allison. "Well, Skip, tell us when you're ready. I better get back to the daily power check. You coming, Ewan?"

Allison grinned at their enthusiasm and returned her attention to the Web.

TWENTY-FOUR HOURS later Allison was pleased to see a partial picture of the hut begin to take shape. As the picture built up, she adjusted the position of the Web. Engrossed in the correct placement of the mother node, she almost missed Rick's excited voice over the ever-present wind.

"Dianne, Alli, come here!" Rick detached his ice axe from his belt and made a cut in the ice as Allison and Dianne strode to him.

Rick stood up and stepped away from the hole. "Look. I was placing out one of the nodes when I noticed a discolouration in the ice off to my right. When I got closer I realised it could only be wood. This is obviously some part of the roof of the hut. There's no need to continue on with the plotting, we can start here."

"It's great that the building isn't as deep as what we thought it was, but don't you think we should find another access way?" Allison asked.

Rick raised his brows and blinked in surprise. "Are you crazy? This could cut days, maybe weeks off our excavation and give us the opportunity to explore other remote sites or caches that might be around here. If this building's configured like most of the other huts of this era, then it will have reinforced skylights for use when the normal entrances were snowed-in. These could form our access points."

"That may be the case if the building wasn't buried under so much ice," Allison said. "I'm worried about the integrity of the structure. Your idea may result in the building caving in on someone who's in it."

Rick threw his hands up and walked away before turning back to Allison and Dianne. "Oh, for heaven's sake, Alli, don't be daft. What happened to your spirit of adventure? You weren't so cautious last year during that cave dig in Perth."

Allison forced herself to remain calm. "That was completely different and you know it. We weren't in the middle of a continent whose closest surgical help is over nine days away."

Rick turned to Dianne. "Come on, Di. Can't you see how much time we could save here? It's a bit risky but we've all been in tighter situations."

"Sorry, but I have to agree with Alli. There're safety issues at stake, not to mention what a collapse would do to the possible artefacts inside. Plus, not all of the workers here are skilled at digging. Take Rob and Ewan. I'd hate to see their enthusiasm accidentally result in injury."

Rick angrily shook his head. "Bloody women, you're all the same. I'd be surprised if we ever manage to find a way into this damn hut. Christ, at this rate, it'll be time to go home before we even have a building framework. If you want to play it super safe then suit your bloody self. But if you think I'm going to spend any more time laying out these bloody nodes in the freezing cold, then you've got another thing coming." Rick shoved his ice axe back on his belt and stomped away.

Allison looked at the nodes in her hands. "It's far too risky. We can't afford to lose another member of the team."

Dianne patted Allison's shoulder. "He's frustrated

that's all. Tell you what. You continue here and I'll go and try to talk to him."

Allison watched Dianne head off in search of Rick and wasn't surprised to see Sarah head her way.

"What was all that about? Rick came into the camp spitting chips."

"He's frustrated over how slow things are and wanted to start entering the hut through a sky-light." Allison looked at the markers already identifying some of the outline of the hut. "You've worked here before. Am I being unrealistic? Would it be safe to dig from the roof down?"

"If this structure's anything like the McKinley expedition hut then it'll be pre-fabricated wooden walls, and pretty strong at that. But I'd caution against cutting into the superstructure. You should try to maintain its integrity. That way, when you eventually start to cut through the ice, there's still some strength remaining in the hut. I guess your biggest task will be finding the actual entrance to the building."

Allison nodded. "This shouldn't be too hard once we've got an outline to work with. If we can only find it before Rick loses his temper and decides to start without the entrance."

Sarah chuckled at Allison's exasperation. "He'll cool down once he sees sense." She pointed to the wiring left behind by Dianne and Rick. "In the meantime, how'd you feel about another pair of hands to help you put those node thingies out?"

Allison gratefully smiled. "Thanks. I had Ewan and Rob helping me yesterday, but I think they both expected immediate results. When things were slow to happen they found other jobs to fill their time."

Sarah picked up the netted bag of electronic nodes. "That's not entirely fair. Michela's directions were that once we'd established the camp, everyone was responsible for specific daily tasks. With the exception of the cooking and the slop detail, this leaves a fair amount of spare time. If you're not getting the help you need, why don't you speak with Michela?"

Allison baulked at the idea. Although things between them had been pretty benign since the incident at Wills Station, they certainly weren't on rosy terms. *Sarah's right.*

After all, she's the team leader and this is part of her job. "I'll do that tonight over dinner, but for the moment I think the two of us can manage."

THE FOLLOWING DAY, after a polite reading of the riot act by Michela, Allison had more than her fair share of workers. While Rick remained conspicuously absent, the rest of the team was helpful in setting out the Web and marking the building's outline.

By late morning the digital tablet in the mess hut displayed a roughly rectangular outline, about thirty-six feet long by twenty-four feet wide. Happy with the progress, Allison called a halt and the team went to the hut and lunch.

ALLISON GRABBED A spoon and fork and sat down at the mess hut table. She picked up a dinner roll, broke it in two, and dipped it into her sauce.

Dianne passed a plate of pasta to Rob as he filed through the food preparation area. "You know. I'd forgotten how much you can do with this dehydrated food."

Rob bent over and took in the aroma of a strong Neapolitan sauce, liberally spiced with chilli and garlic. "This smells great. You sure you don't want to cook next week as well? That's my shift and I hate to say this, but make the most of it, because next week you may starve."

The group laughed.

Sarah nudged Rob as he sat down beside her. "Fibber. I know you can cook. I'm looking forward to that Italian shepherd's pie of yours. Lashings of mince, onion, garlic, and peas in a wonderful beefy sauce, topped with mashed potato and melted cheese."

"If that's your version of 'I can't cook' then I'd hate to see something you can do." Ewan swallowed a mouthful of pasta and blissfully sighed. "Don't get me wrong, Di. This is bloody marvellous."

Di grabbed her bowl and sat down on the last unoccupied chair at the table. "Thanks for your feedback. I thought it made a nice Christmas lunch. Of course, a glass of champagne would go down well too."

Allison looked at her watch and then shook her head. "What do you know. We've been so busy I lost count of the days. I thought it was tomorrow."

Christmas greetings were shared around the group, with extra thanks to Dianne for her effort.

Dianne graciously acknowledged their thanks. "So how did it go out there this morning?"

Allison wiped the sauce that was dribbling down her chin. "Pretty good. Sarah's been keeping an eye on the digital image this morning. We're really beginning to see a shape."

"So, Alli, found any more internal walls lately?" Rob asked.

Alli poked out her tongue at Rob. "Very funny. I thought I'd really found something this morning and it was only a dividing wall. I'd completely forgotten about those."

Rob chuckled. "They're pretty good at holding up ceilings and the like."

"Enough. You've had your laugh for the day," Allison said. "We still haven't cracked the door yet, but I wouldn't be surprised if we find it this afternoon."

Excitement rippled around the table at the realisation of what the discovery of an entranceway would mean.

Dianne sprinkled Parmesan over her pasta. "Then it won't be long before we can get a look at what's inside. I'm sorry I couldn't keep an eye on both the digital tablet and the stove, but I really wanted to give this lunch my full attention." Dianne nodded at Sarah. "Thanks for your help this morning. Once I've tidied up the mess I've made I'll be ready to take over on the tablet if you like."

Sarah twirled another batch of angel hair pasta onto her spoon. "I'm actually enjoying watching the picture take shape. It's a bit like a mystery really, all the pieces coming together. Whenever you're ready though, let me know. Besides, leave the cleaning to the slops lady." She pointed her fork at Michela.

Michela tilted her head. "Is that right? I'll have to remember that, Sarah, especially since tomorrow it's your turn."

LATER THAT AFTERNOON Allison was interrupted from the site by a call from Sarah. With the wind blowing in the opposite direction, Allison couldn't understand what she was saying. She waved back at Sarah and carefully walked through the wind to the hut.

Sarah was hunched over the digital tablet, squinting at the screen. She leant back and ran her hand through her blonde locks. "I think I've been looking at this far too long."

Allison furrowed her brow. "I thought Di was going to replace you when she finished cooking. Where is she?"

Sarah shrugged. "I don't know. She said she'd something to do and that she'd be right back. I don't know how long that's been as I've been pretty preoccupied with the puzzle unfolding right here." She pointed at the tablet.

Allison tried to discern the full outline of the hut, but it was too large for the tablet's screen. "Do you mind if I make a few adjustments?"

Sarah stood. "Be my guest. I've been reluctant to fiddle with anything without you guys giving me a hand. I'd hate to think my fat fingers or voice commands resulted in losing the picture altogether."

Allison chuckled and sat down. "I don't think there's any chance of that. This thing saves on a regular basis."

"Yeah, but you don't know my luck with information technology. Electronics and I haven't always been compatible, and it wouldn't be the first time I've managed to completely crash a program."

Allison tapped on the program's options. "Not to worry. Let me refine the clarity of the picture and reduce it a bit to give us a better view."

The resulting image showed that the external dimensions of the building had slightly detracted from its rectangular shape. Toward one end was a small square structure, extending from the rest of the outline. Allison squinted at the screen. "Tablet, scroll down." She looked at Sarah. "I hope this isn't another internal wall." The mess door opened and a shivering Rob, Michela, and Ewan walked in.

Ewan went to the stove. "See, Michela, it's like I said. They've come in from the cold. I'm going to fix some hot chocolate. Does anyone want some?"

Oblivious, Allison continued to stare at the screen. "I'll be damned."

"You'll be damned what?" Sarah asked, leaning over Allison's shoulder.

Allison pointed at the screen, a smile gracing her features. "I think we've finally found it. See that box-like structure on the end of the wall there? I think that's a foyer, like the McKinley construction." She turned to the group whose attention was now focussed on the small screen. "I think we've found our entrance."

Spontaneous whoops and cheers erupted from the group.

Allison disentangled herself from Rob's bear hug and turned to the next in line, who happened to be Michela. Momentarily sobered by the awkwardness between herself and Michela, she searched for words to hide her reluctance to hug her. "Now this is a Christmas present. Where're Di and Rick? They need to see this. I'll go and check my hut and see if Rick's there." She stopped on her way to the door and turned around. "Maybe it's time we did break out that first bottle of champagne. I'll go and get Rick. Save a glass for us."

Outside, Allison paused as she braced herself against the chilly wind. Pulling her beanie firmly down over her ears, she went to her hut.

She opened the door and could only stare. The wind that had chilled her outside paled into insignificance to the chill that assailed her senses. Dianne's semi-naked form was entwined in Rick's legs and arms.

"What the bloody hell do you think you two are doing?" Allison bellowed.

Dianne quickly reached for her clothes, which were strewn about the cabin.

Rick maintained his position on his back, head resting on his folded hands, in a pose of superiority. "What does it look like?"

Allison's eyes blazed. "You bastard! You bloody bastard. After all these years and you leave me for bloody blimbo."

Dianne struggled to pull on a boot while at the same time maintain some dignity. "I beg your pardon. I may be a lot of things but I'm no blimbo, and yes, I do know what that means."

Allison wheeled—the full force of her anger focussed on Dianne. "Lady, you may be a lot of things but you're going to be something on the end of my fist if you don't get the hell out of here!" She grabbed Dianne by her jeans, opened the door, and threw her into the snow.

Allison slammed the door and paced the floor, attempting to rein in her temper. "How could you? Of all the people to leave me for, how could you pick such an air-head?"

Rick casually reached for the flannel shirt at the end of his bed. "See, that's your problem. You only see things your way. She's not like that at all. In fact she's pretty intelligent."

"How long has this been going on then? A week? A month perhaps? How long have you and that bitch been rutting?"

Rick smugly smiled as he buttoned his shirt. "About nine months and as for rutting, well, that might be what you call it, but I've got another name for it."

Allison did the mental calculations. "You prick! You two have been at this for ages. The morning I was late for work and you were supposed to have come over the evening before. I bet you were with her, weren't you? And let's not forget all those team meetings you had to have at all hours while we were planning this dig. Of course, then there's the 'it'll be okay, I'll walk Di home and then join the others' excuse you gave in Hobart. I bet you never joined the others at all, did you? To think for the whole bloody miserable sea journey down here I washed and looked after you while you puked your guts up. And for what? So you could run off with some bitch. Christ, after all I've done for you!"

Rick stood, his dark eyes aflame as he towered over her. "Bullshit! You've been colder than ice for a long time now. Shit, you've been so preoccupied in this damn dig that everything else has taken a back seat, including me. At least with Di I don't get the cold shoulder every time I try to show a little affection."

"If your idea of showing a little affection is shaking my shoulder after a hard day's work and asking me if I'm awake, then you've got it wrong. Why her? Shit, there was a time when you couldn't stand her." Allison searched her mind for a possible reason and then bitterly smiled. "Of course, how stupid of me. What better way to cement your position at the Museum than getting into bed with the patron's daughter? You lousy, politically minded, scum sucking low life bastard. You can have her. And if it's any consolation, with a prick the size of yours, it's a wonder she gets any satisfaction out of you!"

Rick raised his hand and Allison lifted her arm, to shield herself from the inevitable blow. Almost simultaneously the door slammed open and Michela strode in.

"Rick!" Michela shouted.

Rick sucked in a breath and lowered his hand. Michela quickly stepped between them and faced Rick.

"I don't know the full story of what's going on here. But if I see you raise your hand to a member of my team, male or female, I'll have Sarah sedate you for the rest of the dig or at least until we can get you off the site."

She turned to Allison, who had recovered herself and now wore an equally belligerent expression. "At this point I think it would be best if you went to the mess hut. And, Rick, once you're fully dressed, you're to join us. This needs to be resolved before this dig can go any further." She lightly grasped Allison's arm and manoeuvred her out of the apple.

MICHELA OPENED THE mess hut door and breathed a sigh of relief that only Dianne was there. Dianne looked at Allison's angered features and sank further into her chair. In order to avoid any possible bloodshed, Michela motioned Allison to the other side of the room.

Bloody hell. I mustn't forget that in my report—be wary of the ability of infidelity to potentially drive a wedge through a team. I'll be damned if I'm going to let this occur with this group. These three are going to have to work out some degree of resolution or I'll personally drug the damned lot of them. She rubbed her eyes and traced a path through her auburn locks with her fingers. Rick finally strolled in.

Michela motioned him to a seat a workable distance from Allison and Dianne. "Thank you for joining us. We're all adults here and I'm not about to take sides on who's wrong and who's right. But let me make this clear. We're currently on a dig and the remaining four of us are relying on direction from you three. So, this is how it's going to be. You three can resolve your immediate differences and learn to live with the change in personal circumstances, or we'll strike camp and return to Wills Station. I'm not about to have four innocent people waiting around, freezing their butts off while you three sulk your way through the remaining time here. So, what's it going to be?"

Rick pointed at Allison. "If you think for one moment I'm going to sleep in the same cabin as the ice queen then you've got another thing coming."

Michela swallowed a laugh at Rick's description of Allison. *Ice queen she might be, but she has a mean right hook.* "I don't know that you two have any choice. We returned the spare apple with the BOB. What we now have is all there is, and this hut isn't equipped for you to be sleeping in it."

Rick folded his arms as he leant back in his chair. "The answer's pretty simple. Why can't Allison change places with Di and Di can move in with me."

Allison shook her head. "There's got to be another solution than that. Why can't I set up a sleeping bag in the sno-trak, or pitch one of the tents?"

"I'm sorry. I can't allow you to do either. The sno-trak has no heating unless the engine's running and that'll burn fuel. As for the tent, the reason why we slept four in them in the first place was to increase the body heat inside the tent. With only you, you'd freeze in no time."

"Oh, for God's sake. What's your problem, Alli?" Rick asked. "It's not as if you'd be sharing a hut with Sarah or anything."

Michela held up her hand. "Let's get one thing straight. If you've an issue with Sarah, then you take it up with her. In person." *That is, if you're brave enough.* "Allison, I'm sorry, but there may be only one option open to you. Any other changes will mean disrupting the rest of the group and I think the three of you have caused enough of that already."

Allison suddenly stood, causing some of the table's contents to fall to the floor. "Alright. I'll change bed spaces, but by God, Dianne, you better be out of that damned hut before I get there or I'll start turfing your gear into the snow." She turned to Rick. "As for you, I hope you go to the bloody toilet one night and it's so cold you get frostbite and your old feller drops off."

"Allison." Michela barely muffled her laugh. "I don't expect you to like each other, but are you going to work together or not?" The three mumbled that they would. "Okay. Let's get this move over and done with and get back to why we're here in the first place."

While the change to sleeping arrangements got under way, Michela gave Sarah, Rob, and Ewan the abridged version of events. She reassured them, that for the sake of the dig, professionalism among the three archaeologists would be maintained.

Michela noted tea that evening was a silent affair and the crew retired relatively early to their respective huts. Reluctant to face Allison where she was now living, she took her time in completing her last slops round. Finally, having no good reason to avoid the issue, she headed for their apple.

She found a sullen Allison making an entry in her diary. *I don't want to open old wounds, but I really do need to clear the air or it's going to be an uncomfortable time over the following weeks.* Michela sat on her bed.

"Could I please have a moment of your time?"

Allison raised her red rimmed eyes. "Yes?"

Shit, she's been crying. That bastard. I swear to God if he'd hit her today, I don't think I could've been held responsible for my actions. "I'm sorry things turned out this way. I know it can't be comfortable for you to be bunking with me. But from Rick's comments, it's obvious you haven't mentioned my sexuality to him and for that I'm grateful."

Allison absently picked at a page in her diary. "I really didn't see it was anyone else's business."

"Thanks all the same." Michela took a deep breath. "I'd also like to apologise for what I said that day in the room at Wills Station. It was completely uncalled for and crass. I'd like to reassure you I'd never do anything to compromise you in any way. All I ask is whether we can maintain a strong professional relationship. Is that possible?"

Allison nodded.

"Do you want to talk about it? What happened today I mean?"

"No, thanks. I'd rather put the whole thing behind me, if that's at all possible." Allison stood and went to her bed space. "But right now I'd like some sleep. I'll see you in the morning."

"Okay." Michela turned, giving Allison some privacy. "Pleasant dreams," she whispered. She lay down on her bed for what was the first of many restless nights.

Chapter
Seven

My Darling Charlotte,

It is with heavy heart that I make this entry. We have suffered our first tragedy in this expedition. To understand why the loss occurred, it is first necessary to understand the pull of this continent. The men's urge to explore is strong.

We were barely a week and a half into the preparation of our base camp when four of my team approached me regarding the dispatch of the first exploration party. I explained to them that the priority lay in the completion of our base, long before we could attempt anything else. The discussions were far from cordial, with me finally receiving a begrudging agreement that the crew would wait.

Imagine my surprise and dismay the following morning to find the small group had left in the early hours of the morning, taking half of our dogs and a great deal of our stores with them. We waited in vain for their return, losing all hope when our half-starved dogs staggered back into camp. How the animals found us I'll never know, but their arrival signalled the worst for the men who had left in the night—I am certain they have all perished.

I am sorry my love to bear such sorrowful tidings. I feel as if I have failed in my leadership of this team.

ERF

Antarctica—2009

Sarah closed the mess hut door and headed for the kitchen stove. "I wondered where you'd gotten to. Want a brew?"

Michela put down her pen and rubbed her neck. "I'm about due for one. I've been catching up on my notes. My digital tablet's not working, something to do with the cold I suppose. I'm having to record everything by hand and I'm woefully behind."

Sarah put a cup of coffee in front of Michela and then returned to the kitchen area to prepare a thermos of coffee. "I suppose what's recently happened around here wouldn't be helping much either."

Michela looked down at her notes. "You should be doing my job."

"You wouldn't be doing your work on this table if Di and Rick had their way. Just the other day I caught them on it, in a less than compromising position. Bugger me, they're acting like a couple of sex starved teenagers."

Michela shuddered at the visual image. "I don't think I want to go there. But I'm happy that the three of them have managed to stop arguing."

"I know what you mean. The argument they had the day after Rick and Alli's breakup, over whether or not to dig a trench around the hut was a doozy. It was the safe option though. Alli's keen to ensure the integrity of the building." Sarah paused at the pained look that crossed Michela's face. "What's wrong?"

"I'm pretty concerned about Alli. She seems to retreat into herself a little more every day. She's refused to talk about what's happened, even though I asked her if she wants to. I see how she watches Di and Rick and it's plain she's still hurting over the breakup. That, and the eighteen hour days she's putting in. I wouldn't be surprised if she ends up as a patient of yours."

Sarah screwed the lid on the thermos. "I don't like the sound of that. I'll have a chat with her and see if she'll open up with me." Michela nodded her thanks. "But for now I better get this to the workers outside."

SARAH CALLED DOWN from the edge of the trench. "Hey, you guys are going great guns."

"G'day, mate," Rob called from the nine foot high trench around the hut.

Sarah waved a green metal thermos. "How'd you feel about a break and a nice cup of hot chocolate?"

Rob moaned in delight. "Sarah, if things were different I'd kiss you." Sarah screwed up her face. "All right, all right. I get the picture. Do you think you could bring it down here? Out of the wind?"

Sarah nodded and walked to the cut steps at the other end of the hut. Preoccupied with looking toward where the hut was being uncovered, her foot hit a slick spot. Her arms windmilled and she struggled to steady herself. As she teetered on the edge of the step, her hands found no purchase on the smooth walls of ice and she fell into the trench, landing flat on her back.

Rob ran to Sarah's side, knelt down, and searched for any obvious signs of injury. "Are you okay?"

Sarah tuned her mind to her body. *Legs and arms still pointing in the right direction. A bit woozy in the head, possibly a small concussion, but ribs seem okay. Shit that was lucky.* "I've felt better and I do feel like a bit of an idiot but other than that, oh, crap." As she raised herself into a seated position, the familiar pain of an old back injury made itself known.

"What is it?" Ewan asked.

"I think I've twinged an old war wound. Damn it."

Ewan helped Sarah up. "It's not too bad is it?"

Rob hooked his arm under Sarah's armpit and they gingerly walked to the stairs. "That depends on your definition of too bad, eh, Sarah?"

Sarah cursed, part in frustration and part over the dull pain that had settled at the base of her spine. "God give me strength that I have to be stuck with you again when I do this."

Ewan frowned and looked at Rob for an explanation.

Rob chuckled. "I've been stuck with Sarah before when this has happened. Usually she's laid up for at least a couple of days. If there's one thing she hates, it's being a patient. She's like a bear with a sore head."

She winced at the discomfort in her lower back. "I

bloody-well am not."

"You are, so shut up or I *will* give you something to whinge about." Rob took Sarah's full weight from Ewan. "Mate, both of us aren't going to be able to get her up those steps. Can you go and find Michela and let her know what's happened. I'll get lady muck here to her sleeping quarters."

ROB HAD BARELY gotten Sarah into her bed when there was a knock on the door. "Come in," he called as he placed a folded blanket under Sarah's knees, to elevate her legs and take the weight off the base of her back.

Michela walked in, knelt beside Sarah, and put her hand on her arm to prevent her from moving too much. "How did you manage this?"

"Let's say, it's the last time I decide to play the Good Samaritan to someone at the bottom of a trench."

Michela softly rubbed Sarah's arm. "Do you want me to call Wills Station?"

Sarah shook her head. "Please don't. I'd never hear the end of it from Maddi and besides, this isn't the first time this has happened. The best thing is a couple of days bed rest. From there I'll have to take it easy when I move around camp, that's all."

"Do you need anything for the pain?"

"Yes, although I'm going to have to self administer it. Rob, can you get my bag please?"

Rob fetched the bag from one of the small cupboards and handed it to Michela.

"There's a vial with the label benzodiazepine on it. It's more commonly known as Valium. It'll almost immediately start to alleviate the spasm."

Michela handed her the vial and searched for a needle. "Can you administer this yourself?"

"I don't know I've got any choice. At least I can administer the first shot. After that I'll take the pills for the first twenty-four hours or so. Do you think you can possibly stop people from not getting hurt while I'm in la-la land?"

Michela smiled and pulled an alcohol swab from the bag. "If I can keep Alli away from Rick, that should limit any degree of physical damage. As for the rest of us, we're just going to have to be a little careful. Where do you want me to swab you?"

"My right shoulder, on the meaty bit of the deltoid. That'll give me plenty to aim at. This is going to work pretty quickly. Is there anything you want to ask me before I'm off-line for a while?"

"No, hang on, yes. Who's going to look after you for bathroom visits and the like?"

"Don't worry, Rob's an old hand at helping me with that, aren't you, mate? He knows what needs to be done."

Michela smiled at Rob and patted Sarah's knee. "In that case, pleasant dreams. We'll just have to celebrate New Year's day without you. If you need anything just let me know, via Rob that is."

"That'd be right, hold a party while I'm out to it." Michela winced as Sarah injected herself and watched as Sarah's features glazed over. She took the syringe from Sarah's hands and gave it to Rob.

"Don't worry. She'll be all right," Rob said.

Michela nodded and prayed that everyone else stayed that way, at least until Sarah recovered.

ALLISON SWITCHED OFF off the blade and turned to her co-workers. "This ice has done a great job of acting as packing material around the building."

Ewan rubbed his hand over the bleached wood. "Sure has. The ice has worn the wood a bit, but all in all, it looks pretty good for something over a hundred years old."

Allison nodded and turned to Rob. "How are those joists going?"

Rob patted a joist, supporting the hut's frame. "They're good to go. If you pass me one of the blades, I'll cut away at some of this ice. That should give you a better look inside."

Rob carefully cleared away the excess ice. The team moved closer and stared at the foyer in child-like amazement.

Rick looked around the small entrance. "This looks like an old photograph."

Dianne carefully stroked one of the four frozen wet

weather jackets hanging from a wooden peg on the wall. "Look at these. They look as if they're part of a museum exhibit instead of history itself."

Allison carefully picked up a pair of stiff leather boots. "Look at these snow boots and the shoes down there. They're in fantastic shape, as if they were only put here yesterday."

Rick nodded. "Just think what waits us inside. Why don't we increase the heat and speed of the blades so we can get to what's in there?"

"Mate, the walls may be solid but we don't know what the weight of snow and ice has done to the building's ceiling," Rob said. "We need to take it slow and set up joists as we go. That'll give you a safer environment to work in."

"Suit yourself," Rick said. "But don't come crying to me when you get to the good bits and you find it's time to pack up and go home."

Allison, barely acknowledging Rick's comments, pulled her notebook from her jacket. "Let's get some of this catalogued. Dianne, have you got your camera handy?"

Dianne pulled the camera from its waterproof pack and the two spent the rest of the day cataloguing the antique cache. They then sealed some of the artefacts in specially designed bags for the long journey back to Australia.

FRUSTRATED BY THE speed of the dig, Rick argued almost daily with Dianne and Allison. On the fifth day, he finally threw his hands up in disgust, and went to the mess hut for a cup of coffee. *What's old man Peterson going to say when we arrive home with some bloody old clothes to show for our troubles? These guys would have all kept diaries. That's what we've got to find. Plus there's bound to be other caches around here. We'll never have time to find any of those if we continue to dig at this pace.* He yanked a coffee cup from the wall and slammed it down on the bench.

"What's the matter, mate?" Ewan asked from his seat at the dining table.

Rick rubbed his hands through his dark hair. "It's these bloody women. They're taking too much time—time we can't afford to waste."

Ewan scratched at his three-day growth of beard. "I thought that was to make sure everything was safe."

"If it was any safer we wouldn't be doing anything at all. Trust me, I know about this sort of stuff and we're going far too slow."

"Women do tend to fuss over everything don't they?"

Rick vigorously nodded. "Herr DeGrasse runs this place like a Army camp. I don't know why but she watches me like a bloody hawk. Damn, there's so much more that we could find if we just took the time to do so." He poured water into his cup.

"Maybe we should be a bit riskier," Ewan said.

Rick sat down and surreptitiously gazed over his coffee at Ewan's eager face. "You know the best thing about finding things down here in Antarctica?"

Ewan tilted his head. "No, what?"

"It usually means it's never been discovered before and so you have naming rights." Rick knew he couldn't be further from the truth, but he now had Ewan's full attention. "Come to think of it, I can't really see why Finlayson would build one hut if they were looking at exploring other parts of the continent. Why I bet there're dumps and caches all around here."

Ewan again scratched his stubble, his face a picture of concentration. "What you're saying is if someone like me found such a dump then I'd have first naming rights?"

Rick smiled. "You've got it in one." He went to the kitchen and rinsed his cup before returning it to its place on the wall. "I'll see you around."

Later that afternoon, Rick wasn't at all surprised at the knock on his door. "Come in."

Ewan, juggling a map and one of the emergency kits, stumbled through the door. Rick stood and took the emergency kit from Ewan, before it could fall out of Ewan's arms. "What are you up to?"

Ewan laid the map on the small table. "I've been thinking about what you said and you're right, this is taking too long. I was looking at going on a bit of a quick trip, no more than about six miles or so, to see what's out there."

Rick slapped Ewan on the back. "That's great news.

We'll make a fully-fledged archaeologist out of you yet. Where are you going to go?"

"I think I'll head this way. It's slightly inland, but if they were going to the South Pole that's the way they would've headed. It shouldn't take me that long to cover six miles, should it?"

Rick put the emergency kit on the table. "I don't think so. You'll most likely be back for supper with news of your discovery." Rick picked up a pen and scribbled on a piece of paper. "Here, let me jot down that bearing, just in case. What else are you taking with you?"

Ewan checked the power on the short-range radio. "I'm taking this and a small medical kit. Do you think the radio will cover that distance?"

"No worries, mate. They have a range of at least twelve miles."

Ewan pulled a small orange rectangle from his emergency pack. "I've got this EPIRB thing, as well as some food just in case."

Rick took the cold conditions Emergency Personal Individual Rescue Beacon, or EPIRB, from him and ensured it was set to the correct frequency. "I'll switch this thing on now. That way you can be tracked from camp."

"What do you mean?" Ewan asked.

"These EPIRB's are specifically designed for adverse environments. The regular emission of a passive locating mark allows it to be picked by one of the receivers we've here at the site. Rick handed the EPIRB back to Ewan. "There, it's good to go. Make sure it's strapped to you or the vehicle at all times in case you get a little off track."

A wide grin spread across Ewan's face. "No worries, mate. I'm off before I get roped into some other task." He bundled his equipment into his backpack and headed for the door. Ewan paused at the door and turned. "Get that bottle of whiskey out. I think there'll be plenty to celebrate tonight."

DIANNE LEANT BACK in her chair looking content with the day's proceedings and the evening's meal. "Things moved along pretty well today. The ice blades are proving their worth, despite the need to regularly recharge

them. Tomorrow should see us well past the entranceway." She clasped her coffee in her hands to draw warmth
from the cup. "Oh, and thanks for the meal, Michela, that
was pretty good."

Michela graciously nodded. "I'm glad you enjoyed it.
Speaking of eating, where's Ewan? I've never known him
to miss a meal. Even when he was seasick he still managed
to keep something down." The group chuckled at Ewan's
love of food.

"Come to think of it, I haven't seen a lot of him since
lunch. He didn't end up succumbing to the fate of getting
stuck on the toilet did he?" Rob asked.

Allison placed her knife and fork together on her
plate. "I was there about half an hour ago and I was the
only one."

An uneasy feeling settled over Michela. Searching the
group's faces, her stomach sank at Rick's enigmatic features. "Rick, you wouldn't know where Ewan is, would
you?"

Rick wiped his plate with a bread roll. "As a matter of
fact he did say something to me this afternoon."

Sarah shifted in her seat. "And what would that be?"

"We were talking about Antarctica and the other
explorers who'd been down here. I might have mentioned
to him the idea this camp was a staging base and that there
might be other areas yet undiscovered not far from here. I
think he mentioned something about going and having a
look for a couple."

"Let me clarify something with you, Dr. Winston,"
Michela said in a dangerously calm voice. "You had a discussion with a member of this team, someone you know to
be exceptionally enthusiastic, but relatively new to the
continent." Rick nodded. "Knowing he's been eager to
please since his arrival, you then discussed the likelihood
of what might be also found around here."

Rick folded his arms. "It seemed only fair to let him
know what else is possibly out there. Besides, things here
are going at a snail's pace."

"Have you any idea the danger you may have put that
man into, or for that matter do you really care?" Michela
turned to Rob as he made his way to the door.

Rob held the door as Allison followed him. "I'll check

our lodgings, boss, and the ski-demons. I'll be right back."

"I'll check the dig site and the loo, in case he headed back there." Allison closed the door behind her.

Michela returned her steely gaze to Rick. "Dr. Winston, I swear to God this time you've overstepped the mark. You've potentially risked the life of one of my people. At least tell me you didn't allow him to leave here without a radio or EPIRB?"

Rick held up his hands. "Hang on a minute. I didn't tell him to go anywhere. He's a grown man, for Christ's sake."

"You're quite right. He's a grown man and can make his own decisions. But I've a sneaking suspicion this is one decision he'd have never arrived at had it not been for you. Now, I'll ask you again, did he leave here with a short-range radio and EPIRB, and for that matter, did he give you a direction?"

Before Rick could answer, Allison and Rob, shaking their heads, walked back through the door.

"That means he's still out there. So, where was he headed, Dr. Winston?" Michela asked in deadly calm tones as she rose from the table.

Sarah reached across the table and grabbed Rick's collar, and winced from the pain in her back. "You bloody idiot. Have you any idea what kind of danger you may have put Ewan into?"

Michela quickly leaned across the table and forced Sarah's fingers open. "Stop that right now. Our main effort here should be finding Ewan." After ensuring Sarah wasn't about to resume her grip, Michela turned to Rob. "Can you get me a map and then make up an emergency kit? We're going to have to go and look for him. Now, Dr. Winston, where did he go and what time did he leave?"

Rick straightened his collar and stood. He cast a baleful glance in Sarah's direction and then traced a line on the map on the wall of the hut. "He said this was the route he was going to take and he left about four hours ago."

Allison looked at the map and roughly measured the distance between the camp and Ewan's destination. "That's no more than a twelve to thirteen mile round trip." She raised her eyes to Michela. "He should have been home hours ago."

Michela rapidly calculated the time to reach the extremity of Ewan's location. "What was his radio frequency? Did he have his EPIRB turned on?"

"He's on a 94.20 frequency and, yes, I did turn his EPIRB on before he left. I don't know what you're worrying about, I'm sure he's lost his way, that's all."

Rob stepped up to Rick, his quiet voice barely masking his anger. "Mate, you could really do with a clue right now. There are a million and one things that could go wrong down here. Something as simple as a breakdown, without the right emergency shelter, could mean the difference between life and death. You really are some piece of work."

Michela intervened before Rob did physical damage, although her own fingers were itching to do the same. "This is getting us nowhere. Rob, go and prepare a ski-demon for travel and I'll finish packing the emergency kit."

Sarah put a restraining hand on Michela's arm. "I'll come with you. If he's injured he may need medical help."

Michela shook her head. "No one's better suited, but you've only started to recover. Sitting behind me on a not very well cushioned snow mobile won't help your back." She held up her hand to halt any protest. "I'm sorry. You're going to have to stay here. Besides, if Dr. Winston steps an inch out of line while I'm gone, I want Rob to hold him down while you sedate him."

Rick sat up. "You can't do that. It's against the law."

Sarah wheeled on him and winced at the sudden movement. "You're not in Australia now, mate, you're in Antarctic territory. If you think for a minute I wouldn't take pleasure in sedating your sorry ass then you've got another thing coming." She reined in her anger and returned her gaze to Michela, who was busy packing a small rescue pack. "You sure as hell can't go alone."

"I'll go with you," Allison said.

Michela turned to Allison, aware that the idea of being on the back of a snow mobile with her couldn't be all that attractive. "Okay, but go and get your extreme weather gear on. It's going to be cold on the back of the vehicle. Could you also ensure Rob packs enough rope for about a hundred yard drop and the rappelling gear as well? We may just need it." Allison nodded and Michela picked up the radio from the table.

"Ewan, this is Finlayson site. Do you read me, over?" She released the prezzle switch and received only the static of radio waves. "Ewan, Ewan, this is, this is, Finlayson site, Finlayson site, do you read me, do you read me?" Michela doubled everything, hoping the silence was no more than a bad connection. Again silence filled the room. "Ewan, it's Michela. Do you read me? If you can, but can't speak, press the prezzle switch twice over." The radio remained silent.

She placed the radio back on the table. "Either his radio's run out of power or he's not next to it." Even as she uttered the words, she felt a chill. *I'm getting a bad feeling about this.* She turned on the portable-locating receiver for the EPIRB and she almost immediately got a signal keyed into Ewan's EPIRB.

Michela turned to the others. "At least we've got a pretty good idea of where he should be located. Sarah, Allison, and I will keep in contact by short-range radio. We'll be on Ewan's frequency in case he calls in. I'll give you radio checks every half hour so you can plot our progress in case we have a breakdown. The EPIRB will be on at all times, so you should be able to pinpoint our location."

Rob entered the hut. "Ski-demon's good to go, boss."

"Thanks. Sarah, could you get onto Wills Station and let them know what's going on? Tell the Station Leader I'll give her a full run down when I get back."

Sarah followed Michela out the door and to the now running snow mobile. "Not a problem. Just find him, okay?"

Having added the necessary extra layers of clothing, Allison was ready to go. She handed a bundle to Michela. "I hope you don't mind but I took the liberty of taking these off your bed."

Michela gratefully received her gear and put it on. After conducting one final radio check and confirming the EPIRB and the locating beacon were operating, the two hopped on the vehicle and sped off in the direction Ewan had taken.

THEY MOVED ACROSS the ice as fast as could be managed while trying to search for someone, pausing only occasionally to check their bearing with the EPIRB receiver. Despite their cruising speed, there was no sign of Ewan or his snow mobile.

Michela scanned the white landscape. *By the strength of this signal, we should be on his location any moment now. So why can't I see him?* A chilling thought flashed through her mind. She pulled the vehicle to a fast halt and looked around.

Allison tapped Michela on the shoulder. "Why have we stopped here? I can't see any trace of the ski-demon."

"How strong is the signal?" Michela calmly asked, despite her growing sense of foreboding.

Allison pulled the range finder from her jacket and checked the gauge. "This says we should be right on top of it, or at least within a three feet radius. Why?"

Michela carefully surveyed the ground around her. "Ewan's here all right, but I've got a bad feeling we're in the middle of a crevasse field. Whatever you do, don't get off the snow mobile, not for the moment anyway."

Allison looked around her. "A crevasse field?"

"Yes. These ones are a little different to the ones in Mount Cook. The depth of the ice here means they can be very deep, sometimes over half a mile. The snow bridges that form across the crevasses aren't all that deep, four or five yards or so. This means you can often be right in a crevasse field and never know it. Sometimes the bridges give way."

Allison scanned the landscape and saw a depression in the ground, mere yards away, hidden in the endless white. "Over there, at about two o'clock to where we are, it looks like there's a break in the ground."

Michela turned her head. There was a definite break in the ice. She closed her eyes, a part of her not wanting to go and look down the crevasse, and yet knowing she had to. "I'm going to have to go and check that out. I want you to stay on the snow mobile; you'll be my anchor. I'll also get you to tie off an anchor rope to the ice. This'll embed itself deep in the surface, hopefully with at least some degree of depth."

Michela pulled a hydraulic gun from the emergency

bag and tied one end of her climbing rope to the anchor. "I'm going to rig myself up to check out the hole. Under no circumstances are you to get off the ski-demon, do you understand me?"

Allison's concerned eyes searched Michela's face. "What happens if you fall through the ice?"

"I should be okay. I'll be on a rig and will be able to pull myself back up if anything happens. But, if everything goes to hell in a hand basket, I want you to start the ski-demon and very gently turn the throttle to get any slack out of the rope. Disengage the anchor and then use the vehicle to pull me up. We may be lucky at the moment, the snow mobile seems to be on reasonably firm ground. Hand me that bag will you please?"

Michela took the bag from Allison's shaking hands. She rummaged through it and pulled out the climbing equipment before handing the bag back to Allison. She put the rappelling harness on, hooked on the rope, and checked the xenon light on her headlamp. "Can you get out the mechanical ascenders and the xenon glow sticks?"

Allison rummaged through the bag and pulled out two lightweight left and right-hand ascenders, plus a handful of glow sticks. She tore open the packaging for the xenon glow sticks and handed the ascenders and glow sticks to Michela.

Michela nodded her thanks and stuffed them in one of the pouches hanging from the harness on her waist. "Is there a little hook and spool-looking thing in the bag? That'll allow me to lower one of the glow sticks further into the crevasse if necessary." Allison checked the bag and handed over the small spool as Michela checked her equipment one final time.

"Are you sure you know what you're doing?"

Michela gave Allison's arm a reassuring squeeze. "I'll be okay. I do quite a bit of rappelling back home when I have the time. Besides, I don't intend to lose anyone on this expedition, not if I have anything to do with it."

Michela carefully stepped off the vehicle and gingerly made her way toward the crevasse, scanning the ground as she went.

So far, so good. As she eased closer, she clearly saw the crevasse and the direction in which it went. This would be valuable information when the three of them later negotiated their way out of the field. *God, let there be three of us finding our way out of this, please.*

Michela eased herself onto the snow, leopard-crawling the final yard to the chasm's edge. She flicked the switch on the headlamp, allowing the xenon beam to illuminate the view. She systematically swept the hole with the light and paused at a ledge about twenty yards below. Scattered on the frozen landing were the unmistakable remains of something mechanical. *Damn it. Given we're the only show on this block, it looks a hell of a lot like the ski-demon I rode in on.*

She eased herself back from the edge, stood, and turned to Allison. "I'm going down." After checking her harness and equipment again, she took the climbing rope and threw it into the crevasse. She faced Allison and slowly leant back till she was forty-five degrees to the ledge. She cautiously began her descent over the edge, at the same time using her crampons to take a bite out of the ice wall.

The silence around Michela was almost complete, with only the occasional whistle of wind as it reverberated off the edges of the icy ravine. Her headlamp lit the way, its glow eerily reflecting off the cool blue walls. She shuffled across to the ledge she'd seen only moments ago from above and then eased upright before checking the metal and fibreglass wreckage.

Any doubts to its origin were quickly dispelled. Sitting in its carry pouch, on the side of a piece of fibreglass casing, was an EPIRB. A piece of white tape was stuck to the transponder's side, the words "FINLAYSON EXPEDITION" written in bold letters. Michela bowed her head. *So you've found wreckage. That doesn't mean the worst, not yet anyway. He may have fallen off and is somewhere below you.* Even so, this would mean evacuating an injured person, *and that's going to be a hell of a lot more difficult, not to mention we're not completely equipped for such an evacuation.* Leaning over, she strained her eyes, searching for another ledge below her without success. *It looks as if I'm going down again.*

Using her foot, she pushed the wreckage toward the ice wall, allowing her a firm step-off point for the next part of her descent. She stepped off the ledge and rappelled, scanning her surroundings with the high-powered beam for any evidence of the rest of the snow mobile or Ewan.

As she strained to see further down the chasm's length, her frigid brake hand slipped from the iced rope and the rope raced through the karabiner at a frightening pace. For what seemed like an eternity she fell, as she struggled to regain control. Experience finally overcame fear and she managed to grip the rope, performing an emergency lockout to halt her fall.

She hit the ice wall with a muffled thud, winding herself in the process. As she fought to force air back into her lungs she swung and twirled like a yo-yo parallel to the crevasse's walls. Waiting for her momentum to slow, she watched the light's strobing effect off the smooth surfaces. *What's that?* She squinted and finally stopped moving.

Slightly below her and to the left, the opposite wall was splattered with red, like a single-coloured abstract expressionist painting. She struggled to keep down dinner, swallowing the bile that rose in her throat. The impact had been tremendous, causing blood to be spattered as far as she could see. Looking above her, she could just make out the ledge she'd been on only moments before. Obviously the snow mobile had plummeted through the lightly packed snow, its first impact being the icy outcrop above her. From there, the force of the impact must have dislodged Ewan, before he free fell and hit the opposite wall.

Bowing her head, she fought back tears. *Focus, Michela, focus! You can't afford to lose it now. First things first. See if you can see any trace of his, his body.* She locked out her rope with a prusik knot and pulled one of the cylindrical glow sticks from her pouch. She bent it in half, in turn breaking the gas vial in the cylinder and releasing a light from the plastic container. She hooked one end of the plastic light to the small spool and lowered it into the darkness.

Lower and lower it went, the light casting an unnatural glow off the icy walls. Swinging the small light like a pendulum, Michela strained to see any evidence of either Ewan or the additional remains of his ski-demon. At one hundred yards the light reached the maximum length of its cord, with still no evidence of man or machine. *If he sur-*

vived the fall, the elements and loss of blood would have cer-
tainly killed him.

Michela, on autopilot, wound in the glow light and contemplated how to break the news to the others. *More importantly, how can I get Rick out of the camp before someone, possibly Rob, does him bodily harm?* She knew that Rob and Ewan had formed a steady friendship, relying on one another for support when they felt they were being "over-whelmed by women," as both jokingly put it.

Maybe it wouldn't be so bad if Rick had the living crap kicked out of him. Michela stopped herself. *No. No matter what Rick's involvement is in this, at the end of the day Ewan made his own decision to come out here.* As far as she was concerned, the indirect responsibility for his death would always rest with Rick, but any coroner would rightly see Ewan's death as no more than death by misadventure. *And the bastard gets away with it. I hope you don't sleep well at night once you find out what you've done, you damn low life.*

Michela returned the spool and glow light to her pouch. She then pulled out her left and right mechanical ascenders and another length of rope. The mechanical ascenders small teeth gripped the rope, allowing her to ascend using one for each hand. As an added precaution she belayed the ascenders to her climbing rope, and attached loops for her feet, allowing her to climb, much like a caterpillar would move up the stem of a plant.

Michela's ascent was slow and laboured. Halting at the ledge where she'd found remnants of the snow mobile, she took a ragged breath. The free fall had been physically draining and the shock of Ewan's death had emotionally shaken her. She closed her eyes for a minute and leant against the wall with her crampons locked into the ledge. *You may reach the top, Michela, but we're not out of this yet. You've got to find a safe way out of this field. Then we've got to get back to camp and break the news.* Forcing herself to relax, Michela focussed on her breathing, disciplining it into slow and deep breaths. She relaxed her clenched jaw and rotated her neck, attempting to remove the stress in her shoulders. She shook out her aching arms, centred herself, and resumed her climb.

Finally, she broke over the crevasse's ledge, sprawled over the snow, and tiredly pulled up her rope. Avoiding

Allison's gaze, she looped her rope before making her way to the ski-demon.

Allison looked expectantly behind Michela. "Did you find him?"

Michela disengaged the anchor and the other end of the rope and stowed the equipment. She then took Allison's hands in her own. "He didn't make it. He's dead."

Allison blinked and shook her head. "He can't be. This morning he was helping me on the dig. Are you sure? How did it happen?"

Michela rubbed Allison's hands, as much to warm Allison as herself. "I'm sorry, honey, but he's dead and for the moment you're going to have to trust me on that one." She held up her hand. "Please, don't ask me about it now. I suggest we give Sarah a quick report and then get out of this field."

Allison nodded, seeing the barely concealed anguish in Michela's eyes.

Michela picked up the short-range radio and depressed the prezzle switch. "Finlayson Base, this is Michela. Do you read, over?"

After a short delay the call was answered. "Michela, this is Sarah."

"Sarah, are you alone at the moment?"

"Yes, I am. Rick and Di have gone to their hut and Rob's busying himself with the solar generator."

Michela frowned. "Is there something wrong with it?"

"No, but there's a big storm bearing down on us here. It's due to reach us in the next thirty minutes or so. I asked him to check the anchor ropes on the solar generator, just to make sure it didn't blow away. He's checking those and the blizzard ropes. Did you find Ewan?"

"Sarah, he's gone. By the looks of it he fell into a crevasse and kept on falling. I had visual to about one hundred and seventy yards and couldn't see the bottom of the crevasse." Allison gasped. Michela rubbed Allison's hand.

"The storm's heading your way. You need to find cover where you are."

Frustrated, Michela shook her head. *Can this day get any worse?* "You say it's due to hit you in thirty minutes, which gives us about an hour or so. Sarah, we're on a crevasse field."

"Shit! Can you track your way back again?"

"I don't know if we can safely do that. I really don't know how long we travelled onto the field before we actually realised where we were."

"Have you got your GPS handy?"

Michela turned to Allison who was busy removing the instrument from its docking port. Michela read the figures on the compact screen back to Sarah.

"I'm checking the map." There was a slight pause before Sarah's voice was again heard. "You're right. You're on top of a glacier. But by your coordinates you're close to the edge. Unfortunately, that's the furthest edge."

Michela closed her eyes. "Do you have any good news for me?"

"Yes I do. If you take a westerly heading for about two hundred and twenty yards or so, you should find yourself out of the field. But one of you is going to have to go ahead of the ski-demon and check the ground as you go. Have you got your map?"

Allison handed the map to Michela. "I have now."

"Right. Look at grid reference 8099 4050."

Michela located the relevant easting and northing. "Got it."

"Once you get to the edge, if you plot a bound in that direction, in about three miles you'll come across one of the emergency huts. You'll have to wait out the storm there."

"Hang on a minute." Michela plotted the small westerly move into the GPS before plotting the longer northerly move. Double-checking her numbers, she then placed the GPS in its docking port and activated the button that allowed both GPS and ski-demon to work together to get them to the emergency hut. She depressed the prezzle switch. "Do you have any suggestions once the storm passes us?"

"Yes. The snow and ice should be a lot more stable to cross from higher up the glacier. Once you can leave the hut, plot a bearing to grid reference 9595 4050. This will give you a safe path across the glacier. Once you're on the other side, take a reading and plot a bearing back home. Do you understand?"

"Yes I do. We'd better start before we run out of time.

If we lose communications with you, I'll use the following code. Two bursts of static will mean we're off the glacier and three will mean we've reached the hut."

"Roger that. Michela, you and Allison be careful. I hope to see you soon."

"We hope to see you soon also. Can you radio the information about Ewan to Wills Station? I'll give a full report when we return."

"Roger that, Michela. Now get going, out."

She handed the radio to Allison and eased herself off the snow mobile. "We better get out of here, before the storm hits."

Chapter
Eight

My Darling Charlotte,

The last few weeks have been somber to say the least. The tragic loss of our team members gravely affected the group. As for me, I still feel as if I've failed as the expedition leader. I should have watched my team more closely; this continent and its seductive nature are not to be trusted. We held a service for our comrades who did not return and then we were forced to continue on with life. To do nothing other than to dwell on their passing would not be productive, either emotionally or physically.

We have finished the main hut, marking its completion with a small celebration out of our meager rations. The loss of the others and the food they took with them has meant that I have been forced to ration some of our provisions, aware that not to do so may see us run short before our ship returns.

We have a little wood left and it is my intent to use this to construct a small building, for the purpose of developing a photographic record of our expedition. My photographer Ian Ross is an enthusiastic man, however his equipment is taking up far too much of the internal space of our working and living area, not to mention the awful smell of developing photographs. Hopefully this will keep him happy and the other members of the crew as well.
All my love,

ERF

Antarctica—2010

ALLISON WATCHED MICHELA alight from the ski-demon. "Where do you think you're going?" she demanded.

Michela turned and frowned. "What do you mean? We've got to get out of here and the only safe way to do this is if someone walks in front of the snow mobile and checks the path."

Allison scowled. "I understand that. But, why are you doing it?"

Michela tilted her head. "I'm sorry, I don't understand."

"Just stop and think. You've spent the better part of the last hour going down into the bowels of the earth before having to drag yourself out. You must be about dead on your feet." Allison eased her leg over the side of the vehicle. "Let me do this. Tell me what needs to be done."

"I don't think that's a good idea."

"Why?" Allison asked, her hands on her hips.

Michela forced herself to remain calm. "For a start, you may have a rudimentary understanding of glaciers, but have you had training in this?"

"No, but how difficult can it be?"

"It isn't that easy to do, Allison. It requires a lot of focus and a fair degree of quick reaction. I'll go ahead of you and check the ground. You've got to be prepared to manoeuvre the ski-demon to miss any cracks in the ice."

Allison snorted. "Seriously, it can't be that hard. Give me a quick run down of what has to be done."

Closing her eyes, Michela rubbed the back of her neck in frustration. "Look, I know back at the camp we'd all normally discuss something before we reach agreement, but this isn't the time or place for consensual decision making. I'll do the probing and you drive the vehicle. There's a storm bearing down on us and we really don't have the time to discuss this."

Allison braced her feet and shook her head. "Be reasonable. You said this requires focus and reaction. You can't possibly tell me you're completely focussed now; not after what you've been put through." Michela turned away. "Why won't you let me do this?"

Michela wheeled, desperation on her features, her eyes glistening. "Because I can't afford to lose you too damn it. Please, if you want to argue about this later, then fine. But right now we've got to get out of here, and fast."

Michela grabbed her ice axe and moved to a position roughly three yards in front of the snow mobile. Not looking back, she checked the surface to her front, relieved when she finally heard the vehicle's engine roar to life.

Michela carefully edged across the ice, using her axe to check the ground as she went. More than once she held up her hand to halt the vehicle and prodded the ground until again the axe found purchase.

Meandering across the cold surface at a snail's pace seemed to take forever, further taxing Michela's frayed nerves. *All I want now is a warm bath, a good glass of scotch and, a decent sleep—none of which I'm likely to get in the near future.* She winced as she bent down to check the ice. Her fall in the crevasse had left its mark on her tired body. Only now as her system cooled down did she become aware of how many aches and pains she had. She was certain she'd have her fair share of bruises when she finally removed her multiple layers of clothing.

Allowing her mind to wander, she instinctively prodded the ground, almost losing her balance as the axe broke through yet another thin layer of snow. Feeling herself teetering toward the chasm before her, she threw all of her balance backwards and fell face up on the cold surface. *That was too close. I've got to keep concentrating on the task at hand, if not for me then at least for Allison.*

Allison hovered above her. "Are you all right?"

Michela, trying hard to mask a grimace of pain, sat up. "I'm okay, just a little bit of hurt pride." She leant forward and looked at the break in the ice where her axe had plummeted through. Realising going after it wasn't an option, she rose and turned to Allison. "I've lost the snow axe."

Allison gently gripped Michela's arms with her gloved hands. "Lost the snow axe. Who cares about the bloody snow axe? I almost lost you. Are you sure you don't want me to do this?"

As tired as she was, Michela knew she had to get them off the glacier and soon. "No, I'm okay. I could use another axe if you could possibly let me play with yours," she said, a hint of teasing in her voice.

Allison stepped back and shook her head. "You're incorrigible, but I guess you know that." She retrieved her axe from the vehicle and gave it to Michela. She then returned to the snow mobile. "We better get going then, Superwoman."

Michela tiredly smiled before turning around and again tracking a path across the glacier. It took another ten minutes before she was certain they were out of immediate danger. She keyed the radio and found they'd lost communications, and so used the prearranged signal to let Sarah know they were clear of their first obstacle. *Now all we have to do is find this hut. Out of the frying pan and into the fire.*

They'd barely managed to reach the emergency hut when the increase in wind speed and the closing in of the clouds heralded the oncoming storm. Michela checked the door and found it unlocked.

"I think we've got about ten minutes max before the storm hits. I'll get this gear inside." Michela pointed to two metal points, firmly entrenched in the ice. "Could you take the rope and tie the ski-demon to the anchor points by the side of the hut over there. You know how to tie knots and lashings don't you?"

Allison rolled her eyes. "If what I currently do for a living didn't come with the requirement to tie such things, then I'm sure my old Girl Scout training would help me. Of course I can bloody-well tie knots. Get inside and I'll be in shortly."

A Girl Scout hey? I can just imagine what sort of havoc you'd have wreaked on your poor Scout Master. Exhausted, Michela managed a smile before she stepped out of the wind and cold, and into the building.

She plonked the gear on the table, collapsed into a seat, and scanned the building's interior. It was like their mess hut, except without the solar heating element to generate internal warmth. *It's certainly darned small for a prolonged stay with Alli.*

ALLISON PULLED THE collar of her extreme weather jacket up around her ears as she came through the door.

Despite being inside a sealed container, the sound of the wind was a constant as the storm began in earnest. "Brrrr, it's like an ice box in here. Where's the heating unit?"

Michela tiredly shrugged. "I don't think there is one. We're going to have to rely on the old fashioned method."

Allison gave her a quizzical look. "What old fashioned method?"

Michela rose and looked around the room. "There should be Stinson pressure lamps in here somewhere."

"What are they?"

"They're a kerosene lamp, invented in 1813 and they've been used in Antarctica from the very beginning. They not only give off light, they give off heat as well, at least some degree of heat that is."

Michela lifted the lid of a box, peered inside, and then pulled out two of the lamps. "Here they are." She bent down and pulled out another two. "See if you can find any kerosene."

Allison went to one end of the small building and scanned the cramped surroundings, looking for fuel. She stopped in front of a plastic container filled with a clear blue liquid and turned to Michela, who was busy checking the serviceability of the lamps. "I think I've found some." She dragged the large container from under the bench, opened the top, and sniffed the contents. Pulling back and scrunching her nose, she sealed the container. "Yep, that's kerosene all right. I remember that smell from my great grandfather's heater. No matter how much we wanted to replace it with something more modern he wouldn't be swayed."

Michela smiled. "Stubborn streak, hey? I wouldn't have thought that'd be a family trait."

Allison opened her mouth then just as quickly closed it. "There's a tap at the bottom here. We're going to have to get it onto the table to pour the kero. We should be able to do it together." Allison went to one side of the container while Michela took her position on the other. They hefted the flammable liquid onto the table and, out of the corner of her eye, Allison spied Michela's strained features.

Once the container was stable, Allison moved around the table to where Michela had gingerly sat down. "Are you all right?"

"I'm okay. I got bounced around a bit in the crevasse, that's all."

"Bounced around a bit? What do you mean?"

Michela shook her head. "Not now, please. Maybe later. Let's get these Stinsons' filled." She attempted to stand but Allison put a hand on her shoulder and gently held her down.

Allison picked up the lamps. "No. You stay there. Just tell me what to do. I can cope."

Michela nodded. "I understand, but things will go a lot quicker if we work concurrently. How about you let me try and find the sleeping bags? It's going to be very cold tonight without them."

Allison shrugged. "Either way, I reckon it's still going to be cold. Okay, see if you can find them, but then I want you to rest while I get something ready for dinner." She looked at the cupboards below the small stove. "There's got to be food here somewhere."

Michela walked to the beds. "There always is. These huts are pretty well provisioned for long stays. We'll have to remember to radio Wills Station when we return, and let them know which hut we used. That way they'll restock it before its next use."

Allison filled the first lamp. "How long do you think we're going to be stuck here?"

Michela shrugged. "I really can't say. It could be days or weeks. These storms are highly unpredictable, but at least we're out of the cold."

She pulled two sleeping bags sealed in plastic from the compartment underneath one of the foam mattresses. "Ah, here we are, our sleeping gear for the evening." She pulled both out of their packing and shook them to increase their loft. "They look okay. Hopefully they'll keep us warm."

Allison filled the lamps as she surreptitiously observed Michela. *She looks like she's been dragged through a wringer backwards. And what's this about bouncing in the crevasse? She looks as if she's ready to sleep now. I better finish this and find us something to eat.*

Allison completed filling the four lamps and took them and a box of waterproof matches to Michela. "How about you get these things going while I wash my hands and get some hot water on."

Michela put the first lamp in front of her and pumped pressure into the container. After feeling resistance, she eased the pump back to its original position and lit the lamp, its light reaching the corners of the room. She lit the other lamps and placed them around the hut, attempting to generate both light and warmth.

Allison placed a steaming mug on the table where Michela had been working. "Try that. It's hot chocolate and if it's like any chocolate I'm used to it will at least make you feel a little better."

Michela gratefully lifted the warm mug to her cold lips. The smooth liquid warmed the back of her throat and her stomach. "Marvellous, I think that's all I need before sleep."

"I don't think so. I know we ate before we left, but I think it'd be best if we both had some sustenance before we get some rest." Allison pointed to the pot on the stove. "Besides, I've already started and it'd be a shame to waste good food."

Michela released her cup and held up her hands in mock defeat. "Okay. Food, then bed. Hopefully by then it'll be warm enough in here to strip down to our long johns."

Allison almost dropped the spoon she was holding. "Are you sure that's necessary?"

Michela shook her head. "I hate to say this but it makes more sense to strip down to our long johns. It's a little bit different back at our base camp with the controlled heating and normal bedclothes. While the lamps here will add some warmth, it won't be as warm as what you've been used to. If you hop into the bags with too many clothes on, all you'll do is trap the cold air between the loose layers of clothing. In your long johns, you'll have trapped the warm air close to your skin and then you can rely on the loft of these Antarctic sleeping bags to do the rest. Trust me, I've tried both and long johns are a lot warmer."

Allison placed a plate of food in front of Michela. "Dehydrated chilli con carne. I can't vouch for its taste, but at least it's warm." She retrieved her own plate and sat down. "I'll admit I'm a bit doubtful about this clothes thing."

Michela swallowed her mouthful of beans and wiped the sauce from the edge of her mouth. "I understand, but at least give it a go. If it's too cold, there are other options open."

Allison raised her spoon to her lips. "What other options?"

Michela dismissively waved her hand. "Let's see how this works out and then we'll take it from there." She looked around as a gust of wind buffeted the building.

Allison scanned the walls, half expecting them to cave in at any moment. "Are you sure we're going to be safe in here?"

Michela nodded. "We're a heck of a lot safer in here than out there. These containers are anchored into the ground, so it would have to be the mother of all blizzards to wrench them free." She took another sip of her hot chocolate.

Allison still looked doubtful. "Let's hope so."

Through the meal Allison continued to glance at Michela and was relieved that she looked too tired to care about anything but eating. *I wonder if she knows how nervous I am at the moment. But nervous of what?*

With the meal finished and the edge taken off the cold of the cabin, Michela removed her layers of clothing as she readied herself for bed. Allison preoccupied herself with a detailed inspection of every part of the cabin, except where Michela was disrobing. Her eyes wandered to Michela's back, surprised at Michela's build as she stood and faced the other way in her long johns. *She's got amazingly broad shoulders, and well developed to boot. Hang on, what's that?* Her voyeuristic appraisal halted at a stain underneath Michela's left arm, near her ribs. She went to Michela's side. "What's that?"

Without thought Allison touched the material. She drew her hand away and looked at her bloodstained fingers. "What happened down that crevasse? You're bleeding."

Michela craned her neck in an attempt to see. "I told you, I bounced off the walls a bit, that's all."

"Come here and let me have a look at it. It could require cleaning and dressing." Allison drew Michela to her and lifted up the thermal top. Allison sucked in her breath at the purpling bruises spread over Michela's torso. She gingerly probed the nasty graze from where the blood had come. "Bounced off the walls a bit. I'd say you did more than that."

Michela gritted her teeth, not from the pain but from the effect of Allison's touch.

"This may hurt a bit." Allison swabbed the wound before applying a large adhesive patch to it. Michela clenched and unclenched her fists, the look on her face mirroring her discomfort. "I'll have to have another look at that in the morning, when we'll also talk about how much you bounced off the walls."

Michela murmured her thanks and quickly retreated to the warmth and concealment of the sleeping bag. "Tomorrow, but not tonight. I'm too tired to talk at the moment." She turned her face toward the wall.

Allison smiled at the gesture that allowed her to change in privacy.

Michela turned back as Allison climbed the ladder to her own sleeping bag. "Have a good sleep," she mumbled.

"You too," Allison replied, before making herself comfortable.

For the next half hour Allison fought a losing battle to keep warm. She was beginning to doubt Michela's advice regarding clothing in a sleeping bag. Plus, the lamps didn't seem to be doing that much of a job to keep out the cold. She stared at the ceiling. "Are you still awake?"

"It's a bit hard to sleep with you turning all the time. What's the problem?"

"I'm still cold. Are you certain about the clothes thing?"

"Yes I am."

Allison rolled and leant her head over the edge of the bunk. "You said there was another option. I'm willing to try anything at this moment. My feet and the rest of me are freezing."

Michela opened her eyes and looked up at the face peering down at her. "These bags are interlocking. We can join them together and rely on body warmth." She stifled a laugh as Allison's face rapidly disappeared back over the edge of the bunk.

Allison face reddened as she thought about Michela's suggestion. *What happened when you were that close to her before?* In the tent she'd been so close to Michela the day of Michael's illness. She was certain Michela had meant to do something before she was fully awake and had been told of Michael's heart attack. After that they slept as far away from each other as possible.

This is ridiculous. I can sit up here and freeze or...

"Alli," Michela's voice was muffled by the barrier of the bed, "I know this isn't the optimum solution, but if you're cold, it's one way of combating it. The human body gives off its share of body heat. Between the two of us we should generate enough to keep warm." Michela cringed at the way her words sounded. "Listen, if this has anything to do with my sexuality, I promise you I'd never take advantage of such a situation."

Allison, aware her face was flushed, looked over the side of the bed. "I'm sorry, it's not that at all. I trust you. It's just I wasn't expecting such a means to keep warm."

Michela smiled. "I understand. I think it'd probably be better if you came down here. The two of us on a narrow bunk could be painful if one of us rolls the wrong way and we both end up falling from the height of your bed."

Allison climbed down the ladder, sleeping bag in tow. "So, how do we do this?"

Michela wriggled out of her bag and unzipped the length of the zipper. "Simple, as long as these are male and female bags."

Allison looked at Michela in disbelief. "Now I know you're having me on. There's no such thing as male and female bags."

Michela shook her head. "Sure there is. Firstly, what side of the bag is your zipper on?"

Allison held the bag up. "On the right, why?"

"Mine's on the left and that's a start. They should be able to join together. Now zip the zipper all the way down as far as you can go. Before you get to the box foot element of the bag, there should be a box and pin mechanism, like any old raincoat."

"I see what you mean." Allison disconnected the zipper from the other side of the bag. "So what now?"

"Is your zipper on the top part or bottom part of your

zip, and what side is it on?"

"It's on the bottom, on the right."

Michela took the bag from her. "We have a winner. Mine's top left. This'll allow me to join my zipper to your zip and then your zipper to my zip. Just watch."

Michela quickly zipped the two together. She then laid them on the small bed and unzipped the top of the bag. "Which side would you prefer?" She tried to sound as nonchalant as possible.

Allison mentally cursed at her sudden blush. "You can have the wall if you like," she replied, her voice higher than usual. "That way if I have to get out during the night, I won't disturb your sleep."

Michela nodded. *More like you don't have to worry about me trapping you in and having my wicked way with you. Stop that! What if the situation was reversed and Allison was a man?* Michela winced.

"Is that okay?" Allison asked.

Michela crawled into the bag and faced the wall. "Yes. One of my aches twinged, that's all."

Allison climbed in and put her back to Michela's, immediately grateful for the warmth created. "You're right, this is warmer. Good night, Michela."

"Night, Alli," Michela replied, and within minutes sleep claimed them both.

MICHELA AWOKE AND was grateful for the warm body spooned in front of her. Despite the warmth of the lamps, the hut was cold. Listening, she could still hear the howling of the storm as it buffeted the hut. *It looks as if we're going nowhere, at least not today.* As she made herself comfortable, she felt Allison stir.

Allison awoke, suddenly conscious of the body that spooned her own. The soft breasts that pressed into her back were proof enough that sometime during the night she'd gravitated toward Michela for warmth. As she considered a means to discretely remove herself, she became aware of the uncontrollable warmth filling the pit of her stomach before it made its way southward. *Oh my God. This isn't happening! It's just a natural reaction to how close we are.* Shocked at the sensations Michela's body was causing, Allison scooted away.

"Are you all right?" Michela asked in a sleepy voice.

"Of course I'm all right," Allison replied, knowing she sounded defensive.

"Then what's wrong?"

Allison clung to the edge of the bunk so she wouldn't sink back. "Nothing. Don't think this is going to be a permanent arrangement."

"Nothing could be further from my mind. I like warmth in my women," Michela tersely replied, regretting the words as soon as she said them.

Allison propelled herself out of the warmth of the bag and picked up her clothes.

You insensitive idiot! Didn't Rick call her the ice queen? Why does she make me so angry? She watched as Allison attempted to pull on a frozen shirt. Michela sat up. "I'm sorry. That was uncalled for."

Allison turned her back to Michela. "I doubt it. It seems to be the common consensus around here. First Rick and now you." She struggled with her shirt, her frozen fingers fighting a losing battle.

Michela disentangled herself from the bag and padded to her. She gently touched Allison's shoulder.

"I really didn't mean to say that," Michela said. "It's just I'm not much of a morning person and sometimes my mouth engages well before my brain does."

Michela looked around at the thin layer of ice forming on the walls. "Grab the clothes and come back to bed. It's far too cold and too early to get up yet. Besides we're not going anywhere in a hurry. We can put our clothes in the compartments below the mattress and if we both get back into the bag, this should generate some heat in their direction. They'll be easier to put on when they're warmer." Michela held out her hand to Allison. "Please."

Allison looked at Michela's hand, suddenly struck by the intimacy of her gesture. Searching Michela's face, all she saw was contrition and little more than a need to get back into something that was warm, rather than the cold floor they were standing on. She nodded and grabbed her clothes as Michela picked up her own. After stowing them in the compartment below, they wordlessly returned to the bag and the position they'd woken up in.

MICHELA SUCKED IN her breath as Allison dressed her wound.

"The wound's not too bad, but there are bruises all over your back," Allison said. "What happened down there?"

Michela looked at Allison, realising she'd only be able to delay the conversation, not put if off altogether. "I fell."

"What do you mean you fell?"

"My hand slipped off the rope and I fell a ways before I managed to perform an emergency lockout," she replied, trying to sound casual.

"Hang on a minute. You're telling me you lost your grip on the rope?" Michela nodded. "You could have been killed."

Michela pulled the third layer of clothing over her head before returning her gaze to a worried Allison. "I wasn't and that's the main thing."

Allison returned the medicine kit to the table and sat on the bed. She faced Michela. "What happened down there yesterday? How do you know that Ewan's not alive?" she softly asked.

Michela gazed at Allison and, feeling her eyes water, turned away. She knew, as a psychologist, there was a need to discuss traumatic incidents. To carry them inside could be emotionally and physically destructive. She rubbed her hands together, bent forward, and put her elbows on her knees, as if to protect herself from the reality of what she was about to say.

"There was wreckage on the ledge and when I got to it, one of our EPIRB's was still attached to its side." She looked at Allison. "It had the same piece of tape on it that I'd placed there while we were at Wills Station; it was my writing. I couldn't see anything else and so I started to rappel again when I was distracted. I don't know how far I fell, but I managed to lock out and then I swung back and forth, bouncing off the wall and spinning as I went. The light reflected off the wall and that's when I realised Ewan was dead. The chasm was covered in blood, almost as if someone had hit it and continued falling. I spooled the glow light out to its full length and there was still no end. I couldn't see the bottom of the crevasse. It went on forever, with Ewan somewhere at the bottom of it." Michela's voice broke as she covered her face with her hands.

Allison embraced Michela and slowly rocked her. They sat, the sound of the storm outside enveloping them, until Michela gently broke free from Allison's embrace.

Allison brushed an errant hair away from Michela's face. "So, that's what you meant when you said you couldn't afford to lose me as well. I'm sorry I was so stubborn yesterday, I should've known better."

Michela smiled. "It's okay, I know I can be pretty difficult at times." They shared an awkward laugh. "Can I ask you a question?"

Allison nodded.

Michela searched Allison's face. "What did you mean when you said you almost lost me?"

Allison, not really knowing what she meant, turned away in pretence of getting more clothes for Michela. She handed Michela her vest.

"What would we have done if we'd lost our team leader? We certainly couldn't do without you, that's for sure," Allison replied, a heavy emphasis on the word "we." She rose and went to the stove. "I don't know about you, but I'm starving."

After breakfast Allison stood and took their plates to the sink. "I suppose with Ewan gone that means we'll be ending the dig early."

Michela shook her head. "I don't see it that way at all and I'm sure Ewan wouldn't have wanted that. Understandably there'll be reports to be written and people who'll be called into account, but I think we should continue the dig."

Allison placed a dried coffee cup on a wall rack. "When you say people will be called into account, you mean Rick, don't you?"

Michela nodded. "Yes, except I don't think he can be held to blame. Ewan made his own decision, no matter how much he was coerced into it. But I do intend to see if I can remove Rick from the expedition site. He's a disruptive influence and I really can't guarantee his safety once Rob finds out about his friend's death. I know that'll affect your dig, but I really can't have it any other way."

Allison rubbed Michela's forearm in reassurance. "I understand what you mean. Maybe it's the best thing for all of us."

Both took the time to record their memory of the failed rescue attempt, in case they were required to produce evidence. In their search for paper Allison also found a deck of cards and they almost wore the deck out exhausting all the games they knew.

When the day came to an end, Allison prepared tea, and they retired once again to the warmth of their two-person sleeping bag.

MICHELA COULD NEVER be certain whether it was the storm that had awoken her in the small hours of the morning or some other innate sense. Despite the reason, she was comfortably spooned against Allison, the warmth of Allison's body coursing through her. As she again settled into sleep, she snuggled closer, barely aware that her hand caressed the underside of Allison's breast. *Her breast?* As if hit with cold water, Michela was completely awake, her body wired in response to the intimacy of her touch. Her breathing picked up at the undeniable warmth between her legs. Paralysed at Allison's reaction should she be caught in such a position, Michela fought her own battle between logic and libido.

She's straight, you know that. Now behave yourself and find a way to get out of this, or at least a way to remove your hand. She gulped, warring with a desire to leave her hand exactly where it was. Despite the sound of the wind pounding against the building, she was painfully aware of the beating of her heart as it roared in her ears. She felt Allison tremble and then shift.

"Are you okay?" Michela worked to tamp down the almost uncontrollable urges of her own body.

Allison was agonisingly aware of Michela's hand and missed Michela's words. She twisted her upper body and head, and found herself dangerously close to Michela's lips. Michela's rapid breath caressed her face. "It's okay, I'm a little cold, that's all," she said in a breathless voice.

For what seemed like an eternity but was, in reality, no more than a few seconds, Michela fought to focus on the unsexiest images she could conjure. With concerted effort, she finally managed to get her oversexed imagination under control.

Allison turned away, and Michela pulled her to her, using the action to remove her hand. "Sorry, I didn't realise."

Allison nodded and snuggled her backside into the Michela's groin. Michela sucked in her breath. *This is going to be a long night.*

ALLISON POURED A packet of food into a pan of boiling water, the latest of several chores she had done that morning to avoid being near Michela. In turn, Michela seemed to be deliberately preoccupied with small chores of her own. She turned and found Michela leaning against the table and looking at her.

"Allison, about last night."

Allison turned back to the stove. *Please don't go there. I don't think I could right now.* "I don't know what you mean."

Allison glanced back as Michela walked toward her and stopped a few feet away.

"I think you do, I think we both do," Michela replied quietly. "I think we need to talk about it."

"I don't think I can," Allison whispered, focusing on the food in the pot of water.

"We both know something happened last night, something neither of us planned. Despite this, it did happen and it can't be taken back. I just want to reinforce what I said before. I'd never seek to do something that would drive a wedge between our friendship. Despite our disagreements, I do regard you as a friend. I'd hate to think that's changed."

Allison turned, sensing only sincerity in Michela's words. "No, it hasn't. I wouldn't want that either." She stepped to within arm's length of Michela. "Michela..." Their radio burst to life.

"Michela, Allison, this is Sarah, do you read, over?"

Breaking free of Allison's hypnotic gaze, Michela picked up the radio. "This is Michela. It's good to be back in communications range."

"For a small storm, it packed a punch."

"It certainly did. So it's finished where you are?"

"Yes, the winds have died down to their normal state. I'm guessing that it should end your way very shortly. Do you remember the directions I gave you when you were on the glacier?"

"Roger. We'll follow those once the storm breaks. We'll let you know before we leave the hut. Is everything okay at the site?"

"Yes, no damage here at all, with the exception of snow filling the trenches around the hut. That should be able to be removed in no time."

"We better let you get to it then. Can you radio the station and let them know we've used fuel, water, and food in the hut? Oh, and can you ask them about the feasibility of removing Rick from the team site."

"Roger, will do. We hope to see you soon."

"Same here. This is Michela, out."

WITHIN THE HOUR the storm had abated and, after a rudimentary check of the snow mobile, they were on their way. Their journey across the top part of the glacier was as uneventful as Sarah had predicted—the ice a lot more stable than what they'd traversed three days before. They made good time and were back at Finlayson Base within three hours.

Sarah, wearing a smile of relief, walked toward them. "The things you see when you don't have a gun. It certainly is great to see you two."

Michela gave Sarah a quick hug and retrieved her pack from Allison. "It's great to see you, too. I'd like to call a team meeting but first I think Alli and I need a fresh change of clothes."

Sarah squeezed Alli's shoulder and walked between the two to their hut. "I managed to speak with the guy who's second in command at Wills Station. It seems Maddi's out at one of the remote sites. Anyway, he says they can't fly in and pick up Rick because one of their long range helos is down."

Michela nodded. "Unless there's two, they don't fly, right?"

"Yep. Aside from that, he said he was pretty reluctant to have Rick at the station as there's really nowhere he could be contained. He suggested it'd be better if we keep him out here."

Michela shook her head. "That's the last thing I want to do. Did you tell the others about Ewan? How did Rob react?"

Sarah shrugged. "Rob was pretty calm all things considered. Rick seemed to take the news the worst."

"Serves the bastard right," Allison said. "If he hadn't goaded Ewan in the first place, then none of this would have happened." She opened the door of the apple and walked inside.

Michela turned to Sarah. "She's a bit angry about the whole thing. Could you get the rest of the team together? We should be no more than about ten minutes."

"Sure. Are you okay?"

"I will be after a good night's sleep and a large scotch." Michela watched Sarah cross the snow before going inside.

They silently changed. Allison shrugged into her jacket and went to the door.

"Alli?" Allison turned around. "I thought I'd let you know that there are enough beds now, if you wanted to go and stay in the hut with Rob and Sarah."

Allison searched Michela's face. "Do you want me to?" she asked quietly.

"No, no I don't," Michela answered softly. Allison nodded and closed the door behind her.

The remaining three team members were in the mess when Michela arrived, and after a cup of coffee and the abbreviated version of events, she got down to business. "We're all adults here, so I'm going to get straight to the point. What happened the other day shouldn't have and I'm as much to blame as anyone else." She held her temper as a smug look crossed Rick's features. "It's for that reason, I'm going to implement the following rule. No one, I mean no one, leaves the confines of this camp without discussing it with me first."

Allison jumped out of her chair. "You've got to be joking. Just because idiot features over there stuffs it up, doesn't mean everyone should pay."

"I'm sorry, Alli, but it does. I don't intend to lose anyone else and if that means I have to hide the batteries for the ski-demons and the sno-trak, then that's what I'll do." Allison stomped out the door before Michela barely finished her sentence. "This is a non-negotiable issue people." She stood and hurried after Allison.

She entered their hut and slammed the door. "What is it with you? Why the hell must you walk out of every damn meeting I hold?"

Allison wheeled. "Why must you treat us all like children? It's Rick that's at fault here. Why do we all have to suffer?"

Michela battled to control the level of her voice, remembering the last time they argued in a confined space at Wills Station. "Because I'm the team leader and I say that's the way it's going to be." Allison took a step toward the door.

Michela grabbed Allison's hand and pulled her to her with more force than she'd intended. Allison's hands pressed against Michela's chest.

"Why is it that you're always walking out on me?" Michela asked, her breathing ragged, her body painfully aware of Allison's closeness.

Allison could feel Michela's breasts through the layers of clothing. "Why do you have to always treat me like a child?" Passion blazed in her eyes.

Michela brushed an errant hair away from Allison's cheek and ran her fingers through the back of Allison's hair. "And why do you have to be so damned frustrating," she whispered as she lowered her lips to Allison's waiting mouth.

They broke away at a knock at the door.

"What?" Michela called in frustration.

"Maddi's returned to Wills Station and she's on the radio. She wants a debrief from you. Do you want to speak with her now?" Sarah asked through the closed door.

Allison stepped away from Michela, putting distance between them. "Best you go. After all, you wouldn't want to keep Maddi waiting."

Michela blinked, torn between reporting in and finishing what they'd started. She stepped toward Allison, who turned her back. "I'm on my way," she replied and left the hut.

Chapter
Nine

My Darling Charlotte,

We are woefully behind time. At least two weeks ago we were ready for me to lead another, more organized expedition onto the Antarctic plateau. To our dismay the weather closed in, making any movement beyond the confines of the immediate base almost impossible.

Walking in this weather is to risk life itself, with my men bent over, headfirst into the wind as they endeavor to feed the dogs who so stoically brave the horrendous cold. Just the other morning it was my turn to feed these animals and I felt my leg collapse from underneath me. The doctor says it is a serious tear of the muscles surrounding the ankle and that I must keep my weight off it. Sometimes I feel so helpless out here.

Yesterday the weather finally broke, allowing us to get our second expedition under way. They will spend the next twenty days pushing up onto the plateau, forging a path for our next journey to Antarctica. Alas, with my ankle in such a state, I will not lead them—that I leave up to my second in command. They will take the rest of the dogs and enough rations to see them through their journey. Two others and myself will remain behind, keeping an eye on our base and eagerly awaiting their return. I cannot wait to hear of their adventure!

All my love,

ERF

Antarctica—2010

SARAH OPENED THE door to the mess hut and was surprised to find Michela there. "Now I really do think that people are going to begin to talk about us. What are you doing up at four-thirty in the morning?"

Michela looked at the notes spread out on the table. "Catching up on some work. With everything that's happened lately, I've had very little time to consolidate my research."

Sarah nodded. "I know what you mean. What a week. Getting everyone to sit down and record their version of events in relation to Ewan's death was like pulling teeth. I swear at one stage there I thought I was going to have to physically restrain Rick to a seat so that he gave his side of the story."

Michela slammed her pen down. "That's what frustrates me. We all know that Rick planted the seed of an idea with Ewan. The problem is the coroner's only going to see it as death by misadventure. It frustrates me to hell to think he's going to get off."

Sarah placed the kettle on the gas burner. "I know what you mean. I'm about to make tea. Want one?"

"Hang on. What the blazes are you doing up at this hour?"

Sarah flopped down in a chair opposite Michela and motioned toward the door. "Rob had one too many scotches tonight and he's snoring like a bloody baby elephant. I've gotten up out of bed and prodded him more than once, but he keeps right on going." They shared a quiet laugh. "So, why are you really up this late?"

Michela's features sobered and she idly searched her papers. "As I said, catching up on research. I hate to think what my boss would say if I returned with nothing to show for my efforts but a really great story or two."

Sarah stood and walked to the kettle. "Yes, I don't think anyone would be happy with that. You seem to have gotten through a bit, if that pile's any indication."

Sarah poured tea for them both and handed a cup to Michela before taking her seat at the table. *There's something not right here. She hasn't been the same since the loss of Ewan and, by the looks of it, things aren't getting any easier.*

"Can I ask you something?"

Michela raised her head and looked at Sarah. "Sure, is everything okay?"

Sarah smiled. "I could ask you the same thing. You haven't really been all here since the accident with Ewan."

"What do you mean?"

"Look at you. From the bags under your eyes, it's obvious you've been burning the candle at both ends and have probably had more than one late night over the past few days." She watched as Michela nervously shifted. "Plus you've been like a bear with a sore head. Listen, I know Ewan's death hit the team hard, but you seem to have been affected quite badly. Are you sure you don't want to talk about it?"

Michela looked away as if searching for something. Running her fingers through her hair she returned her gaze to Sarah. "It's not Ewan."

Sarah sat back, a frown on her face. *If it isn't about Ewan then who is it about? Ah, of course, how stupid can you be, Sarah?* "This is about Alli, isn't it?"

Michela vigorously rubbed her forehead. "Yes, it is."

"I suppose that would've been my next question. I don't mean to pry, but is something going on between the two of you? Has something happened?"

Michela shrugged. "You could say there is and you could as easily say there isn't. In the same vein, you could say something's happened but you could as easily say it hasn't."

Sarah lightly grasped Michela's hand. "There's one thing I do know. It's affecting you and the way you are with others. What happened?"

"It started in the emergency hut when we were so cold I suggested we join the sleeping bags together. Sometime during the first night we ended up against each other and Alli woke up and freaked. I opened my big mouth and she shot out of the bag. It took some convincing by me, but she eventually came back to bed. The next night we were in a similar position, but worse. I swear I almost kissed her, but I stopped myself. All the same, she seemed to react differently, I can't explain how. We were both aware something had happened and so I tried to talk to her about it the following morning. Before we could get into the conversation you called on the radio."

Sarah smiled. "Sorry about that, mate. Did you try and speak with her when you returned?"

"Not about that exactly. You remember when the Dianne and Rick thing happened and we made the change to accommodations arrangements?" Sarah nodded. "When we returned from looking for Ewan, and given the extra space in the googie, I gave her the chance to move in with you and Rob. She asked me if I wanted her to leave and I said no. I can't describe it, but something passed between us. It was as if she really didn't want to leave me.

"Then we had that team meeting that she walked out of. I came back into our hut, pretty angry that she'd stormed out and told her as much. She tried to storm out again but I grabbed her hand. We ended up in a clinch and I swear to God that had it not been for you knocking on the door I'd have kissed her. And by the look in her eyes I think she would have kissed me back."

"Bad timing again. So have you spoken to her about that?" Sarah ventured.

Michela shook her head. "I've tried to bring it up, but she seems to want to avoid it, as if nothing's happened between us. I don't want to go down a path that's a dead end. It's too painful. And besides, by the looks of it, she's woken up to what happened and is now more interested in avoiding me than anything else."

So, the strange way Allison's been behaving recently is now falling into place. "Are you sure about that?"

Michela picked up her tea. "I'm not sure what you mean."

"I've been watching our errant archaeologist over the past few days, concerned she may be suffering a little bit of post traumatic stress disorder. When you're not watching, Alli follows your every move. But, the moment you turn her way, she looks elsewhere. There's a need in her face, as if she wants to speak with you, but is afraid of how to raise the topic. I just assumed she wanted your professional advice on something. Maybe Alli wants something more." She went to the sink and rinsed out her cup.

Michela frowned in thought. "Do you think anyone else has noticed?"

Sarah chuckled. "Everyone's noticed that something's

not right with you. They're so used to you being a calm ship in any storm, that when you turned on Rob the other day because he left a dirty dish in the sink I think they were all surprised. As for noticing how Alli's acting, I don't think Rick, Di, or Rob has picked up on the difference. Di and Rick are still too focussed on each other and while Rob's not slow, he's no sensitive new age guy either."

Michela vigorously rubbed her face with both hands. "I don't know what to do here, Sarah. I know I like her. A lot more than I care to admit. But if she's avoiding the issue, then I'm not about to pursue it."

"If that's the way you want to deal with it then that's your choice. But remember, if you want to talk things over or have a rant, then come and see me. I promise what we speak about won't go any further." Sarah patted Michela's hand. "Now, in the meantime you need to get a lot more rest and stop acting like a grumble bum."

Michela rose and mock saluted Sarah. "Yes, ma'am." She stifled a yawn. "I'd better return to my hut and get at least a little sleep before we start the day all over again." She collected her notes and waved a goodbye before heading to her own apple and hopefully some degree of slumber.

After quietly entering the hut, she instinctively turned to Allison. The night light cast a warm glow over Allison's features, making her look at peace. Michela smiled at the rogue strand of hair that always found its way onto Allison's face. She headed toward Allison to brush the hair away, then stopped herself and ruefully shook her head. *I really do need to get a little sleep.* She walked to her bed and stripped down to her underwear. After removing her bra, she climbed into her sleeping bag, oblivious to the eyes that watched her from the other side of the hut.

"I CAN'T BELIEVE we're digging out these trenches yet again," Dianne said in a grumpy voice. "Why can't we leave them that way?"

Rob smiled at Dianne's frustration. "I don't make the rules here, I just follow them. Alli says it'd be a good idea to maintain this trench as a possible indicator of any changes to the exterior of the hut."

Rick walked through the knee deep snow. "I thought this place was supposed to be drier than most deserts on the earth. If that's the case, how can it snow down here?"

"It's dry and very little snow falls in a year," Rob said. "But once it falls it doesn't evaporate like normal snow would. The blizzards on the continent blow the snow around until it comes across a solid object or some sort of natural barrier and it piles up. Explorers have been encountering this problem for years. I'm sure Finlayson and his mob had similar problems with snow drifts."

Rick snorted. "I guess we'll never know. At the rate we're going and all the delays, we're not likely to know what happened to him."

Rob stepped into Rick's personal space. "If I were you, I'd get on with what I've been told to do. Or have you forgotten that one of those delays was due to the loss of one of our team members? Something you're more than accountable for?"

Rick stumbled away from Rob. "He made up his own mind. I didn't make it up for him."

"Bullshit!" Rob roared, rushing forward as if to strike Rick. Something cold impacted on the top of his head and he looked up.

"There you are, you big oaf. Something's gone pear shaped with the generator. Do you think you can have a look at it?" Sarah asked.

Rob glared at Rick before silently walking around Dianne, and out of the trench. He followed Sarah away from the trench. "I swear, if he gives me one more reason, I'll flatten him. Then you won't have to worry about drugging him."

Sarah hugged Rob's waist, since he was too tall to reach his shoulders. "Trust me, he's not worth it. I know Ewan's death has hit you hard. You know if you want to get if off your chest, you can always talk to me."

Rob removed Sarah's cap and playfully ruffled her blonde hair. "I know, sprite. It's just that sometimes I wish Rick would give me a reason. I hear you though. Maybe we can sit down tonight after a few drinks."

Sarah nodded. "No problem. For the moment, can you go and check the solar panels? Michela's doing Ewan's shift for tea and she says she can't see to cook in the hut at the moment."

"I'm right on it." Rob turned and headed in the direction of the solar generator.

Sarah sighed. *Thank heaven's I wasn't a little later on the scene. The last thing I can afford to be doing is patching up Rick after Rob's finished with him.*

AFTER WHAT SEEMED like an eternity of shovelling snow, and a checking of the walls by Allison, the team was again ready to focus its efforts on the hut's interior.

Allison scanned the room with childlike wonder. Makeshift shelves lined the wooden walls. "Look at this. This must have been one of the member's personal space." She lightly ran her hand over the eclectic collection of books on the shelves. "It's like a time capsule from the 1890's."

Dianne opened one of the novels. "*Moby Dick.* My God, it's a first edition."

Allison picked up the pile of loose sheets that were acting as a bookend. She chuckled. "Music hall tunes. At least that was one way to while away the time. And they're amazingly intact." One half of the next shelf contained a man's shaving mug and razor, with a half-used stick of lather stuck in an almost jaunty angle in a willow pattern shaving cup.

Allison squinted at the slightly faded writing on a bottle in a collection of small bottles. "Mason's remedy for indigestion. This must have been their medical stores." She pointed. "And look at those spirit bottles. I suppose that's one way to keep warm."

Next to a small table stood the remnants of a well-used rattan chair. A man's pipe lay on the seat where it had been left. The eerie windswept silence of the sight affected Allison as she walked with care around the building's interior. By the look on their faces, she could tell that the others felt the same.

Rick and Dianne quietly took photographs of everything, while Allison and Rob continued to carefully use the blades to widen the path into the hut.

Rob broke up yet another sheet of ice in front of him

and jumped back in surprise. "Shit!"

Allison turned to see that Rob had uncovered the first of the beds.

Dianne pointed at the long object. "What's that?"

Allison stroked the rough fabric and felt the distinct shape of something hard inside. She stood, wiping her hands on her trousers. "Rob, can you go and get Sarah and Michela?"

Rob disappeared and returned minutes later with the Sarah and Michela in tow.

"Wow," Sarah exclaimed. "You're really getting down to the bits and pieces now. This is like the museum exhibit I saw years ago in Auckland. Someone had gone to the trouble of recreating Scott's accommodations. I thought that was good, but this is like going back in time."

Allison motioned Michela and Sarah to her. "I suspect somewhat too real for my liking."

Sarah sobered and looked at the lump on the bed. She touched the fabric and ran her hands along its contours. "It looks like someone's used a sleeping bag as a funeral shroud."

Rick peered over Michela's shoulder. "What, you mean there's a body in there? That's disgusting."

Sarah shook her head. "No, not disgusting. In fact I'd say it's entirely practical. If someone died it'd be just as easy to sew them into their bag and allow the climate to do the rest."

Dianne put as much space between her and the body as was possible. "Why would someone die in here? And why wouldn't they be buried outside?"

"There could be a number of reasons. There could have been a blizzard that prevented his burial or the person or people who did the sewing may not have been capable of moving the body outside. I won't be sure without further investigation." Sarah studied the stitching at the top of the bag.

"That's what I wanted to speak to you two about," Allison said. "I'm interested to find out what's within, but I didn't know where I stood, it being a possible body and all. Michela, as team leader, what's your call on this?"

Michela looked as if she was taken off guard. "I'm not quite certain, but as long as we're respectful with how we check the body, then this shouldn't be a problem." She tapped Sarah's shoulder. "What do you think?"

Sarah stood. "I think you're right. Of course, it does help that before I studied to become a doctor I trained for a while in forensic anthropology."

Rob scratched his head. "Bugger me, woman, is there anything you didn't do?"

Sarah casually shrugged. "When you're a child prodigy you've got to do something to occupy your time. After I finished my first degree, this seemed like a good way to fill in time before I worked out what I wanted to do next. I studied it for a while but found the whole thing too morbid. But it did prepare me for my medical degree."

Dianne shuddered. "That's awful. Playing with dead bodies."

Sarah turned to Dianne. "I found it pretty interesting. And, in this case, helpful. Allison, I can review the body for you without creating too much of a mess, and at the same time try and determine a cause of death. I've already got an idea regarding the cause of death, but that's all it is at this stage." Her gaze trailed the length of the body and she pointed to a box under the feet. "What's that?"

Allison gently removed the box from its resting-place. "It's a suitcase, as if someone left it there in the hope it would some day be found. It's heavy too. Let me see if I can open it."

She gently put the suitcase on a wooden table and tried the clasps but they refused to budge. She gave the clasps a determined jiggle and it finally opened. "Oh my."

Rob peered over her shoulder. "What are they?"

"They're glass photographic plates. I'd say this belongs to the expedition's photographer, Ian Ross, and I assume that's his body on the bed. This is physical proof the expedition did indeed spend time on the continent. Here's our pictorial history." Allison reverently sorted through the plates. At the bottom of the case her fingers closed around a book, and she pulled it out and opened it. Reading the front page, she nodded. "It's the diary of Ian Ross."

Rick seized the diary from her hands. "This is fantastic. If we find nothing else this will make the museum a tidy sum and more than cement my, er, our position in the museum."

Allison smugly smiled at Rick's egocentricity. "Yes, it'll be interesting to see what kind of information it contains. It'll need to be photographed before we leave the site, in case something happens to it."

Rick put the document to his chest. "Di and I can do that. You can occupy yourself with the body."

Before Allison could object Rick and Dianne strode out of the hut.

"No worries, mate," Rob muttered. "So what do we do now?"

"Alli, do you want me to do a preliminary inspection of the body?" Sarah asked.

Allison drew her brows together and tilted her head. "What, you mean an autopsy?"

"Not exactly. That'd involve inspection and dissection and I'm not really prepared for that. All I'd like to do is inspect the body. I think this will confirm my preliminary assessment regarding death. Is that okay with you?"

Allison thought about it and then nodded. "But where would you do it?"

The room was silent as everyone thought.

"What about the storage container for the sno-trak," Allison suggested. "You know, the container we brought a lot of our gear in. We could rig up some lighting and put up a makeshift table. It would be tight, but it should suit your purpose."

Sarah nodded. "Yes, it should do. Michela, do you mind helping me with this? I'd ask Rob, but he's been known to faint at the sight of blood." She dodged a mock blow from Rob. "And the way Alli's looking at those photographs, I think I know what she'd rather be doing, am I right?"

Allison looked up. "What? Oh, yes. The diary would've been more interesting, but these should prove quite a challenge to wade through. But the next diary that's found is definitely mine. Do you two mind working on the body?"

Michela shook her head.

"We'll have to get the container ready and then, Rob, we'll probably need your help to move the body," Sarah said. "Where do you two intend to study the photos?"

Allison carefully closed the suitcase and handed it to Rob. "We'll be in the mess hut. That way we should be able to spread these out so they can be photographed."

MICHELA AND SARAH shifted the majority of the boxes from inside the sno-trak container to make a temporary morgue. Rigging a string of temporary lighting from the xenon glow sticks, Michela made the container look more like a Christmas decoration than a repository for stores. After setting up a makeshift table in the middle of the space, with Rob's help, they brought the body to the container.

Sarah removed her outer layer of clothing. "Have you ever done anything like this before?"

Michela shook her head. "I can't say I have, although I'm a fast learner."

"Promises, promises." Sarah smiled before holding up her hands. "Only joking. Could you take notes while I dictate? They don't need to be detailed, but should anyone question what we've done, then we'll have a record. Plus, Alli can use it for her research."

Sarah cut the twine that encased the body within the sleeping bag, while providing a running commentary on her actions. She pulled back the flap and smoothed her hand across the fur that comprised the inside of the bag. "Hmm, this looks to be like some sort of animal fur. If it's like the bags made by later explorers, it's probably caribou or something like that."

Michela jotted down her notes. "What makes you say that?"

"Caribou fur's remarkably warm. The hairs are hollow and trap the heat, making for a pretty toasty sleep. Not warm by our standards, but comfortable all the same." Sarah unravelled the rest of the thick twine, revealing the body.

"He looks as if he's just asleep." Sarah lightly ran her hand over his clothing. "And look at these old clothes, they're almost new. In fact, given the amount of time he's been down here, he's remarkably well preserved, but I believe the bag helped to ensure there was no real deterioration of the skin.

"He's a white male. By the greying whiskers on his cheeks and his face, I'd say he's in his late thirties, possibly early forties. However he died it was peaceful, as there are no signs of struggle or rigour in the face to indicate otherwise. Could you give me a hand to get this bag off him?" Michela stood on the opposite side of the table to Sarah, and they peeled the stiff bag from the frozen body.

"Right. I want to check his body." Sarah carefully cut through the man's jumper, and then undid the buttons of his vest and shirt. After spreading them open, she cut through his undergarment to reveal the torso of Ian Ross. "I don't think we need to go any further."

Michela looked down at the body. "What do you mean?"

"See how his stomach's concave?" Michela nodded. "Now look at his ribs. You can count every single one of them. His pelvis is the same as is his collarbone. This man didn't die of natural causes, but he did die of starvation. Hang on, look at the displacement of his left foot."

Sarah felt the length of the Ian Ross' leg. She cut his left trouser leg, revealing a rudimentary splint. "Poor bugger, he broke his leg at some stage. That must have hurt like Hades."

Michela nodded. "Probably the reason why someone as important as a photographer was still in the hut rather than part of any inland expedition."

"You're right," Sarah said. "Without a full dissection, I don't think we're going to get much more out of Mr. Ross. I suggest we re-dress him and re-sew the bag. Once we've done this we'll put him back where we found him. At least there we can preserve his remains."

THE TABLE OF the kitchen hut was strewn with the mess made by Allison and Rob.

"Look at this one," Rob exclaimed. He held a glass plate to the light. The image was of a group of people standing on a wharf, as if in the process of bidding someone or something farewell. "Can you read the name on the banner there?"

Allison held up her magnifying glass and strained her eyes to read the infinitesimal writing. "It says

Christchurch. This must have been taken during their last stop." She slapped Rob's back. "Bless the industriousness of Ian Ross, he's left us with visual proof of what sort of expedition Finlayson led. And bless the person who had the presence of mind to lay him to rest in proximity of his photographic plates. Let's see if we can divide these into some logical sequence."

A half hour later Sarah wandered into the hut. "Bloody hell. He certainly was a shutterbug."

Rob and Allison looked up. "Yep, he sure was." Rob pulled his chair in to allow Sarah access to the sink. "Did you and Michela find out anything?"

"In a way, yes. I think we can assume by what was found at the foot of the bed, if not the diary in the suitcase that the body we're dealing with is that of the expedition's photographer, Ian Ross. He must have suffered a fall at some stage during the expedition as someone's done a pretty good job of splinting his leg."

"Did he die from the fall?" Allison asked.

"Nothing that dramatic. By the state he's in I'd say he died of starvation. His body was pretty thin. I've put him back in his sleeping bag and Michela and I returned him to his bed in the hut. That should keep him well preserved until you work out what you want to do with him." Sarah took a mug from the drying rack.

"Still that's a pretty terrible way to go, getting progressively weaker and weaker," Rob said, a concerned look on his face.

"You're right, but in the end he most likely went to sleep and didn't wake up. It could have been a lot worse." Sarah's words hung in the air. Allison knew that Ewan was still on everyone's mind.

Dianne and Rick, carrying the diary, entered the hut.

"He starved to death," Rick said.

Allison looked up, a non-plussed expression on her face. "We know that already. Sarah told us."

Rick scowled at Sarah. "But does she know there were two expeditions, the first one leaving within days of arrival and in direct contravention to Finlayson's orders. They never returned. Only a handful of dogs made it back. The second expedition left and Finlayson couldn't go with it—he'd badly sprained his ankle."

Allison eagerly sat forward. "Does he say what happened to him? Did he go after the others?"

Dianne shrugged. "We don't know. We only got so far into the diary and then, well," she looked sideways at Rick, "we got sidetracked."

Ugh, too much information and by the look on Rick's face, he's glad she said it as well. The sooner I see the back end of you, mister, the better. Allison maintained a calm outward stance. "I'd be grateful if you could keep working on it. Are you photographing as you go along?"

"Of course we are. What do you take us for? Amateurs?" Rick asked. "When's dinner, I'm starving." He jumped at the voice behind him.

"It'll be cooked as soon as I can get some space in here." Michela walked around him and stared at the photographic plates spread across every flat surface in the hut. "Alli, Rob, I'm sorry but if we're to eat I really do need a little space. The last thing I'd want to do is spill something on those plates."

Rob smiled. "No worries. If you like, Alli, I'll take these back to my hut and see if I can group them as we were discussing. When you're ready you can come and take a look."

Allison smiled, grateful to have her attention diverted from Michela's close proximity to her. "Not a problem. Let me know when you're ready."

The group dispersed, allowing Michela the space she needed to prepare dinner. She hummed silently and started at the movement behind her.

Sarah snagged a biscuit from Michela's preparation bench. "So, did you see that?"

Michela lightly hit her with a mixing spoon. "What do you mean?"

Sarah munched loudly on her ill-gotten gains. "With Alli just then. She changed when you arrived, almost as if she wasn't all that comfortable being near you."

Michela slapped the spoon down on the bench. "And that's supposed to prove what? That she likes me? If anything I think that proves she's not at all at ease in my presence and that's damn great."

"For a psychologist you really don't have a clue, do you? Didn't you ever read that verse, and I'm paraphrasing here: *I search for your face in a crowd and then turn away, afraid of the love others might see.*"

Exasperated, Michela shook her head. "My friend, I think you've been on one too many trips to Antarctica. It's time you found yourself a woman to waste your romantic ideals on."

Sarah chuckled as she walked to the door. "Mark my words, Michela, mark my words."

SARAH WAVED ACROSS the compound at Michela, who was struggling with several bundles. "Hey, do want a hand with that?"

Michela handed half of the bundles to Sarah, relieved to have relinquished some of the weight. "Thanks. This darned frozen food weighs a ton. Besides, I don't know why I'm cooking anyway. No one seems to be bothering eating these days."

Sarah laughed. "Yeah. Things have changed around here with the Ross discovery. It's as if those three have gained a new burst of energy."

"I know what you mean. It's a shame half his diary was ruined by water. The mystery of the expedition's demise remains unsolved." Michela nudged open the door of the mess hut.

They walked in and Sarah closed the door behind her. "At least the mystery of his leg's been solved. Imagine a crate of your own gear falling on your leg. That must have hurt like blazes."

"I'd have preferred they didn't find out that information. The way Rick carried on when he found out there was the possibility of another hut around here, I could have wrung his neck."

Sarah chuckled. "You'll need to get in line with that one. I think Alli would've beaten you to it."

Michela, a wistful smile on her face, looked at the small pile of photographic plates on the table. "She's really begun to stand up to him and I'm glad to see that. So what have they been up to this morning?"

"Di and Rick were bagging and tagging the artefacts they're taking back to Australia and then they were going to join Rob and Alli in the hut. I think they've been trying

to track a course around the internal walls of the hut."
Sarah headed for the door. "Are you coming over?"

"Let me finish here and I'll be there shortly."

AFTER GAINING DIRECTIONS from Allison, Rob
skilfully manoeuvred around the hut's internal walls with
his blade. At one place, the blade sunk a little further, her-
alding a possible entrance that was plugged by ice. As he
peeled away at the barrier, more evidence of a smaller
room came into view, surprisingly free of all but a few ici-
cles that clung to the ceiling. Despite his growing excitement, he continued until he'd uncovered a space large
enough for a human to walk through.

"Alli," he called softly.

Allison got up from the wooden bench she'd been cataloguing on and went to Rob's side. She was lost for
words. Lying within a sleeping bag, his hands calmly
folded over an encased document, was a man, his face
weathered by the exposure to the elements. Unlike the
other body, no one had gone to the trouble to sew him into
his sleeping bag. His pose reminded Allison of one of the
knights of old.

She walked quietly across the small confines of the
room and peered down at the encased document he was
holding. In bold on the document were three letters: *ERF*.
She crumpled to the floor, the shock of the discovery too
much to take in.

Rob rushed to her side, afraid she'd fainted. "Are you
all right?"

She looked up at Rob's concerned face, her eyes glistening with tears. "You've found him," she whispered.
"You've found Eric Finlayson."

"No kidding? Bugger me." He stepped out of the
small room and turned to the others, preoccupied in various corners of the room. "Hey, we've found the man himself." He quickly stepped aside as the group crammed
around the doorway.

Allison stood and cast her eyes around what had been
Eric Finlayson's final resting-place. The personal area
wasn't that dissimilar to the others they'd found. A small
shelf contained his belongings; a faded silk sled pennant,

half family crest, half American flag was tacked to the wall. There was a record on an opened phonograph—possibly the last tune he'd heard before he closed his eyes forever. She reverently touched each of the items before returning her gaze to the man laid out on the small bed, his features surprisingly calm, a glimmer of a smile around the corners of his lips.

Rick forced his way into the room and attempted to pull the monogrammed document from the dead man's hands. "Damn it, he doesn't seem to want to give this up too quickly, does he."

"What do you think you're doing?" Allison screamed in outrage at the desecration of the man whose existence she'd sought to prove for so long.

Rob clasped Rick's shoulder with a vise-like grip. "Why don't you step back, mate. This is Alli's find, not yours. Besides, you had your turn with the last diary."

Rick turned and saw the murderous look in Rob's eyes. Stepping back, he rubbed his shoulder while Rob calmed Allison.

"That proves again the ability of man to conquer all he sees. Here we have the proof." Rick pointed at the bed.

Allison, having recovered from the shock of Rick's attempted theft, laughed. "He can't be too bloody skilful. He died in the attempt."

Sarah chuckled. "Congratulations, Rob, and congratulations, Alli. He must have been the last. Otherwise, I've no doubt someone would have wrapped him in a shroud as well." She looked at the frozen hands that grimly clutched the prize of what could only be Finlayson's diary. "How about we see if we can release that without too much injury to the body itself. Rob, can you tell Michela?"

"I'm here." Michela stepped into the room and stared at the man in the cot. The words of Charlotte Finlayson echoed across the miles before spiritually rebounding off the walls of the small room: "Bring my ancestor home."

His features, although withered, were as Michela had remembered seeing him in the painting behind Charlotte Finlayson's desk. With the exception of the pallor of his skin, the only thing that was missing were the eyes that had seemed to radiate from the painting, now in death, forever closed. She glanced sideways and took in Allison's shaking figure. Without thinking she stepped closer and lightly touched Allison's arm. "Are you okay?" she softly asked.

Allison looked down at the hand softly stroking her arm and then at Michela. "I'll be fine," she quietly replied, giving Michela's hand a small squeeze.

Sarah cast an "I told you so" smile at Michela before turning her attention to Allison. "So what do you want to do?"

"If possible I'd like to try and remove the diary. Once that's done, I think I'll take it back to my hut and see what it holds," Allison said. "Michela, I know Mrs. Finlayson's requirements, but do you think it would be okay if we tried to work out how her ancestor died?"

Michela nodded, only now able to think coherent thoughts as opposed to the ones that had rushed through her head at Allison's gentle touch. "I don't think that would pose a problem, especially if we take it slowly."

Rick took Dianne's hand. "If you think I'm going to give you a hand then you've got another thing coming. Come on, love, we may as well continue with the cataloguing."

"I'll give you a hand to move him," Rob offered.

"First things first," Sarah said. With Michela's help, she managed to carefully pry Finlayson's fingers open enough to pull out the encased document. "Here." She handed it to Allison.

Allison held the document as if it was the most precious thing on earth. "Thank you," she whispered and smiled at them. "This is a dream come true."

ALLISON ENTERED HER hut and carefully placed the diary on the table. *I think this is going to be a long morning, and my camera's still in the mess hut. I better grab that and a coffee while I'm at it.*

On her way to the mess hut, she watched Rob, Michela, and Sarah as they carried Finlayson. Catching Michela's glance in her direction, she waved as her thoughts returned to the interaction in the hut and Michela's reassuring touch. She shook her head to bring herself back to the present and entered the mess hut. She retrieved her camera and a cup of the brew made fresh that morning, and returned to her apple.

Allison photographed the document's jacket. It was made of cardboard, encasing its contents on all sides bar one. "Hmm, a good way to protect the contents." She tilted the open side toward her and the book slid out, its cover obviously once brilliant deep green leather. "Now that is a beautiful piece of craftsmanship."

Only the gold monogrammed letters of ERF and the gold border that formed a boundary to the diary broke the green leather. She lifted the book and a small waterproof pouch fell from the back of the casing.

"SO, WHAT DID I tell you?" Sarah smugly said as she and Michela removed the stiff sleeping bag from Finlayson.

"I still think you're making things up. She wasn't thinking. If it had been you in my place, she'd have done the same thing," Michela replied.

"You can say what you want, Dr. DeGrasse, but I think you *know* she likes you." Sarah dodged Michela's soft punch. "Do this like last time?"

Michela nodded. "Let me get comfortable." She leaned against the wall of the container. "Whenever you're ready."

"It's a male who looks to be a lot older than the other male, but this could be due to the exposure of Finlayson's skin to the extremes over the passing years. Anyway, if we take that into account, my rough guess is that he's about the same age—late thirties to early forties. I'm going down through the layers here and he seems to be wearing a hell of a lot more clothing than Ross was. Mind you, if he's died from the same thing then there probably wasn't that much body fat to keep him warm. I'm unbuttoning his shirt and cutting through his undershirt." Sarah sucked in a breath. "Shit, it looks as if he may have suffered broken ribs at some stage. His chest is tightly bound. Are you getting all this, Michela?"

"Yes, yes, give me a minute," Michela replied as she furiously wrote.

ALLISON PHOTOGRAPHED THE front and back of the pouch and set her camera on the table. She took a long sip of her coffee, allowing the contents to warm her insides.

She set the cup down, took up a pair of long-nosed tweezers, and carefully unfolded the waterproof covering to reveal two photographs, one on top of the other. She put them beside each other, picked up her camera, and photographed them before studying them more closely.

The first photograph was of a woman in a flowing dress of the 1890's, accompanied by a small child dressed in a pinafore. From the extensive research Allison had undertaken on Finlayson, she knew this could only be a picture of Finlayson's wife Charlotte, and their son Robert. She smiled at the family portrait of father, mother, and son in the second photograph. Finlayson stood proudly behind the seated Charlotte, the smiling child on her lap.

She carefully picked up the family portrait, turned it over, and struggled to read the inscription on its back. She turned on the high-resolution lamp, hoping the light would make her reading that much easier.

SARAH TAPPED THE floor as she waited for Michela to catch up. "Are you ready yet?" Michela nodded. "As I was saying, it seems he's suffered some sort of rib damage as his ribs are tightly bound. I'm going to cut through the gauze to see if I can see what the source of the injury is." She cut through the icy material and pulled it back.

Michela, nose in her notes, heard Sarah gasp. "What's wrong?"

Sarah looked down at the seated Michela. "Take a look."

Michela put the notepad on the floor, went to Sarah's side and looked at Finlayson's body. She blinked twice. "Oh shit, what do we do now?"

THE HIGH-RESOLUTION lamp allowed Allison to see the fine copperplate inscription written all those years ago. *My darling Elizabeth may this memory of a happy day tide you through the cold days ahead. My love and thoughts will always be with you. All my love, Charlotte.*

Thinking she'd read it wrong, she scrubbed her eyes and read the inscription again. Her mouth open, she turned the photograph over to reveal the family portrait. "Son of a..." she said out loud. "ERF doesn't stand for Eric Robert Finlayson, the E stands for Elizabeth. Finlayson was a woman!" She put the photograph down, hurled herself through the door, and half-ran, half-slid the distance to the makeshift morgue.

She burst through the door of the morgue and found Sarah and Michela intently studying the body. They turned around and shielded the body from Allison.

Allison struggled to get her words out and breathe at the same time. "You're not going to believe this. I've got the most amazing news."

Sarah smiled, her arms crossed. "I bet our news is better than yours. We've found the first female expeditioner on the Continent and it's Finlayson." Sarah pointed over her shoulder with her thumb to the body. "This makes the Conner-Boyd expedition of 1928 not the first time a female set foot on Antarctica."

Allison laughed, her breath coming a little easier. "You may have found the first female expeditioner, but I can do better than that. Eric's name is actually *Elizabeth*. And by the looks of the photos that fell out of his, I mean her diary, she was married to a woman—she's gay."

"Just because she was living with a woman, doesn't mean she was gay. It could've been a Boston marriage," Michela said.

Allison tilted her head. "What's that?"

"By most modern-day accounts they were intense friendships formed between women who had no interest in marrying, in the more conventional sense that is. As far as we know, they were asexual relationships, but very strong, loving friendships all the same. This could have been the sort of relationship Charlotte and Elizabeth shared." Michela turned to Sarah for confirmation.

"Or, they could be gay, and she was more comfortable dressing as a man rather than a woman. I mean, have you ever heard of a Boston marriage resulting in actual marriage? And heaven knows, it can't have been that easy to be a woman in the late 1800's and one who was an explorer to boot," Sarah replied.

"Either way, how do think we should break this news to the rest of the group?" Allison asked, not receiving any great comfort from the concerned look on both Sarah and Michela's faces.

"Let's do it after dinner. People tend to be a lot more relaxed on a full stomach, and something tells me this news isn't going to go down all that well," Michela ventured.

"What about Di and Rick?" Sarah asked. "They're going to be keen to know what you've found in the diary."

Allison waved her hand. "Leave them to me."

ALLISON CAST HER eyes around the table in the mess hut. "Today, while I was reading the Finlayson diary a small waterproof pouch fell out. It contained two photographs, one had an inscription on the back. It's this inscription that leads me to believe that Eric Finlayson isn't Eric at all, he's Elizabeth."

There was a stunned silence as Dianne, Rick, and Rob absorbed Allison's revelation.

"Garbage," Rick replied. "You must have read it wrong."

Sarah folded her arms. "She did no such thing. I conducted the same investigation on Finlayson as I did on Ross. Trust me when I tell you Finlayson is definitely a woman."

Confused, Dianne turned to Allison. "But in the reading material you gave to me on Finlayson, you said he was married and had a child. How can that be?"

Allison shrugged. "I don't know how to explain the child, but I can tell you that these two women were in a stable relationship of some sort or another."

Dianne looked at Sarah, and then back to Allison. "That's disgusting."

Rick stood and pushed his chair away from the table. "You're damn right it is." He wheeled on Sarah. "So, a damned dyke was the first to establish a base in Antarctica. You must be pretty happy about that. Bloody hell, you're all over the damn place." He angrily jabbed his finger at Sarah. "You and your bloody perverted lifestyle, you don't deserve to be here."

Rob strode toward Rick. "That's it. I've about had it with you, mate. You've had this coming for a long time. No one and I mean no one offends my friends."

Michela stepped between them. "Hang on, Rob." She turned to Rick. "And, Rick, you hang on a minute, too. If you're pointing fingers then you better point one at me as well."

The implication of her words hung in the air. Dianne cast a baleful eye at her. "I should have known. I always had a funny feeling when I was changing in the same hut as you and now I know why."

Michela quickly glanced at Allison, before she turned her steely-eyed gaze on Dianne, who defiantly stood beside Rick. "Ms. Peterson, you've got to be joking." Michela cast a disdainful look the length of Dianne's body. "Please credit me with some taste."

"You're bloody sick, you know that. You're a bloody pervert just like her!" Rick bellowed.

Allison held up her hands. "Please, just stop it. We've discovered a world first. This will make the dig a household name and establish us for future expeditions. Now's not the time for name calling—"

Rick pointed at Michela. "Why are you bothering defending that damn dyke? If she was looking at Di's body, what makes you think you're all that safe?"

Disgusted, Allison rolled her eyes. "Oh for heaven's sake, you uptight prick, get a life."

Rob burst out laughing.

"Hang on a minute, Alli," Rick said, "or have I got it all wrong? Do you like what that damn psychologist dyke puts out?"

"That's it!" Rob hit Rick squarely on the jaw.

Sarah knelt beside an unconscious Rick, while trying to push away a hysterical Dianne. "Shit, mate, you dropped him like a bag of spuds." She arranged him in the coma position and stood. "You know, you really ought to be more careful."

"Yeah," Rob said. "And he really ought to learn some bloody manners."

Chapter
Ten

My Darling Charlotte,

It has been over two months since I last made an entry in my diary, and it is only now through sheer will that I do so. The second expedition that left in such good spirits has failed to return. Their original journey was to be no more than twenty days duration. I knew them to be an exuberant band and didn't really expect to see them before the twenty-five day mark. This day came and went, as did many others. Without the dogs, sleds or ability to man a search party, I can only assume the worst—they have perished also. I thought I had reached my lowest ebb.

The three of us that remained tried our best to maintain each other's spirits, dutifully keeping our diaries so as to have at least something to show for our time here. However, the worse was yet to come. The day came when our ship was to rendezvous with us and yet it did not appear. We waited in vain for one week and then two but still there was no sign of it. I can only assume that it too has been lost and now we are trapped. Trapped with our food dwindling and no possible means of escaping the continent we so proudly set out to conquer.

Where have I led my men? What have I done?

ERF

Antarctica—2010

MICHELA CHUCKLED AS Sarah attempted to divide her time between the overflowing pot on the stove and preparing the dinner rolls. "Need help with that?"

Sarah turned the gas down on the stove. "Aargh! I can't believe you let me loose in a kitchen."

"Yeah it does look a little out of control."

Sarah laughed. "Hah, no more so that what it's been like here over the past few days. Alli's not talking to Rick at all and I can barely get a word out of Di. I swear, meals around here are like pulling teeth. It's a wonder they're getting any work done on the dig."

"I know what you mean. I think we better have a team meeting after dinner, if we survive it, that is." Sarah threw the spoon as Michela rushed out the door.

"Everyone's a bloody critic," Sarah yelled.

"EVERYONE'S BEEN WALKING around on eggshells these past few days. I'm not pointing any fingers here. I'm as much to blame as anyone else. But we've got very little time left to finish the cataloguing of the site and then commence our pack up." Michela consulted her notes. "By my estimate we've two more days of digging and cataloguing. After that we have to start packing or we'll miss our window to get home."

Allison, Dianne, and Rob all spoke at once.

"We've got so much to do inside the hut." Allison's voice cut through, silencing the others. "Not to mention trying to identify where the photographer's hut might lie. For all we know this camp may be right on top of it."

Michela nodded. "I understand and that's why we need to work together these last few days to get as much done as possible. I know there are some here who'll be more than happy to see the last of some of us. But, for the moment, we're a team, relying on each other to get as much done as possible. Now, we can do that or we can all retire to our huts and sulk until it's time to pack up." She scanned the faces in front of her. "What's it going to be?"

Rick pointed to Rob. "Is he going to be able to keep his fists to himself?"

Rob cracked his fingers and made a pretence of picking his nails before staring at Rick. "Depends. Are you going to give me a reason to use them?"

"That's enough, the two of you. There'll be no more of that while I'm in charge."

Sarah held up her hand. "Look, to allow you three to focus on the dig, I'll pick up the slops task as well as cooking."

Michela shook her head. "I know how much you hate cooking. How about I do that and you do the slops?"

Sarah breathed a sigh of relief. "Sounds fine by me."

Michela looked around the team. "Okay, then let's get on with it."

AS SHE CATALOGUED, Allison's mind wandered, as it had done over the past week, to Rick's words: *Do you like what that damned psychologist dyke puts out?* She'd been shocked into silence and was grateful if not a little regretful of Rob's physical defence of her. It wasn't until later, in the silence of her own counsel, that she'd managed to give the matter more thought.

How do I really feel? There was something about Michela that drove her crazy and yet drew her at the same time. That morning in the hut, when they'd returned from trying to find Ewan, she was sure Michela meant to kiss her. She'd waited, surprisingly eager for Michela's intimate touch. Even now, the thought evoked feelings she'd never felt before. But, with Sarah's knock on the door, the spell had been broken. *Maddi was waiting for a report. Of course she'd be more interested in reporting to her than anything else.*

Since the incident in the hut, Michela had been polite, going out of her way to give Allison space. But the more Michela gave, the closer Allison realised she wanted to get and yet she was unsure how to do so. When Michela prepared for bed, she'd secretly watch her undress, marvelling at Michela's toned but powerful body. Now, within days, the dig would be over, they would travel back to Wills Station, and return home. Michela would slip from her life, returning to her own job on the other side of the world. *So how do you feel about that? Yes, but how does a straight woman, broach such a subject without looking com-*

pletely hypocritical?

DIANNE HELD UP one side of the wooden barrier as Rob hammered the other side to one of the posts of the existing hut. "Are you sure this will keep out the snow?"

"I suppose you won't know until you're down here next, but it can only help. When we first got here there was no door and the whole place was full of snow and ice. At least next time you mightn't have so much to dig." He shifted his weight so he could hammer the other side of the door. "So, when do you think you guys will be back?" *Just so I can be forewarned and make sure we never run into each other again.*

Dianne shrugged. "I don't know. It depends on whether father decides it's worthwhile to finance another expedition and that'll depend on what we have to report. Somehow I don't think he's going to be all that happy."

"I don't get it. You've collected a heap of stuff from the site."

Dianne shuffled from one foot to the other. "My father is, well, a little conservative. While he'll be excited by the find and the circumstances around the discovery, who we discovered may set him back a bit."

Rob bent down and hammered the final nail in the door. "What, you mean because Eric's actually Elizabeth and Elizabeth was living with a woman and child as husband and wife?"

Dianne nervously laughed. "Something like that. You have to admit it's a little odd."

Rob straightened and silently observed Dianne. "That's where I think you and I won't ever agree. I see nothing odd about it. Who gives a toss whether it's a man and woman, a man and man or a woman and woman? What's the issue if there's love involved?" He shook his head and, muttering, walked away.

"HEY WHERE ARE you off to big boy?" Sarah called as she crossed the camp from toilet cleaning duty.

Rob held up a blade. "I was going to oil this before I pack it. If I can sea prep the equipment here, it means I don't have to worry about it when I get to Wills Station. And if that's the case, then you and I can have a couple of very quiet or very loud drinks together."

Sarah slapped Rob's back. "Isn't that the truth. Do you want to finish that and head for the mess hut? Michela said she had some news. I'll go and let Di know."

"WE HAVE A little bit of good news," Michela said to the group gathered in the mess hut. "I've been on the radio to Maddi this morning and she's organised two opportunity lifts with the Chinook that delivered some of our stores here."

Rick rested a booted foot on the edge of the table. "So what exactly does that mean?"

"The Chinook has a lift capacity of about sixteen thousand pounds. It means we'll be able to completely transport the camp, excepting the bare minimum, back to Wills Station without having to rely on surface transport. This will give you more time to ensure your artefacts are ready for sea travel," Michela replied.

Rob reached for a couple of biscuits in the middle of the table. "So what's to move, boss, and what's not to move?"

"The first move will be an under slung load of the mess hut and most of what's contained in it. The second move will be all stores and accommodations with the exception of the two apples. Stores that we can't put in the spare space of the mess hut will be placed inside the Chinook, along with the artefacts." Michela turned to Allison.

"Alli, I've spoken with Maddi and she tells me they've a small refrigerated container that'll be capable of carrying Finlayson for the move back to base and the duration of the sea journey. That way we can free up the sno-trak's storage container for when we need to start packing away the remainder of the camp. Is that okay with you?"

Allison nodded. "That should be fine, but I don't think I could get back up in one of those helos so soon. Who's going to look after the artefacts?"

Michela turned to Rick and Dianne. "That's where you two come in. There'll be plenty of space so you two can go back to base to act as an advance party. The rest of us will break down the camp, before I confirm it's clear of any human waste or rubbish. Rob, Alli, Sarah, and myself will be responsible for that."

Rick nodded. "Sounds like a plan. When do we start dismantling that solar generator thing? I'd like to know when my last hot meal is."

Thinking about yourself yet again. "That won't be dismantled as it was put here under trial conditions. Under the agreement, only the people who installed it are qualified to remove it. This fits in well with our plans. It means Rob can disconnect power progressively until there's only power to the two remaining apples. That power will remain until the day we leave for Wills Station."

"What about the impact of the helicopters landing near the site?" Allison asked.

Michela smiled. "That won't be a major problem. We'll establish a LZ on the far side of the site. The only time the helo will get close is when the load master slings our kitchen and carries it on its merry way. The weather forecast indicates the wind should be pretty calm for the move back to the station. It should take about four hours there and back, with the loading taking advantage of the extended light conditions and extra helicopter crew."

Michela turned to Rick and Dianne. "For you two this will be an especially long day, but Maddi assures me there's now enough spare living space in the main building that we'll all be accommodated in there. Any final questions?"

"I'd still like to give it one more try at finding the location of the photographer's hut," Rick said.

Michela shook her head. "I understand, but I don't think we have the time. When we return to the station I'll ensure that the site's marked to prevent any possible site egress or damage. Maybe it's a consideration you can make for subsequent digs, finding the hut that is."

"If you think I'm coming to this God forsaken place ever again, then you've got another thing coming," Rick said.

"And Antarctica will be grateful to see the ass end of you too, mate," Sarah muttered for only Michela's ears.

ALLISON, RICK, AND Dianne confirmed the site was relatively stable until the next dig. Rob, Sarah, and Michela progressively broke down the camp, crating equipment and stores for the journey to Wills Station and Hobart. Rob and Sarah moved into the mess hut when the googie was dismantled, to live in until they took over the second apple when Rick and Dianne departed.

Fortunately the weather held and the first helo lift arrived at eight the following morning.

Allison was surprised at the helicopter crew's efficiency. "What are they doing now?"

Sarah pointed to where the crew was working. "They're checking to make sure the boxes within the mess hut are well stowed or the load may shift during its move to the station. Then they'll rig it within a chain frame which will be hooked onto a lead that will be suspended from the helo. Once that's complete the load master will get off the top of the hut and the helo will carry it away. The load master will then be picked up on the next trip."

Allison frowned. "We put a heck of a lot of stuff in there. What happens if it's too heavy to lift?"

Sarah smiled. "Do you remember the other day Rob was filling out a chart of what we put in the hut?" Allison nodded. "He was raising a cargo manifest. This details the weight or at least the approximate weight of everything in there. He then totalled this and added the weight of the container to make sure it didn't exceed the under slung load tolerance of the helicopter. Trust me, it didn't by a long shot. It'll be fine, don't worry about it."

It wasn't long before the helicopter returned, and set down on the LZ. Using the sno-trak, the artefacts from the dig and the remainder of non-essential stores were transported into the bowels of the aircraft before Rick and Dianne boarded for the flight back to Wills Station.

The team watched the helicopter until it was no more than a speck on the horizon. "Thank Christ they've gone," Rob muttered.

"Rob, that's enough," Michela said. "Remember you've got a sea journey with Rick to contend with yet."

Crossing his arms, Rob smugly smiled. "That may be so but I'm banking on the journey being as rough as the trip down. If that's the case then Rick will spend most of his time in his bed or praying to the porcelain god. But you know the best bit about that?"

Sarah laughed. "What?"

Rob threw his arm around Allison's shoulders. "This time this young lady can enjoy herself instead of playing nurse maid. The idea of Di cleaning up after that bastard does my old heart good."

The group shared a laugh. The long-range radio crackled to life.

"Finlayson Base this is Wills Station. Michela, this is Maddi, do you read me, over?"

Michela went to her daypack where the radio was stored, but not before she saw Allison stalk off in the opposite direction. "Maddi, this is Michela, go ahead."

"Michela, our meteorologists are recording the possibility of enhanced solar flare activity in the next twelve hours."

Michela frowned and clicked her tongue, as she recalled the ability of such activity to render useless their long-range communications. "How long is it expected to last?"

"They're not sure, but you can bank on being out of contact for at least three to four days."

Michela removed her beanie and ran her fingers through her hair. "I guess there's nothing we can do about it."

"That isn't the worst of it. They've also picked up a major storm front heading in your direction that's due to hit within eight hours. There's no way you could make it back to the station in that time. I suggest you maintain your position until the storm's passed."

Michela turned to Rob and Sarah. Sarah held up her hand. "We're on it. We'll check the huts and ensure everything that can be tied down, is."

Michela nodded and returned to the radio. "We'll batten down here. I won't break camp until we can establish communications with you and determine the storm cell's passed."

"That sounds fine. And, Michela, take care of yourself. I'd like to see you back here soon and in one piece."

"I'd like to see *all* of us in your location and in one piece. Keep an eye on Rick and Di, will you."

"Michela, this is Maddi, roger, out."

Michela put the radio back onto her pack and headed to her apple. She entered the hut, put her pack on the bed, and turned to Allison. "Maddi says there's a storm cell coming and it's due to be upon us in the next eight hours. I'm sorry to disturb you, but we really do have to ensure the camp is safe."

Allison closed the book she was reading and quickly stood. "Sorry, I was engrossed in Finlayson's diary. I really didn't want it to go back to the station with the rest of the artefacts. Speaking of artefacts, will Finlayson's hut be okay during the storm?"

Michela held back a terse response when she saw the concern on Allison's face. She gave Allison's arm a reassuring rub. "I don't know, but it's been here for over one hundred and ten years, so I don't think it'll give its place up in history all that easily. Besides, Rob's boarded the hut's entrance, so the worst that can happen is the snow will cover it over again."

"What needs to be done?"

Michela picked up her heavy-duty work gloves. "Rob and Sarah have started checking the anchor points for their building. If you could check out the short range radios for serviceability that would be great."

Allison pulled on her jacket. "Why the short range radios? I thought their distance was limited."

Michela nodded. "They are, but Maddi also said solar flares were expected. This'll cut out our communications with Wills Station. I want to be able to at least talk between the two apples once the storm hits. I'm going to check the anchor points of our apple. Can you tell Rob and Sarah we'll meet in their hut in, say, ten minutes?"

"Okay. I'll grab the radios from the sno-trak and meet you there." Allison turned to the door, halted, and turned back to Michela. "Is there anything else I can do?"

"Can you make sure the blizzard rope around the base is still anchored correctly? Once this storm hits there'll be no telling what will happen." Michela followed Allison through the door. Pausing on the top step, she looked at the deceptively blue sky that displayed no hint of the oncoming storm. *Here we go again. Small spaces and Alli—I hope we don't end up murdering each other.*

MICHELA QUICKLY COMPLETED a check of the camp and entered Rob and Sarah's hut. She pulled her beanie from her head. "The wind's already picking up out there. I don't know if the weatherman got it right this time."

Sarah laughed. "Well, it wouldn't be the first time they got it wrong. What's the plan?"

"If we still had the googie I'd have recommended we all bed down in that. The apples are a little too small for four people over an indeterminate period of time."

"What do you mean indeterminate period of time?" Allison asked. "How long do you think the storm will last?"

"You never know how long these babies are going to last," Rob said. "I've been in one that went for twenty days before it blew itself out. Don't worry though, this one may be as short as the last storm that blew through here."

Michela nodded. "Rob's right, but I'm going to err on the side of caution. We'll pull the emergency rations and power from the storage container in the sno-trak and divide them between us. Once the storm hits I don't want any unnecessary movement outside the buildings. It looks like we're going to have to wait this one out. At least the short range radios will allow limited communications between the apples."

THE STORM HIT the camp three hours before its forecast arrival. While it was uncomfortably close within their apple, Michela and Allison used the time to focus on their respective tasks. Allison occupied the hours reading and cataloguing Finlayson's diary, pausing only when an extra-strong gust of wind buffeted the hut. Michela collated her research notes and made a rudimentary start on her final report. They worked through the early evening, stopping only for refreshments and dinner. As the storm continued to lash the sides of the hut they went to bed, both hopeful that the morning would bring an end to the storm and the forced occupation.

The following morning Michela woke and wasn't surprised to hear the sounds of the storm. *It looks as if we're in here for another day.* Looking around, she saw that Allison had already risen.

Allison brushed her hair and smiled. "Good morning, sleepy head. Feel like some breakfast?"

Michela sat up. "Thanks. What have you got planned for the morning?"

"Oh, more of the same I suppose. I really do want to finish this diary before I have to hand it over. Are you continuing with your research?"

Michela nodded. "Yep. But if I'm to get anywhere I better get up."

Allison carefully placed her brush on her already overloaded makeshift bookshelf. After ensuring it was stable, she walked toward the stove to make breakfast.

ALLISON CHECKED HER watch, surprised to find it was mid-morning. She closed the book and rubbed her tired eyes. "Ugh, this is murder. Elizabeth was a prodigious writer and this cursive text is bloody hard to read."

Michela put down her pen and watched as Allison rubbed the base of her neck. *I could do that for you if you like.* She mentally slapped herself. "I know what you mean. It's been years since I've had to write freehand. I'm sure recording my research would have been a lot easier if my digital tablet hadn't died when it did. It's amazing what we get used to, isn't it?" Allison nodded. "Hey, have you found any reference to whether Elizabeth told the rest of the crew that they were being led by a woman?"

"Not really. From what I can see, she travelled as a male and that makes a little sense. Who's likely to follow a woman to the bottom of the world?" Allison rose and turned to the small gas stove. "Would you like a cup of hot chocolate?"

"If you're offering. Thanks very much." Michela watched as Allison pulled her own mug from the makeshift shelf at the end of her bed. "You know if you put anything else on that it's likely to break."

Allison looked at the shelf and then shook her head. "Nah, I'm sure there's a little more space on it."

Michela laughed and then watched Allison's back as she prepared the beverage. The relative warmth of the hut allowed them to dress in only one layer. Her eyes traced a path from Allison's warm trousers to a long sleeved skivvy that clung to her curves. *Not too skinny, that's nice. Certainly nicely built for her outdoor work. Wonder what it would be like to run my hands over the delicately muscled planes of her back.*

"Earth to Michela, are you there?"

Michela looked up. Allison was on the other side of the table, the skivvy offering a relatively unimpeded view of her shapely figure. Michela forced her eyes away from where they desperately wanted to look and stared at the steaming mug Allison had placed in front of her. "Thanks." She picked up the mug, blew on the liquid, and took a sip.

Allison sat down. "Can I ask you a question?"

Michela took another drink of hot chocolate. "Ask away."

"You remember the night at the coffee house?" Michela nodded. "You said you'd been in a long relationship, four-and-a-half years, I think. Why did you break up? I mean, you don't have to answer if you don't want to."

"It's, okay. It's a little easier to talk about now," Michela said. "My partner, or should I say ex-partner's name is Natalie. We were together for a long time, but most of that time I was away on one field trip or another. I suppose I can't blame her really, breaking up that is. When I think about it now I can't help but wonder whether I was running away from commitment, trying my best to not develop any lasting emotional ties. I'd been hurt before and now I'm wondering whether I was ever true with her in the relationship. Maybe she's better off with someone else."

Allison pondered Michela's response. "Did you love her?"

Michela ran her fingers through her hair and gazed around the cabin as if looking for an answer. She returned her attention to Allison. "I used to think I did but now, well, I'm not so sure. What about you and Rick? That is, if you're okay to talk about it."

Allison dismissively waved her hand. "No, I'm over it. I don't really know what I saw in him in the first place. I suppose there was a time when I thought I loved him and believed he was the only one for me. But recently we'd grown apart. Strangely enough while I'm none too happy with his new choice of partners, it's not that which bothered me the most. I think it was his deceit." She took a sip of her hot chocolate. "I mean, if he'd had enough why didn't he say so?"

Michela nodded. "I know what you mean. Imagine my surprise when I came home from visiting Charlotte Finlayson, to find my work second-in-command with his hands all over Natalie."

"Did you say his?" Allison asked. "That had to be painful. What did you do?"

"I walked out but not before saying that when I told him to keep abreast of the situation it didn't mean fondling my partner's breasts as well." She paused at Allison's reddening cheeks. "I'm sorry. I didn't mean to be that explicit."

Allison rose and turned to the small makeshift sink. "No, that's okay. After all, you were only telling the truth." *And besides, Alli, your reaction has more to do with you thinking what it would feel like to have Michela's hands on parts other than those not covered by clothes.* "I really don't want to go back to the diary just yet. How about a game of cards?"

Michela laughed, happy to break the tension that had been building between them. "Are you a glutton for punishment? Last time we played I beat the socks off you. Are you sure you want to try again?"

Allison curled a finger at Michela. "Bring it on, woman, bring it on."

Oh, Alli, if you only knew. Michela retrieved the cards and dealt the first hand of their card-playing war—one that lasted the stormy afternoon.

MICHELA TRIED HARD not to laugh. "You said nothing of the sort."

Allison pulled on a flannel shirt over her skivvy as a tinge of cold seeped through the warmth of the hut. "I did, too. The deal was whoever lost at the cards not only had to cook tea, but wash up as well. I can't help it if you couldn't focus on the cards."

It was entirely your fault. If I wasn't preoccupied in trying

not to look at you, I'd have whopped your rather pleasant ass.
Michela kicked herself for the fortieth time that day,
reminding herself to keep her mind above her belt buckle.
"Don't worry, we'll try again after tea and I'll leave you
for dead."

Allison shook her head. "Maybe tomorrow. I really do
have to get some more of the diary read. I know once we
get back to Sydney, it'll become the centrepiece of old
Peterson's collection."

Michela frowned. "Peterson, Flinders Museum
patron? Isn't that Di's last name?"

Allison nodded. "*Daddy*'s the museum's patron."

"So that's where Di fits into all of this. That explains a
lot."

"I've no doubt in the near future she'll be the head of
at least one of the Museum's departments. But for the
moment, the diary's under my charge and so I'm going to
make the most of it."

MICHELA WAS STRETCHED out on her bed studying
her notes when she thought she heard a sniffle. She looked
to where Allison was seated reading the diary and
frowned at seeing her silently weeping. She quietly put
down her notes, went to Allison's side, and put a soothing
hand on her shoulder. "Are you all right?"

Allison's distraught tear-stained face nearly broke
Michela's heart. Michela pulled around a chair, sat beside
Allison, and took her hands in her own. "Honey, what's
the matter?"

"I've just read the diary entry where Elizabeth recon-
ciles she's not only lost most of her crew, but their ship
hasn't turned up. They're stranded, with no possible hope
of rescue. The pain in her words is too much to bear. I can't
help but wonder what must have gone through her mind,
knowing she'd never see her wife again. That must have
been heartbreaking." She sobbed. "How could she stand
such a separation?"

Without thought, Michela took Allison into her arms,
allowing her to weep. She could only offer murmured
words of encouragement.

Finally Allison looked up and searched Michela's face.

"Why are you so kind to me?"

Michela brushed away a stray tear from Allison's cheek. "Why shouldn't I be? As I said before, no matter how much we disagree, I'm still your friend and friends do this for one another. They're there when the other needs support."

Allison took a tissue and wiped her eyes. "I don't know what came over me. I was okay until I started thinking of Elizabeth here, dying all alone and away from Charlotte, who'd never really know what happened to her. The more I thought about it the worse things got." She blew her nose. "Do you think they were really lovers in the true sense of the word? Or was it merely a Boston marriage?"

"Does it really matter? I think loving someone has more to do with how they make you feel and how you make them feel in return. Were they soul mates? Most likely. I think being lovers has more to do with the emotion behind the act than the act itself. Boston marriage or lovers in the sexual sense, does it make a difference?" Michela closed the diary. "I think we've both done enough work for today. At this rate, by the time the storm breaks we'll be blind. How about we both get some sleep?"

Allison nodded. "I suppose you're right, yet again."

Michela stood and headed for her bed when Allison grabbed her hand. Michela turned back and was rewarded with a hug.

"Thank you for being my friend," Allison whispered before she broke contact and went to her side of the room.

Michela uttered a small "good night" and prepared for bed. *This storm's got to finish soon. Or I'm likely to implode.*

ALLISON AWOKE AS the relentless wind buffeted the small apple. Snuggled up against the wall she swore she could feel the fibreglass structure flex with the wind. While she knew she was safe, her thoughts were preoccupied with what had been her sole focus for the last eight weeks. *What if the barrier Rob put up doesn't hold and snow gets into the hut? We could have done more harm than good in creating a wind tunnel inside the structure. That wind tunnel has the potential to blow the fragile building across the snow.*

No matter how hard she tried to rationalise Rob's work, she couldn't sleep. She looked at Michela and was relieved to see she was still in a deep slumber.

Allison dressed in her multiple layers, trying to make as little noise as possible. She pulled on her snow boots and snatched at her goggles that sat on the overcrowded small shelf at the end of her bed. Without warning the end of the shelf tilted, and books, containers, and other personal items crashed to the floor.

Allison wheeled to Michela.

Michela frowned and tried to force her sleep-filled eyes open. She rubbed her face, as if to remove the effects of her sleep, and finally opened her eyes. "What's going on?" Michela looked at her watch. "Why are you dressed like that at this time in the morning?"

Allison pulled on her gloves. "I couldn't sleep and I was worried about whether Rob's improvements to the hut have done more harm than good. I'm just going to do a quick check on it and then I'll be straight back."

"What? Don't be stupid."

Allison glowered at Michela, shoved her beanie on her head, and reached for the door handle.

Before Allison got any further, Michela unzipped her sleeping bag, quickly rose, and closed her hand over Allison's, effectively halting her escape. "What the hell do you think you're doing? It's at least minus thirty degrees Fahrenheit out there. You could damn well get yourself killed."

Allison ripped her hand from the door handle and stood toe to toe with Michela. "How dare you raise your voice to me!"

"Don't even go there, woman. What did I tell you, no, what did I tell all of you about leaving the huts in this weather?"

"I heard what you said, but—"

Michela grabbed Allison's upper arms. "If that's the damned case then why did you try to disobey me? In fact, what is it with you? You seem to take a perverse pleasure in going out of your way to do exactly the opposite to what I ask you to do."

"I don't go out of the way to disobey you at all. I'm the only remaining archaeologist here and that bloody hut's my responsibility!"

"That may be the case, but you're my responsibility. As long as we're out here, that's the way it has to be Allison. I don't intend to lose anyone else," Michela yelled, stepping closer to Allison.

"Of course, we couldn't have that happen, could we?" Allison caught herself as she saw her barb had struck home.

This has nothing to do with the loss the camp's already suffered. It's you, Alli. It has only ever been about you. Can't you see that? Closing her eyes, Michela hung her head in defeat. She softened her grip on Allison's arms.

"Have you any idea what I feel for you? What would happen if I lost you? I told you only yesterday that I thought I found love with Natalie, but when I met you, you changed my whole focus. No matter how hard I try to hide my feelings and force them to be otherwise, I can't help but feel like I'm falling in love with you."

Michela stepped back from Allison. "I find myself wanting to know the smallest things about you. What's your middle name, how old are you? Do you have any brothers or sisters, what's your favourite food? That morning here, in this hut, when we returned from looking for Ewan, you don't know how much I wanted to kiss you. If Sarah hadn't knocked on the door then I'd have made a big fool of myself. I'm sorry, you're probably disgusted by this, but I can't take it any more." She turned around and went, arms folded and frustrated at her inability to keep her emotions in check, to her side of the hut.

Mouth agape, Allison was at a loss for words. *She's falling in love with me? So how do I feel about that?* She closed her eyes as images flashed through her mind. Her first meeting with Michela. Their first confrontation. Her disdainful treatment of her and Michela's rescue of her on the glacier at Mount Cook. That night in the coffee house, the touching of hands. Allison's insistence on little meetings during their sea voyage. Her reaction to Maddi and the time in the emergency hut. *I think I feel the same. So where do I go from here?*

Michela felt Allison's arms snake around her waist. She turned and found Allison in her arms.

Allison tentatively brushed Michela's cheek. "Jane, hence my nickname AJ, thirty-two but closer to thirty-three, one brother Justin and he's a doctor, chocolate, always chocolate, and why don't you finish it?"

"Finish what?" Michela asked.

"This." Allison put her hand on the back of Michela's head and drew her close.

Surprised by Allison's boldness, Michela pulled back, only to find her lips pursued by Allison's. Surrendering to the sensations coursing through her, she tentatively mapped Allison's back with her hands. Despite the layers of fabric, she was painfully aware of Allison's muscular strength.

Allison broke the kiss and put her head against Michela's chest, surprised that the rapid beating of Michela's heart matched her own. She'd never meant to react the way she did, but was glad she had. Seeing the pain and honesty in Michela's eyes had shattered her resolve and, despite what she kept on telling herself, she could deny it no longer. The feelings she had for Michela were equally strong. The kiss was sweeter and more passionate than anything she'd ever experienced before. She smiled into Michela's sleeping shirt.

"I don't think I could have said it before but you make me feel the same way," she said. "You've had me off kilter since the day at the crevasse in New Zealand when you held me and called me honey. Not only that, but whether I liked it or not, before things ended with Rick I found myself irrationally measuring you up against him and he was failing dismally. No matter how hard I tried to run from it, when you looked my way I felt as if I was melting from the inside out. And as for that second night in the emergency hut, you were generating so much heat, I severely doubted that we needed a sleeping bag. I was so incredibly aroused it was only doubt and a degree of ignorance that stopped me from doing heaven knows what."

Michela chuckled and kissed Allison's forehead. "Me, too. When you snuggled back into me I thought I was going to die. It was only my promise I wouldn't compromise you that stopped me from taking it further."

Allison shyly leant back from Michela. "I still feel as I did that night in the hut. Where do we go from here?"

Michela slightly leant back and frowned. "Are you sure this is what you want? This has been a very stressful time out here for everyone, not the least of which you. I don't want you to think you have to commit to something you don't—" Allison placed a silencing finger on her lips.

"I've been known to be indecisive, but I think, no, I know I'm sure about this. It's not about stress or being here for as long as we have, it's about how I feel for you. It has been for a while now, I was just too stubborn and proud to admit it." Covering her shyness, Allison leaned in for a kiss just as the final cup that had been precariously balanced on her bookcase fell and shattered on the floor.

Allison bent her head down and chuckled. "I made a bit of a mess, didn't I." She moved out of Michela's arms and turned to the broken cup. "Let me clean it up."

"Leave it." As Michela opened her arms in invitation, Allison eagerly entered them. With one finger, she gently lifted Allison's chin and kissed her. Lightly stroking Allison's face, Michela was engulfed by emotions. Almost tentatively she stroked the tip of her tongue across Allison's lips and smiled when entrance was granted. She lightly teased Allison's tongue and her senses caught fire as Allison's tongue shyly entered her mouth.

Allison was on sensory overload. When Michela had brushed her lips she honestly thought her legs would fail her. The sensations now went far beyond what she'd ever experienced before. The heat in her stomach was a raging inferno that was rapidly engulfing her body. She broke away from the kiss and managed to whisper into Michela's ear, "God, I want so much more. I don't know what to do."

Michela relaxed her embrace. She cupped Allison's cheek in her hand as she lightly stroked it with her thumb. "Do you remember what we talked about yesterday, about Elizabeth and Charlotte?" Allison furrowed her brows. "You asked me whether the two were lovers or in a Boston marriage. Do you remember what I said?"

Allison shook her head.

Stroking Allison's face, Michela gazed into her piercing cobalt eyes. "I said it didn't matter whether they were lovers or not, it was the emotion behind the act and not the act itself." Allison nodded. Michela lightly grazed Allison's lips with her own. "Let your emotions lead you, the rest will follow." She pulled Allison to her and they stood, relishing in the warmth and comfort of each other.

Michela stepped back and held out her hand to Allison. "Let me show you."

Allison took the hand and Michela led her to her bed. Michela slowly undressed Allison, only pausing to scatter feather-soft kisses on her face to convey the depth of emotion she felt.

Allison put her fingers on the buttons of Michela's sleeping shirt, only to have them gently halted.

Michela pulled Allison's hand to her lips and tenderly kissed her fingers. "You don't have to do that."

Allison shook her head, a shy smile on her face. "But I want to. For so many nights I watched you undress, always disappointed when you got into bed." She lightly kissed Michela's cheek. "Please let me help."

Michela softly captured Allison's lips and guided Allison's hands to her shirt. They slowly undressed each other, relieved at the trust and passion that was reflected in each other's eyes. Finally naked, they stood and silently worshipped the other's body.

Michela reached across the small distance, and tenderly traced the curve of Allison's breast with the back of her fingers. "You are so incredibly beautiful."

Allison shuddered at the effect of Michela's touch.

Michela pulled Allison to her and revelled in the feel of skin against skin. She traced a lazy trail down Allison's back and rested her hand on her baby-soft backside.

Allison, hands lightly draped on Michela's waist, gasped at the sensation created by their closeness. Between ragged breaths, she kissed Michela's neck and looked up. "Please, baby, help me."

Michela snagged the sleeping bag off the other bed and put it next to her bag. She held out her hand to Allison and in return Allison silently took Michela's hand. Michela eased Allison onto the bed and climbed in next to her. As she did she offered a silent prayer of thanks at the wider beds now fitted in the apples.

Michela traced a gentle path over Allison's skin, barely touching her. She paused at the bottom of Allison's stomach and lightly played with the downy hair below her navel, before grazing the warm hollow near her waist. She traced Allison's breasts with feather-light touches, lovingly delivered with the back of her hand, intensely aware of Allison's building arousal. Halting her sensual path, she gazed into Allison's eyes. "Honey, I want to make love to you, but if I do anything you're not comfortable with please stop me. I'd never do anything to hurt you."

Allison sweetly smiled. She kissed Michela's palm and then shyly guided it to the swell of her breast. "I don't think you could ever hurt me." She sealed her words with a kiss.

Humbled by Allison's trust, Michela ever so gently kissed a trail of love over Allison's body. She was in turn rewarded by Allison's feather-light touches as they charted a path across Michela's body, tentatively grazing across Michela's breasts before retreating.

As their dance of love progressed, their touches became bolder, more certain, each quietly pleased at the sensations they created in the other. Murmuring words of love, Michela tenderly stroked Allison, barely containing her own response to Allison's ardour.

Sensing Michela's need, Allison captured her lips and shyly moved her thigh to meet Michela's centre. Passionately connected, they sensuously moved together, harmoniously building to a climax. They crested together and continued to move in exquisite synchronisation before finally slowing down, entwined around each other's body.

Regaining her breath, Michela looked at Allison. "Honey, are you all right?"

Allison stroked Michela's face. "Thank you. Thank you for being so patient with me. Thank you for putting up with my bad moods and my tantrums. But most of all, thank you for loving me." Her voice broke as her eyes misted with tears.

Fighting her own tears, Michela pulled Allison to her and tenderly kissed her forehead. "Always, my love, for forever and beyond."

WHILE THE STORM raged outside, Michela and Allison took the time to discover each other and were delighted at what they found. Their days passed peacefully, sometimes doing no more than completing their respective research, sometimes not getting out of bed at all. Occasionally they'd disagree on one issue or another.

Such discussions would lapse into arguments, end with stony silence, and then they would passionately reconcile their differences.

Finally, after seven days of being buffeted by the wind, Michela awoke, her body comfortably covered by Allison. She gently shook Allison. "Alli, honey, wake up."

Allison nuzzled the chest she'd used on and off as a pillow for the past few days. "Don't want to."

Michela smiled and kissed the top of Allison's head. "Okay, then just listen." Allison shifted and a couple of seconds later slumped against Michela. "What's the matter?"

Allison's voice was muffled as she clung to the Michela's body. "I don't want to go. Can't we stay here and let the rest of the world go on without us?"

Michela put her hand underneath Allison's chin and tilted her face up. "It'll be okay, trust me. I think I understand how you feel right now, but we'll work it out." She softly and lovingly kissed Allison's lips. "But if we don't get this place cleaned up, we're likely to have Sarah walk in on us."

Allison almost leapt from the bed. She quickly bathed and dressed and then helped in straightening the hut.

"Michela, this is Sarah, can I come over, over."

Michela and Allison laughed at Sarah's perfect timing—they'd just finished making the place presentable.

Sarah walked into the hut and observed the look that passed between Michela and Allison. "G'day you two. That was some storm wasn't it?" Trying to hide her "I told you so" smile, she looked at Allison and was surprised by a touch of reticence in her face. Puzzled, she glanced at Michela. Michela almost imperceptibly shook her head.

Breaking the slight tension, Michela clapped Sarah's shoulder. "Yes, it was. Now, how about some breakfast? Have we managed to regain communications with Wills Station yet?"

Sarah nodded. "That happened about four hours ago. Maddi suggested we finish breaking down the camp and then head for the station."

Allison slammed her cup on the counter, startling Michela and Sarah. They caught a brief glimpse of her angry expression before she turned away from them. Michela gave Sarah a "don't ask" look.

"She's right," Michela said. "We'll start with breakfast and then pull these huts down. That should take no more than a couple of hours and then we'll be on our way. Alli, how about we try some of Sarah's cooking for a change?"

Allison nodded, fighting back the irrational frustration at hearing Maddi Walker's name. While she was grateful for Michela's explanation of what had occurred between her and Maddi, she couldn't help but wonder if Maddi felt the same way. "That sounds like a plan. Let's go." Allison walked around Michela and Sarah and out the door.

Sarah gave Michela a quizzical look. "What's that about? I'm assuming that by the look you gave me that you two finally sorted out your differences."

"Yes, we did. But ever since this morning when we woke up and found the storm had passed over, she's progressively withdrawn into herself." *And not prepared to admit what's happened between the two of us to the world.*

Sarah rubbed Michela's back. "Give it time. It's got to be a hell of a change for her. Maybe the trip back with the four of us is what she needs to help sort herself out and what this change means to her."

Michela followed Sarah to the other apple. *I just hope that's all it is, and she's not having second thoughts. I don't think I could cope.*

Chapter
Eleven

My Darling Charlotte,

My love, the daylight hours grow shorter here as winter tightens its grip against Ian Ross and myself. Only yesterday our team member Malcolm Pitt, succumbed to the pneumonia that had racked his poor body for the last week. The weather is so forbidding and cold that it took us most of the day to dig any more than a pitifully shallow scrape in the ice. We sewed him into his sleeping bag and built a makeshift sled to take him to his final resting-place. After a short ceremony, we covered him and returned to the cold and loneliness of our hut.

Despite that only two of us remain, our food is slowly running out. As the days progress, even the simplest of tasks become a burden, made even more so by the injury to Ian's leg, which stubbornly refuses to heal. It is only my commitment to maintaining Ian's spirits that force me out of bed at all. However, I fear the day will soon be upon us when neither of us moves, consigning us to our own fate. To have come so far and hoped for so much, only to arrive at where we are now. How did I allow it to come to this?

ERF

Antarctica—2010

THE ABSENCE OF the BOB-trak allowed the team to return to Will's Station in their sno-trak at a comfortable cruising speed of twenty five miles an hour. Instead of the tedious nine days it had taken to get to the site, Rob estimated they would spend no more than two nights on the ice.

Taking advantage of the vehicle's speed, and after a quick discussion with Michela, Rob deviated from the original route and took them to a rookery, populated by emperor penguins and their recently hatched young.

For the first time since leaving the base, Allison surfaced from her introspective mood. The sound of the adult penguins was almost unbearable as they squawked over one another to be heard. She carefully walked to the rookery and smiled at the penguins as they waddled around her, as if her presence there was an everyday event. She took her video from its bag on her hip and filmed the adults, with their resplendent black and white plumage, trimmed by a neck of golden yellow. She softly laughed at their antics and at the sweet grey chicks that followed their parents' every step. Preoccupied in her task, she was startled by a crunch on the snow behind her.

Michela walked to Allison's side. "They're funny, aren't they? Last time I was down here I was taken to an Adelie penguin rookery. The Adelie are small compared to these and much more in keeping with the traditional black and white penguin."

Allison nodded, surprised and yet, awkwardly silenced by Michela's arrival. She finished her filming and returned her camera to its bag.

Michela brushed Allison's arm with her hand. Allison turned to her.

"Is anything wrong?" Michela asked.

Allison looked where Michela's hand rested, lightly grasping her wrist, and then gazed at the vista. *What is the matter with me? Only days ago everything seemed so perfect and now, well, I'm not so sure.* She returned her gaze to Michela. "No. I think I'm tired and a little bit disappointed that we didn't get a lot more done than we did at the dig site."

Michela shook her head. "You and the rest of your crew did wonders. You've established it well for any further excavations. Don't lessen the degree of what you achieved because you didn't uncover the complete hut." Michela took Allison's hand. "And besides, I'm proud of you."

Allison looked at the hand covering her own and then slowly released it. "I know. I wish we were back there, that's all."

Disappointed at Allison's detachment and yet sensing she wanted some time to herself, Michela softly rubbed Allison's back, before leaving her to her own thoughts.

Allison listened to Michela's footfall as she walked away, and winced at her actions. *Why did I do that when she touched me? Not less than twenty-four hours ago she touched me and I welcomed it. What's changed?*

The more she thought about her response to Michela's touch, the more confused she became. *I mean, I really do like her. But everything seems to have gotten a heck of a lot more complex. How am I supposed to act around her? Are we allowed to touch each other in public? Do I want her to touch me in public? What about what other people say? My friends have no idea what's gone on down here, not to mention my parents. And what about my job? What does this mean for my job?* She cursed the loss of the isolation and intimacy she'd shared with Michela during the final days at Finlayson camp and longed to return to the time when it was just her and Michela alone.

Hearing Rob calling her back, she trudged back to the sno-trak for the rest of their return journey.

MICHELA WATCHED AS Allison headed into the main building at Will's Station. Shaking her head, she went to the rear of the sno-trak to help Sarah unhook the container from the vehicle.

Sarah motioned her head at Allison. "So, how're things going between you two?"

Michela let out an exasperated breath. "I really don't know. It seems the closer we got to this place the more withdrawn she became."

Sarah pulled the trailer away from the sno-trak. "I saw

you talking at the rookery. Did she mention anything there?"

"No. She seems to be fine when there's the four of us, but when it's just us, she's almost reticent to discuss anything."

"Are you going to talk to her about it?"

Michela nodded. "Now we're back here and there's a bit more privacy, maybe I can sit down with her and talk this through." She closed her eyes and rubbed the back of her neck. She gazed at Sarah. "I really do like her. I wonder if she realises how much."

Sarah gently patted Michela's back. "Give it time, my friend, give it time."

ALLISON CLOSED THE door of her allocated room and released a sigh. For the first time in a long while she was finally alone. While privacy was a luxury she'd longed for during her time on the ice, it now had a new meaning— being alone with Michela. Now she could no longer look forward to quiet moments alone with Michela.

Allison pulled from her pack clothes that were sorely in need of a decent wash as she tried work through her confusion over her actions with Michela during the return journey. While she felt as if she'd at last found comfort and loving security in Michela's arms, the thought of returning to civilisation and its associated pressures clouded her thinking. *What do I really want?*

She jumped at the knock on her door. She opened it and was greeted by a smiling Sarah. Sarah walked into the small room, jumped onto the bed, and made herself comfortable. Allison smiled. "Come in."

"Thanks, I thought I'd see what you were up to. As surprising as it may seem, Rick and Di made themselves useful while they were back here. Everything's good to go for the trip home." Sarah crossed her outstretched legs. "So, have you got any plans when you get back to Australia? Any possible holiday plans with *someone else* perhaps?"

Allison blushed, strangely uncomfortable that the relationship between herself and Michela was so transparent. "You know."

Sarah waved her hand. "Of course I do and I have to say it's about time. Most of the eight weeks you two spent together were wasted on dancing around the subject. Sometimes the two of you clash, but most of the time you're right for each other."

Exasperated, Allison flopped down on the bed. "How is it you know we're so right for each other and yet I'm not so sure? I mean, I really do care for Michela, but I'm not certain whether I'm ready to commit to anything and everything that goes with it."

"Have you spoken with Michela?" Allison shook her head. "What is it that concerns you the most?"

"There're so many things. As you said, sometimes we argue like cats and dogs. Not to mention, she's on one side of the world and I'm on the other. What does this mean to her job? Hell, I didn't even know I was out and now do I have to be? How do I know this relationship isn't a case of two people being thrown together in the right circumstances and nothing else?"

Sarah took Allison's hands. "I know this is different to what you've experienced before on a personal level, but let me try and clear a few things up. Yes, you argue like cats and dogs, but how long do you really stay mad at each other? Yes, she's on the other side of the world and that's a major hurdle. One that only you and she can overcome. I don't know what it means to Michela's job and as for you, when did anyone say you had to be out? That's a personal choice, Alli, and one I don't think Michela's going to demand as a prerequisite for any relationship."

Allison nodded. "I understand. It's so much to absorb all at once."

"And finally, regarding your last comment, let me ask you one thing." Sarah searched Allison's face. "Do you honestly believe this is no more than a case of two people being thrown together under the right circumstances? How do you really feel about her?"

Allison closed out all the external pressures and centralised her thoughts, her mind surprisingly clear. She smiled. "She moves me like no one else has ever done. She touches emotional depths I never knew existed. She holds me when I hurt and comforts me through the pain. I've never felt this way about anyone before."

"Then I think you've answered your own question. Mind you, I still think you two need to sit down and talk about it. But, for the moment, were you going to the laundry? I've also got a heap of washing to do."

Allison stood and threw her dirty clothing into her laundry bag. "I do. It's amazing the amount of dirt that piles up after only weeks of basic washing."

MICHELA STRETCHED OUT full-length on her bed, disdainful of the request on the back door to first remove her shoes before lying down. *This is so much different to that apple. I particularly like the do not disturb and please make up my room sign that someone snatched from a hotel. Someone certainly had a keen sense of humour.* She nuzzled into her pillow and groaned at the knock on the door. She got up, opened the door, and smiled at Maddi, before seeing her tears. "What is it?"

"I'm sorry to disturb you," Maddi said. "I was wondering if I could speak with you. On a professional basis if I could."

Michela motioned for Maddi to enter and put the "do not disturb" sign on the doorknob before closing the door.

"What is it? What's happened?"

"It's my father. I just got off the satellite phone to mum. He was working on the roof yesterday and he suffered a massive stroke. He died last night in the hospital," Maddi said. "God, he was my rock. He loved me no matter how many times I caused him to consider otherwise. When I came out all he said was 'you're my daughter and if you're happy then that's all that matters.' I'm so lost without him." Maddi sobbed and fell into Michela's arms.

Michela rested Maddi's head on her shoulder, holding her as she grieved. She raised her eyes at the sound of her door opening, slightly annoyed to think that someone would disregard the sign she'd placed on her door. Allison stood in the doorway, taking in the intimate sight before her. Before Michela could say anything Allison turned and slammed the door.

Controlling her anger, Michela continued to comfort Maddi and finally managed to get her to talk through some of her grief. After an hour of consoling, she helped Maddi back to her quarters and some well-needed rest.

Michela strode toward Allison's room and stormed through the door, not bothering to knock.

Allison jumped up from the bed and glared at Michela. "How dare you enter without knocking!"

"How dare I enter without knocking?" Michela countered. "That's a lesson you could well learn. What part of a 'do not disturb' sign don't you understand?"

"Isn't that convenient, or do you carry one of those with you everywhere you go?" Allison challenged. "You must think it's a great opportunity here, getting the best of both worlds. Isn't one woman enough for you that you have to pursue two?"

Michela couldn't believe she was having this conversation. "Not that it's really any of your business but I was consoling Maddi, not engaging in foreplay."

"*Really?*" Allison spat back.

Shocked by Allison's venom, Michela closed the door, took a deep breath, and then slowly released it. "Is that what you really think?" she asked quietly. "Do you really believe that I'd think so little of what happened out there between us?" She took a step forward and Allison turned away from her. "Alli, please tell me what you're thinking." Silence was the reply.

Michela shook her head. *I should have known. On the trip back to base I should have known where this was heading. She's changed her mind.*

"Alli, honey, I can't be in a relationship like this where there seems to be so little trust. I'd never dream of hurting you but you're hurting me now with your silence, can't you see that? Either you trust me or you don't." She put her hand on Allison's shoulder. Allison shrugged it off.

"Please don't," Allison whispered.

"What is it? Speak to me," Michela pleaded.

Allison shook her head. "I can't."

Michela stared at Allison, who continued to focus on the window. "I'm only going to say this once. If I walk out that door, that's it. I'll know that whatever we started out there will have meant so little to you and that I was no more than an experiment." She waited in the silence and then hung her head in resignation. "I suppose it's goodbye." Michela walked out of the room and quietly closed the door.

Allison turned around, tears staining her cheeks. She started for the door and then stopped. She slumped her shoulders, collapsed onto her bed, and wept at how quickly her life had slipped from ideal into a living nightmare.

SARAH CHUCKLED AT the raucous noise emanating from the Wills Station bar. *Is that Michela? It sounds like she and Alli managed to square things away.* She entered the bar and was surprised to find Michela alone, drunkenly crooning to the jukebox for all she was worth.

Michela swayed with the music and looked at Sarah with glazed eyes. "Sarah! Glad you could make it," she slurred and drank from the mug in her unsteady hand. "These people are all party peep, party pop, party poopers. I tried to start a sing along, but they all left me."

Sarah went to Michela's side and stepped back from the reek of alcohol that wafted off her. "Whoa, I think you've had more than your fair share tonight, sailor." She eased Michela into a chair. "Where's Allison?"

Michela flopped into her chair, dropped her mug, and put her head in her hands. "It's over. Over before it even started. She hates me. Won't talk to me," she slurred.

Sarah stared at the change in Michela. "I think you're probably reading it wrong." She pulled Michela from the chair and slung Michela's arm around her shoulder. "Come on, how about we get you to bed and resolve everything in the morning."

Michela staggered as Sarah tried to walk her to the door. "No, she hates me, trust me, she doesn't—" She hiccoughed and collapsed in a drunken stupor.

Sarah cursed as she pulled Michela over her shoulder. "That's just bloody great, where's Rob when you need him?"

MICHELA WOKE TO a knocking that reverberated around the insides of her skull before seeping out through her eye sockets. She sat up and the room seemed to tilt.

Instinctively she closed her eyes and lay back down.

"Come in."

Sarah entered and closed the door. "I think I'll say morning, because you certainly don't look so good." She sat on the bed and touched the back of her hand to Michela's forehead. "No temperature. Must have been something in the ice cubes last night." She wryly smiled and pulled a bottle of pills from the medicine bag.

Michela opened her eyes and attempted to swallow. She looked around, saw a glass of water on her bedside table, and greedily drank it. "Just what I need this morning—a bloody glaciologist with attitude."

Sarah unscrewed the top of a water bottle she'd brought with her. "I've no doubt that's just what you need. Especially when the glaciologist, *who's also a physician,* comes bearing gifts. Here, take these." She gave the water and two pills to Michela.

Michela tried to focus on the pills in her hand. "What are they?"

"They're hangover tablets. While they won't take away the pain completely, they'll bring your system back on an even keel. That, coupled with this," Sarah held up a clear fluid bag, "is going to get you back on track."

Michela frowned. "How do you expect me to drink that?"

Sarah laughed. "I don't. I'm going to cannulate you to replace some of the fluids you've managed to lose over the past twelve hours."

Michela attempted to sit up. "Don't you use big words on me, you damned quack. You're going to stick a big needle into me."

"That's the general idea. Trust me, this'll work wonders. I should know. When I was an intern, I used it after more parties than I care to count. That coupled with the pills should see you good to go in about an hour or so."

Michela winced at the thought of having to tolerate her headache another hour. Watching Sarah, she yelped as the needle penetrated her skin.

Sarah checked the flow of the bag. "Stay there and I'll be back in about five minutes."

True to her word, Sarah strolled through the door a few minutes later with breakfast in hand.

Michela just managed to swallow the bile caused by the smell of food. "What is that?" she asked through gritted teeth.

Sarah put the tray on the bedside table. "It's all part of the cure. It starts with some Vegemite toast. This stuff's chock full of vitamin B and believe me when I say you need all the help you can get with vitamin B. Next, we'll move on to some bacon and baked beans." Michela scrunched her pale face. "The baked beans are another dose of vitamin B and the fat on the bacon will do a great job of lining your stomach."

Michela held her up hand. "Stop. Has anyone ever told you your bedside manner is woeful? Give me the food and let me get this over and done with."

Sarah stood and watched as Michela fought her way through the meal. Michela put the tray on the bedside table, grabbed her cup, and took a sip of black coffee. When Michela was finished, Sarah sat on the bed. "So, do you want to tell me why you got yourself into such a state last night?"

Michela leant back on her pillow. Closing her eyes, she recalled the night before. After leaving Allison, she'd paced the halls in an attempt to vent her frustration and found herself outside the station bar. She opened her eyes and gazed at Sarah. "I'd rather not talk about it."

"I know this must seem like a kind of a role reversal to you, but don't you think it would be better if you did?"

Michela vigorously shook her head and winced. "There's been enough of that already. All I want to do is get on with my life. I want to finish what has to be done here, get on a boat, sail to Hobart, hop on a plane, and head back to the States."

Sarah tilted her head. "Just like that?"

"*Just* like that."

Sarah folded her arms. "You know, you're so full of crap it's a wonder it's not coming out of your eyes. If you think I believe you can switch off your emotions that easily then you're sorely mistaken. I don't know what went on last night and I can't find Allison to ask her. I've no doubt she'd be singing the same tune as you. You *need* to talk about this. We can do it now or later, but you need to get it off your chest."

Michela gently put her head in her hands to halt the hockey game inside her skull. She patted Sarah's hand. "Not now. It's too soon and there's too much to do. Maybe once we're under way."

Sarah shook her head. "There's no maybe about it. We'll be talking, even if I have to beat it out of you." Sarah rose and checked the drip. "You've got another hour before that runs through. Why don't you sit here and work out the flight schedule for the trip to the ship."

Frustrated, Michela raised her face to the ceiling and sighed heavily, and then gazed at Sarah. "That's today, isn't it?"

"Yep, but fortunately for you the helo's been delayed. We're not expected to see it before midday. Time enough for you to be back on your feet."

Michela smiled that at least something was going right for her. "I guess Alli will need your help for the flight. Can you speak with her and see if she wants you to administer a small relaxant for the helo flight?"

"No problem. Will you be flying with her to the ship?"

Although she wanted to, Michela was fairly certain that Allison didn't want to be around her. "No, I think it'd be for the better if you were to accompany her. I'll make sure everything is good to go here and then catch the last flight."

Sarah nodded and went to the door. "We should be under steam by the end of the day. I'll be back in an hour to take that needle out of you. If you give me the crew manifest then, I'll ensure everyone's made aware of when they're flying."

Michela watched as Sarah closed the door behind her. Despite the combination of the pills and the drip working its magic, Michela felt miserable. What was worse was the knowledge that the misery would be with her for a long time.

SARAH LED A lightly sedated Allison to the helicopter, secured her in her seat, and climbed in the other side. After securing her own safety harness, Sarah turned to Allison, whose attention was focussed on something outside. Sarah leant as far forward as the harness would allow and looked across to the edge of the LZ to where Michela was standing, hands shoved into the pockets of her cold weather jacket.

Unable to see Allison's face, Sarah lightly touched her shoulder and Allison turned, her eyes filled with tears. Taking Allison's hand, Sarah leant to her ear to be heard over the engine. "It's okay. It won't be a long flight. We'll be on the ship in no time."

Allison shook her head, her senses dulled by the drugs. "She's leaving me. I thought she'd always be there for me and instead she's leaving me."

Sarah once again stared out the window at Michela on the side of the tarmac. She gripped Allison's hands. "She's not doing that, sweetie. She's going to join us on the boat, you'll see."

Allison shook her head as she wept. "No, she's leaving me, and I don't blame her."

Michela, on the side of the landing pad, patted the pockets of her jacket for her sunglasses to combat the glare of the helicopter's reflective windows. She watched the helicopter rise from the LZ, turn one hundred and eighty degrees and head toward the horizon. She was thankful that Allison was finally safe and on her way.

Maddi waved and crossed the small tarmac to her.

"How are you feeling this morning?" Michela asked.

Maddi sadly smiled. "It's going to take some time before I work through this. I wish you were staying a bit longer so I could talk to you about it."

Michela removed a pen and a small notepad from her jacket. "I think it's about time for me to go. But if you want to talk about it, here's my e-mail address and phone number. Contact me at any time. I'll be happy to help." She tore the page from the notepad and handed it to Maddi.

"Do you have time for a coffee before you go?" Maddi asked.

Michela watched the helicopter that was now a speck on the horizon. "Possibly a quick one. This guy's turn around time is pretty swift."

After a cup of coffee, they returned to the LZ and the waiting helicopter. Michela hugged Maddi and took a final look at the continent that had been her home for about the past eight weeks. After resolutely nodding, she hopped into the helicopter and strapped herself in. At least the first part of her homeward journey would soon be over.

MICHELA SPENT THE sea journey finalising her report. She avoided most of the team by eating outside the standard meal breaks, and usually in her room. When she ventured onto the decks, she often saw a windswept Allison staring at the ocean. Although she wanted to speak with Allison, she always hesitated. For when Allison saw her, she would return her attention to the ocean. Michela finally stopped going to the deck and kept to her room, seeking solace in her own company.

Michela sighed at the sharp rap on her door after six days of peaceful solitude. She opened the door and found Sarah standing there, an exasperated look on her face. Before she could say anything, Sarah strode into the small room.

Michela closed the door, folded her arms, and leant against the frame. "You know, I'm beginning to wonder whether it's got something to do with me. No one seems to wait to be invited in these days."

Sarah shook her finger at Michela. "Don't you start. I've been checking around and no one's seen you for days." She squinted at Michela's face and lightly pinched her stomach. "When was the last time you had a decent meal?"

Michela blushed. "I had a sandwich this morning, I think." She scratched her head. "What day is it again?"

Sarah lightly slapped her. "It's too long since you ate last, that's what day it is. Now, we're going to have something to eat and you're going to explain exactly what happened at the station. And don't give me that look. That's not going to work. Either we discuss this or I'm not leaving until you do."

Defeated, Michela sat on her bed. "It's too painful to go out. When I do, I run into Allison and by the looks on her face she isn't happy to see me."

Sarah leant against the table and gazed at Michela's tired face. "Have you tried to speak with her?"

"I have, but when I approach her, she turns away," Michela said quietly.

Sarah pulled out a chair and sat down. "So, what did happen back at the station?"

Michela ran her fingers through her hair at the none-too-pleasant memory. "As you've probably guessed we argued. Again. Allison walked in on Maddi and me." She held up her hand. "No, it wasn't what you're thinking. Maddi had just learned that her father had died and wanted to talk to someone on a professional level. I don't like to be disturbed when dealing with someone who's grieving. Some past occupant of the room had left behind a hotel's 'do not disturb' sign, so I used that to prevent any unwelcome guests. As I was comforting Maddi in my arms, Allison walked in unannounced, incorrectly summed up the situation and left, loudly."

Sarah cringed. "She really does have something against Maddi, doesn't she? I wonder if from the first day she subconsciously figured her as a potential rival?"

Michela shrugged. "I don't know if that's the case, but I can tell you she wasn't happy with what she saw. I over reacted and yelled at her, asking her why she'd barged into my room and she basically accused me of being with two women at the same time, something I've never, *never* done. I tried to reason with her but she wouldn't let me near her. I assumed she'd changed her mind about our relationship—"

"Are you serious?" Sarah asked. "You see the way she looks at you. Confused, maybe. Changed her mind—I don't think so."

"Then how do you explain how she acted on the journey from the dig site?"

Sarah smiled. "I had the chance to talk to her when we got back to the station. There were a lot of issues going through her mind during that trip. I've no doubt she was on her way to discuss those with you when she walked in on you and Maddi."

Michela laughed. "That's just my luck. Timing has never been one of my strong points."

Sarah tilted her head. "So what are you going to do about it?"

Michela crossed her legs and arms. "Nothing. I've had time to think about this and maybe what happened between us was no more than two people thrown together

in extreme circumstances who were both emotionally fragile and looking for an anchor. I'm sorry, but I've tried
enough. To coin one of your phrases, I think I'd like to let
sleeping dogs lie."

"If you do that, then you're a bigger fool than I
thought you were," Sarah said. "You're mad about her.
She's mad about you. But if you want to throw something
this good away then so be it."

"It's too painful. Between Natalie and Allison, these
past ten months has seen my emotions pulled every which
way and I don't think I can take much more. No, it's up to
Alli now." Michela stood and opened her small closet. She
pulled out a jacket and put it on. "Now, how about we go
and get something to eat so I can get back to my research."

ON THE FINAL night, during a ship's gathering in the
games room, Sarah looked up and saw Allison's wan face.
Despite being in a group of attentive young men, Allison
seemed lost, looking around as if she were looking for her
anchor. *Unfortunately Michela's still in her room.* Realising
Allison was seeking a polite means to remove herself from
the male gathering, Sarah went to her side.

"There you are. I've been looking for you everywhere.
There's a leak in one of the containers from the dig site and
the captain was wondering what you wanted to do about
it." Allison headed to the doorway before Sarah could finish her sentence. Sarah excused herself to the group of
young men, caught up with Allison, and snagged her arm.
"Hey, not so fast. There's no emergency. I made that up.
You looked as if you were keen to get away from that lot."

Allison's face alternated between mild anger at being
tricked and relief. "Thanks, I was beginning to think I was
a fish in a very small pond of sharks. I think I'll head back
to my room."

"No problem, I'll walk you."

The pair silently walked until they reached Allison's
door. Allison opened the door and walked into the room,
followed by Sarah. "As a matter of fact I think I'll come in.
That is, if you don't mind."

"I know what you're doing and I really don't want to
talk about it."

Sarah stretched out on the bed and placed her hands behind her head. "Too bad. I've had about enough of you two. There're some things you need to know before you make up your mind. If you listen to me I promise not to bother you any more. After I'm finished, the decision will be yours."

Allison closed the door. "I suppose it's the only way I'm going to get rid of you."

Sarah smiled. "I'm glad you see it my way. I know something happened between you and Michela after I'd spoken to you and before I found her as drunk as a lord in the Wills Station bar the night before we left." She paused at Allison's surprised look.

"I didn't think she drank that much."

"I don't think she did until then," Sarah replied. "All I could get out of her were ramblings that something had happened between the two of you and no more. It was only yesterday I got a better picture."

Allison's face reddened as she remembered how she'd found Michela and Maddi. "So, you know she was seeing Maddi?"

Sarah's features softened. "Oh, Alli, it wasn't like that at all. Yes, Michela and Maddi had a very brief interlude during the voyage on the way to Antarctica, but that was only one night. Trust me, I know Maddi and she was only really interested in scratching an itch, and Michela was the itch. What you saw at the station before you left was Michela comforting Maddi." Allison snorted. "No, listen, please. Maddi lost her father that day and had only just received the news. Michela was doing no more than comforting her after Maddi had asked for her professional help. Do you really think Michela would overstep her professional bounds and compromise her reputation?"

Allison tried to recall exactly what she'd seen. *But how do I know for sure?* She answered her own question as she remembered Michela's work ethic and their discussions during the storm. Michela had admitted she'd strong feelings for Allison for a long time, but her promise and professionalism meant she'd never acted on them. *So why would she do so now?* Allison raised her eyes to Sarah. "I believe you, but I think it's too late. I let her walk away. What's done is done."

Sarah got up from the bed and took Allison's hand. "Only if you want it to be." She looked at her watch. "It's after two, so now's probably not a good time. Why don't you try and talk with her in the morning? Believe me, I think she'll be willing to listen." Her eyes twinkled.

Allison awkwardly hugged Sarah. "Thanks for having the patience to verbally pound some sense into me."

Sarah returned the hug. "You two were made for each other. Now, if I can only get the two of you to realise this at exactly the same time then I'll be a happy woman."

AFTER THINKING ABOUT how she would approach Michela, Allison finally drifted off to sleep at four in the morning. It was some time later when she finally awoke with a start. She looked at her watch and launched herself out of bed. After a quick shower, she lightly jogged to Michela's room.

"Allison, there you are," Dianne said when Allison was within sight of Michela's door. Allison sighed and turned around. "They're unloading the containers and they want to know where and how you want them laid on the wharf. I'd have asked Rick, but he's still seasick. Do you think you can let them know?"

So, Di, now you know what it feels like to run after that pain in the backside. "I'll head down there now. Do you think you and Rick can manage once I get the load onto the wharf? I've got a couple of things I need to see to."

"I'm sure we can. Once I get Rick onto solid ground he should be a lot better." Dianne turned and walked quickly down the corridor.

"Thanks to you, too," Allison muttered. She stopped at Michela's door and placed her palm on the door, making a silent promise to return.

MICHELA FINISHED PACKING, looked around for any stray belongings, and checked the cupboard one last time. She looked at the door, feeling disappointed that Sarah had got it wrong. She was certain Sarah was going to talk with Allison. *Well, there you go, Sarah. It seems Alli wasn't so interested after all.*

MAKING SENSE OF the unloading of the artefacts took a lot longer than Allison had first expected. She knocked at Michela's door before seeing the access card in its slot.

"Michela," she called, as she pushed on the access card and the door. Her hopes plummeted as she looked at the Spartan emptiness of the room, and she slumped against the wall in defeat. *Surely she hadn't left so soon. Maybe she's on the deck.* She pushed away from the wall and ran down the gangway and toward the bow of the ship.

MICHELA TOOK HER time as she adjusted to solid ground. She shook out her legs, found her bags, and loaded them onto a small trolley.

She watched Rick and Dianne, who were preoccupied with unloading the cargo further down the wharf and her thoughts returned to the dig site.

Michela couldn't help but feel a sense of loss over her failure with Allison. She gazed up one final time at the lines of the ship that had brought her one step closer to her homeward journey and found herself staring straight into Allison's eyes as she stood at the ship's bow.

"Michela," Allison called above the din.

Before she could respond to Allison's hail, Michela felt hands encircle her waist. She turned and yelped in surprise. "Chrissie, what are you doing here?"

Christine laughed. "Can't a sister greet her explorer from the ends of the earth? That's the way it's done isn't it? And besides, I was in Hong Kong for a conference and this was too good an opportunity to let pass."

"You're mad, you know. Greetings were usually done by husbands or wives. Just a moment, there's someone I'd like you to meet." Michela turned and sadness overwhelmed her. Allison was gone.

Houston—2010

MICHELA GATHERED HER notes as Dr. Reilly completed his conference call. He rubbed his hands together and smiled. "That went well. I think the board's convinced that your time in Antarctica was well spent. Your research should exponentially speed up our Mars project. Well done."

Michela nodded. "Thank you. There were days I didn't think I was ever going to get it finished. Between the project and calls from the coroner in Hobart, regarding Ewan McMillan's death, I was surprised I managed to find the time." She'd provided the coroner with a report, as well as the contact details of the rest of the team. Out of professional courtesy and vain hope of a reply, Michela had e-mailed Allison, advising her of the coroner's keenness to interview the team. Although her system identified the e-mail had been opened, there was no response.

William nodded. "So what's next?"

Michela picked up her digital tablet. "Back to the project, I guess. Ms. Finlayson has asked me to come to her country home next week and personally provide a report. If you don't mind, I'd like to take a couple of days to visit her."

"Given her funding made the project worthwhile," Dr. Reilly said, "it's the least we can do."

MICHELA SMILED WHEN the same driver who'd taken her to Charlotte's office before was waiting for her at the small airport. During the drive to the estate, she entertained him with tales of ice flows and icebergs on the Great Southern Ocean.

Michela couldn't help but stare when they drove through wrought iron gates. The car crept up a tree-lined drive and stopped in front of an imposing mansion.

Michela was hard pressed not to stare at the grand home in front of her. Her preoccupation was interrupted as she felt the driver beside her.

"It's beautiful, isn't it?" the driver asked as he pulled Michela's bag out of the car. "It's been in the family for well over a hundred years. Ms. Finlayson's namesake lived here for most of her life. Anyway, we better get you inside before Ella chews my ears off."

Almost on cue, one of the double doors to the mansion opened and a short, elderly woman, dressed in a grey skirt and pastel violet cashmere pullover, stood on the porch with her arms crossed.

"That's Ella," the driver whispered and then walked up the stairs.

"Where have you been, old man?" Ella asked in a soft southern accent. "You must be Dr. DeGrasse, Miss Charlotte's guest. I'm Ella, part housekeeper, part secretary to Miss Charlotte."

Michela extended her hand. "Please, Dr. DeGrasse is my mother. I'd very much prefer if you'd call me Michela."

"That's a lovely name," Ella said. "Miss Charlotte has asked me to place you in the east wing, so if you'll follow me." She turned and walked through the doorway.

Michela took her bag from the driver, thanked him, and hefted it onto her shoulder. "I gather Ms. Finlayson's not here. When is she due?"

Ella lightly chuckled. "Just like people your age. Always the destination, never the journey. Miss Charlotte's here, but she's at the family cemetery. She asked if you could join her there."

Michela nodded. "You're right. I'm sorry for being so direct. How about you show me to my room and we'll take it from there."

Ella gave her a brief tour, taking in what Michela surmised to be only the key rooms of the magnificent home. As she looked at the treasures in the rooms shown to her, she realised that Elizabeth's descendants had followed in her footsteps. The walls of more than one room were liberally dotted with collections from one expedition or another, all with an obvious tale to tell. Ella finished the tour in the kitchen and offered Michela a homemade glass of lemonade before pointing her in the direction of the family cemetery.

Michela crested a small hill and gasped at the view. On the forward slopes was a small cemetery overlooking the wooded valley below. In the distance were mountain ranges, their multi-coloured leaves reflecting in the twilight sun. Returning her gaze to the small family plot, she spied a jean-clad Charlotte bent over a headstone in the cemetery.

Michela walked to a small gate that signalled the entrance to the plot. The gate creaked as she pushed it open, and Charlotte rose to greet her, surprising her with a hug.

"My intrepid explorer returns," Charlotte said. "By the looks of it, the trip took a lot out of you. What have you been doing to look so awful?"

Michela laughed at Charlotte's bluntness. "I've been working too hard and not getting enough food or sleep. But I finished the last of my presentations for the Institute the other day, so maybe my life can get back to normal."

"Maybe it can." Charlotte eagerly grasped Michela's hand. "Let me show you something."

Charlotte led Michela to a pair of gravestones. One was very old with corners touched by the moss and lichen that had leeched into the old basalt. Michela knelt down and read the inscription:

> Here lies Charlotte Louise Finlayson
> Beloved mother of Robert Finlayson
> and Beloved wife of Elizabeth Robyn Finlayson
> Born 1866, Died 1949
> Even in Death I Will Not Be Parted

The other headstone was of freshly cut basalt. Unlike the gilt on the older stone, the gold inscription on the modern one was clear and bold:

> Here lies Elizabeth Robyn Finlayson
> Beloved mother of Robert Finlayson
> and Beloved wife of Charlotte Louise Finlayson
> Born 1858, Died 1897, Laid to rest 2010
> Together at last – Even in Death I Will Not Be Parted

Overcome with emotion, Michela dried her eyes with her handkerchief, then stood and gazed at Charlotte. "You knew all along, didn't you?"

"That Eric was actually Elizabeth?" Michela nodded. "Of course I did. That's why I wanted you as the team leader. I knew I could rely on your tolerance, given your own circumstances."

Michela blinked at Charlotte. "You know about me?"

"Of course I know about your lifestyle choice; and don't look so surprised. You really didn't think I'd have allowed you to lead the expedition if I didn't check your background first? In my wildest dreams, I never thought you'd find my grandmother but I'm eternally grateful you did."

Michela shook her head. "I'm afraid I can't take all the credit. It was the dig team that made the discovery." She gazed at the two stones. Thinking of the many discussions about the two women she and Allison had shared during the storm, she knew Allison would be grateful to see their final resting-place. "I know this is a strange request. Would you mind if I took a picture of the stones?"

Charlotte smiled. "Not at all. But then we should head down to the house. It might be spring, but the late afternoon chill settles quickly on these old bones of mine. And, besides, I'm sure you've a number of questions you're dying to ask."

Michela took three photographs with her PDA. The setting was just perfect, with the rays of the evening sun reflecting off the polished basalt, bringing the gold inscriptions into relief. Despite Allison's reticence to answer her e-mail, Michela knew she'd be eager to see this. After checking the pictures, she placed the PDA in her pocket, and followed Charlotte down to the house and into the drawing room.

After light refreshments, they sat in the comfortable chairs, waiting for the other to start.

"Do you mind if I ask you a question?" Michela asked.

Charlotte chuckled. "I'm sure you've got more than one. Ask away. If I don't wish to answer, I won't."

"Why didn't you tell me the truth about Elizabeth's gender?"

Charlotte pointed at Michela. "Ah, so you think I lied to you, but I didn't. If you remember when we entered the office, you looked at the painting of my grandparents that hung behind my desk. I told you I was named after my grandmother, both of them in fact. My name is Charlotte Elizabeth Finlayson. It was only after you referred to Elizabeth as Eric that I saw no need to correct the mistake."

Michela tilted her head. "But why?"

Charlotte grinned. "People often see what they want to see and little else. You chose to see my grandmother as Eric and I saw no need to change that. Truth be told, I didn't hold out much hope that you would find her remains and now that you have, the secret is well and truly out in the open."

"Does that bother you?"

Charlotte shook her head. "No, not at all."

"You're aware we found her diary down there and it's in Australia at the Flinders Museum." Charlotte nodded. "I know this next question is a bit forward and you may chose not to answer, but were they lovers, or was their arrangement more of a Boston marriage?"

Charlotte chuckled. "Yes, they were lovers in the true sense of the word. My grandmother Charlotte lost her husband shortly after the birth of her child. By her diary accounts, she met my grandmother Elizabeth at a presentation she attended on an expedition Elizabeth had conducted to China. What you have to understand is that when Elizabeth was in the public eye she always dressed as a man and no one knew the difference. By Charlotte's accounts, when the two set eyes on each other it was love at first sight. Elizabeth shied away, aware of the precariousness of her own situation and fearful of Charlotte's reaction. In her diary my grandmother Charlotte speaks of the culminating event in their relationship. Elizabeth had a dinner party here and invited a number of guests, of which Charlotte was one. Throughout the night Charlotte was open with her feelings, but Elizabeth still shied away. It wasn't until late in the evening that Charlotte managed to find Elizabeth alone in the library. She locked the door and took the explorer into her arms. She whispered two words into Elizabeth's ear. 'I know.' She'd known Elizabeth's secret all along, it was just Elizabeth wouldn't stand still long enough for Charlotte to tell her. They married and lived as man and wife or, more correctly, wife and wife."

Michela sat back. *If only Alli could hear that. It's a story worthy of a movie.* "What a lovely story. It's a shame they couldn't live as two women in a loving relationship."

Charlotte nodded. "Yes, it's unfortunate how things turn out. But I think the thing that hurt Grandmother

Charlotte the most occurred when she was told of her lover's death." She took a sip of tea.

"About eighteen months or so after the expedition had departed, which was a good four months after it was due to return, Charlotte was visited by the American National Exploration and Philanthropic Society. They'd sponsored a great deal of the expedition. The reason they visited was to tell Charlotte of her husband's death. Although they couldn't be sure, given how he was overdue, they felt he'd most likely perished on Antarctica. They reassured her, explaining how he'd be lauded as one of the great explorers of his time. It was then that Charlotte let the cat out of the bag so to speak, explaining he was actually a she. As she records in her diary the group was shocked and disgusted, and left shortly thereafter."

Michela sadly shook her head. "That's disgraceful."

"Yes it is, but there's more. Doesn't it strike you as strange that you've never heard much about the failed expedition?"

"Come to think of it, yes, it does," Michela said.

"That's because there was very little publicity about Elizabeth's death made by the Society, given that it would be scandalous to announce that the first explorer on the continent was not only dead but a woman who lived with another woman under the veil of marriage. The memorial service was small and I'm being generous when I say that. Since then there's been little recognition until now. And I have you to thank for that." Charlotte patted Michela's hand.

That would explain why Alli had such difficulty finding out information. It was covered up by a group of men who couldn't bear to think they'd been hoodwinked. "Even though I led the expedition, it was the archaeological team, led by Dr. Shaunessy that really did all the hard work."

"What's this Dr. Shaunessy like?" Charlotte asked. "Can she be trusted? I only ask because I'm looking for someone to possibly oversee any future digs I might finance."

Michela sat back as thoughts of Allison filled her mind. For the past month she'd done a very good job of trying to forget her, but the floodgate of memories was broken. "I don't think you could ask for a better woman than Alli. She's committed to Finlayson. Part of her Doctoral dissertation was on his expedition."

"Yes, I know. I have a copy of it in my bookcase if you're interested."

Michela looked around. "I'd be very interested in reading her work. Thank you for the offer. As I was saying, she's very committed." Michela's eyes shone and a small smile of reminiscence graced her features. "Sometimes she can be passionate and hard-headed about her work, but her heart's always in the right place. I don't think I could recommend anyone more highly."

Charlotte gazed at Michela. "Do you mind if I asked you a question?"

Michela graciously tilted her head. "That's only fair."

"Did something happen between the two of you? Were you more than just friends?"

Michela knew her pain was evident on her face, although she tried to look as expressionless as possible. "Yes, we were, but for a very short time. It's over now."

"I'm sorry to hear that. You speak so highly of her." Charlotte looked around as if searching for something. "As a matter of fact, I'm expecting a call from her tonight regarding the arrangements for grandmother's body. It's been in the damned hands of Australian customs for the past month now. Do you know that the Patron of Flinders Museum called me and asked if he could show the body?"

"No, I didn't," Michela said. "But having had dealings with his daughter, his actions don't surprise me at all."

Charlotte slapped her knee. "I can tell you one thing, that's not going to happen. And if I have my way, I'm going to buy the complete Finlayson artefacts from him, once they've spent a reasonable time in his Museum. That's my grandmother's history he's hawking and I want it home. And besides, her final resting place is waiting for her."

"When are you going to be able to take charge of the body?"

"That's what Dr. Shaunessy's going to let me know." The visual-phone rang. "That should be her now." She walked across the room and pushed a button on a console and an image of Allison materialised.

As Charlotte discussed the matter of her grandmother's body, Michela stayed out of Allison's view. Her heart ached at Allison's gaunt features, and how exhausted she looked.

"In fact, I've someone here you may wish to talk to," Charlotte said. "Michela come here."

Michela's eyes widened and then she tried to relax. She walked to the visual-phone, heart beating in double time. Charlotte patted her arm, stepped away from her, and left the room. She met Allison's eyes and, for what seemed like forever, they stared at each other. "Hello, Alli. How are you?"

Allison wanly smiled. "Okay, I suppose. I've been very busy with the Finlayson artefacts and trying to clear Ms. Finlayson's ancestor through customs. And I thought getting out of Australia was bad when you're alive; this is horrendous."

They laughed although Allison looked as awkward as Michela felt.

"So how are things at the Museum?" Michela asked.

"There've been a few changes since we got back. Rick's been removed. It seems someone got wind of his indirect involvement in Ewan's death. There was a media circus and old man Peterson asked for his resignation. When Rick didn't resign, Peterson removed him. Dianne dropped him like a brick and she's now heading up the Museum's archaeological department. So, you could say I currently work for her. But I'm fielding a few offers which may or may not come off."

But how would I contact you if you left? Michela silently thought, afraid of how to broach such a question. "I saw their gravestones today, Charlotte and Elizabeth's that is. They're beautiful, Alli. I took some pictures of the site for you. Would you mind if I sent them to your work address?"

"I'd like that a lot," she quietly said.

"I spoke with Charlotte today. It seems her grandmother kept a diary and that confirms they were married and were lovers."

"I guessed that. The final entries in Elizabeth's diary answers that question. Her profession of love to Charlotte could only be that of a lover. Her words are so strong, so full of emotion." Allison's eyes filled with such pain and longing that Michela bit her lip to stop from reacting to it.

Michela closed her eyes in resignation. She opened them with the knowledge that it might be the last time she ever saw Allison. "I'd better sign off. Do you want me to get Charlotte?"

Allison shook her head. "No, we've finished our business."

Michela searched for another reason to prolong the conversation and found none. "I'd better let you go. I really hope everything turns out for you down there. Take care of yourself," she whispered, her voice choked with emotion.

Allison nodded, her eyes glistening. "You too." Her image dissolved.

"I love you," Michela said.

Chapter
Twelve

My Darling Charlotte,

There is only me now and every day the chore of keeping this diary becomes increasingly difficult. I do not know how much longer I will be able to write to you, however, I shall continue to do so while I have the strength.

I do not rise any more, instead spending the day in bed, reminiscing over our happy times together. There are so many times between the two of us I can recall and yet I fear there will be no more. Yesterday I dreamt of that first night, when you had the strength to take me in your arms. I am so glad you did, my love, for I fear I would have never possessed the courage to take that first step. Our love making that night was sweet and passionate, such as I had never experienced before.

I have so little time left and yet there is so much to say. Tell our son I love him and that I will always be there for him. More importantly, take care of yourself, my darling. Mourn for what we shared together but look toward the future also. It would sadden me if you did not allow yourself to again find happiness.

I am going to stop now as it tires me to write. I do not know if there will be another entry after this, so know, my Charlotte, that I will always be with you and will love you no matter where either of us finds ourselves. There will come a time when again we will be reunited. I will wait for you, forever, if need be.
All my love

Elizabeth

Houston—2010

CHRISTINE FLOPPED DOWN on the sofa. "Heaven's, sis, don't tell me you've taken a vow of celibacy."

Michela looked up from the pile of mail she was sorting through. She dearly loved her sister's visits, but recently Christine had taken it upon herself to find another woman for her and it was driving her crazy. "I haven't taken a vow of celibacy. I'm not interested."

"It's been almost fifteen months since your break up with Natalie. What are you waiting for?"

Michela waved her hand. "I'm over that and you know it."

Frustrated, Christine shook her head. "And it's been over five months since you returned from Antarctica. Have you gotten over Alli as well?"

Michela shot a warning glare at Christine. "Don't go there, please."

Christine pulled a magazine off the coffee table. "At least let me introduce you to some female friends of mine."

Michela shook her head as she continued to sort through the mail. "Like the last woman you set me up with? What was her name again, Missy or Misty something? The woman was an octopus."

Christine laughed. "She seemed intelligent, with a good sense of humour and, well, reserved when I spoke with her. How was I to know she was a nymphomaniac? Anyone can get it wrong sometimes."

Michela sagely nodded. "So how do you explain Eleanor?"

Christine threw her head back in exasperation. "How was I to know she was a right-wing extremist? How many lesbians do you know who are right-wing extremists?"

Michela chuckled. "That woman had more hang ups than a closet. I couldn't believe it when she launched into a dissertation on the superiority of the white race. I couldn't get out of there fast enough."

"Hmm, she looked so reasonable on the surface." Christine tilted her head, a pleading look on her face. "Let me have one more go. I promise I'll get it right this time. In fact, I'll run a background check if you like."

Michela shook her head. "Chrissie, I'm not inter-

ested." *Not in anyone on this side of the equator anyway.*
"Let's leave it at that." A thick gilt envelope dropped from
the business mail and onto the desk. "What's this?" She
opened the extravagant envelope.

Christine leant forward. "What's what?"

Michela read the contents of the invitation and smiled.
"Charlotte Finlayson's finally secured the complete Antarctica Finlayson collection. She's having an exhibition at
the local museum and, to celebrate its opening, she's having a casual cocktail party for selected guests next week. It
seems I'm invited."

"Is it stag, or do you get to take someone?"

Michela turned over the cream invitation card and
found a hand written note on the back. "It says I'm more
than welcome to bring someone. Charlotte says the exhibit
will be open for a private viewing the day before the
crowds descend."

"God, that leaves me little time to find someone to go
with you."

Michela smiled at Christine. *I'll give her ten points for
persistence but zero for success.* "You're not listening, are
you? I don't want to take a date and I don't want a woman
right now. I'm more than happy by myself." *Except at night
when I can't stop dreaming about Alli.*

Christine turned her best sorrowful expression at
Michela. "Please yourself, but at least take me. I haven't
seen anything except the pictures you brought back from
Antarctica."

Michela laughed. "Okay, we'll go together. But I want
you to behave. There'll be no setting me up with eligible
women or I'll tie you up and leave you in your room for
the duration."

"Where are we staying?"

"Charlotte's note says she expects me to stay at her
home, so I guess that means you as well. I'll have to give
her a call and make sure it's okay." Michela gave Charlotte
a quick call. "She says it's okay."

Christine stood and headed for the door.

"Where are you going?" Michela asked.

"Where do you think I'm going? Just because you
want to live like a nun, doesn't mean I have to. There's
bound to be eligible men at this soiree and I want to make

sure I'm ready for them. I'm going shopping. Something you could try more than once a year."

Michela chuckled. "I just don't see the need for the incredibly large wardrobe you have." She made a shooing motion. "Off with you then, and don't spend all your money."

Michela sat down at her desk, the piles of sorted mail spread out in front of her. She picked up the invite again and lightly tapped it against the side of her head. *Allison would love this. An exhibition of the Finlayson dig and, after so many years, returning again to her home country.*

She leaned back and sadly visualised Allison's features. She pulled a series of loose photographs from her top drawer and found her favourite. Allison, the layers of cold weather gear making her look larger than her well-defined, slighter frame, smiled at the camera as she held the Finlayson diary, next to the cot where it had been found clutched in the hands of its previous owner. Michela traced Allison's features with her finger. "God help me, I still miss you," she whispered, her voice choked with emotion.

"AND THIS PERSON here is Ella, my sanity valve," Charlotte said.

Allison nodded, still taken aback by the size of the mansion. It was like the homes she'd seen in movies—a sprawling estate, replete with lightly wooded areas and lush, green gently undulating meadows, dominated by a beautiful, old family mansion.

Realising Ella was waiting, she put out her hand. "Hello, please call me Alli, everyone else does. I'm sorry to be gawking like a tourist, but this house is beautiful."

"Thank you," Charlotte said. "It's been in my family for generations and was the family residence of Great Grandmothers Charlotte and Elizabeth. If you like, I'll give you a tour later, that is if Ella doesn't beat me to it. Of course, I could have given you a tour earlier in the week, had you not decided to stay in town."

Allison shrugged. "I'm sorry but it seemed a lot easier to be where the exhibit was. I tend to get a little self-absorbed when I'm working on a project and end up keeping very late hours."

Charlotte smiled. "Well, you're here now. Ella, could you show our guest to her room? Alli, once you're settled, come downstairs and we can get down to business." She motioned to the wood panelled door behind her. "I'll meet you in the study if you like."

Allison didn't take long to unpack her small bag and return to the study.

"You've worked wonders with the exhibit," Charlotte said. "This morning, looking at the re-creation of the interior of the hut, I almost felt I was there. And the sound effects of that wind are marvellous."

"I'm glad you like it," Allison said. "I'd have liked to do something similar at the Flinders Museum, but the patron wasn't interested. He seemed more focussed on getting the artefacts on display as soon as possible."

Charlotte clicked her tongue and shook her head. "It sounds like his only intent was to start reaping in the profits from the exhibit. How did you manage to re-create the wind? It sounds like Antarctica itself."

Allison blushed with pride. "It is from Antarctica. Sarah, the glaciologist on the expedition, is back on the Continent. I contacted her and she agreed to record two hours of a windstorm. I looped it so that it repeats every two hours. It really does add to the hut's ambience."

"It certainly does. What are your plans for the rest of the day?"

"There are still some things I have to finish up before the official opening tomorrow evening," Allison said. "Plus, there have been some private visitors through already this morning and so I'm keen to make sure everything is where it should be. I think I'll head back to the exhibit and tinker a little bit more before I call it a day."

Charlotte wagged a finger at Allison. "Make sure you're back here tonight in time for the cocktail party. Now it's informal, but there are a lot of people I'd like you to meet. Your room has all the luxuries of a hotel room, so make yourself comfortable. But don't be late."

Allison nodded. "I promise I won't be. A couple of more hours should be enough to ensure everything is perfect for tomorrow's official opening."

"Michael, my driver, is at your disposal. Have Ella page him and he'll take you back to the museum."

"Thank you." Allison stood. "I'll see you later then."

"IF WE'RE COMING to the official opening of the exhibit tomorrow, why are we here this afternoon?"

Michela smiled. "I want to take a peek without being jostled by a group of curious onlookers. Besides, this way I can talk you through the exhibit without becoming the unofficial tour guide to a group of hangers-on."

Michela held her breath as she walked into the hall. She stared in amazement at an almost full-size replica of Finlayson's hut, complete with artefacts. She glanced at the panels recording the history of the explorer and then walked into the hut itself. She closed her eyes as she recalled the last time she'd stood in the real structure, with Allison by her side. It had been the day before Rob boarded up the hut and they took the opportunity to have one last look at it. Allison recorded pictures of every nook and cranny. It was obvious these pictures had contributed to the room Michela now stood in. Charlotte had spared no expense in recreating this piece of family history. "This is amazing. It's exactly as it was on the continent."

Christine walked around, gazing at the weather-beaten wooden walls. Bottles, tins, and jars from an era long gone adorned the shelves. The wooden table, set with a meal, was covered with a cornucopia of old tins—cocoa, condensed milk, and fruit cake. "I almost feel as if I'm there."

Working in the office to the rear of the exhibit, Allison heard faint voices as they echoed through the empty room. *More of Charlotte's private guests no doubt, otherwise the guard would have never allowed them to pass.* Tilting her head, she listened in on the conversation, her heart almost stopping.

"Michela," she whispered.

She quickly stood and went to a secret entrance in the side of the hut, placed there for emergency evacuation. As softly as possible she slightly opened the door.

Michela nodded. "You're right. Quite a lot of work has been put into this. Whoever has gone to the trouble to rec-reate this deserves a lot of praise."

Allison smiled at the compliment, touched that Michela should feel that way about the exhibit. She couldn't see the person Michela was talking to without making her presence known.

Christine shivered and rubbed her hands up and down her arms. "The sound of that wind. It makes me feel cold just to think about it. You were always a bit of a hot water bottle, can you warm me up please?"

Michela chuckled as she pulled Christine to her and rubbed her back.

Allison stepped back and stifled the noise that rose in her throat. It was the same woman that had met Michela on the dock in Hobart. It was obvious Michela had moved on since their time on the continent. Holding back a sob, Allison quietly closed the private door and softly walked back to her office.

Michela released Christine and looked around the room. "Did you hear that?"

"Hear what? I can't hear anything over this wind."

Michela frowned. "I thought I heard something, and a moment ago I had the distinct feeling I was being watched."

Christine punched Michela's arm. "I think you've read one too many of those ghost stories. There's no one here, you ninny. Come on, we can look at this again tomorrow. But now I want to get to this house you've told me so much about." She linked her arm around Michela and they walked out of the hall.

"YOU SEE, YOU do scrub up well when you want to." Christine made a show of admiring Michela's deep burgundy suit and midnight blue silk shirt.

Michela whistled at Christine's dove grey gown. "You don't look too bad yourself. Ready to mingle?"

Christine grinned. "You bet."

"You were right, sis, this house is absolutely beautiful," Christine said as they descended the winding staircase to the party below.

"Yes, I know," Michela replied. "Walking around here, you almost can feel the presence of Elizabeth and Charlotte."

Christine gently nudged Michela. "There you go again

with your otherworldly thoughts. Next you'll be telling me they've both been invited to the cocktail party." They shared a laugh as they ambled into the crowd already filling the ballroom.

Michela spent the next hour patiently answering questions about her trip, with many of the guests interested in visiting the cold continent. Michela chuckled to herself every time someone mentioned it. They'd never survive an hour there. Wishing she were in an isolated environment, she politely answered their questions, while keeping an ear on the surrounding conversations.

"It's really much colder than Chicago in winter." Michela tried not to sigh at the uncomprehending expression on the elderly woman's face.

"The conditions were harsh," a voice said.

Michela looked around and was stunned to see Allison, dressed in elegant shirt and black pants, several feet away." Excuse me a moment," she murmured to the woman.

Michela walked to where she could watch Allison. *She looks so tired.* She mentally smacked herself in realisation. Of course everything about the exhibition was perfect. Allison had made sure of it.

Allison patiently nodded at an elderly woman's words.

Michela was unsure of what to do next. She couldn't retreat to her room. Besides, she'd waited too long to see Allison again. She recalled the many discussions she had had with Christine about her reluctance to contact Allison. *But where do I start?*

Allison frowned as if she sensed something or someone. She slowly turned her head and her eyes locked with Michela's. She softly smiled as her heart pounded uncontrollably.

Michela approached Allison. She desperately wanted to touch Allison's cheek but was afraid Allison would shy away. "Hello, Alli," she said quietly.

Allison tilted her head and gave her a wan smile. "Hello, Michela, how are you?"

Michela shrugged, silently relieved that the initial awkwardness had passed. "I'm fine. Busy, but fine all the same. How about you?"

"Not too bad. I've finished with the Flinders Museum and am looking at a number of job offers; some of which are very attractive."

None of which could be as attractive as you. Michela nodded. "Any catch your interest?"

"Yes and no," Allison said. "There're some lecturing spots opening up in a couple of universities that are tied in with six months worth of work in the field. But I'm still looking and taking a bit of a holiday break at the same time."

The laughter of the woman Michela had been with that afternoon echoed across the gathering. Allison turned and saw her surrounded by several men. She turned back and watched as Michela smiled at the woman across the room.

"She's lovely," Allison said, although it pained her to admit it.

"Chrissie? Yes, she certainly is. And she's a handful as well. You never know what she's going to do next."

Allison watched as Christine lightly tapped the arm of the man beside her. Masking her frustration, Allison took a glass of champagne from the tray of a passing waiter. "She seems to be engrossed in whatever the discussion is over there."

Michela took a fluted glass and sipped the champagne. "Yes, she's looking for a catch."

Allison was grateful she hadn't yet taken a sip. *How can she be so casual? Is she saying Christine's bisexual? I thought...*Allison mentally shook her head, not quite sure what she thought. "Doesn't that bother you? Her actions I mean?"

Michela chuckled. "No, not at all. After so many years, I'm more than used to the way Chrissie operates. Even when we were teenagers Mom and Dad had their hands full with her. Chrissie's beautiful and has always been the catch of every available man, no matter what age she was."

They're sisters? They're sisters you idiot! You let yourself again see something that wasn't there and now it's too late. If you'd believed for a moment that it was only you she wanted then things would be a hell of a lot different now. I can't believe I was so stupid. She gazed up at Michela. "I'm sorry, what did you say?"

"Allison, my dear, come and meet the CEO of Lindstrom Holdings," Charlotte waved from across the room. "He has a building I'm interested in."

Allison regretfully shrugged. "Excuse me." She walked to Charlotte.

Michela took a step to get close to the conversation just as a middle-aged man stopped her.

"Is it true you rappelled into a crevasse?" he asked.

Michela finally managed to get away from the man. She scanned the room and found Charlotte but not Allison. She went to Charlotte, stopped and sipped her drink while she waited for a suitable break in Charlotte's conversation.

"You never mentioned Allison would be here tonight," Michela said.

"You never asked," Charlotte replied. "Besides, you can't tell me after seeing the exhibit today that anyone else could have recreated it?"

"I thought it had been done from the photos she provided." Michela again searched the room for Allison.

Charlotte nudged Michela. "By the looks of it, she seems happy to see you. Are you happy to see her?"

Michela returned her gaze to Charlotte, realising that she'd planned their meeting all along. "I'm very happy to see her. But where's she gone?"

Charlotte motioned toward the patio. "She's at the cemetery. She hadn't yet seen the graves and the twilight's such a lovely time to view them. With the creation of the exhibit over the past week, she's had little time to see any of the estate." Charlotte, her eyes twinkling, nudged Michela's arm. "You might want to go and find her. It's a big estate and I'd hate for her to get lost."

"Thank you," Michela said and hurried out the door.

Michela approached the knoll where the cemetery lay and her breath caught at the sight of Allison, silhouetted by the aura of the setting sun.

Allison turned at the sound of the creaking gate. "Thank you for sending the photos, they were beautiful. But seeing it now, they don't really do it justice, do they?"

Michela shook her head. "No, they don't." They quietly stood, softly buffeted by the gusting wind.

Allison wiped her eyes with her handkerchief. "You

know, their love was still strong, even at the end. The last entry in Elizabeth's diary was her love for Charlotte."

"You're right. Their love lasted against the odds of distance and hardship," Michela said softly. "No matter what was placed in their way, their love was constant." She moved closer to Allison's side. "So, you mentioned you'd had some offers for employment. Did any catch your eye?"

Allison nodded. "There are a couple. Especially the ones where I can work for half the year and then dig for the second half, while still being sponsored. I was surprised when I was actually headhunted by a couple of the institutions. What was even more surprising was that they contacted me within days of my tendering notice." She secured an errant strand of hair behind her ear. "I'm flattered and excited at the same time."

Michela couldn't help but have mixed emotions. She was pleased at Allison's prospects and yet frustrated that she may never see her again. "It does seem as if you've landed on your feet. You can have everything you wanted."

Allison felt her body buffeted by both her own emotions and the wind that gusted over the open knoll. She took a breath and turned to Michela. "No, I haven't got everything, not at all. In fact, it wasn't until later I realised that the one thing I really wanted, I let slip through my fingers."

Michela tilted her head. "What did you let slip through your fingers?"

Allison crossed her arms, not so much against the slight night chill but as a defence for her words. Meeting Michela's eyes, she sadly smiled. "It was you, only you. If I hadn't been so focussed on seeing things that weren't there, I'd have realised how deep your feelings were for me. Instead I let my jealousy, unfounded fears, and foolish pride get in the way." She lowered her head, released a deep breath, and then gazed back at Michela. "Is it too late?"

Michela engulfed Allison in her arms. "It's never too late, my love, not where you're concerned." She captured Allison's lips with her own and then gazed into her eyes. "God, I've missed you so much. There were so many times

I wanted to call you. I'm so glad you're here tonight. I feel as if I'm truly at peace for the first time in months."

Allison lightly brushed Michela's cheek and rested her hand on Michela's chest. "I've missed you too. Those final days when we were together on the continent—it seemed so perfect and then when we returned to civilisation it was so painful. I was around people everyday and yet I felt more alone than I've ever felt before. It didn't take me long to realise what it was I felt for you and I was an idiot to let you slip through my fingers. I'm not going to let that happen again. I love you, Michela, more than I've ever loved anyone else in my life."

Michela's eyes, glistening with tears, mirrored Allison's. "I think I've loved you since that first meeting in Mount Cook and I don't think I've stopped loving you." She pulled Allison to her, protecting her against the wind. Lightning lit up the horizon. "It looks like rain, honey. We should get back to the house."

Allison shook her head against Michela's jacket. "Can we stay here for a while? If we return to the party we'll have to answer questions about the dig and right now I don't want to share you with anyone else. Surely, the storm's a way off yet." She captured Michela's lips with her own.

For the next couple of hours they all but forgot about the party and held each other, reminiscing on everything that had happened to them since they left Antarctica.

Allison chuckled as she snuggled into Michela. "I can't believe I mistook Christine for your girlfriend."

Before Michela could answer, lightning flashed, shortly followed by thunder. Michela brushed the hair from Allison's face. "We'd better get back to the party. I think the storm's going to be here any minute."

"It's a shame. I could have stayed here all night," Allison replied.

Michela released Allison, and walked to the gate before she realised Allison wasn't beside her. She turned and gave Allison a questioning look.

Allison walked to her and entwined their fingers. "I don't think you understand. I love you and if people can't deal with that then that's their problem. I don't intend to make the same mistake twice."

Michela raised their hands to her lips and gently kissed the entwined fingers. She closed the gate and they walked down the hill, hand-in-hand, to the house. As they slipped through the patio glass door, they were surprised to find the room empty. Now, only a single light illuminated the room.

Looking at her watch, Allison chuckled. "It seems we've been out there for quite a while. I hope we haven't offended Charlotte. She's such a generous woman."

Michela shook her head. "I don't think we did. I wouldn't be surprised if this is what she'd planned all along. Something I must thank her for tomorrow morning. I don't know about you, but I'm about ready for bed myself."

Allison nodded and they walked up the stairs. Michela paused at the top and turned to Allison. "Which one's your room?"

"What does it matter which one is my room? As far as I'm concerned the question is which one is yours?" Allison hugged Michela and gazed into her eyes. "I don't want to be separated from you again. Let me stay with you, please."

Smiling, Michela took Allison's hand and led her to her door.

As Michela reached for the handle, Allison stifled a gasp.

"What's the matter?" Michela asked.

Allison looked around the corridor as if to get her bearings. "Did Charlotte tell you about this room?"

"No. She has an uncanny knack of offering only as much information as she deems necessary. What's the problem?"

"This is their room—Elizabeth and Charlotte's. She told me this afternoon when she showed me to my room. I wondered whether it was used any more and she said only for select guests. I have to say I was a little disappointed not to have been given the room to sleep in." Allison chuckled. "I'm beginning to believe this romantic conspiracy theory of yours regarding Ms. Finlayson is true."

Michela opened the door, revealing a soft glow cast by a single lamp. She took Allison's hand, led her through the door, and closed it behind her. She left Allison in the centre of the room, removed her jacket, and hung it on a chair. She quietly walked around the room lighting enough lamps to create a muted glow.

Allison's eyes misted as she gazed around the room. It looked as if a moment from the past had been captured. Adorning one wall was a large unlit fireplace with a portrait of Charlotte and Elizabeth and their son Robert. Along another wall were matching mahogany dressers and a mirror that reflected the soft glow of the lamps. Opposite the fireplace was an old four-poster bed, its worn, multi-coloured quilt an obvious heirloom. The final wall had two sets of French windows that looked out into the inky black of the night.

Allison walked across the carpeted floor to the windows and paused, staring at her full reflection in the glass. She watched as the lightning came closer, momentarily lighting up the room in brief intense flashes.

Allison watched Michela's reflection as she walked to her. Michela wrapped her arms around her from behind, encasing the smaller hands with her own.

They stood, each caught up in the feeling of reconciliation, of comfort, of finally coming home. Allison snuggled closer and Michela brushed the nape of her neck with butterfly-soft touches. Allison arched her neck in response.

Afraid of rushing the moment, Michela broke off her trail of kisses, and gazed, contented, at Allison's reflection.

While she watched Michela, Allison encased Michela's hands with her own. She, raised them to her mouth, softly kissed them, and guided them to the top satin button of her blouse. Michela unbuttoned the button and Allison lowered her hand to the next one, and then the next. Allison put Michela's hands on the sides of the blouse and together they slowly pulled it from her pants.

Michela gazed at Allison's body reflected in the glass, her sculpted skin accentuated by her rapid breathing, her breasts held within the sleek confines of a bronze satin bra.

Allison guided Michela's hands to her breasts and dropped her hands to her side. She gasped as Michela ever so lightly caressed her nipples.

Michela's breath caught at Allison's reaction to her delicate touch. She traced a sensual line on the material and unclasped the front of the bra. She peeled the fabric back and cupped her hands around the soft breasts.

Gasping at the contact, Allison half-turned, snaked an arm around Michela's neck, and brought Michela's head down to her eager lips. Continuing the kiss, she turned fully to face Michela and moaned as her flesh pressed against Michela's silk shirt.

As the kiss deepened, Allison unbuttoned Michela's blouse, circled her arms around Michela's waist under the loose shirt and undid the bra. Allison placed feather-light kisses on the hollow of Michela's throat and down a path between her breasts. She broke the kiss and smiled at the passion reflected back at her in Michela's eyes. Lightning again illuminated the room and their flushed faces. Allison softly traced the curve of Michela's lips and returned her hand to Michela's chest. "Make love to me, please."

Michela led Allison to the bed and they quietly, almost reverently, undressed each other, their shadows cast on the walls in the low light.

Michela was surprised as Allison took her hand and motioned her to lie down. Allison stretched out on her side next to her as lightning strobed the room, temporarily lighting their bodies.

Allison traced a sensual line across Michela's flesh, pleased at the reaction. She lightly grazed the hair at the apex of Michela's thighs and ran her fingers upward, pausing to softly stroke Michela's tender pebbled flesh. She captured Michela's lips.

Unable to control her rising passion any longer, Michela pulled Allison to her, ran her hands down Allison's back, and softly mapped the crease where silky curve met with thigh. Feeling the warmth there, Michela moaned with pleasure as she placed a leg on either side of Allison's.

Allison searched Michela's face as she slowly moved against the sensuous friction of Michela's legs. "There were so many nights when I went to sleep, thinking of you, of us, together again like this, only to wake in the morning and realise it was only a dream. It's almost hard for me to believe we're together like this now."

Michela lightly kissed Allison's nose. "Trust me, I'm real and I don't intend to go anywhere or allow you out of my sight for quite a while." Smiling, she pulled Allison into her arms.

AN INSISTENT KNOCKING on her door interrupted Michela's peaceful slumber. Her eyes widened as the door's knob turned. She quickly pulled the sheets up to cover herself and more importantly, Allison, who was slowly waking.

"Hi, sis. That was some party last night. I can't believe the number of eligible millionaires that were squeezed into one room. There was one lovely gentleman who followed me around the whole evening. Hmm, such a nice man." She walked across the softly shadowed room and looked out the almost floor to ceiling window. "But that's not the most amazing news. It seems your friend the archaeologist's in town, so my gentlemen friend said. So what do you intend to do about that? I think we should try and track down exactly where she is." She turned to the bed and after a shocked moment, her eyes hardened. "After all these months, you better be telling me there's no one else in that bed except who I think should be there. Because if it's anyone else, so help me, I'm going to give you a bigger beating than the one I gave you when you put laxatives in my brownies when you were thirteen."

Michela slightly raised the sheet and Allison nodded. Michela pulled back the bed sheet enough to reveal Allison's head. "Your timing is impeccable as always. Let me introduce Dr. Allison Shaunessy."

"Hi," Allison said, sounding embarrassed.

Christine blushed and went to the bed and shook Allison's hand. "Thank *God* you turned up. I thought this one," she motioned at Michela, "was about to join a damn convent. She's been like a bear with a sore head since arriving home. In fact, she tends to get like that quite a lot." She sat down on the bed. "I can remember a time..."

Michela gave her a warning look. "Do you think we could discuss this later?" She motioned with her head toward the door.

"Oh, of course. You *do* intend to make it down to breakfast, don't you?" Christine stood and smiled. "Don't be long or it'll be lunch before you get down there." She hurried out the door.

Michela slumped down. She turned and brushed the ever-errant fringe out of Allison's eyes. "That about seals it. I hope you don't mind the whole world knowing about us. Aside from being a magnet to men, my sister could put a telephone company out of business. She should give up her calling as a surgeon and go into the gossip business, full time."

Allison laughed at Michela's frustration. "I told you last night and I'll tell you again, I don't care who she tells. I'm happy with things as they are." She pulled Michela to her and they rekindled the passion of the night before.

ALTHOUGH THEY DIDN'T quite manage to make breakfast, Allison and Michela joined Christine for lunch, surprised by Charlotte's presence. After proper introductions, Christine and Allison took the time to begin to know each other.

After lunch, while Christine took at walk, Allison and Michela retired to the library.

Michela opened the heavy velvet burgundy brocade curtains that held the room in darkness. "Have you done a full tour of the house yet?"

Allison shook her head. "I think Ella started to last night, but Charlotte stopped her, saying there'd be more than ample opportunity to do that in the next few days."

Michela chuckled. "I've had the long and the short tour and believe me, when you get the time we won't see you for days. It seems Elizabeth was the first in a long line of explorers. A lot of the rooms hold the different collections from expeditions. This library holds the first part of the memorabilia of Elizabeth's expeditions."

Allison went from object to object. Like a child in a candy store, she lingered over and savoured every little artefact.

Michela watched Allison and was pleased at the excitement radiating in her face.

Allison turned to Michela and smiled. "These are amazing. It's as if there's a little bit of every expedition she ever went on." She held up to the afternoon light the intricate carving of a dragon—her hands bathed in the warm green of the delicate object. "This jade sculpture is exquisite."

Michela nodded. "By what's contained in this room alone, she must have spent a great deal of time travelling. From what the modern-day Charlotte has said, her Great Grandmother Charlotte spent her a lot of time separated from the intrepid explorer."

Allison carefully returned the jade object to its resting-place. She went to Michela, hugged her, and looked up into her eyes. "So, where do we go from here?"

Michela shrugged. "My tenure is about up with the Institute and so I'm just about free to do what I want. As far as I'm concerned, I'm happy to be wherever you are."

Allison gave Michela a quizzical look. "I thought last night you said there was a lot more to be done with the Mars expedition, not to mention the other projects you had in train. Also, from what you mentioned in Antarctica, I thought there was enough work to keep you entrenched there for years."

"It's work that can be easily done by anyone. The hard part, establishing the projects, is finished. I'm sure someone else can take over. I'm more happy to be where you are than—"

Allison released Michela and stepped back. "I can't ask you to give up your career to follow me. You're a professional with a hell of a lot to offer. You should stay here and see your projects through. It wouldn't be fair for me to expect anything else."

"Are you saying you'd rather I stay here than be with you?" Michela asked. "Is that what you want?"

Allison pushed down her growing anger. "That's not what I said at all and you know it." Michela walked to the window. "Oh, for God's sake, Michela, be sensible about this."

Michela wheeled. "Be sensible? Me be sensible? You're the one who's talking about being on one side of the world while I'm here."

The door opened, and Charlotte stood in the doorway, a concerned look on her face.

"What's going on in here?" Charlotte demanded. "I can hear you half the way down the hall."

Allison pointed at Michela. "She won't see the sense in remaining in a good job."

Michela pointed at Allison. "And she doesn't see the logic in me moving to Australia to be with her."

Allison snorted. "I did nothing of the sort. You're stretching the truth."

Charlotte slammed her hand on a small coffee table. "Time out, ladies, *time out!*" Michela and Allison blinked at her in surprise. "Both of you, come and sit down before I have Ella throw a bucket of water over you." They obediently followed Charlotte to a small couch and sat at opposite ends.

Charlotte stood before them and rubbed her hands together. "Alli, did you not mention to me the other day that you were in between jobs?" Allison nodded. "Do you remember the man I introduced you to last night? The one from Lindstrom Holdings, the one I wanted to buy a building from?" Allison nodded again. "There's a very good reason why I want to buy that building. I've decided to establish a museum. But this one's going to be a little different. In fact, truth be told, I don't know why I didn't come up with the idea years ago."

She turned to the painting of her great grandmothers and smiled. "The human race has been around for such a small period of time and yet within that time both men and women have made such great progress. Unfortunately, we rarely hear about the accomplishments women have made because most of the accolades go to men. Don't misunderstand me, I'm not suggesting for a moment their discoveries haven't been seminal in their own right, but where is the history of women? Where are their discoveries lauded, their papers kept, their deeds remembered? One only has to look back over the past one hundred and fifty years or so to realise how remiss society has been in retaining such history.

"Look at Madame Curie, a double Nobel winner in both physics and chemistry. Then there's Amelia Earhardt and Australia's own Nancy Bird—aviatrixs' in their own right, the latter learning to fly when she was merely thirteen. Of course there are the explorers such as my own great grandmother that more than dot the canvas of the past one hundred and fifty years. What about Maria Mitchell, the first American professor of astronomy, discovering a comet in 1847. In the field of sport there are so many women whose feats are rarely mentioned, if at all. Babe Didriskson–one of history's most famous all-round athletes. The Australian, Fanny Durack, who won the only ladies swimming event at the Stockholm Games of 1912, despite the obstacles put in place by her own country. For each one of these women, there are ten whose stories have never been told. I want to create a legacy and ensure young men and women get not only history, but *her*story as well."

Charlotte tapped to her chest. "So, where is this old woman going with this? Well, the answer's simple. Alli, the museum has a patron and that's me, but if this project is to work then I need a Chairman to run the Museum and you're the first person I want to offer the job to." She held up her hand to halt any comment from Allison. "No, you won't be tied to a desk for your time here. I would see you continuing to engage in archaeological exploration, for at least half of your year. You can choose your staff as you see fit. All I ask is that you make my vision come alive. Give the opportunity for the young men and women of tomorrow to realise the depth and colour in the tapestry that is the history of this world of ours. Oh, and of course, there's always the benefit that you and Michela will only be slightly separated, rather than a hemisphere apart. But if the argument I walked in on is any measure, maybe you two need a hemisphere between you." She smiled and headed to the door. "I'll leave you to think about it for a while."

As the lock clicked into place, Allison scooted over and took Michela's hands. "She's right. We argue like cats and dogs. Can we ever live in the same hemisphere, let alone the same continent?"

Michela smiled and cupped Allison's cheek in her palm. "Do you want the job?"

Allison turned to the portrait above the fireplace, her eyes distant as she contemplated such a mammoth task. She returned her gaze to Michela. "More than anything I've ever wanted, in the professional sense that is."

Michela pulled Allison into her arms and lightly kissed the top of her head. "Then the only remaining question is can you bear to live with me?"

Pulling back, Allison chuckled. "After what I've been

through, that shouldn't be too difficult. I hope in six months time, you're not asking the same question about me."

They kissed and relaxed in each other's arms, secure in their future and the myriad of challenges that lay ahead.

Other titles from
Helen Macpherson

And Those Who Trespass Against Us

Sister Katherine Flynn is an Irish nun, sent by her order to work in the remote Australian countryside of New South Wales. Katherine is a prideful woman who originally joined her order to escape the shame of being left at the altar. She had found herself getting married only because society dictated it for a young woman her age, and she was not exactly heartbroken when it didn't take place. Yet, her mother could not be consoled and talked of nothing except the disgrace that she had brought to the Flynn name. So, she finds great relief in escaping the cold Victorian Ireland of 1872.

Catriona Pelham is a member of the reasonably affluent farming gentry within the district. Her relationship with the hardworking townspeople and its farmers is one of genuine and mutual respect. The town's wealthy, however, have ostracized her due to her unorthodox ways and refusal to conform to society's expectations of a woman of the 1870's. Catriona finds comfort in the friendship of the townspeople and farmers, but at night she pines for the lover she lost long ago–her governess, Adele Cooper.

As a bond between Katherine and Catriona develops and so the journey begins for these two strong-willed women. For Katherine it is a journey of self-discovery and of what life holds outside the cloistered walls of the convent. For Catriona it is bittersweet, as feelings she has kept hidden for years resurface in her growing interest in Katherine.

.

ISBN: 1-930928-21-1

Born and residing in Australia, Helen specialises in lecturing and tutoring in a variety of human resource development and management subjects. Currently living in the harbour city of Sydney, she is working as the Deputy Director of a major Human Resource Management agency. When she isn't tied to her work she enjoys travelling, reading, writing and bushwalking. She's an avid sportswoman, in her younger years having competed in soccer and softball at a representational level, although recently she's more of a spectator than participant. She currently lives with her partner of eleven years and their two cats.

Printed in the United States
33759LVS00005B/54

9 781932 300291